Echo Among Warriors

D1496492

Echo Among Warriors

Close Combat in the Jungle of Vietnam

RICHARD CAMP

CASEMATE

Philadelphia & Oxford

Published in the United States of America and Great Britain in 2022 by
CASEMATE PUBLISHERS
1950 Lawrence Road, Havertown, PA 19083, US
and
The Old Music Hall, 106–108 Cowley Road, Oxford OX4 1JE, UK

Copyright 2022 © Richard Camp

Paperback Edition: ISBN 978-1-63624-034-3
Digital Edition: ISBN 978-1-63624-035-0

A CIP record for this book is available from the British Library

All rights reserved. No part of this book may be reproduced or transmitted in any form
or by any means, electronic or mechanical including photocopying, recording or by any
information storage and retrieval system, without permission from the publisher in writing.

Printed and bound in the United States of America by Integrated Books International

Typeset in India by Lapiz Digital Services, Chennai.

For a complete list of Casemate titles, please contact:

CASEMATE PUBLISHERS (US)
Telephone (610) 853-9131
Fax (610) 853-9146
Email: casemate@casematepublishers.com
www.casematepublishers.com

CASEMATE PUBLISHERS (UK)
Telephone (01865) 241249
Email: casemate-uk@casematepublishers.co.uk
www.casematepublishers.co.uk

Dedication
The sacrifice of the officers and men of 3rd Battalion, 26th Marines,
Semper Fi,
and to
Eric Hammel, mentor and great friend,
Shalom.

Etched in the bronze of time you will find the chronicle of your exploits. The names of Dai Do, Lai An, DMZ, upper Ashau and Khe Sanh will join those of Iwo Jima, Guadalcanal and Bougainville to echo among warriors.

Major General Raymond G. Davis
U.S. Marine Corps
Northern Marine, 1968

Author's Note

Echo Among Warriors is a fictional account of gut-level combat as seen through the eyes of American and North Vietnamese participants. The setting is the dense jungle of the Khe Sanh plateau, where the author experienced the brutality of war as a Marine company commander during the North Vietnamese Army's (NVA) build-up to the 1968 Tet offensive. His company regularly patrolled the grass-covered ridge lines and jungle-canopied valleys surrounding the Khe Sanh Combat Base (KSCB), the western anchor of a series of strongpoints that stretched across northern South Vietnam. The objective of these installations was to close the infiltration routes, but it resulted in ceding freedom of movement to the NVA while fixing American troops in position. Khe Sanh was a prime example. It was located on a major infiltration route that ran from the Laotian border east to the Ba Long and Ashau valleys and south to the population-rich coastal lowlands of South Vietnam.

The hills and valleys surrounding KSCB became a vicious, no-holds-barred slug fest, costing hundreds of lives on either side. In the spring of 1967, there was a series of engagements in what became known as the Hill Fights, which were focused on the four major heights northwest of KCSB—Hill 950, Hill 881 North, Hill 881 South, and Hill 861. By the fall of the year, Marines were reporting an increasing concentration of NVA troops and military equipment around the base. Intelligence reports placed the NVA 325C and 304 divisions, a total of approximately twenty thousand men, in the area. Opposing them were three infantry battalions of the 26th Marine Regiment, a battalion of the 9th Marine Regiment, and an Army of the Republic of Vietnam (ARVN) Ranger battalion totaling some six thousand men. By the time of this story, September 1967, KSCB had become a tempting target for destruction.

Echo Among Warriors is a story of close combat in a life-and-death struggle between two opposing, equally committed, adversaries. It represents just one of perhaps thousands of deadly encounters that reflect the reality of battle—a mind-numbing, intensely personal experience that forever changes the participant. I constructed the narrative so that the reader could experience both sides of the battle. The same battle sequence will roll forward like a movie scene and then be replayed from the opposite viewpoint—through the eyes of the Marines and sequentially through the eyes of the North Vietnamese. The bullet fired from a Marine's M-16 at a silhouetted enemy solider crouched on the jungle path will in the next chapter tear into the flesh of that crouched NVA trooper. The story spans a two-day period covering 13 to 14 September 1967. In war, every action has a beginning and an end.

There has been no intention to portray gratuitous violence or profanity. War veterans know that words are insufficient to describe the destructive power of weaponry and the resulting, horrific wounds, the pain of a lost comrade, and the sudden realization that it could have been him. War causes a visceral, emotional impact on those who fight it. Profanity is like combat humor—both an integral part of the real and fictional combat picture. Veterans will already be familiar with war terminology—"Arty, Arty, Arty," "Shot," "Corpsman"—the greenhorn can refer to the glossary. Nor has there been any intention to depict any similarity between the characters and any veteran of the war. Each character is a composite from the author's sometimes fallible memory. They are rather like a kaleidoscope reflecting a million pieces of colored glass—no one in particular, yet everyone together.

Combat is not for the faint of heart ... and neither is this book!

Personnel Roster

U.S. Marine Corps (USMC)

3rd Battalion, 26th Marines, 3rd Marine Division (Reinforced)

Lieutenant Colonel Perry Aldine, Battalion Commander

The 42-year-old, newly assigned commander of the 3rd Battalion enters the Marine Corps in 1947 after graduating from the University of Pennsylvania with a degree in business. After attending officer training at The Basic School, Quantico, Virginia, he is assigned as an infantry officer (0301), to the 1st Marine Division at Camp Pendleton, California. During the Korean War, he serves as an 81mm mortar platoon commander for six months, completing the remainder of the 12-month tour as the executive officer of a headquarters company. For the next 16 years he serves in a variety of administrative and staff assignments, but he is never again in direct command of troops in the field. Aldine is singularly proud of that fact, having learned in Korea that leading young men in combat is hazardous to one's career and health. Despite his lack of command time, he is advanced in rank at the appropriate times and enjoys an excellent reputation as a staff officer, although there is some concern about his lack of infantry experience. The assignment to the 3rd Battalion is an attempt to correct that oversight.

Major Ron Coffman, Operations Officer

Coffman, a "fresh caught" field-grade officer, has been kicked upstairs from command of a rifle company in the same battalion. The thirty-five-year-old officer is a savvy tactician known for his ability to decipher enemy intentions and devise tactical schemes of maneuver to thwart their ambitions. An inspirational leader, he stands in sharp contrast to Lieutenant Colonel Aldine, who employs threats and rank to cower subordinates. Coffman takes great pride in never having served anywhere but in an infantry unit and, if the truth were known, looks down on staff weenies. He is having a tough time adjusting to the new battalion commander and looks for any opportunity to get to the field.

Lima Company, 3rd Battalion

Captain Andy Anderson, Company Commander

A former enlisted Marine, Anderson is on his second tour in-country, this time as the commander of an understrength rifle company, one of four in the battalion. A tough, well-respected field commander, he is more comfortable shooting the bull with his men than in polite chitchat with the rear-echelon pogues at the officers' club. He doesn't have many close friends—except Major Coffman, because they share the same views. In the summer of 1967, he leads his company in a series of fierce battles along the DMZ, learning how to fight the North Vietnamese. In the process, he develops a healthy respect for his enemies, finding them to be tough SOBs. He has also learned that if you don't have your shit together, the NVA will have your ass, as more than one poor bastard found out. In the long-abandoned agricultural area south of the Ben Hai River, is where Anderson operated, it was a deadly game of blind man's bluff, as opponents blundered into one another, often at point-blank range in the dense undergrowth. Under Anderson's aggressive leadership, Lima excels in this bar-room, no-holds-barred, reach-out-and-touch-someone brawl. In this finishing school of hard knocks, Captain Andy Anderson, U.S. Marine Corps, has become one tough son of a bitch himself.

Gunnery Sergeant Mike Smith, Company Gunnery Sergeant

More than one played-out Marine has remarked in awe, "The gunny loves this shit," as he watches this tireless, indefatigable middle-aged man "soldier on", putting the youngsters to shame. The man is right: Gunnery Sergeant Mike Smith has achieved his lifetime ambition, leading Marines in combat—and he is enjoying the hell out of it. After quitting high school to fight in Korea, he arrives just after the truce is signed and spends the next few months "sweeping up after the parade," bitterly disappointed that he doesn't get any "trigger time." Despite the let-down, he stays in, excelling in the post-war downsized Corps. With three tours in the Fleet Marine Force and two as a drill instructor, Smith is a lean, mean, well-trained fighting machine—a great complement to his hard-charging company commander.

2nd Lieutenant John Littleton, 1st Platoon Commander

A summer graduate of The Basic School, where all Marine Officers are trained, "Little John" Littleton turns down an opportunity for leave to ship out immediately, reasoning that if he arrives before his classmates he will have a better chance for assignment to a rifle platoon. He later discovers, much to his chagrin, there is such a severe shortage of lieutenants because of casualties that he would have been assigned an infantry platoon in any case. Two days after arriving in-country, a helicopter drops him off on a hilltop position where he is immediately assigned to the 1st Platoon—three weeks to the day after completing training. A cold dose of reality jolts his confidence as he faces the prospect of leading men in combat. This is no training exercise, no blanks, no pretend casualties. It is real life, in living color, with real bad guys—combat-hardened North Vietnamese regulars. For the first time, he is confronted with doubt, wondering, *Will I be able to hack it when the shit hits the fan?*

1st Lieutenant Dick Frazier, 2nd Platoon Commander

Called "Tiny" by his close friend, Gary Larson, Frazier is anything but; he's six feet three inches and a svelte 215 muscular pounds—down twenty after two months in the field. An outstanding athlete at Alabama, Frazier starts for the Quantico Marines football team while in training but balks at playing after graduation because he wants to get in the war. He gets his wish—assignment to the 3rd Marine Division, Republic of Vietnam. After a whirlwind ten-day leave, during which he cuts a wide swathe through the hometown honeys, he boards a chartered TWA 727 at Travis Air Force Base, California, for the mind-numbing 18-hour flight to Okinawa and a brief layover. Twenty-four exhausting hours later, he reports to the III Marine Amphibious Force Transient Facility, where he is processed in-country and eventually assigned to Lima's 2nd Platoon. Twenty-five grunts look to him for adult leadership, which he provides, much to their relief. Following a couple of minor skirmishes and numerous combat patrols, he considers himself to be a seasoned veteran, although he has yet to come up against a determined force of NVA regulars.

1st Lieutenant Gary Larson, 3rd Platoon Commander

Like his 2nd Platoon nemesis, Gary Larson joins the casualty-depleted company as a replacement when the previous commander is wounded and evacuated. After two grueling months in the field, he is now a physically hardened, competent infantry officer, a far cry from the wet-behind-the-ears "butter bar" who didn't know his ass from second base when he first reported. Larson's calm demeanor and "fire-plug" stature contrast sharply with Frazier's pizzazz and height, but the two are close friends despite the wrangling over whose platoon is better. If the truth be known, the two share a common trait—an aura of understated self-confidence that inspires men to rally in desperate circumstances. Larson's ability to lead men against overwhelming odds, while struggling with his own mortality, will be sorely tested in the days to come.

1st Lieutenant Tom Napoline, Artillery Forward Observer

Recently attached to the company as an artillery forward observer (FO), Napoline's job is to bring the wrath of God down on the head of the enemy—often the difference between life and death for a sorely pressed infantry unit. Fresh out of the artillery school at Fort Sill, Oklahoma, Napoline is still wet behind the ears and untested. Born and raised in the Bronx, he is a fast-talking, wisecracking, irreverent, five-foot-two-inch ball of energy that often lets his "alligator mouth overwhelm his humming bird ass." A case in point: just after meeting the company commander, Napoline describes his role as "lending dignity to the otherwise vulgar infantry brawl." Anderson is not amused. Napoline is everyone's idea of a city slicker, a real-life Damon Runyon caricature, complete with a New York accent. Well liked by the enlisted men, he has yet to prove himself to Captain Anderson, who considers the untested artilleryman somewhat of a feather merchant—much talk, little action—but will give the little "cannon cocker" the benefit of the doubt, at least for a while.

Staff Sergeant Royal Brown, Platoon Sergeant, 1st Platoon

Still a staff sergeant after 22 years in the Corps, Brown is at his terminal rank. While most of his contemporaries have been commissioned temporary officers or received accelerated promotion, he languishes in grade. Only the Corps' need for men because of its rapid wartime expansion keeps him from being tossed out on his ear. Early in his career, Brown is discovered to be a brutal tyrant who leads through intimidation and fear. He is court martialed and thrown off the drill field for physically abusing recruits, but he somehow manages to avoid being discharged. Packed off to a series of backwater assignments, he disappears off the skyline until the demand for infantry staff sergeants forces his recall. Ordered to Vietnam and assigned to the 1st Platoon, he has picked up where he left off.

Corporal Eric Petrovitch, Machine Gun Squad Leader

Petrovitch volunteers for the Corps to escape the numbing boredom of a small mining town in western Pennsylvania, the first of his extended family to make the break. A hard-rock miner at 14, his massive physique is a tribute to swinging 20-pound sledgehammer ten hours a day. Singled out for his size and quiet leadership style, he is given a machine gun squad as a private first class over more senior men. A month later, he is meritoriously promoted to corporal and awarded a Silver Star for bravery in action during an attack on his platoon's night defensive position, in which he singlehandedly beat the intruders back with an entrenching tool and a pistol after his machine gun jammed, killing at least four NVA in hand-to-hand combat. A quiet and unassuming leader, his size motivates his men; no one wants to piss him off.

Hospital Corpsman Larry Zimmer, 1st Platoon Corpsman

A mild-mannered, caring man, Doc Zimmer appears to be somewhat out of place in the company of macho, foul-mouthed Leathernecks. The appearance is misleading; he is fiercely loyal to them, taking great pride in belonging to this irreverent bunch of armed teenagers. Actually, he considers himself to be more Marine than sailor. He has been heard on more than one occasion to refer to his service brethren as swabbies, a derisive nickname used by his platoon mates. The men of the platoon treat him with respect, knowing that Zimmer is the genuine article. He has proven himself time and time again, risking his life to treat the wounded. Trained to perform limited emergency first aid, he has been faced with horrific injuries that would challenge the abilities of a trained surgeon—and he has saved lives. His normal location is with the company command group, but with the loss of the 1st Platoon's corpsman, he volunteers to accompany them on a patrol—forgetting the old adage "Never volunteer."

Bravo Company, 3rd Reconnaissance Battalion

1st Lieutenant Herb Wilson, Reconnaissance Platoon Commander

After completing six months as an infantry platoon commander and facing transfer to a boring staff assignment, Wilson volunteers for a vacancy in the 3rd Reconnaissance Battalion. The screening board takes one look at his exemplary combat record and immediately accepts him, much to the disappointment of his old commander. He quickly proves to be an adept reconnaissance officer by combining well-developed infantry field skills with a savvy tactical sense. His men claim he is part Vietnamese because of his ability to ferret out the NVA in their jungle base camps. However, at three inches over six feet, with blond hair and blue eyes, his bloodlines are clearly Nordic. He is considered to be one of the best patrol leaders in the battalion, his "stingray" teams achieving impressive results, killing dozens of NVA regulars and disrupting the flow of supplies into the Khe Sanh area. Unknown to Wilson, the enemy has brought in an elite counter-reconnaissance platoon to kill his Marines.

Marine Observation Squadron 2 (VMO-2)

Captain Jim Harper, Aerial Observer

Prior to being commissioned, "Pop" Harper has been a gunnery sergeant and, at 38, is the oldest man in the outfit—and the most experienced, with 20 years' service. One of the first staff non-commissioned officers to receive a temporary commission, he is immediately sent to aerial observer school where he learns the fine art of controlling air and artillery support from the back seat of a flimsy puddle jumper—a single-engine World War II Cessna. He enjoys his new flight status and the perks of his commission, the least of which is that he no longer has to salute 20-year-old second lieutenants. The flying is fun and he discovers a knack for the new occupation. Of course, the extra flight pay doesn't hurt either. All good things come to an end, and, upon graduation, he receives orders to the Republic of Vietnam, where he earns a chest full of decorations for numerous acts of bravery. Now on his second tour and an old salt, he is the subject of a great deal of good-natured kidding from his much younger pilot, who dubs him "Pop" and compares him to Methuselah. Despite the light-hearted banter, however, there is an underlying seriousness, for both men know the NVA hate them and would like nothing more than to shoot them out of the sky.

1st Lieutenant Dan Reed, Squadron Pilot

Ever since he can remember, "Bomber" Reed has always wanted to fly jets, even going so far as to take private flying lessons with the local crop duster in a vintage Piper Cub and racking up enough hours to qualify for a license. Immediately after graduation from a small college in the Midwest, he takes the Marine Corps aviation test, is found qualified, and is shipped off to Pensacola for training. He breezes through the syllabus despite the whirlwind courtship of a local girl, whom he marries in the base chapel before heading off to advance flight training. A new wife, combined with the rigors of the school, take its toll and he graduates near the middle of the class, effectively eliminating him from jet training. Instead, a sharp-eyed assignment officer spots his small aircraft qualification and puts a round peg in a round hole. Before Reed can say, "Aw shit," he is headed for Vietnam, and duty with VMO-2, as the pilot of a Bird Dog, a light airplane somewhat faster than a Piper Cub but 500 knots slower than his dream plane. Not one to piss and moan for long—nobody would listen anyway, his squadron mates were in the same boat—Reed teams up with Pop Harper and tears the NVA a new asshole. Screw 'em if they can't take a joke!

Marine Fighter Squadron 223 (VMA-223)

1st Lieutenant Gary Arnold, Squadron Pilot

On his very first mission in support of troops under fire, Arnold's A-4 is hit by several rounds of 12.7mm machine gun fire, forcing him to make an emergency landing, which he walks away from. A month later he is faced with a similar situation, only now he's at the wrong place at the wrong time.

People's Army of Vietnam (PAVN)

1st Battalion, 803rd Regiment, 324th Division

Lieutenant Colonel Pham Le Duc, Battalion Commander

As a young teenager he joins the Vietminh and sees combat fighting the Japanese during the waning months of World War II. Singled out for bravery, he is selected to be a member of the Liberation Army honor guard that protects Ho Chi Minh during his 1945 "Independence" declaration. Nine years later, he earns the coveted Hero of the Liberation Army award for leading the remnants of his platoon into Outpost Beatrice at Dien Bien Phu. Severely wounded, he spends months in a hospital before being released to watch the defeated French Army march out of Hanoi. He is a natural leader who views his duty as an obligation to his fellow soldiers. Revered by his troops, they refer to him as "elder brother," a sign of deepest respect. Nevertheless, the political cadre mistrusts him for his habit of speaking his mind but is hesitant to do anything because of his war record.

Major Vu Van Minh, Political Officer

Assigned by the cadre to maintain the spirit of the troops, this gutless political hack schemes to wrest control from his battle-tested commander. The son of a senior official, Minh avoids the usual selection process, which is based on talent, virtue, and bravery on the battlefield, and is appointed because of political connections. A coward, he is desperate to keep his moral failure from being discovered, even if it means eliminating the commander and taking control.

Lieutenant Tran Van Doi, Reconnaissance Platoon Commander

This veteran officer is censored by the cadre for failure to display proper fighting spirit during an abortive attack that decimates his platoon. Forced to undergo a *Kiem Thao*—self-criticism critique—he is eventually restored to command but remains unrepentant, blaming his superiors for disregarding his sacrifice. Well respected by his men, he desires nothing more than to lead them well and protect them from needless sacrifice. With orders to eliminate his American counterpart, Doi must not fail or he will be replaced.

Senior Sergeant Nguyen Ba Thanh, Sapper Platoon Commander

Two decades of war have made this senior non-commissioned officer into a ruthless killing machine. Commander of an elite sapper platoon, his well-honed survival skills and battlefield acumen make him an extremely dangerous foe. A survivor of numerous skirmishes, he is completely at home in the deadly close combat of the jungle environment.

1

1st Platoon, Lima Company, Combat Patrol, 0630, 12 September 1967, 7 Klicks Northwest KSCB—The impenetrable triple-canopy jungle formed a green screen, blocking the sun's warmth and trapping the early morning coolness between the steep banks of the concealed stream. The soothing murmur of the shallow water flowing over its bed of mud and pebbles added an air of tranquility to the jungle stillness, a silence so complete that even the drone of an insect disturbed the serenity. Dense undergrowth and stands of bamboo thickets hugged the steep banks, restricting movement to the streambed. Wild boar and deer prints abounded in the soft mud, marking the stream as a pathway for the jungle's larger inhabitants. The imprints recorded their passage, providing visual proof of their existence long after they had passed through.

Near the branch of a long-dead tree, a half-concealed imprint, unlike the others, had attracted the attention of a heavily armed party of men who crouched in the shadows. Barely visible, they scanned the foliage looking for the tell-tale signs of recent activity. Contrasting shades of green vegetation formed patterns of camouflage that played havoc with their surveillance in the soft light. One man emerged from the shadows in a hunter's crouch, rifle at the ready. He squatted near the downed tree limb, stared intently at the streambed. Just behind and to his right another man shifted into position to cover him with his rifle, an unconscious but carefully choreographed move. Rising slowly, the scout cautiously moved back into cover and made a series of gestures with his hands, which were relayed along the dispersed column. His movements telegraphed a signal of danger while silently requesting the leader of the patrol to come forward.

Second Lieutenant John Littleton and his radio operator, Lance Corporal Ken Sanders, stepped out of the shadows and moved forward along the column of men. Neither was distinguishable from the other 25 Marines of the platoon, except that Littleton's uniform was recently issued, the mark of a new man. Both wore helmets with a cloth leaf-patterned camouflage cover, gray-green tropical uniforms, protective flak jackets, and rubber-soled canvas and leather jungle boots. They carried similar green packs, except that Sanders's bulged with a PRC-25 radio, only the handset and cord visible. An old salt, he concealed the radio to keep from being identified as a radio operator. He had even gone so far as to bend its light metal antenna down through loops in his shoulder harness to keep from being singled out by North Vietnamese snipers, who viewed radiomen and officers as special targets. Neither man wore rank insignia for the same reason, particularly the officer, who didn't want his shiny gold bars to attract "the eye" of the sniper. Littleton also carried a rifle, rationalizing that a pistol was an obvious leader's weapon. For him the rifle was a lifeline; he couldn't hit the broad side of a barn with the standard Model 1911A-1 .45-caliber service automatic. Its heavy recoil caused him to shoot high and to the right on a pistol target and, much to his dismay, he barely qualified with the damn thing.

As they reached the front of the column, Littleton squatted next to the lead man, trying to place his face with a name. It came to him: Kelly, a tough Irish street kid from the projects of south Boston, who was reported to be the best point and bush man in the company. Go figure it. Leaning forward, his helmet almost touching that of the point man, Littleton whispered, "Kelly, what's going on?"

"Lieutenant," the rifleman responded, pointing to the tree limb, "there's a print in the mud on the other side, and it looks fresh." Kelly waited for his new platoon commander to absorb the information. At this point Littleton was an unknown to Kelly and the men of the 3rd Platoon. They agreed he had more positives than negatives: he could shoulder his load, didn't pull rank, and was easy to talk to within the bounds of military decorum. Nevertheless, the big question remained: how would he react in combat?

"Do you see anything else?"

Kelly hesitated. "No sir, but it's damn creepy. The hairs on my neck are standing straight up. I can feel gooks out there!"

Littleton made up his mind. He told Kelly and Sanders to cover him as he went out to look. Easing out into the middle of the stream, he bent down, feeling totally exposed. *Jesus Christ*, he thought, *what the hell am I doing here? I'm going to get my ass blown away.* With that encouraging thought in mind, he quickly examined the mud and spotted a fresh print. The damn thing looked like a tire track, puzzling him until he remembered the North Vietnamese often wore sandals made from cut-up car tires, using inner tube strips to hold them on their feet, creating a poor man's Birkenstock-type flip-flops. The troops called them "Ho Chi Minh Sandals" and drolly claimed they were good for 100,000 miles. As the realization hit him that a North Vietnamese rifleman might be aiming in at this very moment, his muscles involuntarily tightened and adrenalin surged through his blood. His head snapped up, eyes wide, trying to pierce the uncertain visibility. *Get the hell out of here, you dumb shit!* his brain screamed. It was all he could do to keep from jumping into the shadows, but he forced himself to slowly pull back into cover.

"Christ Kelly, you're right," he whispered. "That's a tire track, and there's no damn car in the middle of this jungle."

Staff Sergeant Brown, the platoon sergeant, suddenly grabbed the officer by the shoulder and heatedly whispered, "Christ, Lieutenant, what the hell are ya doing? You shouldn't be out here, you'll ..." and left the rest of the sentence unspoken. But there was little doubt in Littleton's mind that he was going to say, "fuck it up."

Littleton felt a flush of anger—it wasn't the first time the impertinent SNCO had tried to undermine him—but kept it in check. Littleton suspected Brown resented him because he had been the platoon's temporary commander until he arrived. A pre-war Regular with more than 20 years' service, Brown didn't want to give it up to some snot-nosed second lieutenant. The word among the officers was that the man must have screwed up big time to remain a staff sergeant at a time of rapid promotion. Still, Littleton had tried hard to establish a professional relationship, but Brown had rebuffed his attempts. He sensed the men were scared of Brown and welcomed the change of commanders.

"What's a footprint doing in the stream?" Littleton asked, ignoring Brown's insubordination because he needed the veteran's input. Misreading his intent, Brown thought the young officer slow to grasp the importance of the discovery. Instead of offering advice, he replied cuttingly, "Lieutenant, you better notify the skipper," implying that Littleton didn't know what to do and should ask the company commander for help. With a sigh, Littleton realized he wasn't getting through to Brown, yet he had to admit the man had a good point. "Sanders, get the skipper on the horn," he instructed his radio man.

Looking Brown in the eye, in no uncertain terms he directed him to move a machine gun team up behind the lead fire team, in case they needed more fire power.

Brown glared at him for a moment and then grudgingly nodded, adding, "Lieutenant, I don't like this place one damn bit. A Girl Scout troop with a BB gun could knock the hell out of us." In a final act of insolence, he spit out a stream of tobacco juice, and stalked off to bring the M-60 machine gun team forward.

"Lieutenant, I've got the skipper on the horn." Littleton took the handset. "Lima Six, this is Lima One Actual. Over." Immediately the company commander's voice filled the earpiece: "Roger, One, I've got you loud and clear. What've you got?" As usual, Captain Anderson was direct, without all the military formality of some of the other officers in the battalion.

3

"Lima Six, we've found a fresh footprint in a streambed heading northwest. Over."

"Roger. Understand. What's your position?" With a start, Littleton realized that he didn't have the coordinates and had violated one of the skipper's key tactical principles: know where you are at all times.

Almost by reflex, he reached into the cargo pocket of his utility trousers and took out the acetate-covered 1:50,000 tactical map. Hastily he traced the patrol route from the company's night defensive perimeter, out along the ridgeline, down its slope to the streambed. The hump down had been a ball buster. More than once, men had slipped on the steep slope, crashing through the vegetation, making a hell of a racket.

Estimating the patrol had humped about a thousand meters, Littleton located where he thought they were on the map. But what if he was wrong? Panic set in as the skipper prodded him for his location. *Calm down*, he cautioned himself. *You can do this.* As he studied the map, the brown contour lines gradually sharpened into focus, and he could see how they related to the actual ground the platoon had traversed. His confidence rising, he realized instinctively that he was right.

Using the company's simple code, a four-digit coordinate designated by a car model, he keyed the handset: "Lima Six. From Ford, right four, up six. Over."

Captain Anderson repeated the coordinates and said, "Wait. Out."

Littleton relaxed for a moment, picturing the captain hunched over his map as he translated the code into a location. It was a simple but effective method for encrypting coordinates, for without the four-digit base it was impossible to decipher a location. As a further safeguard, any model car could be used. The platoon commanders had derived great pleasure from using obscure manufacturers until Captain Anderson clamped down after a radio operator misspelled "Dusenburg" and almost called in artillery on the jokester. The company usually had three or four base coordinates, and Lord help the radio operator who sent them in the clear. Anderson believed the NVA monitored the Americans' radio traffic for just such a screw-up.

Littleton's reverie was interrupted by the muffled sounds of movement. Looking up, he spotted the machine gun team approaching. The man in front was a hulk, well over six feet, with a huge chest that was barely protected by the extra-large flak jacket. His biceps were so large he had to cut the sleeves out of his blouse. Two fifty-round belts of linked 7.62mm ammunition were wrapped around his chest, Pancho Villa-style, and he carried the 23-pound M-60 machine gun like it was a toy. Several tubes of gun lubricant were stuck under a piece of rubber inner tube wrapped around his helmet. Struggling to keep up, his sweat-soaked assistant gunner, a much smaller man, carried only a rifle and two boxes of ammunition. His newly issued utilities gave him away as a new man, not yet acclimated to the heat and humidity. Littleton told them to stay behind the first fire team and be ready to support if the riflemen ran into trouble.

The big man nodded and, in a low, confident voice, replied, "Don't worry, Lieutenant. We'll be there when you need us."

There was something about the big machine gunner that impressed Littleton. "What's your name, Marine?"

"Petrovitch, sir," he responded, looking directly at his assistant. "I'm Irish," he said, the hint of a smile on his broad Polish face. With that, he moved to his position.

Shaking his head and smiling despite himself, Littleton marveled at the chutzpa of the man.

Sanders passed him the handset. "Lieutenant, it's the Six," he said. Littleton keyed it and said, "Lima Six, Lima One. Over."

"Roger, One, I've got your position. Go ahead and follow that track, but be careful. The gooks might be using the area as a base camp. I'm moving off the ridge now to support you, but it's going to take time to get there, so watch yourself. Out."

Littleton flipped the handset back to Sanders, looked over at Kelly, caught his eye, and gave him a head nod.

Kelly rose from a crouch and slowly moved forward along the left fork of the steam. Here and there, others rose from the shadows and moved out, maintaining a five-meter spread along both sides of the streambed. As the last man of the first fire team came past, Littleton and Sanders stepped in behind, only three men back from Kelly. He knew Staff Sergeant Brown would disapprove of this exposed position, but, what the hell, he needed to see what was going on. In the back of his mind he could hear his tactics instructor stressing that a platoon commander should be where he could best control his unit. The instructor, an old Korean War veteran, had cautioned the class that a lieutenant's job was to lead, not fight as a rifleman. That lesson, Littleton remembered, had been taught in an air-conditioned classroom—a far cry from the damn hot jungle. And, besides, he had no intention of getting his ass shot off.

Littleton watched Kelly creep slowly along the streambed. The point man seemed to glide along, noiselessly, his head and eyes constantly moving, searching for man-made signs that disturbed the pattern of the jungle. His partner, on the opposite side of the stream, acted in concert, ready to cover Kelly with protective fire. Both men had their M-16s on full automatic, safeties off.

Kelly stopped, squatted down, and closely examined something at his feet. Standing, he glanced toward the left, looked ahead, and then did a double take. His eyes grew wide, a look of horror on his face. He threw himself against the opposite stream bank, M-16 spitting fire, shouting, "Gooks! Gooks! Bunkers! Bunkers!"

Suddenly, he collapsed in a heap as a high-velocity 7.62mm round tore through the front panel of his flak jacket and shattered a bone in his right shoulder. The explosive power of the steel-jacketed bullet shredded flesh and muscle, and propelled the misshapen slug through the back panel, spraying blood as it exited. The terrific force of the blow lifted Kelly off his feet and knocked him unconscious, face down in the streambed, with tendrils of blood staining the water.

The next man in the column, Lance Corporal Tommy Ward, quickly recovered from the shock of the sudden violence and emptied his magazine into the undergrowth. With the last round, he threw himself against the bank and frantically clawed at his ammunition pouch for another magazine. A loud crashing in the underbrush jolted him to attention, as a North Vietnamese soldier rolled off the bank and fell at his feet. In a blind panic, Ward swung his rifle and clubbed the NVA in the head, again and again, before he realized that he was beating the shit out of a cadaver.

Ward fell back against the bank, his whole body shaking from fear and adrenaline. As he lay there, he heard the distinctive snap of AK-47 rounds breaking the sound barrier as they passed close overhead. The third man, Private First Class Steve Rito, dove into cover without firing a shot, his survival instinct overriding his training.

Registering the shouts and gunfire, Littleton stepped into the middle of the stream, hoping to see what was happening. He eyes focused on Kelly just at the moment of the bullet's impact, the ghastly sight indelibly etched in his mind. He clearly saw the strike of the bullet. A puff of dust erupted from the flak jacket and the blood sprayed as it exited. He would always remember the way Kelly's face grimaced with the shock and pain of the wound.

For long seconds, Littleton stood glued to the spot, oblivious to his own safety and totally focused on his wounded Marine, lying helpless a few yards away, still under fire. *Stop shooting at him; he's hit, out of the fight!* his mind screamed. A rage filled him and, without conscious thought, he ran to the wounded man and straddled him while firing his M-16 on full automatic. Rounds thudded into the bank and snapped through the air around him, but he wasn't hit.

Suddenly, off to his left, the M-60 machine gun opened up and 7.62mm rounds scythed the undergrowth in front of him. "Petrovitch!"

The big gunner was an awesome sight as he charged down the streambed, machine gun spitting fire, every fifth round a red tracer. He swung the muzzle back and forth, firing controlled bursts into the NVA position. The stream of bullets tore at the vegetation, raking the ground and hitting several log-reinforced bunkers. By chance, one round entered an embrasure, striking an NVA rifleman in the face, blowing his head into the faces of his two comrades. Hiding in a spider trap overlooking the two Americans in the stream, another soldier winced at their cries of terror, cradling his head in his hands and ducking down. With the two positions out of the fight, there was a noticeable drop in fire. At the same time, Petrovitch ran out of ammunition and took cover against the streambed. He quickly fed another belt into the gun and opened fire into several bunkers that he could see beneath the trees. His assistant gunner joined in with his M-16.

Overcoming his fear, Rito started firing while Ward crawled up the bank to try to spot other bunkers.

Brown ran forward just behind Petrovitch, gesturing and shouting to the men around him, getting them into position to return fire. Littleton spotted him and, in that split second, realized that that's what *he* should have been doing. *Christ*, he thought, *I'm that rifleman the old vet warned us about, and now I'm gonna get my ass shot off.* The thought became a prophecy as a stick-like object sailed out of the undergrowth and landed with a splash at his feet. For a moment he stood, stunned, wondering what it was. Then, as Brown yelled "Grenade!" it came to him: it was a Chicom grenade. Paralyzed, like a deer in a headlight, he waited for it to explode. Nothing happened; the damn thing just lay there. A dud.

The next thing Littleton knew, Brown grabbed him by his flak jacket and roughly pulled him to cover against the bank, alongside Petrovitch. "Jesus Christ, Lieutenant, you're the luckiest son of a bitch alive," Brown growled. And then he crawled over to Kelly and started to pull him to safety. A torrent of emotions swirled in Littleton as he stared at the wounded man. He forced himself to grab Kelly's flak jacket, the cloth covered with congealing blood. Repulsed by the sticky blood on his hand, he fought to maintain composure.

Doc Zimmer, the platoon corpsman, shoved between the two men. He cut through the shirt to expose a mass of torn flesh. Working quickly, the corpsman covered the wound with large battle dressings wrapped tightly to staunch the flow of blood. After tying off the compresses, he readied a bottle of Serum Albumin for injection into Kelly's arm, hoping the blood expander would stabilize the wounded man until he could be evacuated, which had better be pretty damn quick. There was no doubt in his mind that Kelly was an emergency medevac.

Mesmerized by this drama, Littleton was oblivious to the shouting and gunfire around him. He shook his head, trying to clear it of the jumbled image of pain and suffering. Things were happening too fast. He was at a loss for what to do. The expression on his face reflected a mixture of shock and disbelief.

Brown saw the look and shouted, "Lieutenant, if you don't get off your ass, we're going to be in big trouble."

Petrovitch joined in, "I'm running out of ammo. We better do something quick."

Snap out of it, Littleton chided himself. *They're depending on you.* As he looked at the men waiting for him to make a decision, the realization hit him: he was "the man." This wasn't a training exercise, it was live, and in living color. His indecision could cost lives, including his own.

He forced himself to raise his head above the bank to get a better idea of what faced them. For the first time, he noticed the trail leading from the stream up the slope. How had he missed it? The well-worn brown path clearly stood out against the green undergrowth. Just to the left, about five meters away, he saw the bunker, a mound of dirt three feet high with a rectangular firing slit cut into its face. It was so well camouflaged that he would have missed it if the body lying in front of the position had not drawn his attention. Half hidden by foliage, a dead NVA soldier lay face down, a faded green pith helmet still on his head. Kelly probably killed him in the opening exchange of gunfire, Littleton thought.

A burst of automatic weapons fire cracked over his head, forcing him down, but not before he spotted several other suspicious-looking mounds scattered beneath the trees. Turning to Brown, he exclaimed, "I saw at least six bunkers, and there's probably more further up the slope. It looks like we're in the middle of a big complex."

Brown nodded his head in agreement and added, "The gooks'll shoot the shit out of us if we try to take them head-on. And if we stay here much longer, they'll try to get behind us." Littleton realized that the platoon sergeant had stated the obvious without helping to find a solution.

Littleton looked over at Doc Zimmer, who butted in, "We'll never be able to carry Kelly out. He needs to be evacuated as soon as possible."

As he struggled for an answer, Littleton saw Ward working his way up the column, hunched over, staying out of the line of fire. His uniform was soaked with sweat and he was breathing hard. Obviously keyed up, he squatted down and tried to catch his breath. "Lieutenant, I found the flank of the NVA position, and it wasn't defended," he panted. "I worked my way through the jungle almost to the top of the ridge and didn't see a soul." Littleton listened intently, evaluating the information against what he knew of their situation. His face was a study in anxious concentration as he spoke to Brown. "If we put a squad along this streambed and set up a base of fire, the other two squads might be able to envelope their flank. What do you think?"

Brown nodded, clearly recognizing that it would be the officer's ass on the line, not his, if something went wrong. "It's a good plan, Lieutenant. It'll split the platoon, but I think it's the only thing we can do right now." He hesitated, leaving the obvious question hanging in the air. Who would lead the highly vulnerable flankers? They both knew that Corps doctrine held that the officer would lead the two squads.

Littleton settled it. "You take the 1st Squad and the machine gun team, and I'll go with the other two."

Brown showed the barest trace of a smile as he sarcastically replied, "Roger, Lieutenant, we'll keep 'em busy, but you better watch your ass." Then he turned and shouted for the 1st Squad to come up.

2

Lima Company, Night Defense Position, 0700, 12 September, 6 Klicks Northwest KSCB—"Jesus, Gunny, how the hell can you eat cold ham and muthers this early in the morning?" a smiling Captain Andy Anderson asked the older man, who was casually munching on the remains of a C-ration breakfast.

"It's easy Skipper. I just add Tabasco sauce, a slice of raw onion, throw in a couple of hot peppers, and—*voilá*—a meal fit for a Marine," replied Gunnery Sergeant Mike Smith.

Anderson just shook his head. The easy banter between the two underlay a close relationship stretching back over the past several months. A relationship based on mutual professional respect and trust forged during combat operations along the DMZ in the spring and early summer of 1967. Neither man could quite understand how they had survived when most of the other officers and staff noncommissioned officers were lost, but they took comfort in knowing they could absolutely depend on one another in any crisis. There was one other link between the two: Anderson was a former enlisted Marine with 12 years' service who had been commissioned a temporary officer during the Corps' rapid expansion. This was his second Vietnam tour; he had volunteered to return to the war early in the wake of a failed marriage. Smith was a bachelor whose entire life revolved around the Corps.

The company had been ordered to the Khe Sanh plateau for rest and refit after a particularly brutal engagement in the lowlands, which left it whittled down to barely one full-strength platoon. Replacements flooded in, a mixture of Marines right out of boot camp, returning wounded, and men transferred from other units, all of whom swelled the roster to five officers and one hundred fifty enlisted men—still seventy short of the official Marine Corps table-of-organization strength. Moreover, excluding sick, lame, and those on R&R, the company's actual field strength mustered between 120 and

130 Marines at any one time. Each of Anderson's three rifle platoons had a foxhole strength of 30 to 35 men, even after they had been beefed up with men from the weapons platoon. The remainder of the company served in the small headquarters section as radio operators, clerks, and supplymen.

Following two weeks of manning foxholes along the base perimeter, the company was helo-lifted to the hilltop landing zone it now occupied. The mission was to search the jungle for a reported NVA build-up in the area. Due to of a shortage of helicopters, the lift had not gone well. By the time the last of the company arrived, it was almost dusk. Rather than move off the hill in the dark, Anderson elected to dig in and establish a night defensive position. At first light, he sent Littleton's 1st Platoon down the ridge on a patrol route approximately one klick through the jungle. The remainder of the company was in the process of finishing its morning ritual—chow, cleaning weapons, and undertaking personal hygiene—and was preparing to move out. Anderson was anxious to get off the hill; the NVA had a nasty habit of mortaring the hell out of anyone who stayed in one place too long.

Anderson had just finished shaving, an ingrained habit even in the field, when his radio operator, Corporal Eric Johnson, announced that Lieutenant Littleton was on the horn. Dispensing with the usual formal radio procedure, Anderson quickly learned the patrol had found fresh footprints in a streambed, but it took some time for Littleton to report his location. That was understandable, Anderson thought, as it was the young officer's first time in the jungle, and even experienced patrol leaders get lost. By this time, the command group had gathered around him: Gunny Smith; the company executive officer, 1st Lieutenant Gary Miller; and the forward observer, 2nd Lieutenant Tom Napoline. Anderson located the patrol's position on his map, pointing out the rough terrain, which not only made foot movement extremely difficult but was easy for the NVA to hide in. "I don't like him out there all by himself," he observed as he scanned the faces of his command group. "If the intelligence reports are true, the damn gooks could be there in force."

"You're right, Skipper," Miller interjected, "and if they're in bunkers, Littleton could be in real trouble."

Anderson thought for a moment and reached a decision, "Gunny, pass the word: we'll move out in ten minutes."

"Aye aye, sir," Smith answered and broke away from the group, shouting for the platoon sergeants.

Next, Anderson turned to Miller and Napoline. "Gunny, get the platoon commanders up here, I want to talk with them, and, Tom, start thinking how we can get artillery support in that mess down there."

Next, taking the handset from Johnson, Anderson told Littleton that the company was moving out in support, but wouldn't be there for some time.

He cautioned the rookie platoon commander to be careful, which they both knew was futile under the circumstances.

Anderson thought about Littleton, remembering the young officer's enthusiasm as he prepared to move out earlier that morning on his first independent patrol. The youngster had taken quite a few notes at the patrol briefing, making sure he got all the details that would be needed to give instructions to his squad leaders. It was almost comical to see the look of concentration on his face as he tried to organize the information into his own patrol order. Although he had only been with the company two weeks, the tall, good-looking youngster showed a lot of promise. Anderson had kept a watchful eye on him during the company's stint on the lines and noted that Littleton showed maturity beyond his years and experience. He seemed to have a natural ability to lead Marines—one that might be severely tested in the next few hours.

Lieutenant Dick Frazier, a tall, well-proportioned officer, strode over to the CP from the 2nd Platoon area. The most experienced of the lieutenants, he had been with the company three months and had proven to be a good troop leader, although he had not seen any heavy combat. He was well liked and respected by the men for his plain talk and down-to-earth leadership style. It didn't hurt that he was a former All-American football player, who, at six foot three and a muscular 215 pounds, liked to physically mix it up with the troops. In one memorable football game at Khe Sanh, he had knocked hell out of half the platoon, and they loved him for it. A slow talking Southerner, he was an aggressive, competitive officer who hid these traits behind a studied languid manner. His dry sense of humor and keen intellect livened up the infrequent command group bull sessions.

Lieutenant Gary Larson, Frazier's nemesis from the 3rd Platoon, a Midwest farm boy, arrived a few seconds later from the opposite direction. The two men started up their ongoing but good-natured banter that marked them as friendly rivals, each of whom thought his own platoon was the best in the company.

Anderson cut them short with a sarcastic, "All right, boys, let me know when you're finished." Properly chastised, the two officers apologized but were far from repentant. They understood that Anderson encouraged this sort of rough camaraderie.

Looking at Frazier, Anderson said, "Dick, I want your platoon to take the point and move fast, but watch your ass. I don't want to get ambushed. Use your best squad up front and keep them alert."

"Roger Skipper, I'll use Edwards's 2nd Squad. They're the best in the company," Frazier's tone was the soul of propriety, but he had a smile on his face as he glanced over at his competitor.

Before Larson could reply, Anderson continued, "Gary, you're rear security, but be ready to back up Dick if anything goes wrong." This subtle riposte wasn't lost on either junior officer.

Anderson completed the brief by saying, "The command group will follow in trace of the 2nd Platoon. Any questions?" The men shook their heads, and with that, the group broke up and hurried off to oversee preparations.

3

Lima Company, Movement into the Jungle 0730, 12 September—The move down the steep ridge was even more difficult than Littleton's passage had been. "Slick as owl shit" was how Gunny Smith described the slope the first time he fell on his ass—much to the amusement of the troops, who were smart enough not to laugh out loud.

The point had little difficulty following the trail until it reached the stream, where the water obliterated footprints. Frazier's platoon unknowingly veered to the left, away from the 1st Platoon's route, following the same stream, but in the opposite direction. Twenty minutes later, the point discovered a wide, heavily used trail, leading northwest through the undergrowth.

Anderson was still in the streambed with the command group when he received the report. While he came forward to take a look, he passed the word to hold up. He met Frazier about 20 meters in from the stream, standing just off the trail. The undergrowth had thinned out and he could plainly see the track's red clay imprint against the darker shadows of the jungle floor as it wove through the trees up a slight incline. The pathway was at least six feet wide and reminded him of a country lane more than a jungle path. The only thing it lacked was wheel ruts. "What the hell are they using this for?" he whispered to Frazier.

"I don't know Skipper, but it looks like an NVA interstate," Frazier responded, a hint of uneasiness in his voice.

"It's definitely a high-speed trail, and it's been heavily used," Anderson mumbled half to himself, as he inspected the dozens of overlapping sandal prints in the dirt. "I've never seen anything like this before."

Anderson motioned the battalion radio operator, Corporal Mark Reynolds, forward, and the two squatted in the undergrowth while he contacted the battalion operations officer, Major Ron Coffman. The OpsO was an old friend and a savvy, experienced officer who had been a fellow company commander before being promoted and kicked upstairs. Anderson valued his judgment and wasted little time briefing him on the situation, particularly about Littleton's discovery of the footprints.

Coffman acknowledged the information and then said, "Roger, Andy. Be aware Montagnard tribesmen have reported large numbers of NVA just across the Laotian border, maybe heading this way."

As Coffman completed his transmission, a new voice came up on the net, that of Lieutenant Colonel Perry Aldine, the recently assigned battalion commander.

Oh shit, Anderson thought to himself, *what does he want?*

Aldine had replaced a popular, dynamic commander and, in a very short time, had proven to be a heavy-handed, inept martinet. He had spent almost his entire career as a staff officer, avoiding infantry assignments, which was almost a sacrilege to hard-charging grunts like Anderson. It was common knowledge among the company commanders that the colonel didn't know shit about tactics, and it was the consensus that he couldn't lead a Girl Scout troop to the head. He wasn't a leader; Coffman and the battalion executive officer, Major Jim McGinn, ran the battalion.

"Lima Six," Aldine began, "this is Northtide Six. I don't like you to split up. Over."

No shit, Sherlock, Anderson wanted to scream back, *I don't like it anymore than you do*. Instead, he radioed, "Roger. Understand, Six. I'm trying to hook up now. Over."

All he got was an abrupt, "Let me know when you do. Out."

Anderson wanted to throw the handset. *What bullshit!* Here he was, deep in Indian Country, all by himself, and the colonel pulls that shit. Within seconds, however, Coffman was back on the radio with a promise of artillery support and a forward air controller if he needed it. Anderson felt better knowing that Coffman was doing his best to support him, but he nonetheless still smarted from the colonel's curt dismissal. The major signed off with, "Keep your head down," his favorite expression of good luck.

Anderson motioned Frazier closer for a hurried conversation. "Dick, I want you to follow this path, but we need more fire power up front. Put one squad on each side of the trail and bring the other up behind them." Frazier acknowledged the order and moved off to brief his squad leaders.

Within minutes, the column cautiously moved out, on guard for signs of the NVA. An eerie silence pervaded the jungle, adding to a feeling of impending danger. The tension of the Marines of the two lead squads was palpable; sensing the presence of the enemy, the troops redoubled their vigilance. A man in the right-hand squad glanced upward, attracted by strands of oddly tinted gray vines running through the trees. He pointed it out to his squad leader, who exclaimed, "Vines my ass. That's gook comm wire!"

The news hit the column like a jolt of electricity. The experienced men knew the NVA used telephone wire at battalion level or higher. "This is some serious shit," an old hand mumbled.

As his command group reached the edge of a small open area 50 meters behind the lead platoon, Anderson called a halt. The radio operators took advantage of the stop and immediately crapped out, welcoming the opportunity to take a break. Napoline, Miller, and the two platoon commanders squatted around Anderson unknowingly creating an irresistible target for Private Second Class Nguyen Van Hung, an 18-year-old member of the 3rd Company, 1st Battalion, 24th Regiment of the 304th Division. Hung's mission was to pick out the American leaders and target them for destruction after his company sprang the ambush. From his position in a camouflaged trench, he watched the Americans approach.

Almost beside himself with anxiety, Hung waited for an opportunity to use his RPG-2 antitank grenade launcher. As soon as he spotted the group, he forgot the orders to wait for the signal, stood up, sighted in, and squeezed the pistol-grip trigger. The fin-stabilized 40mm round erupted from the tube with a loud explosion and sped toward the Americans, prematurely triggering the ambush.

Caught off guard, the other members of 3rd Company opened a ragged fire from concealed positions 50 to 75 meters off the right side of the trail.

At the sound of the launcher, Anderson's head snapped up and his eye caught sight of a red ball tracking toward him. The grenade flashed by. It struck a tree limb and exploded, sending jagged slivers of steel downward into the circle of men.

The force of the blast knocked the squatting officers to the ground, momentarily stunning them. Anderson recovered first and stood up, only to drop down again as heavy small arms fire and the snap of close rounds sounded around him. He crawled among the prone men trying to determine how badly they had been hit. Gunny Smith and a corpsman, who had been outside the kill radius, came over to help. The lucky shot had devastated the command group, particularly the radio operators, who were prone on the ground, their bodies entirely exposed to the shrapnel. Reynolds was beyond help; he had unzipped his flak jacket and a shard had pierced his heart, killing him instantly. Johnson lay moaning, blood welling from several leg wounds. A third operator, Private First Class Jackson, hunched against a tree, his face a mask of blood from a scalp wound, his left arm ripped from shoulder to elbow. Two others outside the bursting radius escaped injury.

The officers fared somewhat better. Because they had been squatting, their helmets and flak jackets absorbed most of the shrapnel. Even so, Frazier's nose bled from concussion, his left ear was shredded, and he seemed disoriented, his eyes unfocused. Larson lay on his stomach, a hole in his right buttock, tears of pain coursing down his cheeks. It was Miller who was hit hardest. A piece of shrapnel had struck downward, somehow missing his helmet and the protective shoulder of his flak jacket. It penetrated the fleshy part of his neck just above the clavicle and entered his chest cavity, piercing a lung. As he struggled to breath, a bloody froth welled from his mouth. Napoline escaped without a scratch and, although shook up, was helping with the wounded.

As Anderson stared at the scene, struggling to cope with the loss, weariness threatened to overwhelm him. All he wanted was to close his eyes and sleep, but a voice kept interrupting, and he finally realized that Smith was talking to him. "Skipper, are you okay?"

Anderson shook his head to clear some of the fogginess from his brain, "Yeah, just a little tired."

"Tired my ass. You're hit. There's blood all over your arms, and your leg looks like it has a ding."

Anderson looked down and saw the blood, feeling the pain of the wounds for the first time. He realized that he had been going into shock. *Bullshit*, he thought. *Snap out of it. You've got to lead this company!*

"Gunny, what've we got?" he demanded.

"Skipper, we got heavy fire coming from our right front," Smith responded, "They're in bunkers. Harder than hell to spot. The 1st Platoon is pinned down but returning fire, and the rest of the company is sitting on its ass waiting for someone to tell them what to do."

"Well, that's going to happen right now," Anderson replied resolutely. He shouted over to Frazier, who had recovered, and was tying a battle dressing on his destroyed ear. "Dick, get your lazy ass up there and get that platoon organized. Set up a base of fire along the right side of the road."

Galvanized into action by the vehemence of Anderson's order, Frazier completed the knot and went off to join his men, muttering obscenities the whole way.

Napoline, who was still helping with the wounded, was next to feel the lash of Anderson's tongue, "Napoline, stop playing nurse and get that fuckin' artillery going. I want it right now!"

Standing up despite the fire, Anderson limped over to Larson. His leg hurt like hell, but he forced himself to ignore it. "Larson, get back to your platoon. They need you."

"Skipper," Larson moaned, "I can't. I'm wounded."

"Gary, it's just a scratch," Anderson lied as he scanned the torn flesh, "You're a Marine officer, and it's time to earn your pay. Now get up and do your job. Marines are depending on you." Larson lay there for a long moment, stung by the rebuke, but he rolled over, grimaced with pain, and extended a hand. Anderson took it and struggled to pull him up, grunting with the effort, pain etched on his own face from his arm wounds. The two men looked into one another's eyes.

Anderson spoke first, his voice quivering with emotion, "Good man, Gary. I knew you could do it."

Larson shook his head in wonder. "Christ, Skipper, you're a hard man." Then he turned and hobbled painfully back down the trail to his Marines.

Dick Frazier was pissed. His ear hurt like hell and the thought of losing it made him livid. "What girl will go out with a one-eared man?" he mumbled pathetically to himself. "Shit, I'll be a freak, all because of those goddam gooks!" He was also a little mad at Anderson for getting on him. "Lazy ass. I'll show him," he said out loud just as he reached several of his men who had taken cover behind a fallen tree. "Jesus, Lieutenant, you look like shit," one of the men exclaimed when he saw the officer's bloody face and the large green battle dressing that covered the side of his head. Frazier stared at the miscreant, eyes blazing, nostrils flaring. The men waited for the explosion of his famous temper. They weren't disappointed, "What'd you fucking expect? I got shot in the fucking head," he barked, pointing at the dressing, his hand mimicking a pistol. For several seconds he looked at them, and then he cracked up with a huge belly laugh. His men just stared, not sure whether he was in his right mind. Maybe he had been shot in the head.

Another grenade hit the ground, exploding harmlessly. But the debris thrown by the back blast exposed the enemy position. Immediately, several Marines fired, hitting an NVA soldier several times in the throat and head before he could take cover. Death went unrecorded by his comrades in the 3rd Company, as they continued to pour fire at the Americans.

Napoline and his radio operator, Private First Class Hoenig, lay behind a tree, the young officer shouting over the radio at his counterpart in the artillery battery. Infuriatingly slow, the dipshit wanted a formal call for fire, right out of the book. Napoline, under fire for the first time, his voice registering about ten octaves above normal, gave the essentials and wanted them to shoot immediately. Still unconvinced of the urgency, the artilleryman at base asked how close the NVA were. Fed up, Napoline keyed the handset, held it up so the crack of small arms could be heard, lowered it, and said, "I don't know exactly, but if you wait another minute, you can ask them yourself!" That did the trick. Within moments, a voice announced, "Shot!" to indicate that a high-explosive 105mm shell was on the way. Napoline said a prayer, hoping his coordinates were right. If he was wrong, they'd have the damn thing in their laps.

A massive explosion in the jungle rent the air. He couldn't be sure, but it sounded like it was short and needed deflection. "Hoenig, tell 'em 'add 200 and left 50,'" he ordered. Another pause, and then a noise like a freight train thundering past was followed by a terrific explosion in the treetops, directly above the NVA positions.

"Holy shit! Right on target, Lieutenant," Hoenig screamed and called, "Fire for effect, fire for effect," into the handset.

Gunny Smith took the three radios from the wounded operators and had just passed them to Anderson when the first 105mm round exploded. "Get some! Kill the bastards," he blared as he pressed a battle dressing on Miller's wound, his hands and arms smeared with the officer's blood. "Come on, Lieutenant, stay with me," he growled when he saw the officer's eyes roll back in his head. "Don't die on me, goddam it!"

A corpsman pushed the gunny aside and initiated mouth-to-mouth, but a rush of blood gushed out, forcing him to stop. Miller went limp, no longer struggling for breath. The corpsman shook his head; there was nothing more he could do.

"Fuck," Smith yelled, striking his thigh in exasperation. "Goddam gook bastards."

Anderson heard Littleton call him over the radio. *Calm down*, he told himself. *Don't let the kid know we're in deep shit too. He's got enough problems of his own.* He took a deep breath and keyed the handset, "Lima One, this is Lima Six ..."

4

1st Battalion, North Vietnamese Army, Command Bunker, 0730, 12 September, 9 Klicks Northwest KSCB—As Lima Company moved off the ridge, Lieutenant Colonel Pham Le Duc, commanding officer of the NVA 1st Battalion, put down the Chinese-made Type 63 radio handset and motioned to one of the headquarters runners squatting near the entrance to the underground bunker. "Younger Brother, I want you to take this message to the 3rd Company and deliver it to *Trung Uy* Hoi." He handed the runner a few lines he had jotted down on a field message form. "Hurry. I want this delivered immediately."

Duc watched as the young soldier scurried out of the bunker and then turned to Major Vu Van Minh, the battalion *Chinh-Uy*. "Regiment has ordered us to attack the Americans and keep them from finding out about our preparations for the attack on their combat base," he explained while fully understanding that the cadre probably already knew about the orders through his own chain of command. "Yes, *Trung Ta*," Minh smugly responded, formally addressing Duc by his rank. "I am aware. It has been decided that the 1st Battalion will have the honor of defeating the interlopers." He made it sound like he had been personally involved in the decision. *The only interloper is you*, Duc thought as he stared blankly at the newly assigned political officer, trying hard not to register his distaste for the pompous little insect. The man had only been with him for a few days, and in that short time had proven himself to be an insufferable fool. He was arrogant, vain, and totally lacking in common sense—the antithesis of Duc, who prided himself on being an elder brother to the 450 fighters in his battalion.

"How do you intend to defeat the Americans?" Minh haughtily demanded, further antagonizing Duc, who knew the fight would be a desperate affair with no assurance of the outcome. The 42-year-old battalion commander was a hardened combat veteran. He joined the Vietminh at 16 to fight the

Japanese, four years later he had commanded a platoon, and at 30 he had led a company through the wire of Dien Bien Phu's outpost Beatrice, barely surviving a close encounter with a member of *La Légion étrangère*.

"*Thieu Ta* Minh," Duc answered, unable to keep the scorn out of his voice, "I am going to defeat the Americans with the One Quick and Two Strongs maneuver." It was obvious by the look on the political officer's face that he had no idea what Duc was talking about. "Lieutenant Hoi's 3rd Company will ambush the Americans with a quick attack," he explained, "killing and wounding as many as possible, then squads from the 1st and 2nd companies will strike from each flank and destroy them—quick attack, strong fight, and strong assault." Without pausing, he added contemptuously, "Major, I know you want to be at the heart of the action to inspire the men, so I will have a guide take you to Lieutenant Hoi's position." Without waiting for an answer, Duc summoned another runner and directed him to escort the political officer to the 3rd Company's position.

Minh's expression remained impassive, but his eyes registered shock as he realized he had been outmaneuvered. He tried to put the best face on it by thanking the commander for allowing him to be at the place of honor, but it was obvious he was pissed. "*Lo dit*," Duc muttered as Minh left the bunker.

Major Co, the battalion's deputy commander, stepped away from the corner of the bunker from which he had watched the exchange between the two men. "*Trung Ta*, I believe you have made an enemy," he commented as his commander stomped around the bunker fuming. "Is it wise to alienate the cadre so directly?"

"The man is a *Do cho de*," Duc responded angrily, "an idiot. Reality is what counts here, not political rhetoric. Let's see if slogans protect him from American bullets." Co, who was familiar with Duc's notorious temper, knew it was best to let the older man calm down before addressing a strategy to deal with the political officer. The two men had served together for years and were more like father and son than commander and subordinate. In public they maintained a strict decorum, but in private they shared thoughts that would have gotten them relieved, or worse, if the cadre found out. For long moments, Duc stared out the bunker's entrance, and then turned to his subordinate. "I'm sorry, old friend, I did not mean to take out my frustrations on you. I have a sharp tongue and little will power to curb it."

Co nodded, accepting the apology. He knew that Duc's leadership and tactical savvy should have earned him higher command, but his temper kept him in trouble with the political cadre. "Elder brother, the man is dangerous. He is a party member with much influence. I believe he is vindictive and will try to find a way to get even."

Duc knew his deputy was right, and he chafed with that knowledge. Minh's authority was greater than his own. The military command was subordinate to the *Lao Dong*, the Communist Party, which had the last word over tactical decisions.

The Party's control of the military was particularly onerous for Duc because the cadre reminded him of water buffalos, dimwitted and slow; they had to be prodded with a stick before they would exert themselves. He considered them out of touch with the realities of the battlefield. Since the arrival of the Americans, with their massive fire power and helicopter mobility, Duc thought it was stupid to fight in conventional battle. He had seen what their airplanes and artillery could do and knew a stand-up slug fest couldn't be won. And yet, the Politburo were preparing for just this sort of battle. They called it the 1967–68 Winter–Spring Campaign, whose goal was to lure the Americans to the isolated Khe Sanh plateau, where they could be cut off and destroyed. Many of the cadre called it their Dien Bien Phu strategy and dreamed of a victory that would destroy the American will to resist as it had the French. Duc admitted that the two locations had many of the same military similarities—both were isolated outposts surrounded by dominating hills, and both had but a single runway to serve as a logistics lifeline—but there the resemblance ended. Duc's experience with American air power convinced him that it was the key ingredient for a successful defense that the French had lacked. He and Major Co had discussed the situation many times and were of a like mind, but, as long as the political officers were in charge, they had little choice but to obey.

Despite Duc's misgivings about the forthcoming offensive, he drove his battalion hard, digging fortifications—everything from simple foxholes to bunkers and hundreds of yards of trench lines. Digging was a way of life for his soldiers, and they quickly prepared new positions, completing them in as little as one to two hours, including the all-important camouflage. The positions of his three rifle companies formed a rough circle around his command bunker, taking advantage of good defensive terrain and dense overhead cover to hide the positions from aerial observation. The battalion dug two lines of fighting holes and bunkers 50 to 200 meters apart, so if one line was penetrated, the troops could fall back to the second via connecting trenches. Individual positions were L-shaped, with an open trench on one end, about four feet long and chest high. The short end, at right angles, was covered with tree limbs and packed earth, making it safe from everything but a direct hit. Firing ports were sited so that each bunker could cover others with interlocking bands of rifle or machine gun fire. Duc attached his support company's 57mm and 75mm recoilless rifles to the infantry companies but positioned his three 82mm mortars in the center of the battalion position. As protection against the hated aircraft, Duc located four 12.7mm antiaircraft machine guns on the high ground east of his position, with strict instructions to hold their fire until ordered. They were not to expose their position under any circumstance.

Other units were also busy constructing protected camps, strongpoints, and gun positions around the Khe Sanh Combat Base. Duc heard rumors that at least one other division would join the 304th for the attack on the American base, as well as several artillery and air defense units. Although the addition of the antiaircraft guns made him feel somewhat better, he still had nagging doubts about concentrating so many men in one area. In particular, he worried about the Americans discovering their preparations and launching a pre-emptive strike, so he maintained constant patrols in the jungle around his position and had two-man teams watch all the potential hilltop landing zones. His misgivings were confirmed when one of the surveillance teams spotted American helicopters landing on a hilltop not too far away. He immediately informed the regimental commander, who directed Duc to keep the Americans under surveillance. Duc's scouts reported the Americans leaving the hill and heading in the general vicinity of the battalion, and Duc's battalion had been ordered to attack them. His plan was simple—spring an ambush with 3rd Company, using small arms, RPGs, and recoilless rifles while small groups from 1st and 2nd companies sealed off the flanks, trapping the Americans between them. He counted on the violence of the attack to completely overwhelm the defenders so they couldn't mount an organized defense long enough to bring in the deadly airplanes. In case the opening attack failed to destroy them, 3rd Company's *Trung Uy* Hoi was to have his fighters hug the Americans close, so they couldn't use artillery and air without becoming casualties themselves.

With everything in place, there was nothing else Duc could do except wait for the start of the battle, which for him was the hardest time of all, for he was a man of action. Despite his years of service, Duc still considered himself a *Bo doi* at heart and privately longed to trade his burdensome responsibilities for the uncomplicated status of a rear-rank private. He chafed at having to deal with incompetent political cadre who wanted to play a direct role during battle. *Most couldn't lead children to play*, he thought with a chuckle. His mood brightened as he visualized Minh strutting pompously at the head of a group of unruly youngsters.

Two wiremen entered the bunker, interrupting Duc's thoughts. They unreeled a spool of gray plastic-coated telephone wire and connected it to a Chinese model switchboard, allowing Duc to talk with his subordinate commanders by landline, a more secure means of communication than radio. The gray sheet-metal case was mounted on one of the logs propping up the roof and manned by a radio operator from the signal platoon, who quickly tested it, verifying voice contact with Lieutenant Hoi.

Duc took the sound-powered handset and asked the young officer for a status report. "*Trung Ta*," Hoi excitedly replied, "the Americans are approaching Sergeant Xuan's platoon, and he's preparing to open fire." Duc studied the meticulously hand-drawn map spread out on the rough table in front of him, visualizing the Americans advancing along the trail that led past the 3rd Company's position. They would be spread out in a long column, ripe for the ambush that would split them into small, isolated groups, ready for Hoi's fighters to rush in with bayoneted rifles to annihilate the hapless survivors. Duc knew the key to success lay in catching all the Americans in the kill zone and overwhelming them before they could organize an effective resistance. In the spring battle, his battalion had caught an American company in just such an ambush and inflicted casualties of over 130 enemy dead. It had been a great victory, but not without cost. Dozens of planes had attacked them as they attempted to break contact. Duc vividly remembered the feeling of helplessness under merciless pounding from the air and vowed that it wouldn't happen again. He silently cursed the Americans: *Let their rice bowls be full of shit, and may their children spit upon them in life and on their graves in death.*

"Lieutenant Hoi, remember your instructions," Duc said into the handset. "Don't fire until all the Americans are in the killing zone," he cautioned the young officer for perhaps the fourth time. "The timing is critical; you must overwhelm them quickly so they can't fight back."

"Yes, *Trung Ta*, I understand completely," Hoi quickly replied, anxious to end the conversation so he could get back to the business at hand. This was his first real test as a company commander, and he was determined to do well. But his commander's repeated guidance was making him jumpy. Hoi was beginning to think the colonel lacked confidence in his abilities.

Sensing the officer's anxiety, Duc abruptly ended the conversation with his standard exhortation, "*Nam vung thoi-co*—seize the opportunity." He passed the handset to the operator and turned to Major Co.

"I'm getting to be like an old grandmother," he observed, chiding himself. "I can't seem to let them go on their own." Co smiled, understanding that Duc placed great trust in his subordinates' judgment and gave them a good deal of latitude in decision making, much to the disgust of the new political officer.

"*Trung Ta*," he replied, "the men know you only have their best interests at heart …"

A sudden blast, which they subconsciously registered as an RPG, interrupted the conversation. "*Do moi ro*—son of a bitch," Duc swore. His mind raced. *Something has gone wrong; there should be heavy automatic weapons fire, not just a single RPG round.*

5

1st Platoon, Lima Company, 0930, 12 September, North Vietnamese Bunker Complex—Littleton moved back along the streambed, Ward in tow, until they reached Sanders. The platoon commander retrieved the radioman's handset, keyed the mike, and requested to speak to the Six. The company radio keyed, and Littleton was startled to hear a backdrop of explosions and automatic weapons fire. *What the hell?* he thought. *The company must be in contact.* His thought was interrupted by the calm voice of Captain Anderson, who sounded like he didn't have a care in the world.

"Lima One, this is Lima Six. We've run into a large bunker complex, and it's slowing us down. I estimate it'll take three or four hours before we reach your position. Over."

Littleton acknowledged the information, suddenly realizing that he was on his own. Several hours could be a lifetime, especially if Brown was right and the NVA decided to push hard against his isolated platoon. He explained his situation—the heavily used path, multiple bunkers, and an automatic weapon—and spelled out his plan of action, hoping the skipper would have some tactical words of wisdom. Instead, Anderson's next transmission sent chills down his spine.

"John, based on your information and the extent of the position I'm facing, I believe we're in the middle of an NVA battalion-sized base camp. It's imperative that you fight through and consolidate on the high ground north of your position. Over."

The skipper's use of his first name came as a shock, and then Littleton put it together: Anderson was trying to tell him they were *both* in deep shit. The company was split up in two separate bunker complexes, large enough in all to support three or four hundred North Vietnamese infantrymen. Littleton thought about his paltry 25 men and decided he better get off his ass and get to that high ground. "Roger, Six," he transmitted. "I'm on the move."

27

Littleton passed the word for the two squad leaders, Corporal Duvall and Lance Corporal Stevens. They came up and he briefed them on the maneuver. Satisfied that they knew what he wanted, he told Ward to lead them into position. Behind him, he could hear Brown's men in the streambed open up a steady ammunition-conserving fire, mixed with the heavier report of AK-47s.

Ward climbed the stream bank and cautiously moved out through the forest. Littleton and the two squads followed in column. Visibility was poor; they couldn't see more than a couple of meters through the dense, thickly carpeted undergrowth. Tension mounted, the men all too aware that the terrain was just right for an ambush.

After 15 minutes, Ward held up his hand, and the column halted. Littleton crept forward, surprised to see the undergrowth had been cleared away, leaving an open area more than 50 meters in diameter beneath the jungle canopy. Stretching in front of him were the unmistakable signs of an NVA base camp: bamboo huts with thatched roofs, well-worn dirt paths, and even hammocks strung between the trees. Here and there were the tell-tale earthen mounds, which indicated the location of protective bunkers and trenches. He could even see an outdoor classroom, with its rows of log benches. He realized he and his Marines had come in behind the NVA fighting bunkers and were in position to sweep through and take them in the rear—if they moved quickly.

Littleton rushed to get the two squads on line, facing the NVA positions. Silently, the men crouched behind trees. Several Marines fixed bayonets.

The squad leaders watched Littleton pull the pin of a red smoke grenade and throw it as far as he could. As the striker hit the igniter, there was a distinct *pop*, then the canister struck the ground, bounced several times, and stopped. Red smoke blossomed forth, a signal to let the men in the streambed know the rest of the platoon was about to move into their line of fire.

When Littleton motioned his men forward, everyone immediately started firing into the enemy position. *Let's hope Brown can see the smoke through the trees*, Littleton thought. *We could get shot by our own men.*

Gunfire echoed through the trees, mingling with the shouts of the squad leaders keeping the men on line. As they passed the first bunker, a Marine broke off and pitched a fragmentation grenade through the entrance. "Fire in the hole!" he yelled, then ducked behind cover as the explosion of the M-26 rocked the mud-covered log roof. Debris and gray smoke erupted from the opening.

The line moved forward, a rhythm developing—shoot, frag, and move on. Suddenly, two Marines on the left, Tolliver and Edgar, crumpled as bullets struck the dirt around them.

Edgar screamed in agony, legs thrashing the ground, until a bullet cut off his cries. Tolliver curled into a ball, mumbling, "Help me, help me," over and over. Nearby riflemen who saw the two men fall called out "Corpsman!"

Attracted by the yell, Doc Zimmer sprinted toward them, ignoring the danger. Bullets from an NVA machine gun snapped through the foliage, forcing the line of Marines to take cover, including Zimmer, who crawled the last few feet to the fallen men.

The momentum of the attack evaporated under a hail of enemy fire as more North Vietnamese joined in. Marine fire dropped off, allowing the NVA time to organize against this unexpected threat. Littleton realized that, unless he could knock out the machine gun and regain the initiative, his men were in danger of being overwhelmed.

"Where the hell is that gun?" he yelled above the noise.

Stevens, several meters to his left, shouted back, "It's at your ten o'clock, in a bunker just to the right of the big rock."

"I can't see it from here. Too much brush in the way. I'm coming over." With that, Littleton slipped out of the small depression in which he had taken cover and crawled over to Stevens's position, behind a fallen tree.

A North Vietnamese soldier, attracted by the movement, rose to get a good shot. But before he could, Stevens squeezed off a round, hitting the man in the chest. The light, high-velocity 5.56mm bullet deflected off a rib and tumbled through the soldier's chest cavity, destroying his heart and killing him instantly. The body collapsed in a heap.

Completely absorbed in locating the enemy position, Littleton was unaware that Stevens had probably saved his life. Half-rising to look over the log, he was grabbed by the cartridge belt and pulled down. "What the hell?" he exclaimed. Stevens, a concerned look on his face said, "Lieutenant, they've got this thing zeroed in. You'll get your head blown off." Smiling sheepishly, Littleton nodded and slithered to the end of the log, where he cautiously peered out.

At first, he couldn't see the bunker. Then, the muzzle flash of a gun caught his eye. Squinting, he could make out the firing aperture in what looked like a mound of dirt about a hundred feet away. No wonder it had been so hard to spot; the damn thing was only a couple of feet high and covered with foliage that blended in with the surrounding vegetation.

As Littleton watched, an NVA soldier appeared almost out of the ground alongside the emplacement and heaved a Chicom. It landed short of the log and lay there, giving Littleton a chance to pull his head back before the explosion. He could feel the tree vibrate as chunks of steel plough into it. *Stevens is right*, he thought. *They know we're here. We better do something fast.*

He reviewed his limited options. A charge across the open ground was out of the question; they'd be chewed to pieces within ten feet. Artillery and air were out; they were too close to the NVA position. No one could throw a grenade that far and get it in the firing slit. Maybe the "blooper man" could get one close; at least it might keep their heads down for a few moments. Littleton began to formulate a plan.

First, he told Stevens to collect a couple of LAAWs and then get his M-79 man in position to hit the area around the bunker with as many 40mm grenades as he could. He passed the word for everyone to fire as fast as possible on his command.

As he waited for confirmation that the troops were ready, Littleton inspected one of the LAAWs, realizing as he did that the success of his plan depended on a weapon that had a reputation for not working half the time. This one was pretty beat up; small dents and scratches covered the tube, which had lost most of its green paint. The other wasn't any better. *It better work*, he thought. *I'm not going to get a second chance.*

With that in mind, Littleton turned to Stevens. "When I give the word, make sure everyone fires as fast as they can. I'm depending on it to keep the gooks down while I fire the LAAW." The young Marine looked at Littleton as if he were crazy and said, "Lieutenant, I can't believe you're going to stand up right in front of that machine gun."

"Stevens," he replied, "have you got a better plan?" He then bent over the rocket, pulled the safety pins and extended the tube into the firing position.

Satisfied that he was ready, Littleton took a deep breath and gave the word to open fire. His men responded, sending dozens of M-16 rounds slashing into the enemy bunker complex, forcing the NVA to duck. The M-79 man fired three quick grenades, one of which landed just in front of the machine gun position and sent up a shower of debris, momentarily blinding the gunner.

Littleton saw his chance and stood up, fully erect, with the rocket launcher on his shoulder. Forcing himself to ignore the fear that threatened to overwhelm him, he carefully sighted in on the bunker's embrasure and pushed the rubber-coated detent. Nothing happened! *Christ!* he thought as he pressed it again, triggering a startling explosion as the propellant blew the rocket out of the tube, scaring the hell out of him and causing an involuntary flinch—a miss, he thought. A split second later, there was another explosion as the shape charge impacted the dirt in front of the bunker. The warhead, designed to penetrate the armor of a tank, easily pierced the puny earthen barrier and exploded inside the bunker. A shower of dirt, metal, body parts, and wood flew several feet in the air.

Littleton stared at the spectacle for a few seconds, and then, overcoming his paralysis, picked up his rifle and shouted, "Let's go! Let's go!"

Without even a backward glance, he ran forward. The two squad leaders jumped up, echoing their officer's shout, "Let's go! Let's go!" and charged toward the NVA position. The rest of the men broke cover and followed, caught up in the emotion of the moment. Littleton's actions had turned the tide, the NVA were stunned by the loss of the key to their defense, while the Marines were inspired by the bravery of their leader. The momentum on the battlefield had shifted.

As Littleton raced toward the destroyed emplacement, an enemy soldier, groggy from the explosion, rose from a trench. Armed with an SKS semi-automatic rifle with fixed bayonet, he extended the weapon in the classic "on-guard" fighting position. Almost without conscious thought, Littleton swung the barrel of his M-16 and fired every round in the magazine, stitching the Viet from hip to shoulder. The dead man fell back, landing on his two comrades in the trench, knocking them down in a welter of arms, legs, and weapons.

As he jumped over the men, Littleton took in the scene and realized he was in big trouble as the two living NVA sorted themselves out. He dropped down on one knee and attempted to get a grenade out of the Marine-issue pouch. As usual, the damn snaps were stuck. He struggled to pull them open, but it was too late; one of the enemy soldiers was already bringing his Kalashnikov up, finger on the trigger, ready to shoot. Littleton's muscles tightened. Suddenly, out of nowhere, Stevens leaped up on the berm and emptied his rifle into the two, killing them instantly. Dumbfounded, Littleton locked eyes with Stevens, who nodded slightly and gave the officer a thumbs-up, saying, "Lieutenant, you need a full-time bodyguard." And then he grinned.

As the NCO jumped down from the exposed position, a burst of fire caught him in the chest and neck, dropping him on top of the three bodies. Littleton yelled for a corpsman and leaped into the trench, landing on a corpse, which lay in a mixture of blood and body fluids. Regaining his footing, he took Stevens in his arms and lifted him to the lip of the trench. But there was no pulse. Stevens's heroic act had cost him his life. Littleton held the young Marine's hand, his eyes full of anguish as tears streamed down his cheeks.

Corporal Duvall laid a hand on his shoulder. "You all right, Lieutenant?" For a brief moment, Littleton said nothing. Then he rose and motioned his men forward.

***

A rifleman in the 2nd Squad, Private First Class Gonzales, was momentarily separated from his buddy and turned to locate him. Failing to detect the slightly wilted ground cover three feet to his right front, Gonzales was oblivious to the rifle barrel of an AK-47 stealthily poking through the foliage. A single shot rang out and Gonzales pitched forward on his face, screaming from the pain of the wound. The 7.62mm had entered his lower back on an angle, below the protection of the flak jacket, and passed through his body—a through-and-through wound—without hitting any major organs. A member of his squad saw where the shot came from, ran forward, and fired several times into the ground. Then, cautiously bending over, he used his rifle barrel to push aside a small section of undergrowth, exposing a badly wounded North Vietnamese in a spider trap. A round wicker top plaited with twigs and grass to camouflage it covered the hole, which was just large enough for a man to sit in.

Without warning, a dozen Vietnamese jumped up from a trench and ran through the trees. Shouting "Gooks! Gooks!" in unison, the Marines opened fire with a vengeance, finally able to see a live enemy. Most forgot to aim in the excitement and simply sprayed automatic fire at the rapidly disappearing enemy, praying for a hit—"spraying and praying"—with predictable results: only five of the laggards fell before the others reached the safety of the trees.

All this was played out to the disgust of Corporal Duvall, a former rifle team shooter. He had preached marksmanship until he was blue in the face, and now he watched his men throw it away in their first big firefight. He was pissed and in the mood to kick some serious butt. To make matters worse, one of his fire teams took off after the Vietnamese, another tactical no-no that might trigger an ambush. Duvall called them back, and only Littleton's presence on the battlefield kept him from manhandling the team leader.

When they reached the edge of the forest, Littleton stopped the men from going farther, unwilling to risk losing more of them to NVA snipers who might be waiting in the dense undergrowth. He had a hard time holding the Marines back; they were fired up, emotionally pumped, as adrenaline surged through their veins. They wanted blood to settle the score, and a few NVA bodies weren't going to cut it.

Littleton took a moment to assess the situation. He knew that the platoon had to get to the hill quickly or it would be in deep shit. But the casualties were a major impediment. The platoon couldn't move out until all the wounded had been stabilized, but that would take time—and what if the former tenants came back to reclaim their digs?

Having limited options, Littleton placed the two squads in a horseshoe defense to cover the trail in case the NVA decided to counterattack. He sent a runner back to bring up the rest of the platoon, took a deep breath and tried to wind down.

6

1st Platoon, Base of Fire, Streambed, 0930, 12 September—As Anderson's men moved into position, 1st Squad hurried forward, goaded by Brown's shouts as he stood hunched over in the middle of the stream, waving them on. The four-foot stream bank was just high enough to provide protection for the base of fire, but the crack of small arms close overhead was unnerving.

One new man, Edwards, made the mistake of going to ground just as he reached Brown. The SNCO sprang forward, grabbed the surprised Marine by his flak jacket, and pulled him to his feet. Leaning forward, so they were face to face, Brown administered a short, menacing tongue-lashing in his best drill instructor voice: "Get your sorry ass up and get a firing position, or I'll take your head off and shit in it!" The young Private First Class, not long out of boot camp, flashed back to the "grinder", where men with that same tone of voice had commanded instant obedience. "Yes, sir," he responded, and hastily moved out, ignoring the gunfire.

Brown grabbed the squad leader as he came by and told him to pass the word to open fire but to conserve ammunition. He didn't want anyone on automatic and burning up all they had. "Aimed fire only," he ordered.

The seven men took cover, picking spots where they were fairly well protected, and opened up a steady covering fire to keep the NVA pinned down. Brown moved back and forth behind the men, shouting encouragement and chiding them to slow their rate of fire.

Brown was most concerned about Petrovitch, who was drawing heavy fire. He seemed to live a charmed life. Leaves and small twigs floated down on his head and shoulders, severed by bullets clipping the foliage. The savvy gunner played it smart. After firing a few bursts, he changed positions, never allowing the NVA time to zero in on him. Each new position gave him a different angle of fire, which kept the defenders off balance; they didn't know where his bullets would come from next.

Petrovitch lifted the heavy M-60 and cautiously placed it on the ground with the barrel resting on its fully extended bipod legs. With just his upper body exposed above the bank, he settled behind the gun, pushing his shoulder into the butt of the weapon. Edwards, breathing heavily, flopped down beside him and quickly snapped a 50-round belt onto the link hanging from the gun. Petrovitch glanced at Edwards and grinned paternally. He knew the kid was scared shitless, but was still doing his job. Misunderstanding the smile, Edwards thought, *This guy is crazy. He's actually enjoying this shit.*

Petrovitch gently squeezed the trigger, sending a five-round burst into a mound that was spitting fire. The red tracer showed that he was right on target, but, as his finger tightened on the trigger again, dozens of 7.62mm rounds impacted the ground around him, sending a cloud of dust and debris into the air. Edwards fell back, arms outstretched, helmet flying. He landed spread-eagled in the streambed. Petrovitch dropped down, dragging the gun with him, miraculously unhurt in the hail of automatic weapons fire. Reaching out to Edwards, he pulled him closer to the bank, cradling his head, expecting to find a terrible wound. But there was no blood, and no torn flesh, just a large bruise above the temple. As Petrovitch picked up the helmet, he saw the large tear where a 7.62mm bullet had grazed the side, knocking Edwards unconscious. He gently laid the youngster against the bank, picked up the M-60, and quickly inspected it, praying that it was still operable.

Brown knew he had to do something, but every time he rose to shoot, a hail of bullets forced him to duck. He crawled over to Petrovitch. "Jesus Christ, we gotta do something about that gun or we're finished," he shouted above the noise. The big gunner nodded, looked directly into his eyes, and asked, "Will you feed the gun and spot for me?"

Brown stared back, smiling at the challenge, "You bet your ass, Marine," he said, "Let's get some!"

The two crawled over to a low spot in the bank, where a tree had fallen and created a space beneath it large enough to push the M-60 through. Using his entrenching tool, Petrovitch enlarged the hole, creating an embrasure big enough for the two of them to see out of while behind the gun. They linked four belts together—200 rounds—and carefully arranged them in an ammo can. Petrovitch opened the feed cover of the M-60, inserted a linked cartridge, pulled the bolt to the rear, then pushed it forward. He repeated the process, seating the cartridge in the chamber, and then nodded to Brown. They were ready.

With Brown at his side, Petrovitch wiggled into position and spotted two NVA running across the open ground. He shifted the barrel slightly and fired a ten-round burst, hitting the fleeing men in the back, flinging them through the air like kewpie dolls at a carnival. He let up on the trigger just as Brown hit him on the shoulder, shouting, "Machine gun! Machine gun!" and pointing out a string of green tracers.

Petrovitch just lay there, calmly firing controlled bursts as dozens of rounds thumped into the log over their heads. Brown could barely keep it together. Surely it was only a matter of time until the bastards got lucky and put a burst right into their running lights? Fighting the overwhelming urge to duck, the platoon sergeant braced himself for a bullet in his face. *Christ, he wanted to scream, hold that trigger down and hose the bastards!* Instead, he held the ammunition off the ground and carefully fed it into the gun, making sure a twisted link didn't jam it. Petrovitch shifted the barrel slightly and fired another ten-round burst at the apex of a stream of green tracers.

Petrovitch put two more bursts into the bunker, and a momentary lull ensued as the men waited for the return fire. But there was none. Slapping the gunner on the shoulder, Brown yelled, "You got the bastards, you got the bastards!" Petrovitch turned his head and grinned, giving Brown a thumbs up. "Dumb shits," he said, "They ran out of ammunition Should a' fired short bursts." Still shaky from the close call, Brown just shook his head, amazed at the self-control of the gunner.

A hand settled on Brown's shoulder, startling the hell out of him. "Edwards!" he exclaimed, "What the hell are you doing?"

"That's my job," the assistant gunner mumbled, pointing to the ammunition beside the gun, clearly still dazed from the blow to his head. *He looks like shit,* Brown thought, noting the assistant gunner's pasty white face and the bullet hole in his helmet. But Edwards was determined, nudging Brown aside to take his place. Petrovitch just looked at the kid, nodded, and continued to fire.

No longer needed as assistant gunner, Brown worked his way along the streambed, ensuring that his men were up and in position. The men were returning fire, round for round, but they were running out of ammunition. *Where the hell is the lieutenant?* he thought. *If he doesn't hustle, we'll have to start throwing stones.* Just at that moment, he saw a wisp of red from a smoke grenade curl up through the undergrowth, the signal that Littleton was in position and ready to assault the NVA from the flank. Brown's ear caught the forest-muffled sound of heavy firing. Peering through his binoculars, he saw a line of Marines move out of the trees, shooting into the bunker complex. "Shift fire! Shift fire," he yelled, cautioning his men to fire ahead of their advancing buddies, so they would have the NVA in a crossfire.

He caught a glimpse of Littleton moving forward slightly behind the line of Marines, gesturing wildly, obliviously directing their movement.

Stunned, Brown watched the action unfold in front of him. The rapid stutter of a machine gun pierced the air, and two Marines crumpled. All the others disappeared in the blink of an eye. The enemy gunfire seemed to smother the sound of the Marine M-16s. He knew Littleton was in trouble. *Come on,*

35

Lieutenant, he thought, *you've got to do something.* For long moments, he continued to watch and wait. And then, suddenly, he heard explosions and saw a man stand up in the open, a LAAW on his shoulder. "Jesus Christ, that's suicide," he muttered, "That guy's got more balls ...." The thought hung as he realized the standing man was Littleton. A streak of fire left the tube, then an explosion, and then a remarkable charge across the open ground to the NVA trenches.

7

Sapper Platoon, North Vietnamese Army, 0930, 12 September, Bunker Complex—Opposing Littleton's platoon in the bunker complex was an elite sapper platoon under the command of *Truong Si*—Senior Sergeant—Nguyen Ba Thanh, a savvy 32-year-old veteran commander of several punishing battles with the Americans along the DMZ. His orders were to delay Littleton long enough to cover the withdrawal of the NVA battalion. Thanh was to avoid a pitched battle, but the American machine gun was keeping his men pinned down in the bunkers. He knew that if he didn't withdraw quickly, the imperialists would use their artillery and airplanes against him. From his bunker position, Thanh noted that the Americans moved after firing a few bursts and momentarily stopped firing. Taking advantage of this lull, he slipped out of his shelter into an adjoining trench, and crawled to a bunker manned by three men led by *Binh nhat*—Private First Class—Ba Xa Lien. The bunker contained one of the platoon's two RPD 7.62mm Soviet light machine guns. Lien was under orders not to fire unless the Americans attacked his position, but Thanh changed the orders by directing to destroy the *My nguy*—American puppets. Satisfied that Lien knew what was expected, Thanh crawled back to the command bunker and prepared to order a withdrawal.

Lien blazed away with the RPD, traversing its fire along the top of the bank, forcing the *My nguy* in the streambed to stop shooting, and duck. His accurate, heavy fire overwhelmed them. Holding the trigger down, he fired drum after drum. The action threatened to burn out the barrel, but this was not the time to worry; Sergeant Thanh would get him another. The noise in the confined space of the bunker was deafening. Totally engrossed in firing, Lien didn't hear the shouts as one of his men spotted red tracers streaking out of the streambed. The rounds exploded against the bunker, but they failed to penetrate the thick, hard-packed dirt. Lien instantly recovered, shifted his gun, and fired back. The duel was on.

Lien's first burst at the M-60 was high; it split the air above the fallen tree. He quickly corrected his aim and held the RPD's trigger down, spitting out 150 rounds per minute. Green tracers impacted around the enemy position, throwing up dirt and debris, showing that he was on target.

Lien felt the bolt go home on an empty chamber. He automatically hit the drum release, yelling "Hurry, Comrade! Hurry!" Frightened, his loader struggled to seat a fresh hundred-round drum below the receiver. Lien wanted to pummel the man in frustration. The *Do cho de* was all thumbs. "Hurry!" he screamed again, and then he simply swore.

The fresh drum seated with a metallic click. Lien's right index finger tightened on the trigger just as a bullet zipped through the embrasure and struck the loader in the head with a sickening thwack. The man flew backward, his face a mass of gore.

Lien screamed at the revolting sight. Panicked, he jumped aside, directly into the path of a stream of bullets that all but decapitated him. Private Hoa, the third team member, stared at the mangled corpses and slowly slumped against the bunker's blood-covered earthen wall, paralyzed with shock and fear.

"*Do moi ro*," Thanh swore in frustration, railing against the *My nguy*. The loss of the machine gun was a severe setback in his plan to break contact with the Americans. Without its support, he was afraid he would take more casualties, but he had to get the men out before it was too late. The other RPD was not in a good position to use against the enemy machine gun; he didn't want to risk losing it by shifting it to another location. He made the decision and sent runners out to tell the squad leaders to start withdrawing to the second line of trenches. The platoon had practiced the maneuver many times and knew what to do. Each squad would provide covering fire for the other as they leapfrogged back to safety. Although Thanh worried about the squad facing the American machine gun in the streambed, there was nothing he could do. They would have to make it on their own. He waited until the runners returned and then crawled through a trench that had been dug for just this sort of emergency.

Suddenly, the tree line erupted with gunfire, catching Thanh totally by surprise. Cautiously, he peered out of the trench and discovered a line of Americans coming toward him, firing as they advanced.

Muttering curses, he ducked back into cover and quickly made his way to the bunker that contained the second light machine gun. Peering out through the small embrasure, Thanh saw the Americans were still some distance away. He wanted to "hug" them, close enough so they couldn't bring in artillery without hitting their own men. Turning to *Binh nhat* Le Duc Trung, Thanh pointed out a tree as reference and told the machine gunner to start shooting when the Americans reached it. Trung dutifully acknowledged the order, knowing that he was probably being sacrificed so the rest of the platoon could get away. He knew what had happened to his friend Lien, yet he quickly readied the bunker by lining up spare ammunition drums, laying out Chicom grenades, and directing his crew to take positions in the confined space. The two younger men were in their first action, so Trung took pains to appear calm.

Thanh left the dugout and hurried along the trench until he found the six men of the 1st Squad in a large bunker. Confused by the sudden turn of events, the squad leader didn't know whether to fight or withdraw. Thanh turned them around, ordering them to support Trung's machine gun. The squad split into three-man cells and quickly moved down the trench to take position on either side of the machine gun bunker.

Sergeant Thanh and his three runners worked their way back along a series of trenches to a bunker on the edge of the jungle from which he could observe the action.

To Trung's disappointment, only two Americans were directly in his line of fire. The others were too spread out to hit. As they came even with Sergeant Thanh's tree, he squeezed the trigger and watched as the bullets flung the Americans to the ground. Mesmerized by the sight, he waited too long before swinging the gun and firing again. The rest of the Americans had disappeared in the undergrowth, but he shot anyway, hoping to hit someone. Sweeping the ground in front of the bunker, he fired short bursts, as he had been taught. Suddenly, one of his men shouted that he could see movement near a fallen tree and ducked out into the trench to throw a Chicom. As he stood up to throw it, the movement caught the attention of an enemy soldier, who fired several times at his exposed head and shoulders. Although the bullets missed, they were close enough to make him flinch, interfering with his throw. The grenade landed near the tree and exploded, sending shrapnel harmlessly into the wood and sparing the American.

Trung kept firing, drum after drum, until the bunker's stale air was filled with the stench of cordite mixed with sweat. The walls of the narrow bunker seemed to be closing in; Trung felt as though he were in his own grave. The cotton uniform he wore was soaked; heat and fear forced the sweat out of his body. A terrible thirst took hold he couldn't stop to slake. He had to keep firing. Trung knew the Americans were up to something; he could feel it, and so could his men. Out of the corner of his eye he saw them furtively glance at him, hoping he would tell them to get out, but they couldn't go, not without Sergeant Thanh's approval.

Steam rose from the overheated barrel of the machine gun as Trung swung it from side to side in the narrow aperture, firing burst after burst. The bunker's opening limited his visibility but offered a smaller target for enemy fire, for which he was grateful.

Bullets twice entered the embrasure, narrowly missing him before tearing into the rear wall, raising a large puff of dust. The new men had jumped at the sight and would have run if Trung hadn't been there. During lulls, when ammunition drums were changed, they could hear the reassuring heavy fire of AK-47s from adjoining bunkers. They weren't alone in the fight.

Observing movement in the grass, Trung swung his gun to fire, only to have his vision obscured by an explosion, which blew a cloud of dirt and serrated steel into the air directly in front of the embrasure. A sliver of steel from the projectile flew through the opening and penetrated Trung's left eye, shredding the delicate tissue. With a scream he lurched backwards, hands tight against his ruined eye, desperate to stop the pain.

One of Trung's men moved to take over the gun, but two more blasts followed in rapid succession, forcing him to duck. Recovering, he looked out through the dust and saw a lone figure standing directly in front of the bunker. He desperately flung himself behind the gun, with his right hand reaching for the trigger. Too late. The side of the bunker heaved inward, and a searing blast of fire and molten steel from the exploding LAAW warhead filled the space, instantly killing the three men. The blast destroyed the RPD—ripped it into pieces of unrecognizable metal—and blew the cover off the bunker, flinging logs like jackstraws around the smoking crater.

With the loss of the machine gun and its protectors, Sergeant Thanh knew the rest of the platoon was in great danger. He had to get the men out quickly. He turned to *Chien Si* Ngo Giai, his most trusted runner, and ordered him to tell the remaining squad leaders to immediately break contact and pull back to the rally point.

Giai, a fearless 19-year-old, scrambled down a connector trench and, deciding it was faster, slid over the parapet and started crawling across an open area to another trench, a shorter route. Before the young runner knew what had hit him, a machine gunner—in a million-to-one shot—sprayed the foliage, hitting Giai with two of the ten 7.62mm rounds that were fired. Giai passed out from shock and bled to death, without delivering Thanh's order.

Under fire from two directions, and in the absence of orders, the men decided on their own to withdraw. Fear had overcome discipline. As the Americans got closer, panic ensued, and they broke cover, running for their lives.

From a vantage point in the jungle, Sergeant Thanh watched the destruction of over half his platoon of elite soldiers. Rage filled him as the demoralized survivors streamed by, including several wounded, helped by their comrades. *How could this has happened?* The question hung in the air as he followed his men further into the trees.

8

1st Platoon, Lima Company, North Vietnamese Bunker Complex, 0940, 12 September—Brown quickly led the squad out of the streambed. Joining Littleton near the destroyed bunker, he berated the officer in his usual bullying manner. "Jesus, Lieutenant, that was a damn-fool thing to do—"

Littleton cut him off. "What the hell do you mean?" he rejoined angrily. He was in no mood to take the man's bullshit.

Brown's well-honed self-preservation instinct kicked in and he backed off by covering himself with an ingratiating reply. "Hell, Lieutenant, you could've bought the farm, and then where would we have been?"

This time it didn't fly; no longer the indecisive officer, Littleton shot back, "Staff Sergeant Brown, I'm tired of your lip. There's only one commander here, and it's me. You got that?"

As he stared back at the officer, Brown's anger flared, but he realized any outright insubordination would get his ass in a sling, big time. He'd wait until the right moment and then get this wet-behind-the-ears son of a bitch. He dropped eye contact and mumbled, "I got that loud and clear."

"What'd you say, Staff Sergeant?" Littleton demanded in a voice laced with authority.

Brown's head snapped up. He realized he had gone too far. "Yes, sir, I understand you're the platoon commander."

Littleton almost blurted out, "Then act like it," but decided not to push it any further. He had made his point. He badly needed the NCO's help in the hours ahead.

The approach of a stretcher-bearer team interrupted the "clear the air" tête-à-tête. Four Marines staggered by carrying the severely wounded point man on an improvised stretcher made from two poncho-wrapped saplings. Burdened with packs, weapons, equipment, and flak jackets, the men were having a hell of a time carrying the wounded Marine up the slope over the

41

uneven ground. As they came past, Littleton saw that Kelly was in desperate straits; his face was pasty white, covered with a sheen of sweat, and the battle dressings covering his shoulder were soaked with blood. It was obvious that without proper treatment he wouldn't last much longer.

"We've got to get the wounded collected and ready to move to the hill," Littleton said to Brown. "I'll send a patrol to scout a route so we can move fast when we're ready."

The two split up. Brown went to see how Zimmer was doing with the wounded, while Littleton checked the platoon's positions.

The platoon commander spotted Petrovitch and motioned him toward the trail, telling him to position his gun where he could fire on any enemy using it. The big gunner nodded and looked back for his assistant, who was struggling to keep up and appeared ready to pass out. *Just what the platoon needed, another casualty.* Instead of chiding him, however, Petrovitch went back and half carried him to the new position, encouraging him to keep going. Despite the gunner's fearsome disposition, he had a reputation for taking care of his men.

Littleton went looking for Corporal Duvall. He found the NCO talking softly to Private Gonzales's buddy, who was wiping tears away with the sleeve of his blouse. As Littleton approached, the man abruptly got up and left, not wanting the officer to see his distress. Duvall saw Littleton's quizzical look and explained that the man was still blaming himself for getting Gonzales shot.

Littleton felt a pang of sympathy for the man, but this was no time for commiserating. Opening his map, he oriented it to the ground, and pointed to the high ground about 800 meters from their present location. He explained that the trail they were guarding appeared to lead right to the hill and that he wanted Corporal Duvall to take three men and check out the route. Littleton didn't like the idea of sending them out without a radio, but there wasn't any other solution. The platoon only had one, and it was needed to maintain contact with the company.

Littleton watched as Duvall rounded up the men and left the perimeter, cautiously following the well-defined trail.

In the meantime, Brown took several men and carried the wounded to the center of the position, where Doc Zimmer had established an improvised aid station. No stranger to treating wounded in the field, Zimmer often performed medical procedures that in "ordinary" conditions would only be attempted in a well-equipped hospital emergency room. His time with the company was about up. It was policy, after six months in the field, to rotate corpsmen to the rear, normally the battalion aid station. The doc wasn't happy with the rule because he was quite proud of his "practice," claiming he'd built it up from nothing—leaving it unsaid that the North Vietnamese often increased his patient workload.

After quickly surveying the wounded men, Zimmer initiated a simple three-step procedure: "keep 'em breathing, stop 'em bleeding, and treat for shock." In actual fact, he was up to his elbows in blood and gore, struggling to keep the badly wounded men alive until they could be evacuated. Normally, he would expect to get them out in minutes, but here, in the triple-canopy jungle, it simply wasn't possible. Equipped only with the items in his Unit-1 aid bag and his own skill, all Zimmer could do was stabilize them and pray they'd survive the long hump back to an LZ. In the meantime, he worked in the dirt. There was no time for the niceties of sanitation.

Littleton sent two men over to help Zimmer, which allowed the doc to concentrate on Tolliver and Kelly, the most critically wounded.

Another party brought in the poncho-wrapped bodies of Stevens and Edgar, and gently placed them on line with the wounded. It was a somber sight, with battle dressing wrappers, bloody bandages, and a pile of abandoned equipment littering the ground around them. Sanders came over to gather information for a casualty report, which he radioed to Battalion, using an abbreviated format: initials and last four digits of each casualty's Social Security number.

As Littleton anxiously surveyed the scene, the leader of the search team approached and asked, "Lieutenant, what do you want us to do with the wounded gook?" For a moment he had an urge to say, "Shoot the son of a bitch," but quickly shook off the thought. That would be murder, and he couldn't do that. "Bring him over here, so Zimmer can work on him."

The three men struggled with the limp form, whose only signs of life were the shallow rise and fall of his chest and an occasional moan. As they placed him beside the wounded Marines, Littleton was struck by how slight the Vietnamese appeared to be in comparison with his own men. He attributed this to the Marines' bulky combat gear, but the NVA soldier looked to be about 15 years old and probably didn't weigh over 110 pounds. His small hands and wrists looked like a child's. He had rather delicate facial features, with high cheekbones and a narrow face. His light brown skin was smooth, with no sign of a beard, and he had a close-cropped "high and tight" haircut. His green uniform and black ankle-high sneakers appeared to be new, all in sharp contrast with his Marines, who definitely had the grunge look. One of Littleton's men actually "hung out"; his entire crotch was ripped out of his badly worn-out utilities.

The Viet's appearance caused him to think. He called over to Brown, "What do you make of this place?"

"Well, for one thing, the bunkers are fairly new," Brown replied, "and the gooks are probably replacements, just come across the border."

"What makes you think they're replacements?"

"Hell, sir, fresh haircuts, new clothes and equipment—and look at those weapons, factory fresh!"

They walked over to where the search team had piled a mound of equipment and several Soviet AK-47 Kalashnikov assault rifles. Brown reached down, picked one up, and pressed the magazine release. He pulled back the bolt, and a gleaming 7.62mm copper-jacketed steel cartridge flew out.

"Look at that action, Lieutenant. Smooth as a baby's ass." He reversed the rifle and looked down the muzzle. "The bore's clean. No signs of rust. I'll bet a month's pay this baby just came out of cosmoline."

Littleton looked the AK-47 over and agreed. The thing appeared to be in a lot better shape than most of the rifles his men carried. The 7.62mm AK-47 was certainly more dependable; it never jammed, unlike the M-16, which malfunctioned with maddening regularity, the troops calling it "the Mattel Toy." The old timers, like Brown, longed for the recently replaced M-14, a more dependable weapon that also fired the heavier 7.62mm bullet.

Brown pointed to several items of equipment. "See that pack? Looks brand new, no rips or tears, and it's not faded." He unfastened the strap of the top flap and pulled several items out of the dark green rucksack: a pair of black cotton pajamas, a green uniform, a pair of rubber sandals, a plastic sheet, a cotton hammock, and a small entrenching tool. One of the side pouches contained two large gauze compresses and a rolled-up cotton hat. Another held an olive drab-painted aluminum canteen, and in the third he found a plastic bag filled with rice.

Littleton reached over and spread out the lightweight cotton uniform shirt and trousers. Even after observing the slightness of the Vietnamese casualty, the size of the uniform surprised him;it would not have fit anyone in the platoon. Everything in the pack appeared to be clean and in good shape, except the canteen, which had most of its paint rubbed off. Turning it over in his hand, he was surprised to see the name "Hoa" carved on one side. He showed it to Brown.

"Ya, the gooks usually carve their names on them and sometimes scratch designs in the paint," he answered, "Just like our guys mark up their helmet covers." Brown was no exception; he had printed "Sat Cong" in bold letters on his camouflage cover, which Littleton found out supposedly meant "kill Viet Cong."

They walked over to one of the dead Vietnamese. Ignoring the stench of death in the air and the flies gathering on the horrible head wound. Brown squatted down and examined the body. "Did you notice, Lieutenant, the gooks all got fresh haircuts?"

Shit, how the hell can you tell? Littleton thought, cringing at the sight of the shattered skull and exposed brain. Seeing his discomfort, Brown tapped the gray-colored matter with a stick. "First time you ever seen a brain housing group, sir?" he asked, and nonchalantly continued to point out various body parts before Littleton could reply. "Check his face. No zits. And his hands don't have jungle rot."

Littleton's own hands were covered with lacerations and abscesses that never seemed to heal, scabbing over but always oozing pus. *Hell, everybody in the platoon has the sores,* he reflected. *It's impossible to avoid the damn stuff living in the dirt, with little water and no soap to wash the crud off.* He hadn't washed in days. His blouse was stiff with dried sweat and body fluids, and he stank. His nose told him that Brown was in the same shape, but there was another odor that he tried to place. "What's that smell?" he asked.

"Gook," Brown replied. "A combination of wood smoke and fish sauce. When you smell it, bend over, put your head between your legs, and kiss your ass goodbye, 'cause they're too damn close."

Trying to act nonchalant, Littleton pointed to the dead man's uniform and asked about the white strings that were sown to the blouse. "Tie Ties, Lieutenant," Brown said as he casually pulled at the ends. "They use 'em to tie bush and shrubs to their shirts for camouflage." Then, as casually as if the body were a classroom mockup, Brown searched it, emptying pockets and piling the contents on its chest. A cheap leather wallet yielded a photograph of a pretty Vietnamese girl sitting on a bicycle, wearing a white *ao dai* and a conical straw hat. Littleton figured it was either a girlfriend or sister; in either case, it didn't matter anymore. The girl would never know what happened here, in the jungle. Brown pulled out a rumpled bill and handed it to Littleton. "Here, Lieutenant, keep it as a souvenir." The thin paper currency, wider and shorter than a dollar, had a picture of a farmer behind a water buffalo tilling a rice paddy on one side and some sort of weird-looking bird on the other. The numeral 5 was printed on each corner and had the words "Nam Dong" on front and back. He stuffed it in his pocket, along with three postage stamps that showed an armed Vietnamese mand woman standing in a patriotic pose against a blue background. There were some other bits and pieces of paper, but they didn't seem to be of any intelligence value. Quickly sifting through the pitiful collection and finding nothing of interest, Brown stood up and casually threw it to the ground.

Littleton looked away, instead taking in the sight of one of the well-constructed bunkers, which showed the devastatingly explosive power of a U.S. M-26 hand grenade. The hole had been blown apart, exposing its construction. Littleton estimated it to be around three by six by four feet, and it was lined with leaves and matting. The roof consisted of a single layer of logs, three to four inches in diameter, a waterproof plastic sheet, and two feet of hard-packed dirt. Well camouflaged, with a covering of jungle undergrowth, the hole was almost impossible to see, even at close range. It appeared to be newly constructed, but, as he studied it, something seemed out of place. There was only a small entrance and it commanded a poor field of fire. And then it hit him. These bunkers were not designed for fighting; they were *living* bunkers. He turned to Brown and asked, "What about all these new bunkers? Most of them are for shelter, not fighting."

Brown leveled his gaze. "That's the 64-dollar question, sir. My guess is that they're going to sneak in here some night, gather together, and hit the base."

Littleton nodded in agreement. "Yeah, but then we knock the hell out of them with air and artillery."

"You're right," Brown replied, "but have you taken a good look at the bunkers? They've got enough overhead cover to take anything but a direct hit."

The young officer thought about that for a moment. "So that's why they took off," he said, realization dawning. "They were ordered to avoid a big fight and not attract attention to the build-up."

"Right, sir. It doesn't take a mental giant to see those gooners just slipped back across the border and will come back when they're ready."

The two moved over to one of the larger bunkers, where several aluminum pots and pans lay scattered about. "It's the cook shack," Brown commented. "See the covered fire pit?" Littleton looked in and saw a fire-hardened hollow earth shelf. It had holes cut along its top for the cooking pots. A bellows-like apparatus was suspended from a log in the ceiling, its tip poking into the shelf. "What's this for?" he said, pointing to the contraption.

"That's to blow the smoke along a trench, so it dissipates and can't be seen from the air," Brown replied and pointed to the ground. He scraped the leaves away and Littleton saw where the Vietnamese had cut a channel six inches wide, eight inches deep and fifteen feet long. It was covered with a latticework of twigs and leaves that contained the smoke and allowed it to disperse along the length of the trench—primitive, but effective.

A shout caught their attention and suddenly Sanders was running toward them, gesturing with the radio handset. "It's the skipper," he called, skidding to a halt in front of Littleton. "He wants to talk with you ASAP!"

His heart racing, Littleton grabbed the handset and keyed it, "Lima Six, this is Lima One. Over." There was a long pause. No response. He tried again. Anderson's voice broke the squelch, "One, this is Six. We're in deep shit here. The gooks are all over the place and we're being hit hard. They're in close and got us by the short hairs."

Littleton could hear the tension in the captain's voice. This wasn't good; nothing short of a disaster could rattle the old man, who went on, "I'm trying to pull back to the high ground so we can get air and arty to give us a hand. Bottom line, I can't get through to you. You're on your own. Get to the high ground and hunker down. Over."

Littleton was at a loss. What could he say, except "Roger Six. Good luck."

Anderson came back, "Sorry, John. I'd be there if I could. Good luck to you. Out."

The three men stood there, momentarily stunned. Brown spoke first. "Lieutenant, we've got to move fast, and we'll need every swinging dick just to carry the casualties, unless we leave the gook and the two KIAs behind."

Littleton understood that the entire platoon would have to be used as stretcher bearers, which would leave them dangerously exposed. But he wasn't going to abandon anyone. "Bullshit!" he exploded, "We're not leaving anyone behind, Goddamn it!"

Brown was tight-lipped with anger from the reprimand. He wasn't used to being spoken to like that, especially in front of the men. Littleton heatedly continued, "Get the men ready to move out. Tell Zimmer we can't wait any longer."

"Aye, aye sir," Brown stiffly replied and stomped off, mad as hell, looking for someone to take it out on.

Doc Zimmer was squatting down, checking Tolliver's wound, when someone grabbed his shoulder, violently yanking him upright. Startled, it took him a second to realize it was the platoon sergeant, who still held onto his shirt, pulling him closer. "All right, pecker checker," Brown said in a low, menacing voice, pointing to the wounded Vietnamese with his rifle, "Get rid of that gook. You've wasted enough time on that asshole." The murderous look on his face told Zimmer that he was utterly serious. "We're moving out in five minutes, and I want him dead," he added.

Zimmer couldn't believe it. The callous son of a bitch wanted him to commit murder? Mentally and emotionally drained, he blurted out, "Fuck you." He shook loose from Brown's grip.

Enraged, the staff sergeant brought his rifle up, intending to butt-stoke the corpsman. But before he could swing it, a powerful hand gripped his arm in a paralyzing squeeze. He struggled to break free but found himself held fast. He turned his head and looked directly into Petrovitch's intense eyes. "Staff Sergeant," the big man said evenly, "I think the doc needs to get back to work."

9

3rd Company, North Vietnamese Army, Ambush Position, 1000, 12 September—Lieutenant Hoi, the 3rd Company commander, closely followed by his runner, dashed headlong through the trench, intent on finding out who had fired prematurely and ruined the ambush. As the pair rounded a bend, Hoi collided with the diminutive Major Minh, sending both men crashing to the bottom of the trench. Hoi landed on top, driving his shoulder into Minh's chest, forcing the wind from the political officer's lungs. Hoi's runner, unable to stop, plowed into them and fell, losing his rifle in the process. The AK-47 flew out of his hand and struck Minh in the face. The front sight opened a six-inch gash in Minh's forehead, knocking him unconscious. Horrified at what had happened, Hoi struggled to his feet and attended to the heavily bleeding political officer, delaying his arrival in the front lines for 20 critical minutes.

Without Hoi's leadership, the fighters of the 3rd Company hesitated to leave the relative safety of their bunkers to close with the disorganized Americans, who had gone to ground, leaving few visible targets. Instead, the *Bo doi* opened up a desultory fire, allowing the enemy soldiers an opportunity to recover. Both sides fired indiscriminately, neither seeing the other, as American and North Vietnamese soldiers hugged the ground; exposure meant certain injury or death. The Vietnamese soldiers had the advantage of earthen walls, but the bunkers' fixed firing ports severely limited visibility, while the prone Americans couldn't locate the cleverly camouflaged dugouts. The fight was stalemated; neither side had an overwhelming advantage.

Hoi succeeded in staunching the flow of blood and was bandaging the wound when Minh regained consciousness. "What happened?" the major groggily demanded just as the sharp crack of an explosion rocked the canopy high over their heads. Steel shards tore through the vegetation and smacked into the ground around them. The acrid smell of cordite filled the air.

Hoi snapped his head up at the sound and blurted out, "Artillery." He suddenly realized that Duc's fears had materialized; the ambush had failed to keep the Americans from using supporting arms. As he started to rise, he was stopped by a thoroughly cowered Minh, who grabbed him tightly by the arm and refused to let go. "Please, Major," Hoi begged, "I have to join my men and lead them against the Americans."

"No," Minh vehemently replied. "I am sorely wounded and need your assistance in returning to the command bunker." Minh's wild-eyed look told the real truth; he was terrified, using his injury as an excuse to go to the rear.

Hoi stared at the coward, a look of revulsion on his face, as he pulled away. In a voice heavy with sarcasm, he repeated one of Minh's favorite heroic slogans: "*Muon doc lap phai do mau*—For freedom you have to spend your blood"—and dashed off toward the sound of the fighting, leaving the cadre to his own devices.

Minh pressed his face into the bottom of the trench and screamed as six more 105mm rounds detonated over his head in a thunderous explosion. The violent concussion tossed him into the air and slammed him down hard, momentarily taking his breath away. His bowels loosened and he soiled himself, filling the air in the close confines of the trench with the indignity. An overwhelming fear robbing him of any rationality, he jumped to his feet and blindly ran forward. At a bend in the trench, he ran headlong into his wounded guide, who was slumped against the side, blocking his escape. Minh reached out, his hands like claws, and frantically grabbed the man by the shoulders, roughly yanking him out of the way. The *Bo doi* screamed in agony as Minh trampled over his prostrate form in a mindless attempt to flee the cauldron of fire. Just as Minh spotted the entrance to a bunker, another volley impacted the trees behind him. He threw himself through the opening and scrambled into a dark corner, where he curled up in a ball, trembling uncontrollably as the ground shook from the impact of the heavy explosions.

Hoi and his runner reached the line of bunkers and ducked inside one, barely making it through the entrance before several steel shards tore into the roof, sending dirt cascading through gaps in the log ceiling.

Two men were crouched down beside the apertures, occasionally firing through the openings, while a third pointed out targets for the two riflemen. The restricted confines of the small bunker magnified the heavy crack of the AK-47s and prevented the three from hearing their company commander's unexpected entrance. Hoi reached out and touched Sergeant Xuan, the platoon commander, scaring the hell out of him as he focused on the jungle in front of the position. In a voice tight with evident apprehension, Hoi called out, "*Trung Si*, what is happening? Give me a report."

Xuan hesitated, struggled to put together a plausible excuse for the abortive ambush, then stammered out a half-hearted reply that made it obvious that he didn't know what was going on and had done little to find out. Blaming Private Hung, the errant rocket man, for prematurely triggering the ambush, he omitted the fact that he had left the man all by himself without clear instructions. Exasperated with the response, Hoi knew he had to do something quickly in order to establish control of the platoon and destroy the Americans.

Hoi called the sergeant over to the embrasure, pointed out the location of a forward trench that seemed to be in a good position to enfilade the Americans, and ordered him to take a three-man cell to occupy it. Xuan visibly paled, knowing there was a good chance this would be his last assignment. Mustering his courage, he acknowledged the order and quickly left the bunker to gather his men.

Hoi watched intently as the four men, heavily laden with extra ammunition, snaked unseen through the foliage and gained the relative safety of the trench without incident. They immediately opened fire, taking advantage of the position to rake the enemy, hitting several and forcing the rest to seek better cover.

Satisfied with the deployment, Hoi instructed the two remaining riflemen in the bunker to provide covering fire for Xuan's men. He then left with his runner to give instructions to the rest of the platoon. The two made their way through the trench along the line of bunkers, stopping in each one to encourage the fighters and urge them to be more aggressive. His voice and body language exuding confidence, Hoi was fired up. "*Nam Vung Thoi-Co*— Seize the opportunity," he repeated, over and over again, using the slogan as a rallying cry to inspire his young combatants. Their spirits bolstered, his men rose to the challenge, suppressing the Americans with a heavy volume of fire and seizing the initiative.

10

Southern Hotel/Lima Company, 1030, 12 September—Frazier's ear throbbed with pain as he crawled among his men; the constant movement irritated the hell out of him and added to his misery. There was nothing he could do but keep going. Morphine was out; it would make him too sleepy, and, right now, he needed to be alert. The NVA were pouring a torrent of fire into his platoon, threatening to overpower it by sheer weight of bullets. He already had four casualties, one of them serious. Unless something happened damn quickly, they would all be out of luck. His men were outgunned; he counted at least two machine guns and a whole shit pot full of NVA soldiers firing from several bunkers and trenches directly in front of them. One of the trench positions was really giving them fits; it was angled so the three NVA who were using it could fire across the platoon's entire front. They popped up like jack-in-the-boxes, fired like hell, and then ducked down. The bastards led charmed lives; nobody could hit them, and they had already shot three of his men, wiping out a fire team. The trench was just outside hand-grenade range, and the M-79, the only other weapon that could hit it, was disabled.

As Frazier raised his head to look at the trench, the three occupants jumped up and opened fire. "Jesus Christ," he exclaimed as several rounds cut the air over his head and at least two hit the dirt beside him, "Somebody's got to get those gooks, but fast."

He racked his brain to think of a way to get closer to the trench. He needed a diversion. Suddenly, he heard the distinctive ripping sound of an incoming artillery shell, which exploded in the trees. "Napoline, you wonderful son of a bitch," he screamed, just as six more 105mm rounds slammed into the NVA positions, close enough for him to feel the blast. *My God, I hope those gunners don't stutter*, he thought as he burrowed further into the ground, trying to pull his helmet down to his ankles.

More blasts followed, and he realized that at least one six-gun battery was firing for effect, volley after volley, until told to stop. Between volleys, he could hear his troops cheering. The damn cannon cockers had saved their asses.

***

Anderson lay beside Napoline and Hoenig, watching the exploding artillery, trying to judge its effectiveness. Most of the rounds were detonating high in the trees, making a spectacular blast but doing little harm to the bunkers, with their three feet of overhead cover. The trenches were another matter, however. Steel shards and wood slivers from the airbursts plunged directly into them. As he watched, a round detonated in a treetop, the ground underneath it exploding under the impact of dozens of fragments, but he knew they only penetrated a few inches. The light, 33-pound, 105mm shell was simply not up to the job. Only a direct hit could knock out a bunker. They needed heavier ordnance.

Anderson turned to Napoline and told him to keep the artillery coming while he tried to contact the promised aerial observer. Switching the frequency on his radio to the new channel, he keyed the handset, "Any station this net; any station this net. This is Northtide Lima Six. Over."

The happy-go-lucky voice of 1st Lieutenant Dan "Bomber" Reed, the pilot of a Cessna O-1 "Bird Dog" observation aircraft, came back. "Roger dodger, Lima Six. This is Southern Hotel, your eye in the sky, at your service."

Just what I need, Anderson thought, *a goddam comedian.* "Southern Hotel, we're in deep shit here." His voice intensified. "I'm in contact with gooks in bunkers and machine guns. I have beaucoup casualties and we need help, but quick." Another, more serious, businesslike, voice cut in, "Roger. Understand, Lima Six. We're holding about six miles southwest of your position, waiting for a flight of fast movers. We're going to get help for you as soon as we can."

Forward Air Controller Captain Jim "Pop" Harper, call sign "Southern Hotel," switched over to the Cessna's internal radio. "Bomber, I'll stay in contact with the grunts; you brief the fast movers."

Pop Harper, the backseater, was an aerial observer, not a pilot. He could fly and land the plane in an emergency, although his skill level was a matter of some debate between the two men. His one attempt at setting the plane down had been more of a controlled crash than a landing; it had scared hell out of Reed, who swore up and down that Pop had bent the plane. Pop's nonchalant response that "any landing he could walk away from was good enough" trod on the pilot's sensibilities and put him in a day-long snit. Pop's real aptitude, however, lay in controlling airstrikes and coordinating the use of artillery—pilots didn't believe in the "big sky, little bullet" theory and were loath to fly in the same space as artillery rounds. Tagged close air support this integration of air with the movement of the infantry was a Marine Corps specialty, and Pop Harper was one of its finest practitioners. On more than one occasion he had "saved the bacon" for hard-pressed Marines, as attested by the survivors of a reconnaissance team who narrowly missed annihilation. Run to ground by an overwhelming enemy force, they were saved in the nick of time by the intervention of two Harper-controlled F-4s, which had earned Pop honorary team membership.

Pop was at his best when speaking with the men on the ground, who instinctively responded to his calm, deeply accented southern voice. He projected an unflappable demeanor, even as the shit hit the fan, conveying a feeling that, with Pop in control, everything would be okay. That sentiment was well deserved, for he was a second-tour veteran who had racked up hundreds of flight hours and earned a reputation for professional competence and bravery. The awards section of his officer qualification record showed two Silver Star citations, each noting "conspicuous gallantry and intrepidity in action." A mustang with 20 years' service, he was in sharp contrast to Reed, the young, newly married, hot rocks pilot, just out of flight school, who yearned to fly fast movers and drop bombs. Nicknamed "Bomber," he was a fast-talking New Englander, always in motion, but steady as a rock in the air. The two men were a close-knit team despite their backgrounds. They had flown together almost every day for more than two months, a lifetime in the target-rich environment of Northern I Corps.

They had just arrived on station, after being diverted from coordinating airstrikes on suspected enemy positions around the embattled Marine position at Con Thien. Low on fuel, they were heading for the barn when the controller directed them to Khe Sanh on a priority mission—"troops in heavy contact." They were the only Bird Dog available, and it was an emergency, so Bomber firewalled the throttles, conscious of the fuel-gauge indictor as it fluttered toward empty. Pop talked to the infantry while Reed briefed the flight leader of two VMA-223 single-seat A-4E Skyhawks, call sign "Rampage," that were momentarily due on station. The A-4s were armed with "snake and nape"—Mk-82 500-pound high-drag "Snakeye" bombs and BLU-27 750-pound napalm canisters. They had enough fuel for 15 minutes on station.

Reed flew the Bird Dog in a racetrack pattern while keeping the target in sight, unconsciously varying the altitude to throw off any NVA gunners who might be tracking it, even over the jungle. In an era in which jet aircraft were taken for granted, the World War II-era single engine Cessna was an anachronism. It was the Model T Ford of its day, seat-of-the-pants flying at a little more than a hundred miles per hour, almost daring the NVA to shoot at it, which they did with maddening regularity. They did so at their peril, however, for, while the Bird Dog had only spotting rockets for weapons, its occupants could call down the wrath of God, the fast movers, strike aircraft carrying an assortment of lethal ordnance—bombs, rockets, cannon, and napalm.

Harper's plan, which he worked out with Anderson, came right out of the tactics manual: locate the target, mark it, and destroy it with airstrikes. They agreed that, as the last artillery rounds impacted, Reed would fire a white phosphorus rocket; its billowing smoke would act as a marker for the fast movers, a critical cue for pilots traveling at 500 knots over ground that lacked terrain features and looked like a green carpet. Rampage, after being cleared, would drop its ordnance in accordance with Harper's instructions; a life-or-death decision that weighed heavily on him every time a plane started a bombing run, for an errant missile could be disastrous. The plan was simple, but its coordination was a bear. Reed and Harper were busy monitoring FM and UHF radios, which were incompatible, switching frequencies to pass and request information from ground, air, and various control agencies. Harper's canopy was soon covered with grease-penciled information—frequencies, run-in headings, coordinates, bomb loads, fuel status, and call signs—to help him keep track of the mission. Southern Hotel's airmen were the focal point for the air-ground coordination. Today was one of those days when the two earned their flight pay: Marines were in trouble and Southern Hotel was there to help.

Things were not going well on the ground. Heavy automatic weapons fire from the trench was threatening to overwhelm Frazier's platoon. Only a few Marines were able to shoot back; the devastating fire pinned down the rest. The NVA were fewer than a hundred meters away, and Napoline was afraid to bring the artillery any closer for fear of hitting Frazier's men. Anderson ordered Larson's platoon forward to help Frazier, but it was taking time due to the heavy fire, which forced everyone to stay low. At times, there seemed to be a solid *crack* over their heads as hundreds of bullets split the air. There was no question they were in deep shit and needed help now.

Anderson yelled into the handset, as if shouting could somehow bring help faster. "Southern Hotel, give us the air now or it may be too late!" Pop's composed voice came over the net, "Roger, Lima Six. We're coming in to mark the target. Keep your head down."

Wind whistled through the wing struts; Reed dropped the nose to pick up speed as he lined up the target. His aiming point was the center of the damaged trees. He pickled a 2.75-inch fin-stabilized "Willie Pete" marker rocket. With a loud *whoosh*, the four-foot cylinder left the wing-mounted tube, emitting a puff of smoke as it ignited and then streaked toward the target. Reed pulled out of the dive as Harper watched the impact and burst of white smoke, noting that it was right where he wanted it. "Good shot, Bomber, right on the money," he grunted over the intercom from the g-force, and then switched to the strike frequency. "Rampage Leader, do you have my marker? Over?"

"Roger, Hotel. I have it in sight."

"Rampage, you're cleared in hot, heading 270. Pull out left." The pilot of the A-4 clicked his mike twice to acknowledge the approval and announced, "One's in."

Harper watched the small jet as it streaked toward the target, its gray paint a stark contrast to the green jungle. At the release point, the pilot pressed a button on his control stick and four Snakeyes dropped from the plane's hardpoints. Large fins deployed, acting as air brakes, slowing the bombs down and giving the low-flying airplane time to clear the target. As Rampage One pulled out of its dive, his wingman announced, "Two's in."

Three of Rampage One's bombs hit the NVA's 1st Battalion's line of defense, exploding with a bright orange flash and gouging craters in the soft ground six feet deep and twelve feet in diameter. Two bunkers and 20 feet of trench line took direct hits, obliterating six members of the 3rd Company. Razor-sharp pieces of shrapnel severed tree limbs and scoured the undergrowth, hurtling it through the air into the faces of the survivors, forcing them to stop firing. One bomb hit dead center on a tree and detonated 30 feet off the forest floor. The shock wave toppled one old forest giant that crashed on a bunker, collapsing it and crushing the three inhabitants. The overpressure created by the explosions knocked several enemy soldiers unconscious, punctured eardrums, and gave them nosebleeds. Two badly dazed Vietnamese stumbled out of the maelstrom and were immediately shot to death by a surprised Marine who thought they were attacking him. Other traumatized survivors simply stopped firing as they struggled to cope with the effects of the bombing, leaving an area about the size of a football field without effective resistance. Within seconds, the 1st Battalion had been hard hit, losing 20 known dead, with others unaccounted for, and one of its companies down for the count.

The American position didn't escape unscathed; two men in Frazier's platoon suffered minor shrapnel wounds, even though they were at least a hundred meters from the blast. The force of the explosions lifted Marines off the ground and slammed them back down, hard. Though warned of the airstrike, many of the Marines were shaken up by its sudden, overwhelming violence. They involuntarily pushed themselves into the soft earth, attempting to make a smaller target. Many assumed a fetal position while trying to pull their helmet down for added protection. More than one thanked his lucky stars that he wasn't the target of the airstrike.

Anderson, who was safe behind a log, promised himself that he would never say another bad word about pilots and their comforts.

As Rampage Two came up on the release point, the pilot, 1st Lieutenant Gerry Arnold, was startled to see green tracers streak up from a grass-covered hilltop just off his starboard quarter. "Shit, ground fire," he muttered and keyed his mike. "Two's taking fire," he announced calmly, although his heart rate had increased dramatically. He continued boring in, keeping the plane straight and level, trying hard to concentrate on the drop. As he pickled the ordnance, he felt two distinct thuds and knew the aircraft had been hit. The A-4 shuddered, red lights showed in several gauges, and the cockpit started to fill with smoke, an indication that he was in serious trouble. "I'm hit and on fire!" he radioed, his voice no longer calm.

Startled by the transmission, his wingman and long-time friend came back, "Roger, Two. Can you make it to KSCB?" hoping he could, because bailing out over the jungle was chancy at best.

At that moment, Arnold, was too busy to answer. His controls were sluggish and he was losing what little altitude he had. It was decision time. He pushed back in the seat, reached over his head, and pulled the face curtain down, which activated the ejection system. A split second later, a rocket fired, blowing the seat up the rails and through the canopy—just as the aircraft nosed over out of control.

Reed put the Bird Dog over on its wing and headed for the stricken bomber. Harper saw the pilot eject and held his breath, waiting for the sight of a parachute. Suddenly, a white canopy blossomed, just as the A-4 slammed into the jungle and erupted into a huge fireball. Harper called out over the net, "I've got a chute and it appears he's okay."

Beneath the wildly oscillating parachute, Arnold dangled, struggling with the shroud lines and only a few seconds from hitting the trees. But luck was with him—at least for now—as he managed to steer away from the burning crash site toward a grass-covered hilltop. His luck ran out when he slammed into the trees and was knocked senseless by a huge limb that split open his flight helmet. Plummeting toward the ground, he broke an arm and several ribs, before he jerked to a stop ten feet off the forest floor. His shroud lines tangled in the branches of a tree, he hung, motionless, in the parachute harness, blood running freely down his face and neck from deep cuts.

A thousand feet overhead, Southern Hotel sent out a Mayday to the combat base, setting the stage for a rescue attempt. A CH-46 Sea Knight helicopter cranked up, taxied over to Bravo Recon's landing zone, and rigged repelling lines—in case it was necessary to insert a rescue party into the jungle. It then loaded the Sparrow Hawk—a heavily armed seven-man team, call sign "Knife Edge"—and moved to the end of the runway, where it waited for an escort of helicopter gunships. A flight of F-4 Phantoms was diverted from an interdiction mission along the Ho Chi Minh Trail and directed to check in with Southern Hotel.

As the rescue force assembled, Harper and Reed reviewed their options, trying to work out a plan to both support the grunts and rescue the downed airman. There weren't many options. Time and space compounded the problem; both needed help immediately, but their proximity limited alternatives: supporting one meant not supporting the other. The NVA antiaircraft gun added to the complexity; it had to be knocked out before the rescue attempt, and quickly. Harper knew that Rampage One only had enough fuel for five more minutes on station, just enough for one pass on the gun.

Reed dropped the nose of the Bird Dog, lined up on the hill, and began his run, knowing that he would be within the antiaircraft gun's range before he could fire the marking rocket. "Maybe they've pulled out," he said apprehensively over the intercom, his voice betraying the tension he was feeling.

"Ya, and maybe the war'll be over by Christmas," Harper responded in a deadpan voice, which belied his own nervousness. No sooner were the words out of his mouth than a line of green tracers arched toward them, ending the speculation. "Jesus Christ, that guy's good. He's already on us," he exclaimed, as he knew that if one of the thumb-size rounds hit him, his flak jackets wouldn't even slow it down.

Reed didn't look; he was too busy concentrating on the target, hoping to put the rocket down the gunner's throat, because he sure as hell didn't want to come around again. His finger tightened on the firing button just as a large portion of the front windshield blew out with a loud bang and a huge hole appeared in the cockpit over his right shoulder. Reed jerked reflexively, sending the rocket on its way. Harper twisted around to watch the missile, as Reed honked the Cessna up and away, stressing the hell out of the airframe but spoiling the gunner's aim. Harper's sarcastic comment—"Nice shot, Bomber. You hit Vietnam"—made him involuntarily shudder, thinking they had to make another pass. Then came Pop's relieved laugh: "But close enough for government work."

Rampage One was pissed: the NVA had shot down his buddy, and it was time for a little payback. He nosed the little bomber over, careful to keep the 30-degree angle of attack for the BLU-27s he had selected. Right on schedule, the tracers started. It became a duel, with only one winner possible and neither participant willing to back down.

The A-4 bored in through the deadly stream of heavy .51-caliber slugs, steady as a rock, almost as if the pilot were challenging the gunner to hit him. Two large canisters fell tumbling through the air and exploding into a huge fireball, spreading fire across the hilltop, incinerating everything in its path. The gun continued to fire even as hundreds of gallons of jellied gasoline covered the four-man crew with flame. Mercifully, the exploding napalm sucked the air out of their lungs, suffocating them in an instant, sparing them from the terrible agony of being burned alive.

Rampage One rocked his wings in victory, climbed to cruising altitude, and headed home. Even though he wanted to stay and help with the rescue of his wingman, he was bingo fuel.

11

1st Battalion, North Vietnamese Army, Command Bunker, 1040, 12 September—Lieutenant Colonel Duc patted the runner on the back and smiled. Hoi had reported that things were going better, that the 3rd Company had gained fire superiority and pinned the Americans down, fixing them in position. It was time to pinch them between his other two companies and chop them up.

The American artillery was heavy but ineffective against the overhead cover of the bunkers. So far, casualties were light. With luck, the squads working their way around the flanks through the trench system would not suffer too greatly.

Expecting some losses, Duc had set up a medical bunker in the center of the battalion position, staffed with several medics. But medical supplies, particularly infection-fighting drugs, were in short supply. The problem, as usual, was evacuating the casualties from the front lines. Duc would not allow his fighters to be used as stretcher bearers until after the battle, often too late to save the badly wounded.

The dead would be recovered at the same time, as it was a strict policy of the army to police the battlefield for slain comrades. If there was time, the battalion would conduct a simple burial ceremony for them, but more often than not, the remains would be unceremoniously dumped into a hastily dug unmarked jungle grave. In those rare moments when Duc had time for reflection, his thoughts drifted back to the dozens of friends who inhabited those earthen plots so far from home. He wondered when he would join them, for he was, above all, a realist and knew that his luck could not go on forever.

Four heavy bomb explosions rocked the bunker, snapping Duc out of his reverie, sending him scrambling outside to see where they had hit. The jungle growth limited visibility, but the sound seemed to come from the direction of the 3rd Company. Ducking back inside, he tried to contact Lieutenant Hoi, but the line was out, probably destroyed by the bombs. He called for a runner and directed him to make contact with the officer, find out what was going on, and report back. Turning his attention to Major Co, he told him to contact the crews of the 12.7mm antiaircraft machine guns and release them to fire on the American planes. Normally, he would not expose the crew-served weapons, but now he needed their fire power to keep the aircraft at bay. Duc knew they would become the focus of the planes' attack, and that he was probably signing the death warrant for the gun crews, but "*Muon doc lap phai do mau*—for freedom, you have to spend your blood." It was a tradeoff: the gunners for the infantry and a chance to destroy the Americans in front of them. It was not a decision Duc took lightly, but it was a necessary one. As the commander of a fighting battalion who made life and death decisions on a daily basis, he could not afford the luxury of second-guessing himself. He would leave that for others. With that thought in mind, Duc whispered an old soldier's prayer:

"Suffering in life, pain in death,
The common fate of soldiers.
We pray the sacred souls will bless us,
That we may overcome enemy fire,
And avenge our lost comrades."

Co reported that Corporal Chau's machine gun, "Joyous Victory," was in the best position to fire on the American aircraft. Nodding to acknowledge the report, Duc pictured the face of the young *Bo doi*, who was so proud of his team and its heavy machine gun. He remembered the cheerful fighter because he came from a small village not far from Duc's own rural settlement. The oldest son of a farmer, the boy had volunteered to go south with the Liberation Army and had not lost his enthusiasm for the cause. In one hard-fought battle with the imperialists, Chau had shot down one of their helicopters, for which he been awarded the Military Exploit Medal.

Duc reluctantly shifted his thoughts back to the bombing and hardened his heart. He formally addressed his deputy: "Major Co, dispatch a runner to notify *Ha si* Chau that he has my permission to let Joyous Victory sing for the fatherland."

Recognizing the significance of the order, Co drew himself up straight and saluted. "Yes, *Trung Ta*, I will relay your directive immediately," he replied, and exited the bunker to brief the runner.

Duc stared at the entrance for several long minutes, his thoughts drifting back to other young men he had ordered to their deaths. He shuddered to think of what he had become—a killer of men.

A loud commotion outside the bunker entranceway captured Duc's attention. Before he could react, Major Minh burst inside and stopped abruptly, temporarily blinded as his eyes adjusted to the darkness. Duc was shocked by the disheveled appearance of the officer, whose normally immaculate uniform was mud-crusted and torn in several places. A blood-soaked bandage swathed his head and he held a pistol tightly in one hand, as if he expected to be attacked at any moment. He stammered incoherently and his body shook, yet it was his eyes that told Duc the man was near the edge of sanity. They seemed huge, wide open yet unfocused, darting unceasingly about the bunker in nervous apprehension.

Duc spoke softly and slowly reached out, so as not to spook the shell-shocked officer. He gently took Minh's hand, relieving the political officer of the pistol.

The human contact seemed to quiet Minh. His eyes slowly focused, but he continued to mumble unintelligibly.

"Major Minh, what happened? What are you trying to say?" Duc softly repeated several times, trying to get the officer's attention. "*Trung Ta*," Minh finally managed, "American bombs have destroyed the 3rd Company."

Duc was skeptical of the report; Minh was an inexperienced soldier who may have unknowingly magnified the losses. It was not uncommon for green troops to make exaggerated claims due to battlefield confusion, but there was something more profound that irritated Duc. He simply didn't trust the *Do cho de*. How could a few bombs wipe out an entire company? He scrutinized Minh's face, looking for some clue to determine the man's veracity.

***

Minh slowly sagged to the floor of the bunker under Duc's withering gaze, pretending to be spent by the ordeal. In reality, he was trying desperately to come up with a plausible story for his sudden appearance. He felt Duc's hatred and knew the *Do khon* wanted to expose him to the cadre for cowardice. He wasn't about to let that happen. Then, inspiration came to him. "Trung Ta, please forgive me," he softly groaned. "I felt lightheaded from the wound and needed to sit down." He rested his head in his hands for emphasis. The movement also allowed him to conceal his eyes from Duc's examination.

"*Thieu Ta*, how were you wounded?" Duc asked bluntly, his voice devoid of sympathy. He was something of an expert on battlefield wounds after so many years of service, and Minh's looked like a mere scratch. "I was leading an assault team against the Americans when I was hit in the head and knocked unconscious," Minh related, trying hard to sound convincing. "And when I came to, the bombs had struck our comrades and I was all alone." He stopped and hung his head, as if overcome by the thought of the lost men.

"What happened to Lieutenant Hoi?" Duc demanded brusquely. "The last time I saw him, he was in a bunker."

Minh's response implied that Hoi had remained under cover while Minh exposed himself to danger. Duc nodded dismissively and abruptly turned away, anxious to find Hoi and get his side of the story. Minh seethed with anger as the old *Do cho de* stalked away. He prayed that Hoi would become a dead "hero of the revolution," recalling the *Lo dit's* last words: "*Muon doc lap phai do mau.*"

At that moment Hoi was crawling along the trench. The next thing he knew, he was on his back, choking on a mixture of blood and dirt. He sprawled, deaf and semiconscious, in the partially destroyed trench, eyes open but expressionless, blood streaming from his nose and ears. Several meters behind him, two bunkers had been obliterated along with their inhabitants, in a terrifying explosion that threw debris 20 feet into the air and left a gaping, smoking gouge in the jungle floor. Nearby, a gigantic tree lay across a caved-in bunker, one of its log-like branches suspended over the prostrate officer.

The stink of cordite poisoned the dust-filled air, causing Hoi to cough as he slowly regained consciousness. He ran a hand over his face and found it covered with blood, but, in his dazed state, he could only stare at it, unable to recognize its significance.

At Hoi's feet, his runner, *Chien Si* Nhan, moaned and attempted to stand up. Stumbling, he fell back, unable to keep his balance. The young soldier slowly rolled over and managed to get to his hands and knees, all the time calling softly for Lieutenant Hoi, who didn't answer. Crawling forward, Nhan discovered the dust-covered officer, grasped him under the arms, and pulled him to a sitting position. Then, overcoming his own dizziness, he got to his feet and, with a great effort, tugged the officer erect.

Hoi leaned drunkenly against the side of the trench, dazed by the concussion caused by the falling limb. A wave of nausea swept over him and he doubled over, retching violently. His energy sapped, he struggled to catch his breath. He finally straightened up as the spasm passed and cried out for help, frightened because he couldn't hear and his eyes wouldn't focus. Someone grabbed his arm, startling him. He jerked away, not realizing it was his runner, and staggered down the trench, stumbling over the uneven ground until a fallen branch caught his foot and tripped him. He crumpled to his knees but quickly got up and climbed out of the caved-in trench, unknowingly heading toward the Americans. A feeling that something was terribly wrong permeated his consciousness just as a terrific blow in the face and chest hurled him to the ground.

He lay pressed into the earth, unable to rise, as his lifeblood poured from gaping holes in his chest and head. Hoi's lower jaw had been shot away, leaving a grotesque, bloody mask. Silent screams sounded from the gaping maw that had been his mouth. He arched his back in one final agonizing grasp on life, and then he shuddered and went limp in death. Nhan's lifeless body lay beside Hoi's, killed instantly in the same burst of gunfire.

More heavy explosions rocked the jungle, tearing the heart out of the 3rd Company.

12

Southern Hotel Air Support for Lima Company, 1050, 12 September—
Drifting in and out of consciousness, Lieutenant Gerry Arnold hung suspended, unable to free himself because of his injuries. Every time he moved, the jagged ends of his broken ribs grated against each other, sending shock waves of pain through his body. With the parachute harness squeezing his torso, there was no way to relieve the pressure, and the pain was getting worse. Although his facial wounds had stopped bleeding, the smell of fresh blood had attracted a host of insects, which considerably increased his suffering. He started to hallucinate, calling out to his wife. At one point he thought he heard the distinctive roar of a jet pulling out of a dive. Later, he thought he heard voices, but maybe not.

Suddenly, he felt himself falling, then searing pain as he hit the ground. He passed out. When he regained consciousness, someone was yelling and slapping his face. Dazed, he couldn't understand why he was being hit, and then his eyes focused on the uniform. "Oh my God," he mumbled, "They're North Vietnamese." A surge of adrenaline jolted him fully awake. Before he could react, two of the soldiers grabbed him by the arms, hauled him upright, and stepped back. Racked by excruciating pain, he collapsed, screaming in agony.

One of the soldiers kicked Arnold in the leg, shouting in Vietnamese. An older fighter stepped forward, pointing a pistol at the airman and making a motion with it for Arnold to get up. With a tremendous effort, the airman succeeded in scrambling to his hands and knees, but he could not stand. The gunman shouted and struck him across the back of the head with the pistol, splitting his scalp. Arnold collapsed as fresh blood streamed down his head and neck, momentarily losing consciousness.

When he came to, he lay face-up, staring into the hate-filled eyes of his assailant, who slowly raised the pistol and pointed it directly at his face.

With a sudden clarity that cut through the pain, Arnold realized that he was going to die, and there was nothing he could do about it. At that moment, he thought of his wife and mumbled, "I love you," just as the pistol went off.

Senior Sergeant Thanh bent over and ripped the dog tags from the dead flyer's neck. He studied the oval discs for a moment and then stuffed them into his shirt pocket, intending to keep them as a souvenir of the execution of the American criminal. With a skill born from long practice, Thanh stripped Arnold's body of its personal effects, appropriating the flyer's watch, wedding band, and shoulder holster containing a .38-caliber revolver for himself. Two of his men rifled the contents of the billfold, fascinated with a photograph of a young woman in a bathing suit, which they passed around, giggling at the unusual sight. Under Thanh's directions, they propped the battered remains against a tree and, as a final insult, mutilated it by cutting off the genitals and stuffing them in Arnold's mouth. Finally, they booby-trapped the body with grenades set to explode if it were moved. They divided up the spoils they found scattered around the body and eased back into the jungle.

13

Southern Hotel and Lima 6, Rescue Attempt, 1150, 12 September—Southern Hotel was having a hell of a time. The rush of wind through the gaping hole in the windshield was blowing everything around the cockpit, interfering with Reed's ability to fly the aircraft as loose objects pelted him in the flight helmet. An open map hit him in the face, completely obscuring his vision, and causing him to lose control momentarily as he ripped it away from his head. In the backseat, Pop Harper looked like a rag picker as the debris settled in his lap—at least the stuff that wasn't blown out the hole in the roof. Adding insult to injury, Reed's beloved aviator sunglasses were sucked out into the slipstream and, in a frantic attempt to save them, he knocked his headphones off, temporarily putting him out of radio contact.

***

Taking advantage of the NVA's disarray, Anderson reorganized the company, bringing Larson's platoon up behind Frazier's, in position to reinforce him. Gunny Smith gathered the casualties. The main body of Lima Company was still taking fire, especially 1st Platoon, but it was nothing like it had been before the bombing. Anderson knew he had to break contact before the NVA recovered. Meanwhile, the company needed more air and artillery support to keep the Vietnamese pinned down. The Marines had to get to one of the hilltops and hunker down, but the withdrawal was going to be slow as hell with all the casualties.

Anderson's thoughts were interrupted by shouts of "Gooks, gooks!" followed by a heavy burst of gunfire from the right flank of Frazier's platoon. He looked up just in time to see several green-uniformed figures disappear in the undergrowth. "Shit, they're trying to flank us," he exclaimed and turned to Napoline, "Get that artillery going. The gooks are bringing up reinforcements."

The forward observer shook his head, "Skipper, I can't contact the AO, and he's got everything shut off for the rescue attempt."

***

The CH-46, call sign "Seaworthy 4-1," was aloft and on the way with its escort, two UH-1E "Huey" gunships, call signs "Gunslinger One" and "Gunslinger Two."

Harper quickly briefed them, stressing that while he had seen the pilot go in and had an emergency beacon signal, they hadn't been able to establish voice contact. While he was talking, the Phantoms, "Nightmare One" and "Nightmare Two," checked in with Reed, who put them in a holding pattern northwest of the combat base.

Just as Pop was getting the rescue plan together, Anderson came up on the air with news of the NVA movement. "Christ, what a fucking mess," Harper mumbled to himself and keyed the net, "Roger, Lima Six, I understand your situation. I've got two fast movers on station to help you break contact," he replied without a trace of emotion in his voice. After Anderson acknowledged the message, Harper mentally switched gears, changing the plan by directing Seaworthy and escorts to orbit out of the way, then alerting Nightmare to standby for a marker rocket. Switching to intercom, he asked, "Bomber, you ready to rock and roll?"

Cocky as ever, Reed replied, "Pop, I love this shit." He hunched his shoulders and tightened his sphincter muscles, unconsciously reacting to the danger of the run in. He dropped the Bird Dog's nose. The wind streamed through the shot-up windshield as he made the run for the target.

Nightmare One, flight leader for a pair of Navy F-4s off a carrier on Yankee Station, was good. The first pair of Snakeyes hit right on the money, exploding within feet of Reed's marker. Not to be outdone, his wingman put two more into the same place, firmly establishing their bombing credentials. Pleased with the results, Harper worked over the bunker complex with a vengeance, producing dramatic results. A large swathe of jungle was flattened, creating an opening in which he could see evidence of smashed trench lines and collapsed bunkers. Anderson reported that the NVA had stopped trying to flank him and that he was going to try to break contact.

Harper gave the F-4 pilots a BDA (Battle Damage Assessment): fifteen enemy KBA (Killed by Air) plus two bunkers and thirty meters of trench line destroyed. Feeling expansive, he offered to buy them a round at the Dong Ha Officers' Club the next time they came to town. Nightmare One chuckled, knowing that it would be an extremely cold day in hell before he would ever accept an invitation to the exposed Marine base near the DMZ. Nevertheless, in the spirit of Navy–Marine cooperation, he countered with a simple, "Our pleasure. Call us anytime you need help," and checked out of the net.

Reed keyed the intercom, "Pop, I don't mean to overburden you with petty bullshit, but we're about to become a flying rock. We're zip on fuel."

"Okay, Bomber," he replied, "land just as soon as Recon's on the ground."

The two gunships circled protectively over the CH-46 as it came to a hover over a small opening in the jungle about half a klick south of Arnold's parachute. Two nylon lines dropped from its lowered ramp, followed by the Knife Edge team, which quickly repelled the 70 feet to the ground. Seconds after the last man touched down, the helicopter dipped its nose to pick up forward airspeed and climbed rapidly from the area, followed by the gunships.

The Knife Edge team established a tight circular perimeter and waited, anxiously listening to and scanning the jungle for signs their insertion had been discovered. After some moments, they silently moved out, satisfied there was no immediate danger. The team leader, 1st Lieutenant Herb Wilson, gave the all-clear to Harper, who was monitoring the Knife Edge net, prepared to send the gunships back if the reconners needed help.

Setting a faster pace than normal, Wilson sacrificed stealth for speed. He was under orders from the company commander to reach the downed pilot before darkness, which was fast approaching. They found a well-used game trail, relatively free of noise-making undergrowth, that seemed to head in the right direction. They followed it until they estimated they were in the vicinity of the pilot. After designating a rendezvous point, Wilson split the men into two-man teams and started searching, using compass azimuths as directional guides.

A member of the middle team spotted a portion of a white parachute dangling from a treetop. Cautiously the two men approached it, only to be arrested in their tracks at the sight of Arnold's naked, mutilated corpse slumped against the tree. One man retched, then averted his eyes. The other man instinctively reached out, before his partner grabbed his arm, vehemently shaking his head in disapproval. Clearly the body had been tampered with. After taking a quick look around, the two melted back into cover and quickly returned to the rendezvous site, where they picked up the other teams and led them back to retrieve the body.

Forcing himself to ignore the mutilated corpse, Wilson set up security. Then he cautiously felt around and beneath the corpse, trying not to disturb it. He quickly located the two booby-trapped U.S.-made grenades and carefully removed them by holding the spoons tightly so the striker wouldn't release. He replaced the missing cotter pins with a pair he kept on his bush hat for emergencies like this and motioned for one of the men to help him put the lifeless man in the body bag that he had laid out. The two struggled mightily with the stiffened body, rigor mortis had set in, and finally succeeding in stuffing the cadaver in the green nylon bag. As they finished the grisly chore, the younger man turned away and vomited the contents of his stomach into the undergrowth, tears streaming down his camouflaged cheeks. "Lieutenant, why'd they do that?" he asked, after recovering his composure.

"They're trying to scare us, hoping we'll lose our nerve," Wilson responded, his voice taut with suppressed anger, "but it won't work. It just makes us want to kill more of the bastards, especially the ones who did this."

Wilson radioed the news of the discovery and, in a barely controlled voice, described the scene in gruesome detail. As Harper listened, the events played out in his mind, sending him on an emotional roller coaster. "I should have brought the rescue team in first," he mumbled over the intercom, second-guessing himself.

"Bullshit," Reed replied, "Then you'd have a company of dead Marines. It's not your fault, it's not my fault, it's nobody's fault. Shit happens in combat. You did the best you could, and it's no time for a pity party. We've got work to do, Pop."

Harper was startled by Reed's intensity; it was out of character for the happy-go-lucky pilot, who was usually on the receiving end of counseling. He felt blood rush to his face and anger welling up inside, threatening to explode in a burst of rage. *Who the hell do you think you are?* he wanted to scream. *You don't know shit about combat.*

Just as Harper was about to verbally take Reed apart, the younger man's contrite voice came back, "Sorry, Pop, you didn't deserve that. I lost it for a minute."

Harper calmed immediately, realizing Bomber was right: there was nothing they could do for the dead pilot but everything for the grunts on the ground. "Thanks, Chaplain. I needed that. Now fly this damn plane home," he quipped, earning a chuckle of relief from the front seat. The pressure of the mission was getting to both of them.

Reed climbed to 3,000 feet and headed for Khe Sanh, with its 3,900-foot runway. He prayed the tank held 15 additional minutes of fuel, dreading the thought of running out of gas over the jungle. Safely landing a Cessna in the treetops was right up there with walking on water. "Come on, baby. I know you can do it," he pleaded silently as the engine purred on. He picked out the base on the horizon and calculated that in a couple more minutes he could glide in. The runway took on definition—a long strip of gray steel matting outlined against the plateau's distinctive red clay.

Time to check in. "Tower, this is Southern Hotel requesting clearance to land."

"Southern Hotel," the controller replied, "the field is closed. Vector 150 to Dong Ha."

Not now! Reed wanted to scream in frustration. "Tower, I'm running on fumes and declaring an emergency."

"Southern Hotel, the field is torn up. You can't land." Before Reed could answer, the engine coughed, as it sucked up the remaining fuel. It sputtered for a long moment and then died.

"Mayday, Mayday," he anxiously broadcast as the Cessna fell out of the sky.

Harper's stomach lurched when the aircraft's bottom dropped out. He unconsciously grasped the sides of the cockpit as his mind screamed, *We're going in!* A jolt of adrenalin shot into his bloodstream, jump-starting his heart. He tensed for the crash.

Suddenly Reed's shaky voice came over the intercom, "Place your tray tables up and in a locked position. We're experiencing some minor turbulence."

Harper laughed despite himself. The kid was never out of character. "Minor turbulence, my ass. If you can't fly this piece of shit any better than this, I'll take over," he quipped.

"Sorry Pop, we're encountering a little technical difficulty: no power. But not to worry. We're going to glide in—trade altitude for distance. No sweat. I'll get us home."

Harper opened his mouth to reply but thought better of it; Bomber had his hands full without trading any more quips.

Reed struggled to keep the bird in the air, unconsciously calculating the distance to the runway, praying they had enough altitude. As the wheels cleared the last of the forest giants, he felt a small jolt. Jungle turned to scrub growth and red clay as they crossed the perimeter foxholes. His mind registered the surprised look on the defenders' faces as the aircraft silently passed overhead, gliding toward safety. Sweat poured down his face as he willed the Cessna to cover the last few feet.

And then they were down, wheels barely touching the edge of the matting, inches from sinking into the soft red clay.

The intercom exploded with a warning. "Look out, Bomber!" Harper shouted as they headed for a large hole in the runway matting.

Reed had barely enough time to recognize the danger when the front strut hit the hole and gave way. The nose hit with such force that it crumpled the cockpit, trapping him in the wreckage. Harper was luckier. After wriggling free from his harness, he managed to escape. He scrambled around to the cockpit and saw Reed hunched motionless in his seat, bleeding from facial cuts. With his bare hands he attacked the wreckage but couldn't budge the twisted metal. His heart racing, he looked around frantically, breathing a small sigh of relief as a team of rescuers approached, armed with pry bars and sledgehammers. Edging their way in, they deftly maneuvered the metal just enough to get access to Reed.

A large crowd gathered, including two corpsmen and a doctor, who quickly took charge, refusing to allow the pilot to be extracted until he was examined. One of the corpsmen climbed into the wreckage, checked vital signs, immobilized Reed's neck, and unfastened his harness. Two burly Marines lifted the unconscious man out and placed him on a stretcher.

As Harper bent over him, the pilot's eyes fluttered opened. "I told you I'd get you home," Reed whispered.

14

Reconnaissance Platoon, North Vietnamese Army, Rally Point, 1300, 12 September—Thanh and his small party made good time, using a series of jungle trails to reach the rendezvous, a camouflaged weapons storage site, where the survivors of his platoon waited. He found them in poor shape. The medic was treating four seriously wounded men, one of whom was expected to die. Several others were nursing minor injuries. The rest were traumatized by their narrow escape, dispirited, in no condition to fight. Thanh looked them over and decided to have these men carry the wounded to the field hospital while he continued on with just the four men who had arrived with him. He placed the larger group under a senior private and sent it off carrying the three wounded who had the best chance for survival.

Concerned that the Americans would use the trail and find the weapons cache, Thanh had his small party dig a large pit to hide the weapons; such a small force couldn't haul them away. Struggling to think of a way to conceal the ad hoc dump, his attention was drawn to the medical debris scattered on the ground. Suddenly he had a plan. While his men stacked the weapons and ammunition in the hole, he walked over to the seriously wounded man, Private 2nd Class Ton. Unconscious and in shock from a chest wound, Ton was barely breathing.

Thanh kneeled over the soldier. With his back to the working party to conceal his actions, he looked Ton in the eye, and calmly suffocated him. He straightened up and, in a voice dripping with sorrow, announced that Private Ton had given his life for the liberation. Thanh led the men in a hurried Buddhist funeral service, asking Ton's ancestors to accept him into their spirit world. Then, without further adieu, he had the men place the body in the hole, only partially camouflaging it, as if a hasty burial had taken place. After surveying their handiwork, the five men formed up and faded into the jungle, back toward the Americans.

15

1st Platoon, Lima Company, Hill 540, 1300, 12 September—Staff Sergeant Brown was still pissed, still vowing to get even with Littleton. But, in the meantime, he worked off his anger by "vigorously" organizing the platoon for the move, or, in troop parlance, Brown "kicked ass and took names." Not wanting to earn a place on his shit list, the troops rushed to carry out his orders. He organized them into four four-man teams to carry the wounded and two two-man teams for the KIAs, who were each wrapped in a poncho and lashed to a pole. Unable to carry all the captured equipment and weapons, the troops did their best to destroy it. Weapons and ammunition were piled in a bunker and prepared for demolition using several quarter-pound blocks of C-4, which the platoon always carried, primarily to heat C-rations. After it was picked over for souvenirs, the NVA equipment was piled on top. Another working party spread several hundred pounds of rice on the ground and then pissed on the grain, "to give it flavor," in case the NVA came back to reclaim it. Finally, after dividing up several pounds of captured documents, Brown passed the word to move out. "Saddle up, saddle up!" he barked, galvanizing the platoon into action.

There was a flurry of activity as the stretcher parties shouldered their loads and moved out with Littleton and Sanders on point and Brown bringing up the rear. The three men were the only ones not burdened with a casualty. Such a small security element, violated every tactical principle in the book, because it exposed them to annihilation if the NVA ambushed them.

Littleton prayed that Duvall's team had followed the trail out without incident and were on the way back, which would give the platoon a little more fire power. Deciding it was best to scout ahead, he started up the trail with Sanders in tow, noting footprints in the dirt. The patrol's jungle-boot imprints overlapped those made by the Ho Chi Minh tire tracks. After several yards, the trail curved to the right to follow the terrain up the finger to high ground.

The forest seemed to close in behind them, the thick vegetation cutting them off from the noise of his men. An ominous stillness surrounded them as they advanced cautiously, scanning the trail for some sign of danger. *Where the hell is Duvall?* Littleton thought. *He should've returned by now.*

A heavily camouflaged NVA soldier cautiously stepped out of the jungle onto the trail, looked both ways, and bent down to inspect several footprints in the dirt. The foliage that was tied to his uniform and pith helmet blended perfectly with the undergrowth, concealing him from Littleton and Sanders. After a long moment, he rose and moved forward along the edge of the trail, joined by three others, who stepped out of the jungle as he passed by. They took positions on both sides of the path, assault rifles at the ready, covering each other as they noiselessly made their way along the path. Every few moments they stopped to listen intently to the jungle noises, and then they moved on, satisfied that it was safe to proceed. After reaching a bend in the trail, they moved several feet into the undergrowth and squatted down. For several moments, they listened and observed before removing ankle-high branches through the brush all the way to the trail to create fire lanes to see and shoot through. Completing the task, they settled down to wait until the Americans entered the kill zone.

Suddenly, without conscious thought, Littleton's senses fired a warning, and his muscles tensed. He sucked in an involuntary lung full of air. As the aroma of wood smoke and fish filled his nostrils, the hair on his arms literally stood up. *Fish and wood smoke, fish and wood smoke ...* he thought. *Gooks!* his mind screamed.

Both men instantly froze, weapons pointed up the trail, fingers tightening on triggers. Littleton glanced down. *Shit. Tire tracks over boot prints.* He nodded to Sanders. They moved off the trail and squatted down in the dense undergrowth, invisible to anyone on the path.

"The gooks must have doubled back," the lieutenant whispered. "How many do you think there are?"

Sanders, a rancher and part-time hunting guide from Montana, instantly replied, "Three or four, and they're fresh."

Littleton thought for a moment. The Vietnamese must have cut through the trees, spotted the patrol's footprints, and followed them. The patrol was in danger of being ambushed on the way back, and there wasn't any apparent way to alert them.

What a hell of predicament, Littleton thought. *I could lose them if I don't do something.*

"Come on, Sanders," he said, "We're going to get the bad guys." He stepped back out on the trail, mumbling, "Here I am, playing rifleman again."

The undergrowth brought forth the usual collection of blood-sucking insects attracted by the promise of a meal. They buzzed, hummed, and droned around the ears of the four men in ambush, making their wait a miserable experience. They couldn't even slap the damn things for fear of making noise. One pesky bloodsucker attached itself to a vein on the side of a soldier's head, inserted its stylet, and began siphoning its meal, causing an intense itching sensation. Half asleep because of the heat and inactivity, the insect's host unconsciously reached up, violating procedure and slapped the insect. This caused a noticeable movement in the undergrowth. The team leader, hearing the sound, shifted his body slightly, faced the offender, and muttered an order to let the insects have their lunch.

Working to stay in the shadows, Sanders took the left side of the trail, with Littleton across from him and a few steps behind. Carefully, they worked their way up the track, conscious of the fact that the NVA could be just ahead, waiting in ambush. The tension was palpable. Sweat was streaming down Littleton's body, his shirt soaking under the heavy flak jacket. His index finger exerted a steady pressure on the trigger of his rifle, which he had switched to full automatic with the safety off. *Where the hell are they?* he thought as he peered across at Sanders, who stopped and stared intently at a patch of grass at another bend in the trail.

In one fluid motion, the radioman brought up his rifle and pressed the trigger, emptying the magazine in one long burst of fire. Even though Littleton couldn't see anything, he also opened up, spraying the same area.

Both men hit the ground as Sanders yelled, "They're in the grass on the left!" He pulled a grenade from his belt, yanked out the cotter pin, and jumped to his feet. As he heaved it, a burst of fire erupted from the grass. The rounds snapped by, missing him by inches. Flinging himself to the ground, he saw the grenade land in the grass, just off the trail. It exploded with a terrific crump, spraying debris in every direction. Screams erupted from the undergrowth and then abruptly stopped.

Littleton figured that two grenades would be good insurance, so he pitched another. After the explosion, the two men stood up, ready to assault the Vietnamese, but they were stopped by an eruption of automatic weapons fire. It took a second for Littleton to realize that it was Duvall and his team.

The ambush leader had just resumed his position when a fusillade of 5.56mm bullets tore into the undergrowth, raking the ground and striking flesh. Half the ambushers were killed before their minds registered the sound of the rifle. One of the survivors reflexively swiveled around, pointed his weapon in the general direction of the Americans, and cut loose, barely missing his target. The other, momentarily stunned by the shockingly violent scene being played out in front of him, froze in position. Another hail of bullets clipped the shrubbery. Several bullets hit the two bodies but spared the others. Before they could react, a terrific explosion shook the undergrowth, sending shards of metal hurtling through the vegetation, killing another soldier and painfully wounding the last man in the legs. Realizing he had to escape quickly, the wounded NVA soldier forced himself to crawl away, leaving a blood trail through the undergrowth. Behind him, another explosion sent debris and metal flying through the air.

After sweeping through the grass, Duvall joined Littleton and reported finding three dead NVA and a blood trail, evidence that at least one other had been hit. "We also found these on one of the bodies," he said, holding out a Marine ID card, a photograph, and a set of pilot's wings. "There's also some survival gear in their packs, I think these bastards got a pilot."

Littleton took the card and read the name, trying to remember if he knew anyone by the name of Arnold. He turned to Sanders and told him to radio Battalion and report the find.

Reaching into the pack at his side, Duvall brought out a Soviet Tokarev pistol and leather belt with a brass buckle, which he handed Littleton. "Sir, we'd like you to have these," he said, "I think one of the gooks was an officer." It took Littleton a minute to realize the significance of the gesture; the gift was a treasure, a souvenir of inestimable value. This simple act of giving was, in fact, a statement that he had earned the professional respect of his men. Struggling to keep his composure, he stammered out "thanks" to the equally embarrassed squad leader. As he stuffed the weapon in his pack, he happened to look at the pistol and noted a name etched on the grip: "Thanh."

The wounded NVA soldier crawled several meters from the ambush site and forced his way into the center of a thick clump of shrubbery, almost passing out from the pain as his wounded legs bumped against the branches. His pursuers were close enough for him to hear their footsteps, but he remained safe. No one checked his hiding place. Despite the pain and the onset of shock, he had the presence of mind to bind up his wounds, which stopped the bleeding. Exhausted by the effort and half conscious, he took a set of aluminum tags out of his shirt pocket and held them up, his lips forming a maniacal smile, and then passed out, the metal tightly clenched in his fist. As he slid in and out of consciousness, his slender hold on life was strengthened by a terrible thirst for revenge. He would kill the Americans who had destroyed his soldiers.

Touched as he was, Littleton had a job to do. He turned to Sanders and asked him how he had spotted the NVA. "One of them shifted position and I caught the movement," Sanders replied, "and I saw the trail they made in the grass."

"They didn't bother to straighten it up because it was the back side of the ambush. Dumb shits." Littleton shook his head in wonder. Luck was with them. After telling the men to spread out and keep watch, he took Duvall aside and asked about the patrol.

80

Duvall squatted down and used a stick to draw a rough sketch of the patrol route in the dirt. He pointed out a small open area under the trees, where he had found used bandages, empty medical vials, and a large blood trail, evidence of a hastily evacuated aid station. He traced the route to the base of a steep slope where the Vietnamese had carved a series of steps to ease the climb. The steps looked well used. Then he drew an oblong circle representing the hill. "Lieutenant, I've been to a lot of weird places, but that hill takes the cake. The grass is trampled flat and there's big piles of shit all over the place. The damn stuff is as big as cannon balls."

Littleton broke in. "Piles of shit? Cannon balls? You're kidding me, right?"

"No, sir. I think elephants have been on that hill, but I can't figure out why."

Littleton nodded. He *had* heard a story about a recon team that had spotted a whole caravan of elephants being used as pack animals by the NVA. The team had brought in an airstrike, killing several, which they found loaded to the tusks with heavy weapons.

Duvall continued, "The whole damn place is ringed with spider traps—must be two or three dozen—and it smells like the NVA have been there in force."

"Can helicopters land there?" Littleton asked.

"It's as bald as a billiard. Not a tree on the damn thing. But the zone is small, only enough for one bird at a time. And one other thing, Lieutenant," Duvall added. "I couldn't shake off the feeling that I was being watched the whole time. It was really spooky."

"What other options do we have?" Littleton asked rhetorically, and then answered his own question. "We need that hill to get out of here."

He ordered Duvall to send two men back to the platoon as guides and to help with the wounded. The two others would lead Littleton back to the hill.

Duvall set a fast pace until they reached the abandoned aid station. While one man maintained security, the two others spread out to search the site and the surrounding undergrowth. Littleton collected half a dozen small vials that were lying about and noted that the labels were printed in Russian. It was common knowledge that the damn Soviets supplied the NVA with everything from weapons to medical supplies. Another vial, half hidden in the grass, attracted his attention. The label was in English, and the bottom line read, "Supplied by Friends of the Vietnamese People." He couldn't believe it. What a crock! All he could think of was the phrase "providing aid and comfort to the enemy." And here it was, shepherding three severely wounded Americans who badly needed aid and comfort while Americans back home supplied the enemy.

Duvall approached, interrupting his thought to tell him that he found what looked like a grave. The two went over to the edge of the small clearing, where a rifleman in the 2nd Squad, Private First Class Paul Gregg, pointed out a large mound of freshly disturbed earth, half hidden by dead grass.

"What do you think, Corporal Duvall?"

"Lieutenant, I think a couple of their wounded died and they buried them here. They didn't have time to haul them away."

Littleton studied the mound. Something about it seemed off; it was too exposed. He made a decision. "Get your e-tools out. We're going to dig it up."

One of the Marines let out a small groan, then caught himself too late to avoid earning a scowl from his squad leader.

The four men turned to, finding the loosely packed soil easy to scoop out. A foot below the surface, Littleton's shovel hit something soft and spongy. As he cleared away the dirt with his hands, his fingers scraped the face of a dead North Vietnamese soldier, sending a shudder of revulsion through his body. Backing away quickly, he was about to stop the digging when Duvall's shovel struck the dirt with a resounding thunk. Working quickly, they pulled the body out of the hole and uncovered a long wooden box, which was heavy as hell. Duvall excitedly pried the top off and discovered a cosmoline-protected 12.7mm heavy machine gun, which the NVA used as an antiaircraft weapon. They turned to with a will and soon pulled several more boxes from the pit—another machine gun and several hundred rounds of ammunition.

After lifting the last crate from the hole, they took a short break, physically exhausted from the hard work and covered from head to toe with mud.

Duvall took a long pull from his canteen, then turned to the officer and asked, "Lieutenant, how in hell did you know the gooks had stashed weapons in the grave?"

Littleton looked up from examining one of the guns, smiled and replied, "I didn't. It was just a hunch. They usually hide graves so we can't find them. This one was only half camouflaged. Too obvious."

Duvall shook his head in wonder. "So what the hell are we going to do with all this?" he asked.

"We'll leave everything here and come back for them," Littleton replied, "I don't want to waste anymore time. Let's get on to the hill before the platoon gets here."

Within a few moments the small group reached the steps at the base of the hill, where they stopped while two scouts went forward to make sure the NVA weren't waiting in another ambush. After receiving the all-clear, Littleton led them to the top, above the canopy, where he could see for miles. He felt strangely relieved to be out in the open, under the bright sky, following the confinement of the jungle. Turning to Sanders, he told him to switch radio frequencies and establish contact with the battalion COC.

As the radio operator shrugged out of his pack, Littleton's attention was diverted by a shout that the platoon was at the base of the hill. Grabbing a couple of men, he ran to the trail just in time to see the head of the column break out of the trees.

16

Lima Company, 1500, 12 September—Anderson squatted stiffly behind an uprooted tree as he spoke into a radio handset. "Three, this is Six. Move out. Over."

The periodic crack of small arms fire reminded him that the NVA were still around despite the terrific pounding they had taken from the air.

After a brief delay, Larson's pain-racked voice came back, "Roger, Six. Moving now."

"Good man," he mumbled, picturing the wounded officer organizing his men for the move, barely able to hobble but still in command.

Anderson's own wounds had stiffened, making it difficult to walk and move his arms, but the pain was bearable. He turned to Napoline. "Tom, I don't know how much further Larson can go, so I want you to be ready to take over his platoon."

Taken aback, the artilleryman visibly blanched but gamely responded, "Roger, Skipper." *Christ, what have I gotten into?* Napoline thought. *I'm an artilleryman, not a grunt. What do I know about running an infantry platoon?* His self-pity quickly evaporated as he realized the obvious—there wasn't anyone else, and he better learn damn fast.

***

Larson was getting weaker, the loss of blood and the onset of shock threatening to overcome his best efforts to keep going. The platoon corpsman had done his best to patch him up, but the constant movement had aggravated the wound, causing it to bleed freely, soaking the battle dressings. The wound hurt like hell, at times bringing tears to his eyes, but he forced himself to keep going, refusing to give in to the pain.

As the column got underway, Larson leaned heavily on his radio operator, who took his arm and helped him up the trail behind the lead squad. They moved warily forward, staying low as enemy fire cracked overhead. Behind them came the rest of the platoon, now relegated to the role of stretcher bearers, carrying the company's dead and wounded.

First Platoon brought up the rear—except Frazier and one squad of five men, who remained in position to cover the withdrawal, still under fire from several NVA in a trench.

Frazier lay in the shallow depression with his radio operator and, for the umpteenth time, tried to figure out how to knock out the NVA who were giving his men such fits. The bastards had survived bombing, artillery, and everything else that had been thrown at them. Now it was decision time. The company was pulling out, and in order for his platoon to get away, the North Vietnamese had to be eliminated. From where he lay, he could make out the flash of gunfire from the trench in the waning late afternoon daylight. It was getting darker under the trees, the filtered light forming shadows that made it difficult to see into the scattered undergrowth.

"It might just work," Frazier mumbled, loud enough for his radio operator to hear.

"What might work, Lieutenant?" the radioman asked, wondering what craziness Frazier had in mind this time, thinking the blow to his head had done more than just ring the officer's chimes.

"I need a diversion so I can get to the trench," Frazier responded as he slipped off his flak jacket and web gear, "and you're it."

The young Marine crawled along the line to brief the men on the lieutenant's plan, receiving their commiserations for his role in the scheme. He had to go to ground several times as the NVA spotted him and directed their fire in his direction. Each time, he swore to himself that, if he survived this madness, he would get as far away from the lieutenant as possible.

When he reached the end of the line, he took a deep breath, said a little prayer, and stood up, firing his rifle on full automatic in the general direction of the trench. He dropped, just as return fire impacted the ground around him, but one bullet smashed the plastic hand guard of his M-16, sending shards of the material into his hands and face. He curled into a ball as dozens of AK-47 rounds slashed the air over his head.

The other Marines opened a concentrated fire, diverting attention long enough for Frazier to slip out of the depression and crawl forward, using the scattered undergrowth and poor light as concealment. Unencumbered with the bulky flak jacket and web gear, he gained several meters without being seen and finally reached a point at which the vegetation ran out, leaving a wide stretch of open ground to the trench.

Frazier carefully reached into his pocket and drew out a hand grenade. He pulled the pin and let the spoon fly off, which started the five-second delay.

As he rose to a half crouch, the NVA spotted him and started to swing their rifles. Frazier threw the grenade and fell to the ground as it left his hand. No more than two seconds remained in the firing chain.

The missile hit the berm, rolled into the trench, and exploded, killing its two occupants before they could fire.

Frazier jumped to his feet and sprinted toward the trench, fumbling for the .45 automatic he had stuffed in the waistband of his utilities. Grasping the butt, he yanked it out and thumbed back the hammer just as another NVA soldier appeared in the trench, aiming his assault rifle. In a desperate act of self-preservation, Frazier pointed the heavy pistol at the man and squeezed the trigger as fast as he could, still on a dead run, screaming at the top of his voice.

It worked. The NVA ducked back into the trench without firing his rifle.

Frazier reached the lip of the trench, hesitated, and jumped down on the back of the cowering NVA soldier, striking him repeatedly on the head with his pistol. Suddenly, a terrific blow across the shoulders threw him off the man and onto his back in the bottom of the trench. For a split second he lay there, looking directly into the eyes of another Viet who was about to drive a bayonet into his chest. Reflexively, he raised the .45 and fired into the man's face, blowing him backward in a spray of blood and brain matter. He scrambled upright just as another soldier lunged at him. He fired again, knocking the man down, and then glimpsed others trying to force their way forward in the close confines of the trench. Frazier pulled at the trigger, but the .45 didn't fire. He saw the slide was locked to the rear; the pistol was empty. It was the last thing he saw as he was clubbed to the floor of the trench.

Anderson grabbed the prone Marine by the shoulder, sending a spasm of pain up his arm. "Where the hell's the lieutenant?" he angrily whispered, upset that Frazier hadn't withdrawn the last of his platoon. "Captain, I don't know. The last I saw of him, he was running toward that trench," the Marine responded, pointing toward the silent NVA position barely visible in the fading light.

Anderson was thunderstruck. "What the hell happened?" he managed to utter, not quite ready to believe what he had heard. Lance Corporal Donald, the squad leader, ran over and, in a voice filled with emotion, told how Frazier had ordered him to stay put and pull out as soon as the gunfire stopped, with or without him.

"Christ, I don't believe this," Anderson huffed. "And you let him go alone?" Anderson immediately regretted the comment when he saw the crestfallen look on the man's face. It was obvious the young enlisted man was distraught, thinking he had somehow let his officer down.

"Sorry Donald," Anderson said in a calmer tone, trying to take the sting out of his remark. "It wasn't your fault. The lieutenant knew what he was doing."

Before he could say more, Gunny Smith strode out of the darkness. "Skipper, you ready to move out?" he asked. "Everyone's on the trail and we're the last ones."

"Plans have changed, Gunny." He took Smith aside to brief him on the situation.

Ignoring the pain, Anderson led the six men stealthily through the undergrowth, trying to maintain direction in the gathering darkness. He paused every few meters to listen intently for man-made sounds, all too aware that his own men were far from quiet.

Sensing at length that he was close to the objective, he signaled the squad to form a line and advance to the edge of the trench. Once there, they all knelt down, hardly believing they had made it. The two outboard men on either side took up firing positions, ready to shoot anything that came down the trench.

Anderson and Donald warily dropped into the dark hole, weapons at the ready, bayonets fixed. The stink of death was overwhelming in the confined space, forcing Anderson to struggle mightily to keep from gagging. As soon as he overcame the reflex, he crept forward a few steps and stumbled, knocking him off balance. He put out a hand to steady himself. A feeling of revulsion coursed through him as his palm touched cold, clammy skin. He jerked his hand back, rubbing it hard against his shirt, unconsciously trying to wipe away the sensation. "Shit," he mumbled, feeling his knee press into the corpse. He took a flashlight from his webbing and turned it on, carefully shielding the red filtered light so that it shined on the body. He prayed it wasn't Frazier. Inches away, the grotesque face of a dead Vietnamese lay silhouetted in a pool of congealed blood. Quickly shifting the light, he saw two more dead NVA jumbled together in the mud, which was deeply trampled and torn up, as if there had been a struggle. Looking closer, he spotted the gleam of a brass .45-caliber cartridge partially embedded in the bottom of the trench. With a start, Anderson realized he was looking at the spot where Frazier had waged his last fight.

Donald gripped the captain by the shoulder and whispered, "Skipper, I hear 'em coming."

Vietnamese voices sounded close in the still night air. "Quick, out of the trench," Anderson ordered, helping Donald scramble over the berm. "Warn the others and pull back to the company. I'll cover you." He yanked out two hand grenades, pulled the cotter pin from one, and placed the other on the berm next to his face.

As the young Marine took off, Anderson waited for the Vietnamese to get closer. He knew it was pointless to continue the search for Frazier; he would only lose more men. For nothing. The lieutenant was gone.

When he judged the distance to be right, he flung the grenade, feeling the sudden pain as the wounds on his arm reopened. He pulled the pin from the second and grunted with the effort as he threw it with all his might in the hope of catching more of the enemy in the kill zone.

He dropped to the ground just as the first grenade detonated, erupting in a flash of light that silhouetted several figures in and around the trench. The second grenade went off to the accompaniment of screams of agony.

Anderson leaped to his feet, clambered out of the trench, and sprinted back to the start point to assure himself that his men had gotten away.

He had progressed only a few feet when several AK-47s opened up, the rounds coming close enough to make him think the NVA must have seen him. Then he heard the sound of Donald's voice coming out of the darkness—"Over here, Captain. Over here"—and he veered toward it.

"I thought I told you to take off," he lightly chided Donald when he found the squad leader kneeling behind a shrub near a trail.

"Captain, I've lost one officer today, and I damn sure ain't gonna lose another," the younger man heatedly replied, his voice taut with emotion.

Anderson squeezed him on the shoulder to acknowledge Donald's grit, saying, "Thanks for covering my ass; it was getting a little lonely out there. Now we better get the hell out of here."

Both men rose, rifles at the ready, and started back. But they had gone only a few feet before they heard the heavy footfalls of running men.

"Shit," Anderson whispered, "the gooks are after the company. We'll be cut off if we don't hustle." He broke into a pain-laced jog, taking a chance the NVA wouldn't recognize them in the dark.

After getting swatted by tree limbs, they found a clear trail that seemed to lead in the right direction. They followed it, Anderson gasping from the physical exertion. Then, out of the corner of his eye, he saw a dark shadow just ahead and heard a Vietnamese voice call out. Instinctively, he brought up his bayonet-tipped M-16 and drove the blade it deep into the NVA's chest, propelling the screaming man backward. Unable to stop his own forward momentum, Anderson crashed to the ground and lost control of his rifle. Before he could react, the night exploded with shouts and gunfire all around him. Forgetting the rifle, he rolled on his side and desperately grabbed for his holster, which had twisted underneath him in the fall, fully expecting to be shot or stabbed at any moment.

Anderson grasped the leather holster, pushed the flap back, and yanked out the .45 automatic. He pulled the slide to the rear, then released it. The forward momentum stripped a cartridge from the magazine and pushed it into the chamber. The pistol was ready to fire. Just as he raised it to shoot, a body fell on him, pinning him to the ground. He twisted around, trying to get at his assailant. Donald's whispered voice penetrated his senses, "It's me, Captain. Stay down. The gooks are all around us." He passed Anderson his missing rifle, omitting the fact that he had literally pried it out of the dead NVA soldier's chest.

The two lay absolutely still, listening to the shouts and occasional gunfire. The NVA were spooked, shooting at each other, thinking the Americans were attacking. After a few moments of observing the location of the Viets, the two Americans noted a gap and crawled through to the main trail. An American voice whispered, "Who's there?" Relief flooded the two men as they passed through the rear-guard position. It was the first time either of them had felt the least bit safe in several hours.

Gunny Smith and Lieutenant Napoline waited for them just off the trail, "Skipper, we thought you'd bought the farm," the SNCO said, concern evident in his voice.

"I would have if it hadn't been for Donald ... but they got Frazier," Anderson responded, his voice cracking with emotion as the words tumbled out. "Dick took on that trench so his platoon could get away. He got at least five gooks before they killed him and hauled his body off. We couldn't find him. The rotten bastards ...."

Smith could see the skipper was close to the edge. He handed Anderson a canteen, "Skipper, take a slug. It'll do you good."

Anderson tilted the plastic container back and took a long pull, his throat burning as he swallowed the fiery liquid. "Jesus, Gunny, you could have at least warned me," he gasped, eyes watering from the 90-proof hand-made Kentucky sippin' whisky that Smith favored.

When he smelled the booze, Donald interrupted, "How about me, Gunny," as he reached out to try to take advantage of his sudden rise in status from squad leader to captain's savior.

Anderson chuckled, "What d'ya say, Gunny? The kid deserves it."

Outmaneuvered by the brash youngster, Smith handed over the canteen, but he got in the last word. "Take more than one swallow, Marine, and you're a dead man."

After calling in the rear guard, Anderson, Smith, and Donald started up the trail, following the diminished company. Napoline called an artillery mission in the hope of sealing off pursuit.

Within minutes they overtook several of the heavily burdened men who were struggling slowly along in the dark, exhausted by the events of the day. The uneven trail caused them fits; roots, half-buried rocks, and low branches took a toll in falls and barked shins. The stretcher bearers were having even more trouble; several of them had fallen, dumping their burden of wounded to the ground. Anderson turned to Napoline. "Christ, Tom, with this rough treatment and the slow pace, we'll kill some of those men if we don't do something quick. I want you to light this trail up. Constant illumination."

Taken by surprise, Napoline blurted out a reply. "Skipper, they won't like that, expend too much ammunition."

Even in the dark, he felt Anderson's fury. "I don't give a shit what they like. If it saves one of my men, it's worth every round. Now, get it done!"

Properly inspired, the artilleryman got on the horn and coaxed, pleaded, and threatened his counterparts in the rear. Within minutes, the first illumination round burst over the column, floating gently beneath its nylon canopy. Rated at 150,000 candlepower, the burning phosphorous provided enough light to see by, even under the trees. The separated canister made an unreal *whoop, whoop, whoop* sound as it tumbled through the air, thumping into the ground somewhere alongside the column. As the first illume round burned out, another floated in the air, illuminating the weary men as they trudged through the jungle carrying the wounded men.

17

1st Platoon, Hill 540, 1800, 12 September, 10 Klicks Northwest KSCB—The platoon was just about used up by the time everyone climbed to the top of the hill. Many of the fit-for-duty men were nearly as bad off as the wounded. Two passed out halfway up the rise, adding to the burden of the over-worked stretcher bearers. Petrovitch proved to be a godsend, making several trips up and down the slopes, helping carry the wounded to Zimmer's makeshift aid station. Littleton was amazed at the big gunner's strength and stamina; he seemed inexhaustible, serving as an inspiration to the rest of the platoon. Many of the men were out of water, but Littleton couldn't let them rest. He established defense sectors for the depleted squads and cautioned all hands to dig fighting holes and clear sectors of fire under the baleful eye of Staff Sergeant Brown.

While Lieutenant Littleton briefed the squad leaders, Sanders established contact with Battalion and requested an emergency medevac, which was immediately relayed to Seaworthy 4-1, a CH-46 that was sitting on the runway, waiting for orders to extract the recon patrol. The big helo cranked up, taxied to the Charlie Med LZ, picked up a doctor and a corpsman, and took off like a bat out of hell. Gunslinger One and Two joined up, just in case bad guys tried to interfere with the rescue.

As soon as Sanders spotted the inbound helos, he shouted a warning to the stretcher bearers, who were lined up in the grass with the wounded, ready to run them out to the helo. He keyed the net: "Seaworthy 4-1, I have you in sight. I'm at your 12 o'clock. Popping smoke. Over." He pulled the pin on an eight-ounce metal cylinder and pitched it into the makeshift LZ, watching as it blossomed into a billowing cloud of yellow smoke that was clearly visible against the green vegetation.

Seaworthy immediately responded, "Roger, Lima. I have yellow smoke," thus positively identifying the friendly LZ, an important ritual inasmuch as the

NVA had been known to use captured smoke grenades to lure unsuspecting pilots into ambushes.

As the 46 started on final, the gunships circled protectively, ready to suppress ground fire with their 7.62mm miniguns and 2.75-inch rockets.

Aboard Seaworthy, the two enlisted crewmembers manned the .50-caliber waist-mounted machine guns, thumbs lightly touching the butterfly triggers of the heavy weapons, ready to fire at the first sign of danger. Meanwhile, the aircraft commander eased up on the power and pushed down on the collective, preparing to land the big machine in the center of the hill. An old pro at bringing in helicopters, Sanders stood on the edge of the LZ and, using hand and arm signals, helped guide the landing. Maintaining forward momentum until the last moment, the pilot flared the aircraft, bleeding off more speed, and settled down with a gentle bump.

The whirling blades stirred up a maelstrom of grass, elephant dung, dirt, and tendrils of yellow smoke, as well as blasting the stretcher bearers as they rushed toward the helo's rear ramp. The lead team passed through the searing engine exhaust and struggled up the ramp, trying to keep from jostling the wounded man. Unable to be heard because of the engine noise, the crew chief grabbed one of the bearers and pointed toward the front of the aircraft, where another crewmember motioned the litter team to place their burden on a canvas stretcher. The other teams followed suit, placing the rest of the wounded on other stretchers that covered one side of the passenger compartment. As the men struggled to and fro, a momentary bottleneck ensued in the crowded aircraft, but soon the last of them jumped off the ramp as a crewman started to raise it. The pilot increased power and prepared to lift off just as four heavily burdened men scuttled out of the grass with the two poncho-wrapped corpses. Bludgeoned by the blast of air, one of them fell, losing his grip on the corpse and sending the second man sprawling. As the corpse rolled on the ground, the poncho blew off and sailed through the air, just missing the rotor blades and uncovering the bloody remains of Lance Corporal Stevens. The two men quickly recovered, picked up Stevens's body, and had just enough time to throw it on the ramp as the helo lifted off.

Inside the swaying troop compartment, the passengers were having a hard time staying upright as the aircraft dipped off the hill, struggling to gain airspeed and altitude. A crewman lay on the deck, desperately trying to keep Stevens's body from falling off the ramp into space. The other crewman manned the .50-caliber mounted in the starboard hatch.

Kneeling over Kelly, the doctor tried to insert a needle from an IV bottle he had suspended from the nylon webbing of one of the troop seats that ran along both sides of the aircraft. The corpsman worked on another unconscious man, preparing him for an IV, but he had trouble finding a vein. He looked around and motioned for the gunner, but the man was torn between helping him or his buddy, who was still struggling on the ramp with Stevens. Making a quick decision, the gunner grabbed the other crewman by his leg, pulling him and Stevens further inside the helo, then he rushed to help the corpsman. As the pilot cranked on speed, his co-pilot radioed the base, alerting them to the emergency and requesting permission to proceed directly to the Charlie Med LZ.

After ten minutes in the air, the CH-46 set down on the perforated steel matting of the runway, where it was met by several corpsmen, who quickly loaded the wounded into an ambulance—"meat wagon" in troop parlance—and sped off to the medical triage for evaluation and treatment. A second ambulance took the two dead Marines to the morgue, where they would be prepared for the sad voyage home.

***

Littleton felt a great weight lift from his shoulders as he watched the medevac helicopter disappear into the late afternoon haze. He had done everything he could to get the wounded out. He knew their fate was now in hands of the doctors. Knowing it would take a miracle to save them, he said a silent prayer. "Merciful Lord we place our wounded into your hands and humbly ask that you restore them to health again. Amen."

Corporal Duvall interrupted his musings, "Lieutenant, we found what those elephants were hauling. Rockets. There's a big pile of them in the trees on the other side of the hill."

Littleton felt a surge of excitement. "Christ, this place is an NVA weapons dump," he muttered, half to himself. "Let's take a look." He motioned Duvall to move out. "And, for Christ sake, don't let anyone touch anything. They might be booby trapped."

Duvall led Littleton along the trail, stopping a few meters inside the tree line, where he pointed to what looked like a stack of black telegraph poles, seven feet long and fifteen inches in diameter.

"Have you checked the area?" Littleton asked, thinking the stash of ordnance was just too obvious in view of the NVA's penchant for leaving surprises.

"Hell, Lieutenant, I didn't want to get any closer. Those things could blow my ass away." As any dolt could plainly see, they were enemy rockets, thus, by definition, dangerous. *Oh shit*, Duvall thought, noting the look in Littleton's eyes. *He wants me to check the damn things out.*

"I need a volunteer," Littleton muttered, then paused, as if the request were almost too difficult to ask.

Before Duvall could say anything, Littleton continued, "Cover me. I'll check the rockets."

Duvall couldn't believe it. No officer ever put himself out like this. That's why there were junior enlisted men, to handle the crap details—like checking rockets for booby traps.

Suddenly aware that Littleton was staring at him, waiting for an answer, Duvall nodded dumbly, then blurted out, much to his astonishment, "Lieutenant, I'll do it. It's my job."

The young officer reached across and patted Duvall on the shoulder. "Thanks, but this one's mine. Anyone dumb enough to goad the bear should be the one to get clawed." With that, he turned away and cautiously approached the pile of rockets, leaving Duvall open-mouthed.

Littleton cautiously studied the ground before he took a step. He was looking for the thin filament the NVA attached to their booby traps. He knew they stretched the barely visible wire ankle-high across a trail, anchored on one end by a stake, with the other end attached to an American hand grenade stuffed in a C-ration can. Snaring the line tugged the explosive out of the can, releasing the safety spoon and starting the five-second firing sequence. Often, the unsuspecting victim never realized his error until after being struck down by the "surprise-firing device"—a military euphemism used on the next-of-kin telegram because it was softer than, "Your son was maimed/ killed by a booby trap."

Littleton advanced closer and closer to the stack of rockets, expecting at any moment to hear the sudden tell-tale metallic sound of a released safety lever. Sweat poured down his face and neck, soaking the blouse beneath his zipped flak jacket, at times obscuring his vision. He reached the stack, wondering what the hell he was going to do. He hesitated, then made a decision. *Fuck it*, he thought as adrenalin coursed through his blood steam—and he lifted one of the heavy missiles, unconsciously holding his breath and tightening his stomach muscles in anticipation of the explosion.

Duvall hit the deck. He knew the lieutenant was a dead man. When nothing happened, he looked up sheepishly to see Littleton cradling one of the massive weapons in his arms, walking nonchalantly toward him with a strange grin on his face. With the missile in hand, Duvall thought, the guy looked like a damn giant. Like "Little John," his favorite character in *Robin Hood*. And from that moment, the nickname stuck.

18

Recon Team Knife Edge, 1800, 12 September, 12 Klicks Northwest KSCB—Lieutenant Herb Wilson froze mid-step, alerted by the sound of Vietnamese voices just ahead in the undergrowth. He slowly sank into the knee-high grass at the side of the game trail, invisible to even the most vigilant observer. The team followed his example, leaving the body bag in the middle of the narrow track while they took up firing positions. After listening for several minutes, Wilson backed out of the undergrowth, crawled to the next man in the column, Corporal Tim Rohweller, the assistant team leader, and whispered instructions. "I'm going to see what the gooks are up to. If anything happens, shag ass and meet me at the last rally point."

Rohweller nodded and watched as the big man shrugged out of his heavy pack and crawled away, disappearing into the scrub without making a sound. After crawling several meters, Wilson stopped in a clump of bushes and carefully raised his head to look around. His heart stopped, for directly in front of him, no more than 20 feet away, four NVA regulars squatted and jabbered away like they were in their own backyard, without a care in the world. Wilson was struck by how young they looked, almost like teenagers, except these youngsters were carrying AK-47s. Several other squad-size units had gathered near the first group, more than he had ever seen before. As he sank back into cover, adrenalin surged, jump-starting his heart and causing it to thump wildly, almost painfully, in his chest. *Get a hold of yourself*, he silently chided, *or you're a dead man*. With a great effort, he willed himself to calm down, restoring his breathing to a nearly normal rhythm.

He lay there for several minutes, debating whether to pull back or take another look. *I've got to see what they're doing*, he argued with himself. *They've got us cut off from the pick-up zone*. With that thought in mind, he cautiously raised his head.

Wilson's camouflage-painted face, with its black and dark loam striping, blended perfectly with the shadowed foliage in the late afternoon sunlight. Trying to stay as still as possible, he was careful to use the surrounding brush to break up his silhouette. He relied on moving just his eyes to check the area. As he watched, the NVA broke out rations for their evening meal, making it obvious they weren't going to move for some time. *Shit*, he swore to himself. *We're screwed. There's no way we can make it to zone before dark, and we'll miss the pickup.*

He had seen enough; it was high time to rejoin the team and get the hell out of there before something bad happened, like half the North Vietnamese Army jumping on his back.

Wilson slowly edged out of his hiding place, crawled back to the team, and briefed them on what he had seen. He contacted base to let higher authority know that Knife Edge couldn't make the pick-up and would beat feet for the alternate site. "Roger, Knife Edge," base responded. "Be advised your alternate is in friendly hands. Northtide Lima is holding the fort. I'll let 'em know you're on the way."

Reacting to that good news, Wilson broke out his map and studied the route, trying to memorize the terrain so he could visualize it in the dark, which was fast approaching. Next, he oriented the map with the ground as best he could, laid a lensatic compass on its acetate-covered surface, with straight edge on the grid line running north, and obtained the azimuth to the hill. He gave those directions to the point, with instructions to follow them as best he could and to use the trail they were on as a guide. With luck and by pushing it, Wilson estimated the hump would take three to four hours.

Wilson broke up the seven-man team into a four-man carrying party and three on security—two on point and one bringing up the rear. They retraced their route along the game trail, struggling all the way to maneuver the unwieldy body bag through the undergrowth without making too much noise. Despite their best effort, the nylon carrier rubbed against the low-hanging shrubbery, producing an unnatural man-made sound, disturbingly out of character in the quiet jungle. Walker cringed at the sounds but knew there was nothing he could do; they had to hustle if they were to make it to the rendezvous before dark. Even now, the shadows were lengthening, creating pools of darkness and making it difficult to see in the fading light. The team was losing its edge; they were tired and unnerved. Arnold's mutilated body served as a reminder of their own mortality—and it was starting to smell. The excitement of the rescue attempt had long since dissipated, replaced with a growing resentment at having to lug the body through the jungle, especially with the NVA so close. Everyone took their turn at the carrying straps, sharing the load, but the effort was placing a heavy burden on their strength and vigilance.

Private First Class Ronald Campbell had just rotated as the point from his carrying stint when the sudden pain of a knotted muscle in his shoulder distracted him long enough to walk right into the middle of an intersecting high-speed trail. Like a deer caught in the headlights, Campbell froze, aware of his blunder. He heard a noise and turned toward the sound, automatically keeping his M-16 aligned with his body. Standing 20 feet away was an NVA infantryman, who was staring at him with a stunned look on his face, not quite believing that an American was in his backyard. The NVA started to bring the muzzle of his rifle up, but the Marine had a split-second edge. Campbell fired from the hip, unconsciously centering his aim on the enemy's chest and hitting him three times in the upper body. The man dropped to the ground.

As the firing sounds died away, there was a momentary stillness, broken seconds later by Vietnamese shouts and the sound of men crashing through the undergrowth. No sooner had a thoroughly shaken Campbell jumped back to cover with the rest of the team than heavy firing broke out, making it obvious that Knife Edge was up against a considerable enemy force. Wilson knew his small team had to break contact immediately or risk being pinned down, surrounded, and annihilated. A reconnaissance team's main defense was stealth, not brute strength.

The team leader signaled the Marines to return fire and get ready to start their immediate-action drill for breaking contact. Nevertheless, one thought kept going through his mind: *What do I do with the body? There's no way we can carry it* and *get away. It's too heavy, and we've got to move fast.*

Suddenly, the unmistakable sounds of men crashing through the undergrowth caught his attention. Two NVA burst into view, firing at Rohweller, who was lying on the ground trying to clear a jammed rifle. Before the assistant team leader could react, another Marine opened fire, killing the two, but it was too late to save the NCO. Wilson crawled over to the fallen Marine, who was lying on his side, blood covering his face from a terrible head wound. It was obvious Rohweller was dead, but Wilson still picked up his limp arm and checked for a pulse. Nothing.

Now there were two casualties to carry. Although Wilson knew what he had to do, he hesitated. The Corps never left anyone behind—it was a solemn pact—but so was saving the lives of his men. Gradually, the firing seemed to slacken off. *Now's the time*, he thought, *before they get organized to really hit us.* Reaching a decision, he stripped the dead NCO of his weapon, ammunition, compass, dog tags, and map; and rolled him further into the undergrowth, along with his pack, hoping to conceal the body until they could come back for it. He shouted for the team to leave the body bag and start pulling back, covering each other.

Wilson grabbed Rohweller's Claymore mine and set it up, pointing at the main source of enemy fire. After jamming the plastic legs into the ground, he screwed the blasting cap into the top of the mine and crawled backward, playing out the electrical cord. Seeing that the team was clear, Wilson hugged the ground and squeezed the plastic firing device, sending a small electrical charge through the wire into the cap. A terrific blast shook the ground as the C-4 plastic explosive detonated, propelling hundreds of steel pellets through the undergrowth like a huge shotgun. The shock effect of the detonation was instantaneous: NVA fire immediately stopped, as if someone had turned off a switch.

The young officer jumped to his feet, calling for members of the team to run for it, and followed them as they escaped along the game trail. As Wilson leaped over the nylon bag in the middle of the trail, he felt a great sense of frustration and humiliation for leaving the two Americans behind, but he didn't have any choice.

19

1st Platoon, Hill 540, 1900, 12 September—Littleton worked his platoon hard, constantly walking the small perimeter, checking positions. He wasn't satisfied. He made the troops dig their two-man foxholes deeper, made certain they cut grass and brush to clear fields of fire, and chided them whenever they tried dogging it. At one point, he walked down the slope to look at the hill from the enemy's perspective and, afterward, moved two half-finished positions to better cover the terrain, royally pissing off the four residents. To add insult to injury, he made them fill in the unfinished holes, just in case the NVA got into the perimeter and tried to use them against the Marines.

Petrovitch waited at the head of the trail, which he felt was the best location for the machine gun, because it was the most obvious avenue of approach into the position. Following two circuits of the hilltop, Littleton came to the same conclusion as Petrovitch and joined the gunner so the two of them could carefully select just the right spot for the M-60. They lay on the ground, trying to judge the weapon's field of fire, and decided that anyone coming up the trail would be dead meat, although the location exposed the gunner more than either of them liked. The gun position jutted out from the lines, the foxholes on either side slightly to the rear, but any other location dramatically cut down its field of fire. Littleton looked at the gunner, who nodded in agreement with the choice. Both men understood the significance of the decision.

Littleton trudged to the top of the hill to survey the entire position. He was pleased with what he saw; the platoon's ten fighting holes were sited on the military crest with good fields of fire. The troops had taken him at his word and dug them at least chest-deep and camouflaged the spoil with grass and twigs. They were ready, except for a few minor housekeeping chores.

Littleton dispatched Staff Sergeant Brown, who had only grumped around, with a detail to collect the captured heavy machine guns and ammunition.

Excited about the prospect of getting one of the enemy's .51-caliber weapons in his hands, Petrovitch volunteered for the patrol.

Another detail carried the captured rockets to the edge of the landing zone. Major Coffman had radioed that he was sending a helicopter to pick the rockets up, but this news was received with disgust from the men who had to lug the heavy missiles.

Littleton took the opportunity to request a resupply of ammunition, water, and medical supplies, rationalizing that *as long as the helicopter was coming anyway ....* Coffman had chuckled to himself, thinking, *The kid's got balls*, and made a mental check mark beside Littleton's name, noting that the rookie lieutenant had his head and ass wired together. He promised to honor the request.

When the helicopter arrived, it was crammed to the gunwales with small arms ammunition, several wooden boxes of hand grenades, and more than enough water in five-gallon cans to supply the platoon. Petrovitch looked like a little kid in a candy store as he and his ragged assistant lugged two heavy crates of linked 7.62mm machine gun ammunition—1,600 rounds—to the M-60 position.

The landing zone was taking on the appearance of an ammunition dump, which bothered Littleton because it would take only one mortar round to set off a spectacular explosion. Another working party was formed to spread out the ammunition and distribute water, which took most of the early evening.

At the platoon command post, located about 20 meters behind Petrovitch's machine gun position, Sanders was busy monitoring the radio, gathering snippets of information, which he passed on to Little John.

The lieutenant's nickname had swept through the platoon and caught on, although the men were careful to keep it from him. They used it only among themselves as a mark of respect for the young officer. His bravery in the bunker complex was common knowledge among the young enlisted men, who added their own embellishments with each telling, until Littleton was almost a larger-than-life figure. They were proud of him and, by extension, themselves, developing a platoon espirit in the process or, as one rear-rank private quipped, "We're the meanest muthers in the valley."

The troops also kept the lieutenant's new moniker from Staff Sergeant Brown, because they knew, by the snide comments he had made behind the lieutenant's back, that he resented Littleton's leadership of the platoon and his easy rapport with the men. In actual fact, Brown was pissed; he was losing his authority and felt threatened by the "snot-nosed butter bar." His hold on the platoon, which he had gained solely through intimidation, was gone; the troops now looked to Littleton for guidance. Brown was smart enough to give grudging support to the officer, avoiding open conflict, but that was all. As one Marine overheard Brown mutter, "Littleton is on his own, so fuck 'em!"

Littleton felt like he had been hit by a Mack truck; his body was one big ache. Even his hair hurt. Scratches swathed his face and arms—a few were deep enough to require stitches, if he had had the inclination to let Zimmer sew them up. After completing his umpteenth circle of the perimeter and finding the troops alert, he felt a break was in order. It was finally quiet. He welcomed the silence for its calming effect, particularly after the mind-numbing clamor of the resupply helicopters. Cautiously, he sat down on the edge of the foxhole that Sanders had dug for them—God bless him—almost sighing with relief, then wincing as his cartridge belt rubbed against a large, ugly black-and-blue bruise on his hip that he had picked up in the bunker fight when he'd landed on his canteen.

Littleton caught a whiff of burning heat tab and bent over, noting a tiny flickering light in the bottom of the hole. Chow. Sanders was heating a C-ration! The platoon commander's mouth watered, and he realized he hadn't eaten since early morning and was starving. Before he could move, Sanders held out a can. "Careful, Lieutenant, it's hot," and handed him his favorite meal, beefsteak and potatoes with gravy.

"Damn, Sanders, if you didn't need a shave, I'd kiss you," he quipped, fumbling for the plastic spoon he carried in the pocket of his blouse.

"Careful, sir," the radioman chuckled, "my girlfriend will get jealous."

"Is that the nice-looking girl in the photo you've been passing around?" he asked as he wiped the dirt off the spoon and ravenously dug into the contents of the green can.

"Yes, sir. Met her my second year in college, just before I joined the Corps. What about you Lieutenant, got anyone waiting?"

"Not really," he replied, thinking of the blonde bombshell who had professed her undying love until he had shipped out to Quantico for six months of training. He'd pined for about two minutes, confusing love with lust, until a screaming drill instructor snapped him out of his little pity party. "I'm married to the Corps," he joked, which brought a laughing comeback from the radioman.

"Damn, Lieutenant, you're not a lifer, are you?"

Littleton had a smart-ass answer on the tip of his tongue, but bit it off. "After today, all I want to do is get everybody home in one piece."

He finished eating the calorie-packed ration, licked the spoon clean, and stuck it back in his pocket, surprised that the short break and a little chow had revived him. Continuing the conversation, he asked, "What are you going to do when you get out?"

Sanders pondered the question for a moment before replying, "I'd like to go back to school, but I don't know whether I can put up with the petty bullshit after going through all this."

"I know what you mean," Littleton responded, "Humanity 101 is a little out of reach after you've put four rounds through the chest of your fellow man."

"Right on, Lieutenant. Can you imagine some dipshit professor lecturing us about the sanctity of life when he hasn't wallowed in blood up to his asshole? What a joke." Both men chuckled at the thought, playing the scene out in their minds, knowing their carefree academic days had ended with the first crack of an incoming small arms round.

The conversation tailed off as Littleton took a couple of slugs from his canteen, swishing the tepid chlorinated water around in his mouth, wishing it were anything else, or at least cold. Getting to his feet, he turned to Sanders. "I'm going to take a whiz. Hold the fort until I get back."

The lieutenant ambled several meters from his hole, unzipped his trousers, and relieved the pressure on his bladder. As he stood on top of the hill, staring at the sky, he was struck by the beauty of the evening. A clear night sky framed a full moon, bright against the inky blackness that was broken only by the twinkling lights of a million stars. The heat of the day had dissipated, replaced by a gentle breeze that barely stirred the grass, but was strong enough to cool him down and keep the mosquitoes at bay.

His mind wandered back to the blonde and the good times under the same moon in the back seat of the old '52 Ford. *Man, I sure as hell wish I was back there*, he thought. *No responsibilities, free as a bird, and, best of all, no one trying to kill me.* He suddenly shivered, the image of a dead Stevens intruding in his thoughts, a picture he would carry with him for the rest of his life. Tears came to his eyes and he choked back a sob, his body shaking with the effort as the terrible stress of the day finally caught up with him. He struggled for control, taking deep breaths and hoping no one could hear him. He looked again into the night sky, and a terrible feeling of loneliness came over him, as if he were all alone on the hill. *How am I going to keep going?* he agonized, feeling overwhelmed by the responsibility of leading the platoon. As he struggled for an answer, the image of Stevens returned, standing on the berm as the others charged through the fire, following his lead. The realization that he was not alone steadied him; the platoon needed him as much as he needed it. They were a team.

As he stared into the blackness, sorting through his emotions, the sudden light of a parachute flare off in the distance broke his reverie. Sanders saw it too and called out, "Lieutenant, the company's on the move. They're using flares to help find the way."

Littleton jumped into the hole and asked, "Have you heard anything else?"

"Yes, sir. They finally broke contact, but it sounds like they've been hit hard. Lots of casualties. And they're headed this way."

Littleton thought about his own platoon's struggle that afternoon and wished there was some way to help, but there was nothing he could do; the company had to make it on its own.

20

Lima Company, 2100–0100, 12–13 September—"Lima Three's down!" The radioman's frantic voice came over the air, forgetting proper procedure in his distress.

"Acknowledge," Anderson told his operator as he started forward toward the head of the column, accompanied by Napoline, Smith, and the surviving radiomen. As the column had stopped, many of the men collapsed on the side of the trail with exhaustion, nearly blocking the narrow path and slowing Anderson's progress.

"Stay alert, stay alert," the company commander ordered. He knew how vulnerable they were, all strung out on the trail, "Face outboard and get your weapons up!"

In Anderson's wake, Gunny Smith took more direct action, grabbing the fire team and squad leaders to remind them, in no uncertain terms, to "get your ass in gear and do your job." It had the desired effect; tired men jolted to attention and took up firing positions to defend the column.

Anderson finally came upon a small group of men bending over Larson's prostrate form in the middle of the trail. Feebly, he struggled to rise, but the platoon corpsman held him down, pleading with him to stop resisting. Even in the uncertain light, Anderson could see that Larson was plainly out of it—incoherent, eyes unfocused, facial muscles tight with pain. *Shit, it's my fault*, he thought. *I shouldn't have pushed him to keep going.* Looking into the wounded man's eyes, he took Larson's hand and gently squeezed it, his voice thick with emotion as he said, "Gary, can you hear me?"

Larson's eyes slowly focused in reaction to Anderson's voice. Never out of character, he weakly responded, "Skipper, get the license number of the truck that hit me."

Despite Larson's insistence that he was okay, Anderson had him loaded on a makeshift stretcher and gave Napoline command of the platoon. "Tom, you've got the helm," he said. "I want you to move as fast as you can, but keep the point alert. I don't want to run into an ambush."

"Right Skipper. I'll be right behind the lead squad, so I can control their movement and make sure they don't outpace the stretcher bearers."

Anderson nodded. "Okay, Tom, move 'em out." He watched as the column slowly shook itself out and moved forward. As they filed past, he talked with Larson, who was in tears, not from pain, but from having to give up his platoon. "Skipper, I can handle it," he pleaded, "The men are depending on me."

Anderson hesitated before he said, "I'm sorry. Gary, I can't do it. You've done a great job, but you've lost too much blood. The doc says you have to ride." Noting the hurt look on Larson's face, he added, "Napoline's going to pinch hit until you come back." He held out hope for a return, but he knew full well that Larson was out of the war and would be lucky if he didn't limp for the rest of his life.

"Thanks for trying, Skipper, but I know how bad it is. The doc told me."

Struggling for the right words, Anderson said, "I'm sorry, Gary. You're a hell of an officer and a good friend, and I'm going to miss you."

Larson grasped Anderson's hand. "I feel like I'm running out on you and the platoon," he said as tears coursed down his cheeks. "Everyone's depending on me, but I've let them down." Anderson attempted to reply, but Larson cut him off. "Christ, Skipper, when I was first wounded, I wanted to quit, but you shamed me into going back. I cursed you to high heaven. My ass hurt like hell, and I was scared, but deep down I knew it was the right thing to do. I'm just sorry you had to remind me to ...." He tailed off as a spasm of pain took his breath away.

Anderson used the break to reply. "Gary, you have nothing to be ashamed of. If we had been near an LZ, I would have sent you out as an emergency medevac. It took a hell of a lot of courage to keep going. I'm proud of you." The two shook hands both sensing this would be their last meeting.

Anderson patted Larson on the shoulder and nodded to the stretcher bearers, who stepped into the column of men. As he turned away, Larson got in the last word: "Skipper, don't let that little cannon-cocker screw them up."

Anderson chuckled. Just as he raised his hand in a final wave, the sudden crack of small arms fire erupted from the rear of the column, followed by the dreaded cry of "Corpsman!" At the sound of the bullets ripping through the foliage, the company went to ground, seeking cover. Anderson stood in the middle of the trail, ignoring the peril, trying to gauge if the firing signaled an assault.

He hobbled as fast as his wounded legs could carry him toward the firing. Silently cursing the pain as he made his way back down the column, he heard

Gunny Smith's unmistakable bellow above the gunfire: "Shoot, goddam it! What the hell you waiting for? Aim at the flashes. Don't give 'em a free shot. Make 'em pay."

The sharp report of several M-16s answered the command, drowning out the sound of the AK-47s.

Anderson saw that Smith was standing in the middle of the flare-lit trail, oblivious to the danger, directing fire against the enemy snipers. "Gunny, you're going to get yourself shot if you stand here much longer," he chided, motioning the SNCO to follow him to cover behind a large tree trunk. "Come over here and tell me what you've got."

Smith nonchalantly followed, as if he didn't have a care in the world and calmly reported, "Skipper, half a dozen of the little bastards are following us." Then, after pausing long enough to let loose a stream of tobacco juice, he continued, "Third Platoon's got one man down, shot in the leg. Doc's with him now."

Anderson thought for a moment. "Gunny, we can't afford this. The gooks'll nickel-and-dime us all night long if we don't knock 'em out. I'm going to bring in a little artillery and dust 'em off. You get the company off its ass and move out. We'll catch up."

"Roger, Skipper," Smith acknowledged. "But don't play the hero. We need you to get us home."

Anderson marveled at Smith's unflappable demeanor as the veteran Marine ambled up the trail, calling the men from cover like some modern-day Pied Piper. Inspired by the gunny's composure under fire, they responded and quickly moved out of sight, leaving Anderson and the remnants of the 3rd Platoon to deal with the snipers.

While the troops kept up a covering fire, Anderson took the handset from Private First Class Hoenig, inherited when Napoline took the platoon, and called in the fire mission. His carefully scripted request was acknowledged with an abrupt, "Wait. Out." After several anxious moments, an anonymous voice came back with, "Request denied. Those coordinates are in a no-fire zone. Out."

Incredulous, Anderson mumbled, "The goddam gooks are close enough to bayonet us, but that rear echelon son of a bitch wants to play it by the book. I'd like to take that book and shove it where the sun don't shine."

"Roger that, Skipper," a worried Hoenig responded as several AK-47 rounds tore though the foliage over their heads.

"Gimme that phone," the thoroughly pissed-off Marine captain ordered, and proceeded to challenge the no-fire decision up the chain of command, reaching the final authority within moments. Hoenig listened to the one-sided conversation and witnessed a lesson in leadership he would remember for the rest of his life as Anderson blistered the airways: "I don't give a damn what your map says, I am in contact and have taken casualties. My boys need help. I can see the assholes that are shooting, and if you don't fire right now, I'm going to come back there, twist your head off, and shit in it." Hoenig couldn't hear the response, but a second later Anderson responded, "Of course I'll take personal responsibility. That's what Marines do. Now shoot! Out."

It seemed like only seconds before Hoenig heard the terrifying sound of an incoming artillery round, followed by an earth-shattering explosion and the sound of steel cutting through the undergrowth. A large tree limb crashed to the ground a few meters away, sheared cleanly by shrapnel. He looked over at the captain, who lay beside him, wearing a big shit-eating grin.

"Oops. That one was a little close," the officer said in a strained voice. "Better drop the next one 50 meters."

Hoenig gave the correction and tried to burrow further into the ground as the second round came in, landing further away but still close enough to cause his ears to ring. He lay there shaking, praying the gunners didn't make a mistake. Another terrific explosion bounced him on the ground, and another, and another, "For God's sake, how many more," he mumbled, as two more explosions rocked the earth.

As the reverberations of the last round subsided, the men of the platoon stirred, their movements slow as their senses recovered from the overwhelming violence of the bombardment. The smell of cordite and freshly turned earth permeated the air, and a white cloud-like vapor floated through the trees, creating an ominous background in the shadowy undergrowth. They cautiously stood up, carefully screening the undergrowth, alert to the presence of the NVA snipers. One man lay still on the ground, curled into a ball, as if waiting for another shell to land. A concerned buddy nudged him, saw blood staining the leaves underneath his head, and yelled for a corpsman. Anderson heard the shout and ran over, praying that he hadn't killed one of his own men with the artillery.

"Rifle shot right through the head," the corpsman pronounced as he inspected the hole in the camouflage-covered helmet. "Never knew what hit him." Sorrow mixed with relief surged through Anderson. Another man lost and they weren't safe yet.

Napoline and Smith were pushing hard, but the casualty-laden column was slowing the pace, as the stretcher bearers struggled to keep up. "How much further, Lieutenant?" the gunny asked Napoline, aware the company was about played out.

"I estimate another half klick," Napoline replied. "The point should make contact in a few minutes. I'm letting First Platoon know we're coming in, so we don't have an intramural firefight." He gestured to his radio operator for the handset.

The gunny nodded. Turning to go back down the trail, he said, "Right, Lieutenant. I'm going back to the rear with a couple of men to wait for the skipper."

Napoline spoke into the handset, contacted Littleton, and alerted him that the company was approaching his position. Picking up the pace, he and his radioman made their way forward until they were directly behind the point. The trail was becoming noticeably steeper as they approached the hill. He hoped Littleton had passed the word they were coming in. The point slowed down, not wanting to startle the hilltop defenders by suddenly popping out of the jungle.

The trees were thinning and Napoline could finally see the night sky, but dark shadows cast by the parachute flares made it difficult to see anything in the undergrowth. A sudden horrible thought sent chills down his spine: *Is this the right hill?*

Gunny Smith stood in the middle of the trail, waiting for the rear platoon, while two riflemen covered him from positions in the undergrowth. After several moments, he saw several indistinct figures step out of the shadows, their footfalls loud on the hard-packed trail as they came on fast. He couldn't make out who they were in the uncertain light of the illumination round. Taking a chance, he called out, "That you, Third Platoon?"

The lead figure stopped and Smith heard a startled Anderson say, "Damn, Gunny! You scared the shit out of me. Couldn't you have made some noise to alert us?"

"Hell, Skipper, you were making enough racket to wake the dead. You wouldn't have heard me anyway," Smith joked, and then quickly sobered as he saw the poncho-wrapped figure of the dead Marine. "Who's that," he asked gravely.

Anderson responded, "Hall, one of the new men. Took a round through the helmet."

Before he could say another word, a burst of automatic weapons fire interrupted him. "That sounds like it's the column. Come on!" he shouted to the men as he broke into a trot up the trail.

Napoline halted the men at the edge of the jungle while he crept forward to get a better view of the hill. The artificial light playing off scattered brush and knee-high grass kept him from seeing much. *The damn stuff can hide an NVA battalion*, he thought.

There was only one thing to do. Tense with anxiety and with his heart in his mouth, Napoline stepped out on the trail in full view of the hill. He took several tentative steps forward, his senses on full alert, straining to detect movement. The slight breeze through the dry grass made a rustling sound, keeping him on edge. The sound played mind games with his imagination as he pictured NVA riflemen erupting out of the brush intent on grabbing his sorry ass. His finger tightened on the trigger of his rifle just as a low voice whispered an urgent challenge. "Who's there?"

Startled, Napoline involuntarily jerked the trigger, sending half a magazine of 5.56mm into the ground at his feet. Two figures jumped out of the grass, tackling him before he could swing his weapon around, and shouting, "Don't shoot! Don't shoot. It's First Platoon."

The shouting finally got through to Napoline, who quit struggling, his body limp with relief. As the three men untangled themselves, he recognized Littleton and the huge machine gunner, Petrovitch. No wonder he felt like a freight train had hit him. And then it sunk in: *I could have killed someone and started an intramural firefight. What the hell was I thinking?*

Littleton put the thought into words. "Jesus Christ, Napoline, what the hell you doing on point? You almost got somebody killed."

Before Napoline could reply, the head of the column trudged up, alerted by the shouts that 1st Platoon held the hill. As the men stumbled past, Littleton saw how bad off they were. Most seemed to be out on their feet, barely able to place one foot in front of the other. Several men fell out near him, unable to climb the steep trail without help. Littleton turned to Petrovitch and told him to round up half the platoon, one man from each foxhole, to lend a hand.

As Littleton fought to get things organized, Anderson's unmistakable voice grabbed his attention, just as the familiar figure limped into view. The captain's appearance rattled Littleton: blood-encrusted battle-dressings covered his arms, one leg of his trousers had been slit open, and a battle dressing wrapped his upper thigh. Most disturbing of all was the haggard look on his bearded, dirt-caked face, fatigue etched in every feature. It was obvious the officer was about out of gas and drawing upon his last reserves of strength, but Littleton knew that Anderson would never give in as long as he was in command. Catching the skipper's eye, Littleton smiled and reached out to shake his hand, saying warmly, "Skipper, am I glad to see you. It was getting real lonely on this hill."

Anderson grasped the younger man's hand tightly, studying him for a long moment before speaking, "John, you and the platoon have done a great job. I'm proud of you. If you weren't on this hill, the company would be in a hell of a fix." The two stood without speaking, hands clasped. The young officer knew instinctively that the seasoned veteran had accepted him as an equal.

Anderson broke the silence. "John, we've got to move fast, before the gooks get organized and come after us. You get the request in for the medevacs while I take a look at the hill and set in the company. Staff Sergeant Brown can show me around your position."

Littleton acknowledged the order and hurried off, telling Anderson that he would have Brown meet him on top of the hill.

A flurry of activity followed as the company main body, with help from the 1st Platoon, made its way to the crest. There, the new arrivals crapped out while Anderson took Napoline and Smith to meet Brown.

Anderson didn't have any trouble picking out the SNCO; his pugnacious stride and fire-plug silhouette were unmistakable in the light of the parachute flares. As he approached, Anderson thought about the staff sergeant's character, which was something of an enigma. Brown was competent and experienced, but he was overbearing, with a mean disposition. There was a rumor he had been thrown off the drill field for his brutal treatment of recruits, which would help to explain why he was still a staff sergeant in a time of rapid promotion. At one point, Anderson had asked Smith to keep an eye on Brown, but the gunny couldn't come up with anything except that the troops were afraid of the man. Shrugging off his thoughts, he directed Brown to show them the platoon's lines.

As the four men hurriedly made their way around the hill, Anderson pointed out the general location of each platoon's defensive sector, leaving the specific placement of fighting holes to Napoline and Smith. Admonishing them to hustle, Anderson left the two leaders while they moved their men into position.

Brown followed, having awaited an opportunity to speak to Anderson alone, so he could drop a dime on Littleton. His resentment of the young officer's influence within the platoon had turned into an irrational attempt to get even.

"Captain, have you got a moment?" Brown asked, confident the officer would grant his request.

"Sure, what've you got?" Anderson replied, thinking the SNCO had some advice or question on the tactical layout of the lines.

"Well sir, it's about the lieutenant. He had a real tough time this morning in the bunker complex," Brown said, pausing as if it pained him to keep going.

"And?" Anderson guardedly asked, turning his full attention to the man standing in front of him, sensing in his tone that something wasn't right.

Brown continued, lowering his voice conspiratorially. "Captain, I hate to talk bad about an officer, but it's best you should know." He paused again for effect. "He froze, sir. Couldn't make a decision and got people hurt." His face remained an impassive mask, but inside he smirked. *I've settled that young shit's hash*, he thought, oblivious to the disgusted look on the captain's face.

"Let me get this straight, Staff Sergeant Brown," Anderson immediately responded, a sharp edge to his voice. "Are you accusing Lieutenant Littleton of being a coward?"

Taken back by the vehemence of the response, Brown realized he had made a mistake, then compounded it by waffling an answer. "Well, ah … no, sir. What I meant was the lieutenant was a little slow in reacting."

Eyes blazing, Anderson shot back, "That's not what you said, Staff Sergeant. You blamed your platoon commander for causing casualties because he couldn't make decisions under fire. Am I right?"

Brown felt the temperature rise but realized that Anderson wasn't an officer to fuck with. He held himself in check. Feigning humility, he said, "Sir, I misspoke. It's been a bad day, and I guess I got carried away. I lost some of my best men, and it got to me."

What bullshit, Anderson thought. *This guy doesn't give a shit about anything but himself.*

"It's been a tough day for everyone, Staff Sergeant Brown. I suggest you think carefully before making a statement like that again. Now get back to your position."

Brown stiffened, taut with anger, on the verge of insubordination, when Gunny Smith appeared. Choking off his retort, he reluctantly acknowledged Anderson's order and stalked off, avoiding a confrontation that would have gotten him in hot water.

"Skipper, what was that all about?" Smith asked. He had heard enough of the conversation to know the old man was pissed.

"Brown tried to drop a dime on Littleton," Anderson replied, still tight-lipped with anger. "Said he froze and got people hurt."

"Hell, Captain, his men think he's a superman. That's all they're talking about is how he saved their ass in the bunker complex. They call him Little John, after some damn storybook hero."

Anderson nodded, "Ya, one of Littleton's squad leaders told me a few minutes ago. That's why I knew Brown was full of shit. Gunny, I want you to keep an eye on Brown. I think he may need a little of your 'up close and personal' attention."

"Roger, Skipper. If he tries anything like that again, I'll put a boot up his ass. He's giving SNCOs a bad name."

Before they could continue, a voice called out, "Captain Anderson, Captain Anderson."

"Over here," he shouted, as one of Littleton's men jogged over the crest of the hill. "Captain, the lieutenant sent me to get you. There's a recon team running from the gooks, and they're headed our way."

21

Recon Team Knife Edge, 1900–0130, 12–13 September—"They're getting closer," Campbell whispered when he heard the rustling in the brush. NVA were moving through the undergrowth just a few meters away from the prone men. After running through the jungle for the past hour, they were exhausted and had sought refuge in a stand of bamboo just off the trail, hoping to catch their breath. They had only been resting for a few minutes when they heard the tell-tale sounds of pursuit and knew it was only a matter of time before they were discovered.

Who are these guys? Wilson thought as he attempted to remain calm. *How the hell did they find us in the dark?* And then he answered his own question: *They must have brought in special trackers. Shit. Just our luck to run into the first team.* He would have tried the old Claymore routine, but the team had been forced to dump their heavy packs in order to stay ahead of the pursuit. They kept only the radio and their weapons and ammunition. He remembered thinking, as he threw his pack into the thick undergrowth, *At this rate, we'll be lucky to get back to base in our skivvies.* Now, he wondered if they would get back at all. "Christ what a fucked-up mission," he mumbled to himself.

The slight odor of fish and wood smoke reached Wilson. *Gooks. They're close. Time for Plan B.*

He quickly whispered instructions to the rest of the team: "On my signal, fire one magazine. Full automatic. Throw your gas grenade and run like hell up the trail." He knew the CS, a stronger military variant of tear gas, would not have much effect in the open jungle, but he hoped it would surprise and delay the NVA long enough for the patrol to get away.

Carefully rolling onto his side, he unwound the duct tape that affixed the CS grenade to his webbing, and waited for the others to signal they were ready. He flashed back to the gas training at Quantico. It was a terrible experience for the student officers, but a real side splitter for the enlisted instructors.

The officers were made to unmask in a CS-filled shed and sing the "Marines' Hymn" before exiting with eyes burning, snot pouring, and puking their guts out—a great show for the enlisted men. *I hope it fucks up the NVA as bad,* he thought as he gave the signal.

The six Marines opened fire, shattering the night stillness, sending a dozens rounds of 5.56mm ammunition down range. Then they all threw the gas canisters and sprang to their feet. Momentarily blinded by the bright flashes of their weapons, they hesitated to run through the thick brush until Wilson bellowed out, "Get your ass in gear." The stand of bamboo exploded as they crashed through the thorny branches, heedless of the two-inch spikes that ripped clothing and tore flesh.

Screams and shouts of panic echoed in the brush behind them as they pounded up the trail at a dead run, trying to get a good lead on their pursuers. Suddenly, an AK-47 opened up, and Wilson heard the distinctive splat of a bullet hitting flesh as the Marine in front of him collapsed to the ground. Unable to stop in time, the lieutenant tripped over the fallen man and landed heavily, knocking the wind out of himself but saving his life as several rounds slashed the air over his prostrate form. He rolled over, gasping for breath. To Campbell, he sounded like he was dying. He knelt down beside him. "Were you hit, Lieutenant," the radioman asked worriedly as he ran his hands over Wilson's uniform, trying to find the wound in the dark.

"I'm okay. Just help me up," Wilson wheezed, embarrassed for having fallen on his ass and anxious to find out about the wounded Marine, who lay softly moaning a few feet away. "How bad is it?" he asked the patrol's corpsman, who was tying a battle dressing around the wounded man's side.

"Through-and-through Lieutenant. I don't think it hit any bones, but he's losing blood." Another burst of fire cracked over their heads.

Shit, Wilson thought, *we've got to get out of here before the gooks recover.* He kneeled to talk to the young enlisted man. "Davis, we've got to get you on your feet. The gooks'll pin us down here if we don't get going. Can you hack it?"

The youngster hesitated and reached out to grasp Wilson's hand. "Help me up, sir. Marines don't quit."

***

"Northtide Lima, this is Knife Edge. Over," the radioman panted into the handset as he struggled to keep up with the fast pace. Not only was he weighed down with the 25-pound radio, the damn thing slapped him in the back at every step, throwing him off balance. He had fallen once, bruising the hell out of one of his knees on a rock, but luckily he hadn't broken anything. Like the others, he had run out of water and was badly dehydrated, although his jungle utilities were soaked with sweat, chafing his armpits and crotch.

The team had been moving fast for the past hour and was approaching the point of exhaustion, forced to take turns half carrying, half dragging a barely conscious Davis over the rough trail. The effort had kicked their ass. Security had almost gone by the board as they struggled to put one foot in front of the other. They would have stopped if Wilson hadn't driven them so relentlessly. He knew the NVA were hot on their trail, trying to catch them before daylight. By Wilson's reckoning, they were close to Lima's hill. Not wanting to stumble in on the company, he ordered his radio operator to let the company know they were coming in from the west. The message was acknowledged: "Roger. Lima will keep the lights burning for you."

"What the hell did that mean?" Wilson mumbled, too tired to understand the significance of the information until a half hour later, when he suddenly realized it didn't seem so dark. He could see several meters around. And only then did he make the connection: Lima was using parachute flares to help the recon team find it way. A surge of adrenalin hit Wilson as he understood they were almost there. Just another few minutes, and they would be safe. He passed the word, which seemed to bring new energy to the men. They quickened the pace, shrugging off some of their weariness.

The increasingly steep trail slowed them down somewhat, but the brighter light helped them as they climbed out of the forest toward the hill. Wilson turned to check out the back trail just as a flash of light and a terrific explosion shook the night stillness. He hit the ground, his reflexes conditioned to react automatically to any blast. The sharp smell of cordite permeated the air as he looked up to see two of his men lying motionless on the trail.

Booby trap! his mind screamed. *The gooks mined the trail.* Dashing forward, he called for the corpsman, only to find him lying in a pool of blood, dead, his lower body perforated by shrapnel. Further on, the radioman lay unconscious, bleeding heavily from wounds in the back of his legs. The PRC-25 had stopped several large shards of metal and had thus been turned it into a useless piece of junk.

Wilson quickly directed one of the surviving members of the team to cover the back trail and had the other hold a red-filtered flashlight while he cut off the radioman's trousers, exposing the wounds, one of which was pulsing blood. A severed artery. Grabbing the dead corpsman's Unit One, he took out several battle dressings to bind the radioman's legs. "Shit," he mumbled, "what the hell do I do now? All I know about first aid is to yell for a corpsman." Settling down, he realized he had to stop the bleeding, and pretty damn quick, or he'd lose the man.

I've got to clamp off that artery, he thought as he rummaged through the Unit One in search of something to cut into the wound. He found the doc's packet of scalpels and took one out. His hand trembling, he held the sharp knife on top of the wound, steeling himself for the ordeal, Then, with his teeth tightly clenched, Wilson made a tentative cut, surprised that he had to push so hard to penetrate the flesh. Blood spurted over his hands and wrists, making the scalpel slippery and hard to hold. The radioman moaned and moved his leg, which spoiled the first attempt. *Fuck it. Quit pussy-footing around*, Wilson ordered himself. *If you don't hustle, he's going to die.* Cautioning his helper to hold the flashlight steady, he tried again to cut into the wound, using his fingers to hold it open. He found what he was looking for. He closed one of Doc's scissors over the artery, shutting off the flow of blood, except for a small amount that oozed out. He quickly taped the scissors to keep it in place and then covered it and the other wounds with battle dressings. As he leaned back, shaking with effort, but proud of himself, one of his men whispered, "Lieutenant, I can hear someone coming down the trail."

The three Marines took up firing positions, prepared to defend themselves and their two wounded buddies. Wilson whispered, "Don't shoot until I open up, but watch your ammunition; it may have to last for a while."

The sounds grew closer, several men moving fast, as if they knew where they were going. *Gooks*, Wilson thought. *They know the area and are coming back to see the results of their booby trap.*

The team leader's finger tightened on the trigger as a figure stepped out of the shadows just a few meters away, presenting an easy target for the three prone men. Wilson tensed. His pulse raced as adrenalin flooded his system.

Wait! Wait! he cautioned himself. *Let a few more into the kill zone.* A second man appeared and turned his head, presenting the silhouette of a U.S. helmet. Relief surged through Wilson. *Marines!* He called out to them, "Don't shoot! It's Lieutenant Wilson."

In any other situation, the reaction of the newcomers would have been funny, but here it was deadly serious. Immediately, the men dived to the ground, a chorus of grunts and thuds echoing through the jungle as their bodies slammed down. Helmets flew off from the impact, rolling idly on the trail. But no one fired, which in itself was a minor miracle.

Wilson stood up, repeating, "Don't shoot." One of the dark figures rose and came forward, reaching out his hand in greeting. "John Littleton. First Platoon, Lima. And you're Dr. Livingston, I presume."

Wilson warmly grasped Littleton's hand. "I'll be anybody you want me to be if you'll just help me get the hell out of here."

Doc Zimmer hurried forward to examine the two wounded men while the rest of the platoon took up defensive positions under the menacing eye of Staff Sergeant Brown. The two officers stood off the trail to discuss the situation, firming up plans to pull back to the hill as soon as the corpsman was finished.

"How did you know we needed help?" Wilson asked, still amazed that the platoon of infantry had arrived so fast.

"We didn't. Captain Anderson guessed you were in trouble when we couldn't raise you on the radio after we heard the explosion," Littleton explained. "First Platoon was the most rested, so he told me to saddle up and get down here fast."

"Yeah, very nearly *too* fast. We almost blew you away. I thought you were NVA, coming back to see what happened."

Before Littleton could reply, Zimmer approached and briefed them on the status of the wounded, stressing that both men were in bad shape and needed to be evacuated as soon as possible. Littleton acknowledged the report and called Brown over to tell him to move out with the lead squad while he brought up the rear.

Within minutes, the platoon was up and moving along the trail, slowed for the second time that day by casualties, but spurred on by the need to get them evacuated and the sure knowledge that the NVA were hot on their trail and would show them no mercy if they caught them.

22

Reconnaissance Platoon, North Vietnamese Army, 1900–0130, 12–13 September—The slightly built Bru Montagnard tracker stepped warily over the tree limb lying across the trail. The tribesman carefully studied the surrounding jungle, his senses fully engaged, as he searched for some anomaly that disturbed its resonance. He glided noiselessly along the root-strewn path, his precise movements marking him as a skilled woodsman. Two companions followed silently, while, farther back, a troop of men tagged along, their movements in sharp contrast to his. The occasional sound of metal on metal as a rifle stuck a piece of equipment or a heavy footfall as someone stumbled on the rutted trail upset their guides, who were afraid their clumsiness would alert the Americans. The Montagnards had been following the faint trail all afternoon, picking up signs that would not have been detected by the Vietnamese they guided. Now, in the gathering darkness, they sensed the Americans were close. It was time for Lieutenant Tran Van Doi to move his fighters to the front.

The Montagnards didn't trust the officer. They believed that he would sacrifice them to save the lives of his own men, so they deliberately slowed the pace by scrutinizing every potential ambush site. The Americans were extremely dangerous because of their artillery and air support. They were like a cornered tiger, ready to kill the unwary and they didn't want to stumble onto them.

Lieutenant Doi was upset. He wanted the *Moi*—savages—to move faster, to catch up with the Americans before daylight, but they seemed to be stalling. He didn't trust the little tribesmen, whose AK-47s were almost as big as they were, but he admired their superb tracking skills and wished his own men were as competent. He knew, however, that without their help his men would still be combing some remote corner of the jungle without a chance of finding the Americans. He suspected the Montagnards were deliberately slowing the pace and was about to have his own men take their place when the column stopped again. Totally exasperated, Doi noisily stalked to the front, directly behind the last Montagnard, and started to ask why he had stopped. Suddenly the night exploded with automatic weapons fire.

Before Doi could react, the tribesman was flung backward, knocking him to the ground where he lay momentarily stunned. Recovering, he pushed the dead body away, feeling the man's blood soak into his uniform, and got to his feet, shouting for his men to open fire. Afraid to shoot for fear of hitting their own men, only one soldier responded by emptying his magazine in two long bursts.

Doi leaped forward, toward the Americans' position, when he smelled an irritating odor that caused his eyes to water and his throat to burn. He suddenly felt sick to his stomach and doubled over, retching, as mucus ran copiously from his nose. He was totally incapacitated. Several others were also affected, screaming with panic in between puking their guts out. The advance was in chaos.

The men's symptoms subsided, and they slowly recovered, finally realizing the Americans had used an irritating gas to help their escape.

Precious minutes were lost before a badly shaken Doi recovered and established control of his disorganized platoon. Then, more time was wasted when he sent a search team to find the two remaining Montagnards, who were reported missing. Both men were found dead of multiple bullet wounds within a few feet of the American position.

Doi worried about the loss of the three trackers. He knew that his commander would be furious with him. In his mind, Doi could already picture the *Kiem Thao* session in which he would be critiqued and criticized for this leadership failure. He still felt angry over the way he had been treated the last time, promising himself that it wouldn't happen again. His superiors had criticized him for having a passive attitude during a night attack on an American position south of the DMZ. His platoon had been almost wiped out by one of the defenders, a huge giant of a man, who proved to be invincible, single-handedly stopping the attack with a pistol and a small shovel. After that terrible night, Doi was plagued by a recurring nightmare in which he is lying helpless beneath the feet of a terrifying ghost clutching a blood-encrusted shovel, poised to deliver the killing blow. As the apparition's arm descends, Doi mouths a soundless scream, helpless to protect himself. Just as the shovel's edge touches his face, he always awakens with his pulse racing, bathed in sweat. He was afraid to tell anyone, knowing that, if the cadre learned of the dream, they would judge him unfit to lead and he would lose command of the elite reconnaissance platoon. *The cadre didn't care that I had run out of ammunition and most of my men had been killed*, he reflected, *only that the position hadn't been destroyed.* He was still disgusted with himself for kowtowing to the senior cadre, but, in the end, they had allowed him to keep his command.

The platoon was the only thing that mattered to him; he loved his men and took great pride in being their commander. His *Bo doi*, in turn, followed him willingly, knowing that he would take care of them, despite the criticism he'd received after the artillery attack. He was also secretly proud the platoon had been honored with the Commendation Bearing Dead Heroes' Names for the action, the only such award in the battalion. He suspected, however, that it had been granted to raise morale because of the horrific casualties. Only two men had survived to wear the medal. Afterward, he was given the task of training the replacements who arrived after weeks of hard marching down the Ho Chi Minh trail.

Often the teenage soldiers arrived sick and dispirited, having barely survived the dangers of the Trail—frequent air attacks, tropical diseases, and inhospitable terrain—compounded by acute homesickness. The majority of the youngsters—sons of rice farmers who lived along the Red River and the South China Sea—were unprepared for life in the forest. It was their first experience, and for many, their last.

Doi trained them hard but with compassion. He knew instinctively that a firm but fair hand resulted in a more cohesive unit than repressive treatment. He organized them into three-man cells that were expected to share all aspects of a soldier's life, forming a bond closer than brotherhood. As the training progressed, they were indoctrinated with stories of self-sacrifice, of cellmates risking life and limb for one another, retrieving a comrade's body under fire, or tending a sick teammate. The men quickly came to realize that the cell was more important than the individual and was absolutely essential for surviving the harsh demands of combat. Doi painstakingly taught them the skills of the reconnaissance fighter—observation and patrolling, movement, penetration of defensive lines, selecting and marking avenues of attack and withdrawal, stealth and camouflage. He trained the eager young men to encircle the perimeter in steadily smaller circles, searching for American listening posts, command bunkers, and machine gun positions that would be targeted for elimination.

Even though the platoon practiced using realistic mockups of American defensive perimeters, complete with obstacles, live mines, and booby traps, Doi knew that nothing could prepare them for actual combat. Several times, as he watched them practice, he thought back to that horrible night when he'd lost the platoon. He vowed never to let it happen again. Finally, after several months, he declared the renewed reconnaissance platoon ready to rejoin the 1st Battalion, whose commander had sent them against their American counterparts on their first mission.

Doi heaved a sigh of relief. The fleeing Americans had left a clear trail in their haste to get away, making it easy to track them, despite the darkness. He placed his best man, Combatant Xuan, on the point, with instructions to advance as quickly as possible in hopes of catching the Americans before daylight. Doi knew he was risking another ambush, but he thought if he pushed the Americans hard enough, they would make a mistake that he could use to his advantage. Their use of gas had taught him not to underestimate them, but he thought his highly trained men could beat the Americans, once they were brought to bay.

The column halted, and a man whispered to Doi that Xuan had found something important. Doi made his way forward and found Xuan squatting in the middle of the trail, shining a hooded flashlight on several wrappers from American wound dressings. Moving the light to illuminate a large dark spot in the dust, Xuan remarked, "Blood, Comrade Leader. One is badly wounded."

Doi recalled a Montagnard proverb—*A wounded tiger is the most dangerous enemy*—and thought about the young infantryman at his side who would be the first to feel the Americans' bite. He put a hand on Xuan's shoulder and whispered, "*Chien Si* Xuan, I believe it is my turn to lead."

The word that their officer had taken the exposed point position quickly swept through the platoon, increasing Doi's stature in the eyes of his faithful soldiers. His willingness to share this danger marked him as a "man of the people," whose humble origins reflected their own backgrounds and experience. He too was the son of a rice farmer, with limited formal schooling, and had been conscripted into the army for the duration of the war in the south. After completing two months' training and political indoctrination in the "school of the soldier," Doi had infiltrated South Vietnam along the Ho Chi Minh Trail—coined the "10,000-mile trail" by his compatriots and the "Truong Son Strategic Supply Route" by officials in the North. He had rapidly advanced through the ranks based on the army's dual principles, bravery in combat and leadership ability. To his men he was an "elder brother," a mark of deepest respect and affection among Vietnamese males. They were prepared to follow him unquestioningly.

Doi set a fast pace, convinced the Americans would be forced to stay on the trail because of the wounded man. Rounding a bend, he was startled by the deep boom of an explosion some distance away, although it was difficult to tell because of the sound-dampening effects of the foliage. Unsure of what it meant, he slowed the column down, cautiously picking his way forward, alert to the danger of an ambush.

Doi stopped abruptly as the faint scent of stale tobacco and body odor permeated his senses. *Americans!* his brain screamed. Very carefully, he pulled back several meters and briefed his men, designating two of his best to crawl forward and determine the Americans' strength and location.

After what seemed like hours, the scouts returned to report that a platoon-size force was located about 50 meters away, but that it appeared to be leaving.

Doi was disappointed. There were too many Americans to attack with his 15 soldiers, so he decided to follow them and find out where they were going.

23

Prisoner of War, Chu Loc Hospital Complex, 2000–0630, 12–13 September, 9 Klicks Northwest KSCB—Frazier was terrified.

Lying in utter darkness, trussed up so tightly he was losing feeling in his hands and feet, he hurt like nothing he had ever experienced before—a pain so intense that nothing seemed to moderate it. He almost screamed out several times. He suspected his nose was broken and maybe his jaw, because he couldn't open his mouth without tremendous pain. He tasted blood from badly split lips, and he could feel the jagged edges of several broken front teeth with his tongue. His head felt like it was going to explode, and the rest of his body was one mass of agony. But, as bad as his wounds were, he was most frightened by the feeling that he was in a grave and had been left to die. He couldn't see, but he had been in enough foxholes to know that he was below ground, in a cave maybe. Occasionally, a clump of earth fell with a soft thud, sending his pulse racing as he imagined the entire ceiling giving away and burying him alive. He could actually feel the walls closing in as he struggled to breath in the fetid air. As claustrophobia took hold, he blacked out, unaware that a flashlight's beam was penetrating the gloom of the chamber.

He woke with a start. Rough hands held his sweaty head in a firm vise-like grip, and he felt someone grab his nose, sending a fresh jolt of pain. Frazier tried to twist his head away, but he couldn't; he was held too tightly.

Christ, his mind screamed, *they're torturing me!* Overwhelmed by the realization of his predicament, he lay helpless at the hands of a merciless enemy. Suddenly, the pain ceased—except for a dull body ache—and he was released. He twisted his head and looked into the face of his tormenter, shocked to see it was a woman.

What the hell? he exclaimed to himself, totally confused, then noticed that she was holding a bag with a red cross on it. It finally registered: she was a nurse and had straightened his smashed nose and packed it with gauze.

Feelings of relief surged through him as he realized the NVA weren't going to torture and kill him, at least not yet.

The woman continued to examine his face, gently probing his mouth and removing broken tooth fragments. She covered the exposed nerve ends with a substance that dulled the pain, making it more bearable. Finally, she removed the dirty battle dressing on his chewed-up ear and replaced it after washing the area with some sort of smelly liquid that Frazier took to be disinfectant.

Despite the pain of the examination, Frazier took the opportunity to look around his dimly lit surroundings. He was shocked to see the underground room was now filled with recently wounded Vietnamese. He counted more than a dozen men stretched out on bamboo cots, stacked from floor to ceiling and crammed into a space 20 feet square. One badly wounded young soldier stared unblinkingly at Frazier, his pain-filled eyes causing the officer to feel a twinge of remorse as he wondered if the boy had been wounded in the action against his own men.

Frazier shifted his gaze back to the chamber. One wall was covered with rough wooden shelves containing bandages, aluminum utensils, a few glass containers, and assorted vials, which he took to be medical supplies. Several lanterns hung from pegs driven into the dirt ceiling. These furnished the only light except for the flashlights two tough-looking soldiers in green uniforms and pith helmets were holding for the nurse. Frazier could see their AK-47s leaning against the far wall, within easy reach—as if he were in any condition to make a fight of it.

As the nurse poked and prodded various parts of his anatomy, the two soldiers kept up a steady, indecipherable chatter, which Frazier thought was probably a long recitation of his medical condition.

He knew the NVA must have beaten the shit out of him, because almost everywhere the nurse touched brought forth its quota of pain. But he didn't remember anything beyond emptying his pistol in the trench.

How the hell did I get here? I should be lying dead in that ditch, he wondered, oblivious that his capture was a major coup for the 1st Battalion. Capturing an American on the battlefield was almost unheard of, particularly an officer. Lieutenant Colonel Pham Le Duc had issued specific orders to protect the American captive, treat his wounds, and march him north as quickly as possible. A squad of soldiers was detailed to guard him, and the nurse, Thu Do, was assigned to treat his wounds. Duc had called the young nurse aside and told her in no uncertain terms that he was holding her personally responsible for ensuring the American captive reached the north alive and well.

After finishing her inspection, the nurse opened a metal container and brought out a hypodermic needle that she inserted into the rubber tip of a small vial. She carefully measured out a dose before injecting it into Frazier's arm, causing the pain to recede. As he started to drift off, his last thoughts were of his men, praying they got away in the confusion of the attack.

He slept restlessly, his dreams interrupted by the nightmarish scene of a bullet-ruined face hovering over him. He woke hours later, groggy from the effects of the powerful drug. As his eyes focused, he found to his horror that he was staring directly into a soldier's freshly amputated stump as a medical orderly changed the dressings. In the cot above, a man lay moaning, his intestines neatly folded on his chest, covered only with what looked like cheesecloth. An aide held the man's head and shoulders slightly raised while he attempted to cough deliberately in an agonized effort to prevent his lungs from filling with fluid. A rush of nausea hit Frazier as he saw firsthand the devastating consequences of high-velocity metal ripping through flesh.

He turned his head away from the gruesome sight, afraid that he would throw up. Despite his best efforts, he could not take his mind off the suffering men that surrounded him. He felt sorry for all of them. They were all quiet for the most part, patiently waiting for treatment.

He must have fallen asleep; he didn't see the two soldiers until they suddenly began to hoist him out of the cot. They succeeded in getting him to his feet, although the sudden movement made him dizzy and he almost collapsed. One grabbed him by the arm and cuffed his wounded ear, sending a wave of pain coursing through him. *Shit*, he thought, *no more kid gloves. Where's the nice nurse when you need her?*

The two frog-marched him to a three-foot opening in the wall and pushed him down on his hands and knees. One of the guards untied his hands and motioned for him to crawl into the dark tunnel, encouraging him with a boot in the ass. The Vietnamese in front had little trouble negotiating the narrow passageway but, at six-four, Frazier filled the space. At times he had to twist sideways and crawl on his stomach to pass a narrow section. These contortions only intensified his agony, and as he struggled to breathe in the foul air, the exposed nerve endings in his broken teeth vibrated with pain.

They traveled further into the pitch-black tunnel, his imagination taking hold of his senses. He was seized with a terrible feeling of claustrophobia. *Calm down*, he cautioned himself, trying to maintain self-control. *You can do it.*

Reaching ahead, he felt the leg of the Vietnamese. The tactile knowledge that he wasn't alone made him feel a little better.

As they turned another corner, he saw a glimmer of light. They had reached the end of the tunnel.

Frazier had difficulty climbing out and finally had to be helped. One of his captors pulled while the other pushed from inside the tunnel. He was as weak as a kitten and, on top of everything else, had a splitting headache, which seemed to get worse every time he exerted himself. *I wonder if I have a concussion?* he thought, as a wave of nausea hit him and he doubled over to vomit bile.

The spasm passed and he straightened up, just as the guards grabbed his hands and tied them behind his back. A young guard stood in front of him and made a big show of tying a loop in a ten-foot-long piece of woven vine. The soldier stared angrily at the American, a cruel smile on his face, as his hands fashioned the knot. When he finished, he dropped it over Frazier's head and pulled it tight, forming a noose, which he yanked a couple of times to show off for the other guards, who laughed at the spectacle. "Sadistic son of a bitch," Frazier mumbled through split lips, beside himself with anger. "I'd like to have you in my sights, you piss-ant." Noticing his reaction, the soldier yanked the rope, choking the Marine as the noose tightened around his neck.

Frazier had fallen to his knees, about to black out, when the noose loosened. As he fell forward, gasping for breath, he looked up to see the same nurse who had treated him earlier. She knelt beside him and untied the rope, casting it aside in a display of anger that was not lost on the guards. The group broke up, suddenly finding something important to do—except for the younger one, who continued to glare at Frazier, his eyes blazing with rage.

With the help of the nurse, Frazier finally succeeded in struggling to his feet. Dizzy from the effort, he went down on one knee. The woman shouted at the irate soldier, who grudgingly took one arm, squeezing the hell out of it, and yanked him to his feet. "Goddam it, that's about enough," Frazier muttered as he angrily twisted his arm away. The soldier drew back to hit him, but the nurse stepped in between the two and stared the tormentor down.

At that moment, an older soldier approached and said something that caused both Vietnamese to stiffen to attention and then bow to one another, as if apologizing. He then turned and cuffed Frazier on the jaw with the back of his hand, hard enough to stagger him and bring tears to his eyes. Frazier struggled to keep from crying out while inwardly cringing at the thought of another blow to the face.

The older Vietnamese just stood there watching, as if evaluating the effect of the slap. Then he said something to the nurse and walked away. It dawned on Frazier that he had just been the subject of a leadership lesson. The older soldier, obviously an NCO, had shown the youngsters that dissension in the ranks would not be tolerated. Furthermore, it was clear that a captive who displayed anger would get his ass kicked.

As he pondered that lesson, the rope noose was slipped over his head again, but this time it wasn't pulled tight. Startled, he turned and saw the nurse holding the end of the rope, an apologetic look in her eyes, as if to say, "I have to do my duty."

The NCO returned with five heavily laden soldiers armed with brand-new folding-stock AK-47s, a weapon Frazier knew belonged only to elite NVA units. They each carried three extra 30-round ammunition magazines in chest pouches and Chicom stick grenades in heavy cloth containers that hung by their sides. A pumpkin-shaped one-liter canteen, suspended by thin cotton straps, hung on the other hip. They wore a pressed cardboard pith helmet camouflaged with foliage, and carried bulging canvas rucksacks. One lugged an extra pack and canteen that he dropped on the ground at Frazier's feet, leaving no doubt who was expected to carry it. The captive's hands were untied and he was allowed to briefly massage them, restoring some circulation, before having to shrug into the 30-pound pack. In his weakened condition, the damn thing felt like it weighed a ton; he didn't know how far he could carry it, because it was obvious, they weren't on a little day trip.

The tall *Linh My*—American puppet—caused quite a stir as the small group made its way through the hospital complex. Several medics stopped what they were doing to stare open-mouthed at the strange sight. These men had never seen a *My*—American—before, especially one being led on a rope by a diminutive female soldier/nurse.

In an attempt to take his mind off his pain—and his predicament—Frazier concentrated on his surroundings. He was amazed at what he saw beneath the trees; the well-defined path they followed wound through a small jungle village that included bamboo barracks, cookhouses, and at least two open-air wards, filled with dozens of patients. The area had been painstakingly camouflaged and was almost invisible from just a few meters away. A maze of trenches, spider traps, and strategically located bunkers provided evidence that the NVA were prepared to defend the site from an infantry assault. *This would be a real bitch to fight through*, Frazier reflected as he studied the positions from an attacker's point of view. *Definitely have to soften it up with air and artillery first, or we'd lose our ass*, he thought, recalling Lima's fight in the jungle. Frazier estimated the complex covered about ten acres, but he sensed that there were probably extensive underground facilities in case of air attack.

The group halted near a well-camouflaged bunker where the NCO handed a document to two soldiers who materialized out of the jungle. Frazier surmised that it was some sort of pass. He watched the guards examine it closely before handing it back and waving the group forward. The old soldier gave a hand signal and two men started up the trail, one on either side in a patrol formation. He then motioned for Frazier and the nurse to follow but held them up until they were about ten meters behind the leaders. As they moved out, the NCO took the rope out of the nurse's hand and gave it to Frazier's old antagonist.

126

Just great, Frazier reflected angrily, *Piss-ant will choke the shit out of me just for grins and chuckles.*

The last two guards brought up the rear, while the NCO moved to a position between the two leaders and the captive officer.

As they moved north along the trail, Frazier knew he had to find some way to escape or he would be dead meat, stuck in some prisoner-of-war camp, existing on fish heads and rice—assuming he even survived the march.

24

Chu Loc Hospital Complex, 2000–1200, 12–13 September—Senior Sergeant Thanh lay unconscious on the rudely fashioned operating table as the doctor examined the wounds in his legs. The fighter had been recovered from the battlefield after a patrol happened to stumble across him while visiting the site of an earlier ambush. As they were heading back to headquarters, the smell of death caught their attention. Stopping to discover its source, the soldiers found three dead comrades and a faint blood trail. They followed it to the wounded man, whom they immediately carried to the jungle hospital.

When Thanh arrived, a medical orderly saw something in his tightly clenched right fist and pried it open to discover a set of American identification tags. As he removed them, the wounded man suddenly opened his eyes and seized his wrist, squeezing with such strength that the orderly cried out with pain and dropped the tags back into the man's hand. The look in Thanh's eyes was so menacing that the frightened orderly stumbled back from the table and fell against the side of the tunnel.

The doctor who examined the wounded fighter was taken aback by the numerous scars and lacerations that covered his body. Of particular concern were two obvious bullet wounds that puckered the flesh on the left side of his chest, near the heart. The doctor was amazed that the man had survived them, knowing that a large number of men died from shock on the battlefield before even reaching a hospital. He surmised the old veteran had a tremendous will to live and the constitution of a water buffalo. Continuing the examination, he found that the fresh shrapnel wounds in Thanh's legs were through-and-through penetrations of the soft tissue that had missed the bones entirely. They would heal quickly unless infection set in, which it often did in the unsanitary conditions of the jungle hospital. To guard against the threat, the doctor instructed a medical orderly to scrub the torn flesh with a strong antiseptic while he gave Thanh an antibiotic injection, compliments of the South Vietnamese puppet soldiers. There was nothing to be done for the loss of blood except to keep him quiet and provide nourishing food.

As the doctor finished bandaging the wounds, he was thunderstruck when Thanh opened his pain-filled eyes and asked if he could be released from the hospital.

***

The sound of metal on metal woke Thanh with a start. Sitting up straight, he automatically reached for the assault rifle at his side. It wasn't there. Only then did he remember where he was—in a hut, in an outdoor ward. He relaxed slightly. He felt weak and his wounds hurt like hell, just like the other times, but he was familiar with the feeling and knew that it was all part of the process of healing. Nevertheless, the thought of remaining in a cot for days at a time left him depressed. He vowed to leave as soon as possible and return to duty.

As Thanh lay there planning the escape, his attention was drawn to the trail outside. Three fully equipped fighters passed by, then a fourth holding a rope around the neck of an impossibly tall *Bo Doi*. An overwhelming rage filled him as Thanh realized the soldier was an American captive.

Thanh struggled to get out of the cot, determined to kill the Westerner. His thrashings caught the attention of two medical orderlies, who rushed over and held him down despite his shouts and curses.

Thanh gave up and lay back against the thin, straw-filled mattress, exhausted with the struggle. He realized that further effort was futile and would result in being placed under close observation by the cadre if they thought he was suffering battle fatigue.

A familiar voice calling his name interrupted these thoughts. Thanh looked across the aisle and saw Toan, one of his men who had been wounded in the action with the Americans. "Combatant Toan! Are you well?"

"Yes, Comrade Sergeant. It was only a minor wound in the arm," Toan replied as he got up and walked over to Thanh's cot. "Combatants Nhien and Phu are also here, but they are out digging trenches," he added.

"They were not badly wounded, then," Thanh inquired as he put together a plan to make his getaway.

"Yes, Sergeant, and the rest of the platoon is camped about an hour's march from here," Toan replied, bringing a smile to Thanh's face. The young soldier stayed for several more minutes while Thanh fully outlined his plan.

Later that day, Thanh and his three soldiers carefully made their way through the undergrowth past several guard posts, which was almost child's play for men trained to infiltrate heavily defended positions even in broad daylight. The fact that his men knew exactly where the guards were located and that it was lunchtime only made it easier.

Thanh was having a tough time walking because of the pain, so he leaned heavily on his men for support. The wounds had re-opened and he felt blood trickling down his legs, but he was determined to rejoin the platoon. As he thought about what they were doing, he smiled at how strange it was to be escaping from his own people to fight the enemy, but the orders were perfectly clear: a patient had to be fully recovered before release, and that wasn't going to happen soon enough.

After making their way through the camp's defenses, Thanh sent a soldier ahead for more help. By early afternoon they had reached the bivouac, just as a courier arrived with orders to report to *Trung Ta* Duc.

25

Lima Company, Hill 540, 0130-0430, 13 September—The medevac helicopter's red anti-collision lights faded into the night sky as the second bird began its approach, guiding on the strobe light set in the middle of the LZ. Suddenly, the helo turned on its landing lights, dazzling everyone on top of the hill, ruining their night vision and illuminating the position for NVA gunners.

As the CH-46 sat down and turned off its lights, the first of the stretcher bearers headed toward the lowered ramp through a storm of debris thrown up by its whirling blades. Other teams lined up behind them, anxious to place the wounded aboard and get the aircraft the hell out of there before it attracted mortar fire.

Captain Anderson stood off to one side, watching the evacuation, as Gunny Smith walked over and carefully looked him up and down before speaking. "Skipper, you look like shit," he said, concern evident in his voice. "I think you should get on that bird and go back to get those wounds fixed up."

Anderson was taken aback. He hadn't even thought about evacuation. Sure, he hurt, and he was a little stiff too, but Lima was his company and he damn sure wasn't going to leave it unless it was feet first. He heatedly responded to the suggestion, "Damn it, Gunny, I'm not leaving, and that's that."

Smith shrugged his shoulders and nodded. "Skipper, you're as stubborn as a mule, but I knew that's what you'd say. Just don't come bitching to me when your arms fall off."

Anderson couldn't help laughing. "You old fart; you're not worried about me. All you want is to command the company."

Smith snorted indignantly. "Shit, Captain, I already run the company. I just let you think *you* do." And with that last word he ambled off to rejoin 3rd Platoon.

Anderson was still chuckling when he spotted the recon officer heading for the helicopter with the surviving members of his team. "Lieutenant Wilson!" he yelled above the noise. "Hold on a minute, I want to talk with you." The officer stopped in mid-stride and jogged over, motioning for his men to keep going. Anderson knew the younger man was about done in from fatigue and dejection over leaving the two KIAs behind. He blamed himself, even though there was nothing he could have done.

"Herb, I just wanted to tell you that you did a good job out there. You did all you could to bring your men home. I think you ran into some of the same gooks that gave us such a hard time."

"Thanks, Captain, I appreciate that," Wilson hesitantly replied, "but the real credit goes to my men. They're true professionals. I'm just damn sorry I left Rohweller and the pilot out there."

Anderson reached across, gripped Wilson's shoulder, and looked him in the eye. "Herb, you aren't the only one to leave someone behind," he said with emotion. "I left a good friend, and I feel like shit wondering if I could have done more to bring him back." He continued passionately, "But I'll tell you one thing—tomorrow I'm going back to get him, even if I have to shoot my way through the whole NVA army."

Wilson straightened, visibly throwing off his lassitude. "Captain, don't go without me. I'll be back with a new team," he vowed, then turned, ran for the helicopter, and climbed aboard just before it lifted off.

The silence was a welcome relief after the deafening roar of the helicopter engines. At least now they might hear an incoming mortar round and be able to react. Before, with the helo "churning and burning" in the landing zone, they couldn't hear shit. An explosion would be their only notice—and then it would be too late. More than once the NVA had waited until a helo's clatter covered the sound of their weapon before lobbing in the deadly explosives, catching the troops unaware and fully exposed.

Anderson was relieved. So far, Lima Company had escaped the attention of the NVA mortar crews. Now, with the casualties evacuated, it was time to focus all their attention on the defense of the hill. He looked at his watch, noting that it was still three hours to daylight—little enough time for the things he had to do. He called a command group meeting. As he sat waiting for the others to arrive, he leaned back and rested his helmet on the edge of the foxhole, careful not to move his wounded arms. He instantly fell asleep.

Littleton was the first to arrive. Seeing Anderson sleeping, he moved to intercept the others, so as not to disturb the exhausted officer. The four met some distance away: Littleton and Napoline, Gunny Smith, and Private First Class Hoenig, the acting artillery forward observer. They agreed to let Anderson doze unless or until there was an emergency.

Actually, there was little to do. They had already instituted the company night SOP, which put the men on 50-percent alert, one man in each two-man foxhole awake with weapon and grenades at hand. The trick was to keep them that way. The men were exhausted and, like infantry everywhere, could literally fall asleep on their feet in an instant. It would be up to the exhausted officers and NCOs to move along the perimeter and force the men to stay awake.

Before breaking up, the gunny brought up whether to send out listening posts, because there was so little time remaining before daylight. Littleton seemed to express everyone's thought: "It'll take an hour to get them out there and in position, and by that time it will be almost daylight. I don't think it's worth the effort." They all reluctantly agreed, knowingly violating one of Anderson's basic night-defense tenets—to place three to four men near likely avenues of approach into the position. The LP was generally located 50 to 100 meters beyond the lines, on terrain features the enemy might use to get close to the perimeter—a trail, a gulch, or a tree line. Its mission was to provide early warning of NVA movement. It was a thankless assignment but a critical one, for if the enemy was detected soon enough, the defenders would have time to prepare a warm reception. Timing was everything for the men on the LP, because if they were recalled too soon, the defenders wouldn't know what they faced, and if they were withdrawn too late, they might not make it. The men were well aware that enemy doctrine called for locating the LPs and taking them out, which often led to a deadly game of hide and seek.

A bone-tired Tom Napoline, on his second perimeter check in as many hours, heard the distinctive metallic sound of the safety spoon flying off a hand grenade. He automatically hit the ground, pressing his body into the dirt, knowing the missile would explode within seconds. He was not disappointed. A burst of light and sound shattered the night stillness, the blast sending up a shower of debris. He scrambled to his feet and jumped into the nearest two-man foxhole, landing on one of the occupants amid a stream of abuse until the man realized who it was. Ignoring the offended Marine, Napoline turned to his partner. "What the hell's going on? Who threw the grenade?" he demanded in a low voice.

"I did, Lieutenant. I heard something out there," the Marine responded excitedly. "It sounded like someone slithering through the grass."

"Keep your voice down, I'm right here," Napoline warned, then added, "Did you see anything?"

Chastened, the youngster whispered, "No, sir, but I could have sworn it was someone out there."

Napoline was at a loss. Nothing in his artillery training had prepared him for this. *Maybe the kid was just spooked*, he thought as he stared into the darkness. *But I don't want to blow him off either.* He could easily envision NVA sappers crawling toward the position. Unable to reach a decision, he said, "Okay, be alert and let me know if you hear anything else before you do anything. Understand?"

The two men acknowledged the off-the wall-order, wondering what they would do if a battalion of NVA suddenly sprang up and attacked them.

***

Anderson woke with a start at the sound of the grenade, bolting upright, fighting to untangle himself from the poncho liner that someone had draped over his head and shoulders. He cursed mightily as the sudden movement tore open the blood-crusted wounds, sending waves of pain radiating from his arms and leg and bringing tears to his eyes. "Fuck it," he mumbled through clenched teeth, throwing off the liner and scrambling to his feet as anger overcame the pain.

With his radio operator in tow, the captain hustled as fast as his stiff leg would allow to Napoline's CP, where he found the young officer slumped against the side of his foxhole, sound asleep. Anderson shook him roughly by the shoulder and called his name several times before Napoline responded. "Skipper, what's wrong?" Napoline asked, groggy from lack of sleep, wondering why the captain was shaking him.

"Tom, what was that explosion?"

Napoline hesitated, trying to gather his thoughts. "One of my men thought he heard something in the brush and threw a grenade, sir. But we couldn't tell if there was anyone out there or not. I waited for a few minutes but didn't hear anything, so I came back here."

"Tom, did you pass the word about the noise?" Anderson asked, knowing full well that Napoline didn't have the slightest idea what might be happening.

"No, sir, I didn't think ..." and stopped as the significance finally registered. "I guess I screwed up," he replied in a remorseful voice.

Anderson, who was not one to kick a man when he was down, let him off the hook, "Tom, it may have been nothing, but it may also have been the gooks scouting the perimeter. They probably followed us and took advantage of the helicopter distraction to get in close. You better alert your LP and let them know what's happening."

Napoline's head snapped up as an adrenalin rush drove away the fatigue. He swallowed hard. *Oh, shit. Why me?* he thought, dreading to be the one to tell the old man there were no listening posts. "Skipper—" he began, just as another explosion shook the perimeter.

Petrovitch strained to pinpoint the faint sound of movement in the elephant grass. He closed his eyes and concentrated on the sound, tuning out everything but the slight rustle of grass as the stalks were parted. He had heard the sound before, in a night position south of the DMZ, just before NVA sappers rose out of the grass to attack. The scene was frozen in his mind: black-clad figures emerging out of the darkness, screaming insanely, tongues of fire spitting from their automatic weapons, sweeping closer and closer. He shuddered, remembering the jammed gun and the helpless feeling as he rose to meet them with a pistol and entrenching tool.

He shook off the thought as he felt a slight vibration of the rubber-coated wire in his hand, confirming his suspicions. Without hesitation he squeezed the plastic detonator, sending an electric charge to the blasting cap, which detonated the Claymore in a huge explosion. Even as the shock wave rolled over him, he was up and moving fast—into the smoke and falling debris.

He dropped to his hands and knees in the center of the charred blast area, searching for remains. The heavy smell of plastic explosive and burnt flesh assailed his nostrils as his hand came in contact with the shattered remains of a body. Most of the upper torso was missing; only the legs remained. A few yards away, he discovered a second body that was relatively intact. Overcoming a feeling of revulsion, he ran his hands over the bloody remains and found a cloth bag containing a small notebook.

Suddenly, the hair on the back of his neck stood up. He froze. After several nerve-racking moments in which nothing happened, he soundlessly stood up, raised his pistol, and backtracked up the slope, expecting to be shot at any moment. As he cautiously approached the gun pit, he heard the click of a rifle safety being released, then a soft whisper.

"That you, Corporal Petrovitch?" Relieved that the youngster remembered the instructions, he responded more calmly than he felt. "It's me, Private Edwards. Don't shoot."

After briefing his assistant gunner, Petrovitch climbed out of the gun pit and started for the platoon command post to brief Little John. He nearly ran into a knot of several men that included Littleton, Captain Anderson, and two radio operators.

Anderson recognized the big gunner and spoke first. "What's going on, Petrovitch?"

"Sir, gooks are checking out the perimeter and playing games with the Claymores," he quickly replied, anxious to get the word out.

Instantly recognizing the significance of the brief statement, Anderson took the handset from his radioman and passed the information to the other platoon commanders, with a warning not to use the Claymores or fire the machine guns unless directly attacked, so as not to give away their positions. He also ordered a stand-to: every man awake with weapons at hand.

Turning his attention back to Petrovitch, Anderson requested a detailed account. "Sir, I thought the gooks might try to check out the perimeter, so I put out a Claymore and held the wires so I could tell if they fucked with it," the NCO pithily replied, thinking he had about covered the whole incident.

"And?" Littleton interjected, encouraging the laconic NCO to elaborate on the details.

"Well, sir, I had a feeling the gooks would try something early in the morning, so I left Private Edwards with the gun and moved down the hill to hear better. When I felt the tug on the wire, I knew one of the little bastards was turning the Claymore around, so I detonated it and blew the shit out of two of them. I think there was more, but I didn't stay to find out. Guess I got a little spooked."

Littleton was stunned. *Petrovitch must have balls the size of grapefruits*, he thought, trying to imagine what it must have been like to be all alone, out in front of the lines with the NVA only a few yards away.

Anderson broke in. "What were they wearing?"

"I couldn't tell on the first one," Petrovitch replied. "The blast took all his clothes off. But the second wore just a pair of black shorts and was barefoot, just like that time near the DMZ."

"Yeah," Anderson acknowledged, "where you saved my ass and received the Silver Star."

Overlooking the comment, Petrovitch continued, "I took this off his body," and handed over the open notebook.

Anderson shined his blacked-out flashlight on the rough hand-drawn sketch and studied it for a moment before exclaiming, "My God, these are our positions."

26

Reconnaissance Platoon, North Vietnamese Army, Hill 540, 0200–0630, 13 September—*Chien Si* Xuan carefully pulled the long cord he had attached to the top of the stout bush, bending it toward him. Then, he released the cord. The shrub snapped back, making a noise like something had brushed heavily against it. Seconds later, Xuan saw a dark figure rise out of the ground and heard the distinct sound of a safety device fly off a hand grenade. He pressed his face into the crook of his arm and closed his eyes tightly, so the flash of the detonation wouldn't destroy his night vision. As he expected, the grenade exploded harmlessly. The American had fallen for his ruse, and now Xuan had located another position.

The Americans were careless, they were noisy, they didn't camouflage their positions, and they moved around too much. It was never difficult to pinpoint their fighting holes.

Xuan's location on the lower slope gave him an advantage. As he looked up the hill, the Americans were silhouetted against the night sky. All he had to do was watch as they went from position to position. It was almost too easy. In two hours, his three-man cell had reconnoitered half the perimeter without being detected—until he decided to test their reactions with the bush ploy. The response confirmed his suspicion that the Americans were unseasoned amateurs. As a final indignity, he turned several of their directional mines around.

Lieutenant Doi will be pleased with tonight's work, Xuan thought as the three-man cell made its way to the rally point. They had located all the fighting positions in their sector and marked them by tying pieces of cloth painted with luminous arrows to trees. Xuan had carefully inspected each marker to make sure the Americans couldn't see the luminescence, which his fellow *Bo Doi* would use to pinpoint the positions for destruction.

He could imagine the defenders' shock as accurate automatic weapons and rocket-propelled grenades destroyed their puny defenses, opening a path for the assault force. After penetrating the perimeter, they would focus on knocking out command posts and machine gun positions with satchel charges or direct action. On signal, they would withdraw under the cover of automatic weapons and mortar fire. Xuan had practiced the technique many times under the watchful eye of Lieutenant Doi and felt confident of success against the Americans.

A whispered challenge interrupted his thoughts. As Lieutenant Doi stepped onto the trail, a loud explosion split the night stillness.

Chien Si Tam lightly picked up the rubber-coated wire and smiled to himself as he thought of the American reaction when they detonated the mine and its deadly contents exploded in their faces. Reaching out as he had been taught, he cautiously felt around the mine to make sure it was not boobytrapped. Then he carefully lifted it out of the ground. As he started to turn it around, the wire straightened. The slack was taken out and there was a slight tug. The last thing Tam saw, as his life ended, was a brilliant flash of light as the C-4 detonated. His upper body absorbed most of the explosion, but several of the steel pellets passed completely through him, striking Corporal Huan in the head, killing him instantly.

Private First Class Loan, who was covering Tam and Huan from about 50 meters away, escaped injury. He realized something had gone dreadfully wrong and started back to locate them. As he crept silently through the undergrowth, guiding on the strong odor of explosives and burnt flesh, he sensed a foreign presence in the undergrowth. Loan knew instinctively it wasn't either of his comrades, so he settled down to wait, his keyed-up senses alert to the slightest noise. Finally, a slight rustling told him the other hunter was withdrawing, so he moved forward into the killing zone, where he found the remains of his comrades. Loan was shocked. This was his first action. He felt all alone, unprepared for the violent death of close friends. As he struggled to get a grip on his emotions, he finally realized he had to go back to the rally point for help.

When Loan brought word of the two deaths, Doi knew exactly what he had to do. He was never going to leave comrades behind again, even if he had to take extraordinary risks. Now, as the team approached the killing ground in the growing light, Doi realized he could lose more men if they made a mistake. His plan depended on whether the Americans suspected there would be a recovery attempt and if they were especially alert. Nevertheless, based on Xuan's report of the enemy's lax habits, he imagined they would be asleep.

Lieutenant Doi and three men slithered, as fast as they dared, through the undergrowth, intent on recovering the remains of their comrades. They were taking a big chance with dawn rapidly approaching, risking exposure as they lost the advantage of darkness.

Just as the sickly-sweet smell of death wafted on the breeze, Loan signaled they were close. Doi crawled forward and stopped at the edge of a large opening in the undergrowth, blasted clear by the mine's explosion. In the gathering light, he clearly saw Corporal Huan lying face-down in the dirt. Tam's remains were a few feet away.

Motioning the others to remain under cover, Doi crawled to one side until he was directly below Huan's body. There, he unwound a length of cord from around his waist. With as little movement as possible, he threw one end of the rope with its homemade wooden hook, hoping to snag Huan and drag him into the undergrowth. His first two tosses weren't successful. With growing impatience, he tried again, this time catching the hook in Huan's loincloth. He moved further back into the grass and pulled on the rope but found he didn't have the leverage to move the body. He signaled for his men to join him. With three of them pulling, they managed to slowly drag Huan into the grass.

Just as they gave a final tug, a machine gun opened fire. Bullets snapped over their heads; the gunner on the height was naturally inclined to fire high. But then clods of dirt and foliage flew into the air as the gunner adjusted his aim, forcing the four men to burrow into the forest floor. Doi, who was directly behind the body, felt it heave as several rounds tore into it. It saved his life. The others were lucky to find cover behind fallen logs and small mounds of dirt.

The machine gun stopped firing, giving the men an opportunity to escape.

Doi and Loan quickly dragged the body further down the slope, then hoisted the grisly remains and carried them further into the forest. After they reached the rally point, Doi found a secluded spot nearby. There they wrapped Corporal Huan in a hammock and buried him following a brief ceremony. As Doi watched his comrades conceal the grave, he was overcome with emotion. He had left Tam behind for the Americans to gawk at.

27

Lima Company, Hill 540, 0530–0830, 13 September—Edwards wished Petrovitch would hurry back; the night sounds were making him jumpy, and his imagination was running wild with scenes of screaming gooks. He almost fired the M-60 a dozen times, thinking the NVA were creeping through the grass to get him. One time, he actually started to pull the pin from a hand grenade, but he remembered the corporal's admonition: "Don't do anything until you see the whites of their eyes." *Real funny*, he had thought. *Just like Bunker Hill.*

As Edwards stared wide-eyed at the spot at which the Claymore had detonated, he saw for the first time what he took to be a log lying in the middle of the blast area. The sky was getting lighter, enabling him to see better. He checked his watch, noting that it was almost 0600. As he glanced back at the log, he could swear it was moving. He shook his head, thinking he was seeing things, then looked again. The damn thing *was* moving! With shocking clarity, he realized it wasn't a log at all; it was a body, and someone was dragging it into the grass.

Adrenaline surging, Edwards snapped the butt of the machine gun into his shoulder and aimed toward where he judged the gooks to be. Just as he pulled the trigger, he mumbled, "I see the whites of their eyes."

The sound of the gun captured everyone's attention, but Petrovitch was the first to react, taking off at high port toward the machine gun position. He leaped into the hole just as a twisted metal ammunition link jammed the gun. Edwards jumped back in an attempt to swing the M-60 around and shoot the intruder, thinking that Petrovitch was an attacker.

Petrovitch brushed the heavy weapon aside and grabbed the panicked Marine by the shoulders, holding him until he calmed down. "What happened?" he demanded. "Why did you shoot?"

"I thought I saw something," Edwards exclaimed, knowing his statement sounded stupid and feeling like a fool for disobeying orders. But instead of the ass chewing he expected, Petrovitch quietly asked what he saw and where. Feeling more confident, Edwards pointed to the opening in the grass, which was now clearly visible in the morning light. He described the moving corpse. In the midst of this explanation, Littleton and Anderson arrived in time to get the gist of the story.

Looking up at the officers, who were standing in plain view, Petrovitch calmly warned them to get down—because, as he put it, "you could draw fire, which might hit one of the enlisted men."

Both chuckling men did as he suggested, realizing that whoever dragged the body away might still be in the area, wanting a little revenge.

Quickly taking charge, Anderson ordered Littleton to send out a detail to investigate, then left to check the rest of the lines. Littleton announced he was going to lead the patrol, which Petrovitch immediately volunteered for, along with Edwards, who desperately wanted to find something out there to justify his actions.

After alerting the lines that they were going out, the patrol—now increased by the addition of the 1st Platoon's 1st Squad—cautiously approached the area of the mine blast. The cloying stench of death was overpowering, causing several of the men to gag. One man tossed an early C-ration breakfast into the weeds.

"Spread out and keep alert," Littleton cautioned as they approached the putrefying, fly-covered lower torso.

"Not a pretty picture," he mumbled, trying hard not to breathe through his nose as he gave it the once-over. He could see nothing of intelligence value.

"Lieutenant, over here," Edwards called out excitedly, pointing to the flattened grass leading away from the site. "It looks like a trail."

As the two studied the trail, Petrovitch stepped out of the undergrowth below them and announced, "You're right. It intersects the main trail about 25 meters from here. There were four of them, judging from the footprints, and in a hurry, because they usually don't advertise their presence."

"Let's take a look around," Littleton declared. "Maybe we can find out what they were up to."

The patrol followed the faint path to where it intersected the main trail, stopping to inspect the footprints. Littleton didn't like the idea of following them any further into the jungle with his small force, so he decided to cut back along the edge of the perimeter.

After notifying Anderson of his intention, he left the trail and headed into the undergrowth. Almost immediately, the point discovered a length of black communications wire that paralleled the hilltop position. They followed the wire into a gully, in which it was wrapped around a tree, where it continued at an abrupt angle toward the company's position.

"What the hell is this all about?" Littleton pondered out loud as he stood in the hollow, noting that the black wire also ran up the hill.

He motioned for the point to continue to follow the wire. Shortly, they discovered that it tied into another length at the end of the gully, forming a T about 30 meters below the line of foxholes. The cross piece was about 20 feet long.

"Look at that, Lieutenant." Petrovitch was pointing to a piece of cloth wrapped around a small tree. Peering closer, they saw that was a painted luminous arrow, pointing directly toward one of the 3rd Platoon's foxholes.

Littleton suddenly realized that they had stumbled into preparations for an attack.

Following Littleton's request to meet in the 3rd Platoon's sector, Anderson and Gunny Smith met the patrol as it crested the hill. As soon as he had caught his breath from the arduous climb, Littleton quickly told them what the patrol had found, ending the brief by pulling the painted cloth out of the cargo pocket of his trousers.

Anderson inspected the marker for a moment before speaking. "Ever see one of these before, Gunny?" he asked knowingly.

"Just like the ones we found after the gooks hit us that night in the DMZ," Smith responded. "The comm wire fits right in too; they used it as a guide into our position."

Anderson nodded, adding, "The notebook Petrovitch took off the body couldn't make it plainer. The gooks plan on hitting us. They'll probably come in on the main trail, then branch off by using the wire as a guide into the gully. My guess is they'll stage there, hit us with mortars while their sappers get close enough to knock out the machine guns, and then throw a mass attack through the 3rd Platoon's area."

"Skipper," Littleton interrupted, "if we know what they're going to do, why don't we get the hell out of here?"

28

Recon Team Knife Edge, Khe Sanh Combat Base, 0530, 12 September—
Herb Wilson led eleven volunteers across the dark runway to the revetments
where the helicopter crews were busy pre-flighting their aircraft for the
scheduled 0600 liftoff. The men were ready; he had personally checked each
of them, carefully inspecting their weapons and equipment. All that remained
was to brief the pilots.

Wilson ran over the plan for the umpteenth time in his mind, trying to
discover some important detail he had forgotten in his rush to get ready for
the mission. The framework of the plan was simple: recover the two bodies
and bring them back. But the devil, as always, was in the details, so he went
over it one more time.

First, everything depended on getting in without being spotted. The odds
of that happening, he estimated, were less than 50 percent. Then they had to
find the bodies, assuming the NVA hadn't gotten them first—or staked them
out to await an all-but-inevitable rescue attempt. Finally, they had to make
it back to the pick-up point without being discovered. "Talk about mission
impossible," he muttered aloud inadvertently.

"What's that Lieutenant?" Gunny French, the assistant patrol leader, asked
as he strode alongside the officer.

"Nothing, Gunny. Just talking to myself," he casually replied, not wanting
to let on that he had doubts.

An old campaigner, French also knew the odds. "Hell, Lieutenant, the
whole company knows this ain't going to be a picnic, but every swinging dick
volunteered, even the cooks. I thought we were going to have a riot after you
picked the team. They *all* wanted to come."

Wilson reflected back to the team's return after the patrol. Captain
Reynolds, his boss, and the company first sergeant had waited in the dark as
the helo lowered its ramp. The old man didn't say much; he simply grasped

147

Wilson's hand and placed an ice-cold Coke in it as a wonderful welcome home. The simple gesture was enough to make him tear up, speechless with emotion. The older officer had noticed Wilson's distress and taken him aside so he could get himself together, while the first sergeant handed similar treasures to the enlisted men and then shepherded them to the company area.

After Wilson regained his composure, the two officers had walked to the operations hut, where Wilson gave a blow-by-blow account of the patrol, praising the actions of his team members but taking personal responsibility for leaving Rohweller and Arnold behind.

Before the company commander could reply, Wilson gave an emotional pitch to lead a recovery effort, reasoning that he knew where the bodies were located and that he was intimately familiar with the terrain and the enemy situation.

Reynolds had acknowledged the report but remained noncommittal on the recovery effort. He told the disheveled patrol leader to clean up, get something to eat, and come back in an hour. When Wilson returned, Reynolds was talking into a double E-8 telephone and, covering the mouthpiece with his hand, said, "The mission's a go. Regiment just approved it."

Wilson marveled at how fast the news had spread. It seemed that within minutes fully dressed Marines just happened to have business in the ops hut, despite the fact it was 3 o'clock in the morning. On one pretext or another, they all managed to say hello and let it be known that they really didn't have anything going on and needed a little exercise … say a hike in the jungle. Several, including the survivors of his team, made no bones about it; they walked right up to him and volunteered for the mission. Gunny French was something else; he simply announced that he would be the patrol's assistant leader and would take care of picking the team. Wilson remembered being so surprised that he simply acknowledged the statement and watched as French walked out of the hut, calling out several names as he hit the company street. The gunny was a godsend, for Wilson badly needed a good NCO to organize and equip the 12-man team while he worked with Captain Reynolds to develop the mission plan.

As the two officers wrapped it up, Wilson looked at his watch and discovered it was 0500, time to inspect and brief the men. He hadn't even had time to prepare his own gear. Panic city! He jumped to his feet and threw open the door, only to find French standing in front of two ranks of fully equipped and camouflaged Marines. The gunny called them to attention and reported in his best parade ground voice, "Sir, Reconnaissance Team Knife Edge prepared for inspection." With that, French executed a crisp salute, as if it were a Stateside training exercise.

Wilson noted that French had chosen well; the men standing before him were the best in the company, all skilled jungle fighters and veterans of numerous patrols in the Khe Sanh plateau's jungle vastness.

Wilson was halfway down the second line of men when he recognized Harry's familiar canine shape lying on the runway matting, several paces from the formation. As usual, the brute exhibited a calm, relaxed disposition, which had lulled more than one dog lover into range. Harry's calibrated eyeball told him exactly when to lunge to get the maximum effect of scaring the shit out of his intended victim. The sight of a ninety-pound German Shepherd leaping in attack, lips curled back to expose impossibly long teeth, all emphasized by a roar like the banshees of hell, was guaranteed to bring on "the big one." More than one thoroughly shaken Marine needed clean trousers after an up-close-and-personal encounter with Harry. The hell of it was that no one could ever remember Harry actually biting anyone; he simply seemed to revel in scaring the shit out of humans rather than biting them—that is, except for Vietnamese. Harry was a scout dog, trained to accompany Marines on patrol, to silently alert his handler when he smelled Vietnamese. On command of his handler, Corporal Bill Block, he would savage his victims with terrifying abandon, no playing around, until ordered to stop. Harry had been credited with two confirmed kills and four thoroughly mauled captures, and he had accumulated numerous citations for detecting ambushes, which had saved Marine lives.

As Wilson approached Harry and Corporal Block, he was smart enough to wait until Block uttered a command and pulled back on the short leash, causing Harry to sit up, motionless.

"How's Harry?" Wilson asked, trying to sound pleasant, hoping the dog picked up the positive vibes.

"Great, sir. He just got over the shits, I think he gnawed on someone that didn't agree with him," Block responded with a straight face.

"Oh, glad to hear it, Corporal," Wilson guardedly answered, unsure whether the handler was yanking his chain but suspecting there was more truth than exaggeration in the comment. "We're going to need his nose to help us get in and out. The area's overrun with gooks."

"We're ready to go, Lieutenant. If anybody can keep us safe, it's Harry." Wilson studied the young NCO, knowing he wasn't bullshitting; the two were a great team, inseparable, much to the dismay of Block's wife, who had sent an ultimatum "me-or-the-dog" letter after Block extended his tour for the second time.

After completing the inspection, Wilson had the men drop their packs and gather around to hear the patrol order. He carefully led them through the formal five-paragraph order (SMEAC—Situation, Mission, Execution, Administration, and Communication) to ensure that every detail of the patrol was covered and that the men understood their responsibilities and individual assignments. He started by describing both the friendly and enemy situations, while highlighting NVA tactics they could expect to encounter. The mission remained straightforward: recover the remains of Corporal Rohweller, a well-known and popular member of the company, and the A-4 pilot. The execution phase was going to be much trickier. Wilson drew a rough sketch in the dirt, showing the patrol route from the LZ to the last known location of the bodies. He didn't spend too much time going over the patrol formation, because the thick jungle vegetation dictated a column. Nevertheless, Gunny French reviewed immediate action drills for various scenarios: ambush right or left, breaking contact, surprise encounter, and setting up their own immediate ambush. The gunny continued with paragraph four, prescribing ammunition load—six twenty-round magazines per rifleman, 400 rounds for the machine gun, three magazines per pistol, 40 rounds for the M-79, and more than that in their packs. In addition, each man was to carry four fragmentation grenades and one smoke canister. Four Claymore mines were distributed among the team. French advised all hands to carry a minimum of four canteens, but most had six and a bottle of halizone tablets to purify any water they found in the mountain streams. The men also carried two C-ration meals, or at least the parts they favored, usually cans of fruit. The gunny turned the brief back to Wilson, who went over the chain of command, in case there were casualties, and gave a list of call signs and frequencies to the two radio operators.

When Wilson completed the formal brief, he asked if there were any questions—and was surprised by the number. Normally, there weren't any. He smiled, thinking of his first patrol brief, when he had laboriously covered every possible detail and was quite pleased with himself until he heard one old timer sum it up for a latecomer: "SOS"—Same Old Shit. This time was different; the men had absorbed the details and seemed intent on memorizing them, because their lives might depend on the information.

Shit. Time to go. How am I going to get my gear ready? he wondered. Just then, the gunny stepped forward with his recently cleaned weapon, pack, and cartridge belt. "Thought you might need these, Sir," French said without a trace of smugness in his voice, although Wilson noted a mischievous sparkle in his eyes.

Wilson introduced himself and the gunny to the pilots, who had gathered next to one of the gunships, waiting for him to brief them on the plan. They moved close around him as he spread an acetate-covered map out on the deck of the aircraft, pointing out the landing zone, which he estimated to be roughly a thousand meters from the bodies. The pilot of the troop bird, Captain Ross Olson— man Wilson had worked with before and trusted—let out a low whistle. "Awfully small, Herb, I'm not sure I can set down. You may have to jump," which meant the patrol would have to leap off the ramp into ten-foot-high elephant grass.

"That's what I was afraid of," Wilson replied, adding by way of explanation, "but it's the only open area that's close enough without having to hump for a couple of days." The pilot nodded. He understood the facts of life in difficult terrain.

One of the gunship drivers followed up with, "How do you want to work the insertion?"

"Very carefully, like porcupines make love," Wilson quipped, an old joke that always triggered a few belly laughs that worked to break the tension. He continued, "I'd like to go in low and fast, to make it hard for the gooks to spot us."

"That'd make it hard to see the zone," Olson declared, then nodded toward the gunship pilots, "unless you guys stay high and guide us in."

"Roger that. We'll stay at about 1500 feet and talk you in. That'll be a good altitude if we have to roll in and give you a hand, if the zone is hot," one of them replied.

"Okay," Wilson acknowledged. "We'll wait on the edge of the tree line for five minutes to see if we've been spotted. I'll radio an all-clear before moving out." The pilots nodded and Wilson continued, "I guess that's it, unless somebody has something else?"

After a slight pause, the senior man spoke up, surprising him. "Herb, we want you to know we'll do whatever it takes to support your team. Good luck, and bring those Marines home." He stuck out his hand.

Following handshakes all around, the group broke up. The pilots manned their helicopters and cranked them up while Wilson and French joined the team, which was on deck, waiting to board.

On a signal from the CH-46 crewman, Wilson led the team up the ramp. He was shocked to see Captain Reynolds and the first sergeant calmly watching from the forward-most troop seats. It was obvious they were intent on giving moral support to their Marines, sharing the danger of the insertion, and, if necessary, adding a little fire power, for both carried weapons.

Once airborne, while crewmen loaded the two big .50-caliber machine guns mounted in the hatches, Wilson unstrapped and positioned himself between the two pilots so he could get a good view of the landing zone when they approached it. Gunny French signaled the team to load weapons by holding up his rifle and inserting a magazine. It was too noisy to try to pass the word.

After circling the base once, the CH-46 dropped down to treetop level and headed for the landing zone at max speed, using a heading as reference. The gunships flew above them as escort until one minute from the LZ, when one pulled ahead to let the pilot of the '46 know they were approaching it. Inside the aircraft, a crewman held up one finger, indicating the time to touchdown. The men tensed, mentally preparing themselves for the landing, and unstrapped so they could get out as fast as possible.

Wilson had trouble keeping his feet as the early-morning winds buffeted the helo, bouncing him from side to side. But it was worth it as the aircraft flared for landing and he saw the zone. "Damn," he exclaimed, seeing how small it was, knowing the heavily laden men would have to jump into the elephant grass and risk injury.

Gunny French didn't wait for a signal; he simply launched himself off the ramp into the thick grass, feet together and knees slightly bent, rolling as his feet hit the ground. He was a Force Recon-qualified parachutist and knew how to land. Others weren't so fortunate, landing in a welter of arms and legs, Wilson among them. Block cradled Harry in his arms and received a lick on the face just before the handler stepped into space.

Fortunately, the grass acted as a mattress, cushioning their fall, and, except for bruised egos, Team Knife Edge escaped injury and moved into the trees with alacrity, hoping they hadn't been discovered.

All hands immediately assumed defensive positions, each man facing outboard, rifle at the ready, for this was the moment in which the team was most vulnerable. Their only protection against an overwhelming attack lay in the two gunships, which circled protectively in a holding pattern some distance away, so as not to bring attention to the patrol's exact location.

Following the roar of the helicopter engines, it took the team several minutes to get attuned to the jungle's stillness. Wilson took the opportunity to take out his map and orient himself to the sound, verifying the direction in which he wanted the team to head.

After waiting five minutes without detecting any signs of the enemy, Wilson signaled the radio operator to send the all-clear message. Next, he caught Block's eye and motioned him forward with a head nod. One by one, the camouflaged men quietly stood up, taking a five-meter interval as the radioman cryptically whispered into his handset, "Knife Edge moving. Out."

29

North Vietnamese Prisoner Guard, 0730–1200, 13 September—Frazier staggered along the trail half conscious and nearly at the end of his strength. He stumbled again, almost falling over as his foot caught an exposed root, and triggering a sudden wave of nausea, which he struggled to control. His body was a throbbing mass of pain, but it was his injured mouth that tormented him the most. Forced to inhale through it because of his smashed nose, the air hitting the exposed nerve ends in his broken front teeth was pure, unrelenting, all-consuming agony. He prayed for relief. The guards had untied his hands, but he still carried the heavy pack, which was sapping his remaining strength. He would have stopped, but the soldier behind him made it plain that he wouldn't tolerate it by jabbing Frazier in the ass with the point of his bayonet every time he faltered. The guards were in a hurry; they were not about to let him slow them down.

Frazier's nemesis had moved ahead, pulling on the rope looped around his neck in an effort to make him keep up with the fast pace. Every so often, the son of a bitch yanked the rope, knocking Frazier off balance, often causing him to fall. There wasn't any rhyme or reason to the harassment; the asshole was just plain mean, and he got his rocks off picking on the helpless American.

Unnoticed by Frazier, the column stopped, so he blundered into the guard, who swung his rifle and caught the American on his wounded ear. The blow sent him crashing to the ground, out cold.

As Frazier slowly regained consciousness, he was faced with the trauma of this new head injury. Hearing Vietnamese voices, he opened his eyes and saw only blurred images. He rubbed his eyes with the back of his hand and blinked several times; this helped to clear his left eye, but the right one refused to focus. A sudden fear surged through him as he realized the blow might have damaged his sight. In that instant, a terrible feeling of hopelessness seized him, as the reality of his predicament sunk in: he was helpless, completely at the mercy of a brutal, sadistic enemy who gloried in abusing the defenseless. In the depths of despair, he contemplated suicide, but he lacked the means to do it. *Maybe I can get the guards pissed off enough to beat me to death*, he thought. *Anything is better than this.* Nothing in his 23 years of life had prepared him for the utter degradation of his situation. Being wounded or killed were real possibilities, but neither he nor any Marine he'd ever met had ever contemplated captivity.

Tears flowed as his thoughts shifted to home and family. *They'll never know what happened*, he groaned, consumed with self-pity.

Suddenly, the shrill sing-song voice of Piss-ant intruded on Frazier's gloomy thoughts. He could just make out the soldier gesturing and laughing at him. "You son of a bitch," he mumbled to himself. As rage overcame his despondency, he desired nothing more than to get his hands around the asshole's throat. Then, with sudden clarity, he realized that Piss-ant might have saved his life in a perverse sort of way—by rousing him out of his depression.

Frazier slowly gained control over the pain and was surprised to find that the will to live gave him renewed strength. *I almost gave up*, he thought, remembering accounts of Korean War POWs who died because they didn't have the will to live. *That's not going to happen to me*, he vowed.

Noting Frazier's changed demeanor, the soldier stepped closer and kicked him in the leg, uttering a Vietnamese oath. Then, seeing the look of pain on the American's face, he drew back to deliver another blow but was stopped by a sharp command from his leader, who had returned to check on the prisoner. The NCO spoke again. When the young thug was ordered back to his position, he gave Frazier a look of pure hatred, leaving no doubt that he wasn't through, not by a long shot. Remembering the last time, Frazier was careful to keep his face expressionless. He had no desire to antagonize the old veteran.

After studying Frazier carefully, the NCO called Thu Do. She came over carrying a first aid kit and an open container of liquid, which she placed beside Frazier before she squatted down next to him. She took the AK-47 from her shoulder, leaned it against a nearby tree, and turned back to the American, concern etched on her face. As Frazier looked into her eyes, she rolled them toward Piss-ant and shrugged her shoulders slightly, as if to say, "We're not all like that jerk." He nodded back, thinking, *What a madhouse. One beats the shit out of me and another fixes me up. I can't tell whether she sympathizes with me or just wants to keep me fit enough to be a punching bag.*

Thu Do applied an ointment on Frazier's teeth, which eased the sharp pain. Then, she took a hand-carved wooden spoon from her pack and began to feed him, careful to keep the liquid away from the stumps of his teeth. *God, that tastes good*, he thought. As he greedily sucked the soup down, he realized that he hadn't eaten in more than 24 hours. He felt better almost immediately, seeming to gain strength with each spoonful. After feeding him the soup, Thu Do gingerly examined the large knot near Frazier's temple, evidence of where Piss-ant had cold-cocked him. Her light touch felt almost soothing. He could tell that she was taking pains not to hurt him unnecessarily. Next, she carefully removed the large battle dressing from his ear, prying it loose from the congealed blood and pus.

"Shit, that hurts," he mumbled. And at the very instant, the undergrowth exploded with automatic weapons fire that instantly killed all the guards, except for the three closest to him.

The sudden, violent attack was overwhelming. Frazier lay there, completely stunned, trying to make sense of the bewildering onslaught. He looked up as the girl jerked back, eyes as big as saucers, and rose to her feet. He made a desperate attempt to pull her down out of the line of fire, but she twisted out of his grasp and grabbed her assault rifle. She pointed the big AK-47 at his chest, determination in her eyes, as her finger tightened on the trigger. Frazier steeled himself, waiting to die, but she didn't fire. Instead, she lowered the barrel and gave him a sad smile, as if to say goodbye.

Frazier shouted "No!" as she turned and lurched away, firing the big gun as fast as she could toward the concealed assailants. Seconds later a single shot struck her in the chest and violently flung her to the ground at his feet. Her vacant eyes stared at the sky.

Kneeling beside her, Frazier frantically checked for signs of life, praying that she was only wounded. But there was no pulse. As he held her lifeless hand, a hate-filled shriek caught his attention. He looked up, just in time to see a wild-eyed Piss-ant lunge at him with a bayoneted rifle. He froze, unable to do anything but stare as the long triangular blade swept toward his chest.

Suddenly, the rifle plunged to the ground as a huge, snarling black dog knocked the soldier down, sank its teeth into Piss-ant's throat, and shook him violently, severing the juggler. Piss-ant screamed horribly and died, as his blood gushed onto the ground.

Frazier watched, horror-struck, as the beast gave the Vietnamese a last shake and turned toward him, growling low in his throat, lips curled back to expose blood-stained teeth. He desperately looked for a weapon as the animal tensed, preparing to spring.

A low command issued from the undergrowth. "Harry. Guard." The dog immediately sat down, keeping a wary eye on Frazier.

Three camouflaged men stepped out of the brush, weapons at the ready, carefully scanning the carnage on the trail. Their eyes rested on Frazier.

30

Reconnaissance Team Knife Edge, 1100–1500, 13 September—Harry froze in mid-stride. The hair on the back of his neck stood up and his ears pointed forward as he became alert to an unknown threat. Block signaled danger to the men behind him and carefully moved into concealment at the side of the trail. He commanded the big animal to follow.

Wilson made his way forward along the column of men to join Block, who was scanning the undergrowth in front of him. "What d'ya think?" Wilson whispered as he intently watched Harry's tense form. The dog continued to sniff the air.

"I think he smells gooks, and, by the way he's acting, they're not too far ahead."

As Wilson considered options, he suddenly heard the faint but unmistakable sound of a Vietnamese voice. That settled it: they had to get off the path or risk discovery, which would blow the whole mission. He told Block to turn off into the forest and parallel the trail until he and Harry had come alongside whoever had made the noise. Then, he urgently passed the word to the others and stepped off into the undergrowth, following Block's lead.

Slowly, they inched their way through the foliage, conscious of the fact that the slightest man-made sound could be disastrous this close to the enemy. After they had advanced several meters, they came across a game trail clear of ground cover, which enabled them to move faster without making noise.

As the voices grew louder, the patrol stopped and went to ground on the edge of a cleared area beneath the trees that was plainly an NVA way station.

Wilson signaled French, and the two crawled toward the sound until only a thin screen of foliage separated them from the edge of the clearing. Carefully pulling the ground-level fern boughs aside, they saw, not 30 feet away, an NVA soldier walk over to another and deliberately kick the prone man in the leg, all the while muttering in Vietnamese.

The guy must be pissed off about something, Wilson thought. Just then, as the assailant drew back to kick again, a low, guttural voice drew his attention to another rifle-toting soldier walking toward the two men. Following a brief discussion, the assailant walked away, but his body language indicated that he was still pissed.

A third soldier came over and squatted next to the man on the ground and took off his pith helmet, releasing a cascade of long black hair.

A woman? Wilson was taken aback by the scene. *What the hell is she doing here?*

His attention was drawn to the big NVA next to her as she lifted the man's head and shoulders off the ground.

Wilson took in the guy's jungle uniform and Western features. *Holy shit! That's an American!*

He poked French in the side to get his attention. The gunny looked back and nodded, mouthing the word "American," to confirm the lieutenant's suspicions.

Wilson's pulse raced. *An American POW. We've got to get him out of there,* he thought, putting the recovery of the KIAs on the back burner in the face of this new development. The rescue of one of their own triggered an unambiguous impulse—*nothing* was more important than bringing him out—but first he had to learn what Knife Edge was up against.

The two men scanned the area, counting an additional five NVA. When they were satisfied that that was all there were, they crawled back to the others and hurriedly briefed them. Wilson determined that the plan of action had to be as simple as possible, so he split the team in half, one section under Gunny French's control and the other under his control.

French and five shooters would take out the NVA on the right and Wilson's team would kill those on the left, using the POW as the midpoint. He cautioned all hands to avoid firing too close to the POW. He designated Corporal "Dead Eye" Jeppeson, a former rifle team shooter, to eliminate any threat to the captive. Block and Harry were relegated to a support role behind Wilson's team.

Sensing that the NVA were preparing to move out, Wilson gave the men ten minutes to get into position before he opened fire, which was the signal for everyone to shoot.

The men were keyed up, ready to take on the whole damn NVA army to rescue the American, well aware that the slightest mistake could cost the man his life. The NVA would kill him in a heartbeat rather than allow him to be rescued.

Wilson crawled into a concealed position beside Corporal Jeppeson, from which he could see the prisoner and still have a good shot at the three enemy soldiers who flanked him. The NCO signaled that he would take the soldier holding the rope, leaving Wilson the one on the right, who was holding an AK-47 loosely cradled in his arm. That left the woman, but she didn't seem to represent much of a threat and was too close to the POW to risk taking a shot. With luck, she'd panic and either freeze or run away.

Pushing back thoughts of all the things that could go wrong, Wilson instead trusted that his well-trained team could handle the unexpected.

As the last few seconds counted down, he carefully sighted in on his target, praying that his men were in position and ready to shoot. Rivulets of sweat ran down his face, stinging his eyes. His heart pounded as he pulled the M-16 tightly into his shoulder and concentrated on centering the front sight blade in the rear aperture. He struggled to get a good sight picture, using the center of the NVA's chest as the point of aim. Satisfied, he took a breath, let out half of it, and slowly squeezed the trigger with the pad of his index finger.

Wilson's weapon discharged, sending the 5.56mm round downrange. The roar of automatic weapons drowned out the sound of the single gunshot as the team poured a concentrated fire into the stunned guards.

The fusillade killed the five men instantly, dropping them where they stood; they never knew what hit them. Wilson's man was luckier; he had started to turn away just as the weapon discharged, causing the bullet to strike the steel receiver of his rifle, a million-to-one stroke of fortune. The collision deflected the bullet harmlessly into the air. Fragments of the smashed rifle, however, struck the NVA in the face and upper chest, gouging flesh in a spray of blood. For all that, the man had the presence of mind to leap into the undergrowth.

Before Jeppeson could take his shot, the woman jumped up, grabbed an assault rifle, and sprayed bullets dangerously close to the line of Marines. Switching targets, Jeppeson quickly lined her up in his sights and squeezed off a round that struck her in the center of the chest.

Corporal Block sensed what was going to happen even before the fatal shot. He watched the third soldier bring up his bayoneted rifle and start for the prisoner. Commanding, "Kill, Harry," he released the big dog and watched as the animal rocketed toward the Vietnamese soldier in great bounding leaps, covering the distance in a blur of movement. At full stride, the snarling ninety-pound fury leaped onto the man's chest and sent him crashing to the ground, screaming in terror. The dog grabbed the victim's throat and tore at it, severing the juggler and esophagus, cutting off his screams. Then, Harry turned toward the prisoner, growling low in his throat, tensing to spring

With no other targets in sight, Wilson shouted the order to cease fire, which was echoed by French at the other end of the line of riflemen. Within seconds, the battlefield fell silent.

The gunny took charge of security and directed the men to search the bodies for documents.

Wilson and his two men rushed forward to check out the prisoner. The man sat motionless, a terrified look on his face as Harry growled menacingly a few feet away. As they warily approached with weapons trained on the man—just in case—Block commanded, "Harry, guard," and advised the figure to sit still so the dog wouldn't attack.

"Who are you?" Wilson requested, for the first time noticing the man's badly disfigured face. "Marine. I'm a Marine," the man mumbled. The words were nearly unintelligible as they sounded from between shattered teeth and grotesquely swollen lips. "Frazier. Lima Company."

Wilson looked at the man in shock. "Oh my God. Lieutenant Frazier," he exclaimed as he dropped to his knees to cradle the big man in his arms. "Get Doc over here. Quick," he called out to no one in particular.

Frazier slumped against Wilson's chest as tears streamed down his cheeks. He mumbled over and over again, "Thank you. Thank you ..." until he passed out.

"Doc, how bad is he?" Wilson asked as the corpsman completed a quick examination of the unconscious man.

"Well, Lieutenant, his nose is busted, along with all his front teeth. His ear is shot to hell and infected. He may have internal injuries. But what bothers me most is the possibility of concussion. I think someone slugged him alongside the head and knocked him senseless. There's not too much I can do for him here, and if we don't get him to the field hospital pretty damn quick, I don't think he'll make it. It's a wonder he's still alive."

Wilson looked closely at Frazier's battered face and made a decision. "Okay, Doc, do what you can to stabilize him; we're going to get the hell out of here." He immediately turned to the radioman. "Any word yet from Company?" he asked impatiently, yet hopeful that headquarters would send instructions after the rescue.

"No, sir, not since you called in the sitrep. They just said to wait," the operator responded.

French approached. "Lieutenant, I think we got big problems," he reported. "One of the gooks got away. We found a shot-up rifle but no body. Just a light blood trail that we lost about ten meters into the brush."

Wilson mulled over the information for a moment, then asked, "What d'ya think, Gunny?" He was all too aware of the obvious answer, but he wanted to hear the more experienced NCO's thoughts.

"Well, sir, I bet that gook is high-tailing it back to his buddies right now and screaming like a banshee. They're not going to like us rescuing their prize catch, so the whole kit and caboodle is going to ride in here like the cavalry. I think the most we have is an hour head start, but then things are going to get really interesting."

"Thank you, Gunnery Sergeant French, for your positive assessment of our situation," Wilson quipped to take some of the sting out of the obvious truth.

"You're right. We don't want to get caught in their backyard. Get the troops ready to move out. I'll let the company know we're out of here."

With Harry in the lead, the patrol made good progress, trusting that his keen sense of smell, 40 times more sensitive than a human's, would alert them to danger. Block was worried because the big dog was tired and starting to lose his concentration in the heat and humidity. Harry was panting heavily, trying to cool himself off, but Block knew from experience that it wasn't enough. The dog needed a couple of hours' rest—except there wasn't time, with the NVA no doubt hot on the trail or maybe even up ahead, waiting in ambush. And that's where Harry came in.

The three-year-old German Shepherd had spent four months in training at Fort Gordon, learning the specialized skills of a scout dog, when he was paired up with a young Private First Class William Block and sent to Vietnam. The two joined the 2nd Marine Scout Dog Platoon and were immediately assigned to accompany reconnaissance teams. They had earned a reputation for never having led a patrol into an ambush. Now, a year and a half later, these veterans of more than 50 patrols were again being put to the test.

Suddenly, Harry froze by the side of the trail, ears forward, intently studying the ground immediately to the front. Block signaled the others and carefully kneeled down, trying to see why the dog had alerted. At first he couldn't see anything, but then, following Harry's line of sight, he spotted the slender, almost invisible nylon fishing line stretched across the trail three inches above the ground.

"Booby trap," he mouthed to the Marine behind him and gestured for the patrol leaders to come forward.

While Block covered them with his rifle, French and Wilson cautiously approached the trip wire, meticulously scanning the undergrowth to make sure there wasn't another hidden surprise. Wilson carefully peeled back the foliage to reveal a freshly staked Chinese Claymore mine. Its lethal cone of fire pointed down the trail. If someone had tripped it, half the patrol would have been killed or wounded. Harry had saved their asses again.

After backing away from the deadly trap, Wilson and French discussed the situation in whispers. "This doesn't look good," Wilson breathed. "I think the gooks are ahead of us. They knew we'd head for the high ground, so they've sent troops to the possible hilltop landing zones to ambush us."

French nodded in agreement, stating what was foremost in their minds: "We've got to get Lieutenant Frazier evacuated, and quick. He's unconscious and, according to the doc, getting worse."

In response, the officer took out his map and traced a route with his finger toward a meandering stream, a shaded blue line about a klick away, cross-country. Thinking aloud, he murmured, "Gunny, remember the river we flew over, where we could see water through the break in the canopy?

There must be other openings along this stream where a helicopter could hover and lower a jungle penetrator to pick us up."

Before French could reply, Block caught their attention by pointing to Harry, who was frozen in position, ears forward, neck hair standing up—his standard Vietnamese alert pose.

Wilson pointed to the map and signaled the gunny, who nodded to acknowledge that he was to take the lead to the river.

The patrol silently withdrew without incident. Harry continued to alert as they struck out cross-country through the dense undergrowth. The stretcher bearers had to slow down considerably as they traversed the increasingly steep terrain that led down to the stream. They were spelled often, but the physical effort of carrying Frazier in the heat and humidity was taking its toll. Even though they sucked down their tepid canteen water like it was going out of style, the tired men were soaked in sweat and dehydrated.

Block emptied four of his canteens in an effort to keep Harry hydrated, but the big dog was becoming noticeably weaker, appearing to lose interest in what was going on and struggling to keep up the pace. He was placing the patrol in danger, which forced Block to make a decision. If Harry couldn't keep up, the patrol would have no option but to kill him, because there was a standing order to not allow a scout dog to fall into enemy hands. Block was determined not to let that happen, even if he had to carry Harry—and that's just what he intended to do.

As the handler strained to lift Harry's dead weight, he heard Wilson's low voice. "Block, what the hell do you think you're doing with that dog? Put him down." In a panic, Block hugged his beloved animal close, determined to protect him. "Sir, I can carry Harry. You don't have to shoot him," he pleaded, watching as the officer raised his rifle. Wilson stood there, stunned. Block had completely misunderstood his actions.

"My God, man, I'm not going to kill him," Wilson emphatically replied as he slung the M-16 over his shoulder. "We're going to help you carry him." He motioned another Marine forward and helped put the motionless dog onto a makeshift stretcher. As they lifted it up, Wilson patted Block on the shoulder and said, "After what Harry has done for us, it'll be a cold day in hell before we let anything happen to him."

Sensing that they were being followed, Gunny French pushed the tired men hard, setting a fast pace, while Wilson urged them on from the rear. They had to reach the river quickly and locate an opening in the trees so they could get Frazier and the dog team lifted out.

As they moved further from the trail, the ground became even steeper. Near to the bottom of the valley in which the river flowed, the men had trouble keeping their footing, having to grab onto shrubbery to avert a tumble down the slope.

The stretcher bearers weren't as lucky; they were lugging 180 pounds of shifting dead weight that often threw them off balance. More than once, as one or the other stumbled, Frazier's unconscious form nearly rolled off stretcher, and only quick reflexes kept him from plummeting down the gradient.

The patrol's disorganized movement through the shrubbery threw noise-discipline out the window. Wilson was constantly on edge as he imagined the sound giving their position away. *Shit. We'll be lucky if the bastards aren't waiting for us,* he thought.

Just then, the low voice of his radio operator interrupted his musings. "Lieutenant, it's the Six." He passed Wilson the handset.

Captain Reynolds's calm voice came over the air to inform Wilson him that helicopters were on the way to pick up the entire team and return it to base. Wilson was dumbfounded. It had not entered his mind that the recovery mission would be called off. Surely there was some mistake. He keyed the handset and omitted formal radio procedure to make an emotional plea: "Skipper, I just can't leave those Marines behind. All we need is a few more hours, and we'll bring 'em home."

Reynolds's reply was curt and unequivocal: "Negative Knife Edge. Get on the helicopter. Your mission is cancelled."

Swearing softly to himself, Wilson vowed he would never leave the remains of the two Marines. He would find a way to recover them.

The *whop-whop-whop* of the incoming helicopter caught his attention, just as French passed the word that he had reached the stream and had found an opening for the extraction. Wilson worked his way along the line of men to the gunny, took out a small pencil flare, and prepared to launch it through the break in the canopy. He screwed the small, one-inch aluminum cylinder into the barrel of a thick five-inch-long pencil-like device and pulled the internal spring-loaded steel pin back, cocking it. At his nod, the radio operator contacted the pilot and told him to watch for their marking flare. Wilson released the cocking handle, which flew forward and struck the primer, launching a small yellow flare a hundred feet in the air.

Ross Olson, returning for the rescue, acknowledged the sighting and maneuvered his CH-46 into position over the opening as the crew chief prepared to lower the jungle penetrator. The second crewman manned the port .50-caliber machine gun, staring intently down at the jungle, ready to fire at the first sign of trouble.

With a smoothness brought on by long practice, Olson eased the big machine into a steady hover just ten feet over the jungle canopy. The crew chief slowly lowered the bullet-shaped metal rescue apparatus through the hell hole in the cabin floor, carefully guiding it through the opening in the trees toward the two men standing on the stream bank. The tremendous downward thrust of the rotor wash flattened the tops of the trees, pelting the men below with leaves and broken branches, which forced them to shield their eyes as they peered upward through the maelstrom.

Gunny French put the team in a tight defensive circle while Wilson helped the doc secure the unconscious Frazier in one of the small pull-down seats of the penetrator. At a signal, the crew chief started the winch, reeling the cable upward while Olson skillfully kept the bird steady over the jungle opening.

Wilson heaved a sigh of relief as he watched Frazier being pulled safely into the cabin. Moments later the penetrator was back down, and it was Block's turn. They strapped him in, placed the limp dog on his lap, and signaled the crew chief to hoist away.

They were halfway up when a fusillade of small arms fire suddenly erupted from the surrounding jungle, the sharp crack of bullets almost drowned out by the noise of the helicopter. Block lurched from a hit and fell back against the holding strap. Harry slipped out of his grasp. He made a desperate grab and, at the last moment, caught the dog by his hindquarters, saving him from falling to his death. Holding on for dear life, he wrapped one arm around the cable and the other around Harry. Wind buffeted him unmercifully as he swung precariously from the cable. The helo was still just above the treetop trying to gain altitude.

He hunched over, trying to shield the dog from the enemy riflemen as they continued to hammer away at the helicopter. Despite the engine noise, he could hear the snap of rounds and the metallic pings as they tore into the aircraft, passing completely through the fragile aluminum skin.

The gunner yelled they were taking hits and pressed the butterfly trigger of the big .50-caliber, hosing down the jungle in a desperate attempt to suppress the gunfire. AK-47 fire sawed into the left side of the ship and struck the gunner in the chest, the impact throwing him to the deck.

All hell broke loose in the cockpit when the instrument panel shattered and bits of aluminum, paint chips, dust, and debris filled the air. Several rounds tore through the flight deck and smacked into the pilots' armored seats, ricocheting in all directions. Bullet splinters sliced into the co-pilot's lower legs, punching through the skin and deep into the muscle of his calves, incapacitating him. He jerked forward in severe pain and shouted over the intercom that he had been hit.

Olson instantly keyed his mike and declared an emergency, which alerted the escort gunships that the CH-46 was receiving ground fire and had casualties aboard. He added power just as another burst raked the bird, causing it to vibrate heavily. The aircraft started to sink toward the treetops, but with great presence of mind, Olson gently pulled back on the collective, to stop the descent. As he applied more power, the helicopter rose straight up until the crew chief announced the penetrator had cleared the canopy. Still exercising remarkable airmanship, Olson eased the cyclic forward and transitioned into flight, rapidly putting distance between the helicopter and the NVA gunners.

The crew chief frantically worked the hoist until Block finally came up through the hellhole. He pushed Harry onto the floor and attempted to free himself from the rescue harness, but he couldn't move his arm to free the snap link. When he tried to move it, his right shoulder hurt like hell. Then he spotted the heavy stream of blood flowing down his arm and pooling on the deck. "Christ, I'm hit," he mumbled, as the crew chief propped him up against the cabin bulkhead and wrapped a battle dressing on the wound, trying desperately to staunch the flow of blood. Feeling faint and incredibly tired, Block leaned back, closed his eyes, and slipped into a coma—a prelude to death. The crewman recognized the signs and shouted at him to hang on as he slapped his face, hoping it would bring him around. It didn't work. He tried again, only to have his wrist seized in Harry's powerful jaws as the big dog growled a warning deep in his throat. Scared shitless, he frantically backpedaled pulling the dog with him across the aluminum deck.

Satisfied that the stranger no longer posed a threat, Harry released the man's arm and started barking furiously in Block's face, pawing his leg, instinctively aware that his master was badly hurt. Block stirred; something inside him could still respond to Harry's insistent demand for attention. His eyes opened and he lifted his arm to pat the dog on the head. Harry whined, nuzzled his master, and licked him on the face.

The CH-46 was a beat-up wreck. Olson knew he was going to be flying a rock if he didn't set it down quickly. The controls were shot up, hydraulic fluid had pooled on the deck, and the smell of JP-4 jet fuel reminded him that his gas tanks were leaking like sieves. His Mayday brought news of a small hilltop LZ, in friendly hands, just over the next ridge. *Great*, he thought, *if I can just get this son of a bitch over the hump* …. It would be a minor miracle, because the bottom of the aircraft was already skimming the tops of the trees.

"Okay, baby, here we go," he mumbled, willing the big machine to gain more altitude as the green jungle filled his windscreen. Olson increased power as much as he dared and pulled back on the collective, clearing the ridge with only inches to spare as the last of the hydraulic fluid drained from the lines. Without hydraulic pressure, he lost control of the helicopter and it dropped like a rock, pancaking into the top of the hill with a tremendous crash.

The impact forced the whirling rotor blades to strike the ground and break into jagged sections, which sliced through the air like giant buzz saws, cutting down several men in the immediate vicinity. One was very nearly cut in half as he desperately sought cover. The aluminum skin crumpled, trapping the passengers and crew inside the twisted wreckage, which was quickly awash with fuel from the ruptured cells. As the heavy smell of avgas permeated the air, it seemed like it was only a matter of seconds before the shattered debris caught fire.

31

Lima Company, Hill 540, 1200–1500, 13 September—The sound of an approaching helicopter caught Anderson's attention as the corpsman finished dressing his wounds, chiding him for not turning in to sickbay. "Damn it, Skipper, think of my reputation if you die. The boys won't come to me anymore. My practice will suffer."

"Christ, Doc, the last thing I want is for you to suffer professional embarrassment," he mocked. "I'll make a deal with you. If anyone asks who treated me, I'll say it was that pill pusher in Kilo Company. That'll save your reputation."

"Thanks sir, I knew I could depend on you," the doc responded drolly.

The radio operator interrupted their banter. "Skipper, it's the six. A helicopter's on final."

"Oh shit, I wonder what he wants," Anderson mumbled to himself. *I better get my ass in gear and meet him in the LZ*, he thought, knowing the colonel would be pissed if he wasn't there.

As he rolled his sleeves down over the fresh bandages, the corpsman looked him in the eye. "Skipper, I'm serious. Those wounds need treatment. They're already infected."

"Thanks, Doc. I'll take it easy," Anderson replied, touched by the corpsman's concern. Then he turned and limped to the landing zone.

The Huey gently touched down and tipped slightly on the uneven ground. As the pilot reduced power, its passengers exited.

Lieutenant Colonel Perry Aldine alighted first. Bending low to avoid the whirling blades, he came straight toward Anderson, an angry look on his face. Major Coffman, the battalion sergeant major, and two headquarters radiomen with their equipment followed him out of the helicopter.

"What's the meaning of this, Captain?" Aldine shouted heatedly over the sound of the helo as it took off, gesturing toward the line of foxholes on the perimeter.

Anderson had no idea what the colonel was talking about, and he made the mistake of saying so.

"Captain, your men are unshaven and filthy," he answered sarcastically. "Their uniforms are disreputable. They look like a bunch of rag pickers. Being in the field is no excuse for sloppiness. It's obvious that you've let things get out of hand, and I want it corrected, right now—or I'll find someone who can."

Anderson stiffened, his face reddened, and he opened his mouth to speak. Major Coffman cut him off. "Captain Anderson, before you start, why don't you brief me on yesterday's action for my report. The sergeant major will escort the colonel around the perimeter," he said forcefully, quickly moving forward to guide the furious captain away.

The sergeant major, an old salt, quick on the uptake, gestured to Aldine. "Right this way, Colonel. I know the troops will be inspired to see you here sharing their danger."

Coffman knew the company commander was close to insubordination. As the pair walked away, he whispered, "Keep your mouth shut, Andy."

As soon as the colonel and sergeant major were out of earshot, Anderson unloaded. "Who the hell does that son of a bitch think he is dropping in here and saying things like that? Doesn't he know we were in a hell of a firefight yesterday? How does he fucking expect us to look?"

Coffman watched Anderson closely as he raved on, noting in his eyes the hurt that had been inflicted by Aldine's callous, patronizing remarks. At length, he wound down, which gave Coffman an opportunity to speak. "First, Andy, that SOB happens to be the battalion commander and a senior officer. Remember that when you talk to him," he counseled sternly.

Anderson, who was sorely taken aback by his friend's lack of empathy, started to object. Coffman abruptly cut him off. "Listen to me, goddammit. That man is looking for some pretext to relieve you, so don't give him an excuse to fire your ass!"

"Major, I don't understand. What's he got against me?" Anderson asked, shaken up by what he had just heard.

Coffman explained, "The colonel thinks you showed poor judgment yesterday by splitting the company and sending out a platoon-sized patrol under an inexperienced lieutenant. He also thinks you compounded the mistake by blundering into an ambush and getting the company shot up. Dick Frazier's loss put him over the edge. He can't understand how you could have left him behind."

Anderson was dumbfounded. It was beyond his comprehension that the battalion commander would find fault with his performance. It was particularly galling because Aldine lacked any combat experience and went out of his way to avoid leaving the base, preferring instead to launch company-size operations to avoid jeopardizing his own reputation.

As Anderson struggled to digest this information, Coffman went on, "The real story is that Aldine's scared shitless that something will happen to impact his sterling reputation and keep him from getting promoted. The regimental CO is already sniffing around, wondering why the battalion never goes to the field. So, he's out here now trying to keep his reputation intact and eliminate anything that might be trouble. Don't give him a chance to cut his losses. Relieving you would show he's a bad ass that won't tolerate poor performance. Got the picture?"

Anderson sadly shook his head. "Major, it's not fair."

"What's 'fair' got to do with it, Andy?" Coffman replied. "That's the way it is. Live with it." He paused and smiled, adding, "Don't mean nuthin'"—the all-purpose response to everything from disaster to personal loss.

Despite his feelings, Anderson chuckled. He knew that Coffman was trying to keep his spirits up while making him aware of how things were.

"Now that we've got that behind us," Coffman said, "how about letting me know what happened yesterday, so I can keep the wolves away from your door?"

On the other side of the perimeter, Aldine toured the line of foxholes with the sergeant major, struggling to keep his temper as he came in contact with their occupants. While he understood why no one saluted, they could at least stand at attention. Most seemed to slouch, and they were altogether too familiar. One even had the audacity to speak before he was addressed. The men were filthy—their faces, hands, and arms crusted with dirt—and he shuddered to think of what lurked in their matted hair. Their uniforms were sweat-stained and torn; one man's crotch was completely ripped out and his privates hung disgustingly in plain view. At times, their stench was so overwhelming, especially if they were upwind, that he wanted to retch. He found it difficult to talk with them, so he stuck with innocuous questions: "Where do you live, Marine?" or "Are you getting your mail?" or "How long have you been in-country?"

The sergeant major cringed as he ushered the colonel around the perimeter, his sense of professionalism sorely challenged as he watched the floundering, inept officer. *What a disaster*, he thought. *This man doesn't have a clue about dealing with troops in the field.*

One of the 1st Platoon's squad leaders stared at the colonel's spit-shined combat boots and pressed utilities, so out of place on the jungle hilltop. He wondered what it would be like to feel clean again. While his mind was elsewhere, he missed the colonel's question and had to ask for it to be repeated.

"Are you getting enough to eat?" the officer asked.

Without thinking, the young lance corporal replied, "Shit, Colonel, I'm getting all the ham and motherfuckers I can eat. Nobody else likes them."

Aldine stood speechless while the sergeant major let out a huge guffaw, his body shaking with the effort to control the laughter that had destroyed his composure.

***

Anderson had just completed his account of the action when he heard the sound of a helicopter in trouble. Instinctively, he turned toward the landing zone—just in time to see it plummet into the ground. A cloud of dust and debris erupted, temporarily obscuring the LZ. "Oh my God!" he exclaimed and sprinted toward the crash site, followed by Coffman and several other would-be rescuers.

As the air cleared, the LZ looked like a scene out of hell. The shattered airframe, barely recognizable as a helicopter, lay in the center of a debris-ridden field that stretched for dozens of yards. Pieces of aluminum and chunks of rotor blade were strewn in the grass. One large piece hung from the limb of an old tree—mute testimony to the force of the crash. Tendrils of smoke curled up from the wreckage, threatening the rescue effort with the risk of a catastrophic fire. The rotor blades had sheared off, tearing up the ground around the wreckage before cleaving the air as deadly missiles, which wreaked havoc with the nearby mortar crews. A mutilated corpse sprawled across the berm of the mortar pit. The man had been caught by fragments as he was trying to take cover. Another Marine lay in the grass, surrounded by stunned buddies, while a corpsman worked desperately to staunch the bleeding from a severed artery.

The helicopter had crumpled in on itself, blocking the side hatch and trapping the passengers in a space only three feet high. A jumble of torn metal, the cockpit had been partially torn away by one of the rotor blades. It had cut through the airframe like a hot knife through butter, killing the wounded co-pilot. Blood from his mangled body splattered the inside, pooling near his lifeless feet. The unconscious pilot, still in his seat, hung forward, suspended from his shoulder belts.

An NCO shouted, "Get back, it might blow!" as several rescuers pulled pieces of aluminum skin off the side in an effort to gain entrance. One man ignored the warning and crawled through the opening, grabbed the crew chief under the arms, and heaved him to safety.

Another rescuer took his place and found Block, unconscious and trapped in a welter of debris. As he struggled to free him, Block stopped breathing. Yelling for help, the rescuer administered mouth-to-mouth resuscitation until a corpsman forced his way into the small space and took over. After some anxious moments, Block revived and started breathing on his own, although it was obvious he was in a bad way. As they started to pull him free, a menacing growl from underneath the loose wreckage brought their effort up short.

Coffman and Anderson waded right in, struggling to wrest open the severely jammed pilot's door, ignoring the overpowering stench of aviation fuel that permeated the air. A voice called out, "Stand back!" and a huge man muscled the two aside and took hold of the doorframe. Stunned, Anderson glanced over and watched Petrovitch grasp the metal and give it an exploratory tug, measuring the resistance. Then, placing one foot on the fuselage for leverage, the immense machine gunner tightened his hold and heaved with all his might. Veins stood out on his neck as he strained with the effort. The door gave way with a sound of tortured metal, separating from the frame enough for Anderson to reach into the cockpit and release Olson from his shoulder and lap belts. Free from the restraints, the pilot was pulled out of the wreckage. As he gasped for breath, he was rushed to a temporary aid station. A corpsman quickly hyperextended his neck while another inserted an airway into his throat, allowing him to breathe freely.

As Anderson watched the docs work, he heard someone yell for a pistol and saw two men hurriedly scramble backwards out of the crumpled passenger compartment. *What the hell is going on now?* he sighed as he ran toward them.

"Skipper, the dog won't let us touch his handler. He about bit my head off when I tried to pull him out," one of the frightened rescuers explained. "We'll have to shoot him."

A sudden memory struck Anderson—about a dog team that had been attached to his company near Cam Lo. The dog had alerted in time to keep them from walking into an ambush. "No. Stand back. I'll give it a try," he resignedly offered, the image of the ferocious animal's attack on one of the NVA still fresh in his mind.

Fuel-soaked Anderson's clothing as he crawled into the crumpled wreckage. There was just enough space to snake through the tangle of crushed aluminum, electrical wiring, and miscellaneous debris. Sunlight flooded the interior through rents in the helo's skin, enabling him to see the dog lying protectively alongside the handler, chin propped on the man's shoulder. The animal watched intently as Anderson crawled forward. Suddenly, Harry raised his head and growled menacingly. In a frightening display of ferocity, he curled its lips back to show huge teeth. *Jesus Christ, I'm a dead man*, Anderson thought as he looked into the maw of the enraged animal from a distance of three feet. He froze, afraid that even the slightest movement would precipitate an attack. He tried to think of a plan, but he was brain dead. *Don't show fear. Don't show fear*, his mind screamed, even as he realized the trite phase was bullshit. The dog was going to tear him a new asshole, maybe two.

The handler unexpectedly moaned, breaking the stalemate. The Shepherd stopped growling and shifted his attention to his master. He began to lick

Block's face and whined piteously, knowing that his partner was hurt and needed help. "It's now or never," Anderson mumbled to himself as he inched forward. "Easy, big guy. I'm here to help," he said softly over and over, hoping the dog would be soothed by his voice. He reached forward, gently hooked his hand under the handler's shoulder, and slid the unconscious man toward him.

The brute leaped to its feet, as if to attack, sending a shot of adrenaline through Anderson's bloodstream. The dog advanced, stopping inches from the prone officer's upturned face and stared, waiting for the human to react. Anderson froze, praying the animal wouldn't attack. *My God*, he thought, *he'll rip my face off.*

Then, to Anderson's surprise, the dog suddenly leaned forward and licked the captain's face. It was as obvious a gesture of acceptance and trust as could be demonstrated between species.

Anderson came unglued, nearly pissing his pants, shaking all over from relieved tension. "Jesus Christ, you scared the shit out of me," he croaked from a cotton-filled mouth as he warily patted the animal on the side of the head. Minutes later, he emerged from the side of the aircraft with the handler in tow. Several rescuers came forward to help but stopped at the sight of the big dog eying them from the wreckage.

"It's okay. He won't hurt you," Anderson declared.

"Right sir," one of them skeptically replied, edging behind a corpsman, who unreservedly stepped forward to help. Many willing hands loaded Block onto a stretcher and gently carried him away, all too aware of the huge canine that ambled alongside, guardedly watching every movement.

Another rescuer crawled inside the wreckage and, after a few minutes, backed out, yelling excitedly, "Skipper! It's Lieutenant Frazier, and he's alive. Unconscious, but alive!"

Anderson whirled around and stared at the sight of his missing platoon commander being tenderly lifted from the destroyed helicopter. He ran forward, taking Frazier's limp hand as Doc Zimmer quickly checked the badly injured lieutenant's vital signs.

"God, he's a mess," Anderson mumbled. Tears came to his eyes as he gaped at the battered face. "How is he, Doc?" he asked.

"I got a pulse, sir, but it's weak. He's lost a lot of blood." As Zimmer reported, he ripped a bottle of Serum Albumin off the straps of his Unit 1. "Hold this bottle," he ordered the company commander as he prepared to insert a needle into Frazier's arm. He jabbed and swore, "Shit, I can't find a vein," and tried again, finally succeeding in locating a blood vessel. He expertly inserted the needle and taped it down, then started a more detailed examination.

"Skipper, Mister Frazier's got a possible concussion, blood poisoning in his wounded ear, and I think he may have internal injuries from the crash, but I can't be sure. He needs immediate treatment by specialists at a field hospital."

"Doc, we're trying to get a chopper in now," Anderson replied, "but it may be a while. With the LZ blocked by the wreckage, they're diverting one from down south with a hoist. Do what you can for him and the rest of the wounded."

Word of Frazier's miraculous appearance made the rounds of the perimeter, reaching the 2nd Platoon within minutes. A cheer went up and, as one, they jumped out of their foxholes and started running toward the LZ, only to be stopped dead in their tracks by Gunny Smith's booming command, "Stop, goddam it! Where the hell do you think you're going? Get back to your holes till I tell you otherwise. Stay on guard."

32

1st Battalion, North Vietnamese Army, 1500, 13 September—Lieutenant Colonel Duc stood alongside the trail with Majors Co and Minh, watching as guides from the reconnaissance platoon directed the men into the heavily camouflaged assembly areas. He scrutinized the soldiers closely, trying to detect any signs of weakness as a result of yesterday's heavy bombing that had decimated the 3rd Company. Duc knew most of the men by name and spoke softly to them as they passed. Many of the older men responded shyly, trading good-natured quips with their elder brother in the relaxed manner of combat veterans. Duc enjoyed the easy camaraderie; such exchanges usually boosted his spirits. It was his way of gauging morale. To his trained eye, the fighters appeared alert and ready for battle.

Satisfied with what he had observed, Duc turned to his runner and ordered him to pass the word for the unit leaders to join him at the command bunker. Lieutenants Chiem and Khuong, the commanders of the 1st and 2nd companies, were the first to arrive. They were followed by the reconnaissance platoon commander, Lieutenant Doi, and finally Senior Sergeant Thanh, who struggled up the trail barely able to walk because of his wounds but still refusing to relinquish command of his sapper platoon.

They gathered around a large earthen mock-up of their objective, the American-held hill two kilometers west of their position. Lieutenant Doi's men had painstakingly constructed the detailed replica based on the information they had gathered during their reconnaissance of the American position. It showed the location of the perimeter foxholes, machine gun and mortar positions, landing zone, and the general location of the command post. The mock-up also included the approach routes the battalion would use in the attack, as well as natural obstacles that might interfere with their movement. The terrain model was standard procedure in the army, as it provided an excellent opportunity for the officers to study the ground and defenses without exposing themselves and alerting the enemy. In this manner, they maintained secrecy, stealth, and the element of surprise.

Duc began the brief by repeating the orders from the regimental commander. "Little brothers, we have been chosen to strike the first blow against the Americans on the plateau. Colonel Anh has directed us to kill all the imperialists on the hill. The loss of so many will terrify their comrades, making them too fearful to come here again. Our preparations for the attack on Khe Sanh will remain secret."

Duc watched their reactions, wondering if they really understood the significance of the order. The older veterans, Co and Thanh, knew it meant possible death or horrible injury, while the two young company commanders only saw the attack as a proving ground for themselves. They were still naïve enough to regard it as an opportunity to strike a major blow for the fatherland and liberation.

Holding a slender bamboo stick to point out key features, Duc outlined the general plan of attack, which used a scheme of maneuver they had practiced dozens of times. "The battalion will attack here," he began, moving the tip of the makeshift pointer to indicate the draw that led into the middle of the hill. "Lieutenant Chiem's 'Glorious Victory' Company will lead the attack, followed by Lieutenant Khuong and his 'Southern Liberation' Company." He stopped to see if there were any questions, then continued. "Senior Sergeant Thanh's *Dac Cong* will precede each company, infiltrate the American position, and destroy weapons and communications." Then, pointing to an opening in the jungle, he said, "Major Co will support the infiltration and main attack with the 82mm mortars from this position. Doi's reconnaissance platoon will give us guides to take us to the objective and provide security during the march. We will withdraw only after the Americans have been destroyed."

Duc continued with a more detailed discussion, beginning with the two company commanders. In the lively dialogue that followed, the officers thoroughly reviewed all aspects of the plan, ensuring that everyone knew exactly what was expected. Duc had each man verbally walk through his unit's role several times, throwing in "what ifs" to test their ability to react in case of unforeseen circumstances. He wanted them to act independently in case something went wrong, and he encouraged questions—much to the surprise and annoyance of Major Minh, who would never have allowed subordinates to probe his plan.

Deep down, Minh knew that he lacked Duc's tactical and leadership competence and covered his own inadequacies with bluster and threat. He loathed the ease with which Duc wore the mantle of leadership and looked for ways to undercut him, albeit without bringing attention to himself. Minh hated Duc, but he was terrified that Duc would discover and expose his cowardice under fire.

Finally satisfied that the leaders knew the plan, Duc directed the attack group of 300 *Bo doi* to depart for the objective just after dusk. The reconnaissance platoon would lead them over a carefully selected route, which provided ease of movement as well as concealment from observation, to a final assembly area a hundred meters from the base of the hill. Duc indicated that he would be with the 1st Company and would establish a command post in the assembly area. After addressing various communication signals, he then set the time of attack for 0100, giving them more than five hours to get in position.

Senior Sergeant Thanh waited patiently for Duc to finish outlining the plan for the two company commanders. He expected that his turn would come next, and he was not disappointed. Duc turned and looked intently into his eyes, searching for some indication that Thanh was not up to the task. The depleted sapper platoon was to be the spearhead of the attack, a critical element of the plan. These elite troops were to infiltrate the American position, open a hole for the *Bo doi*, and create a diversion. If they failed, the main attack would be exposed to the full fire power of the defenders. Thanh held his commander's stare, refusing to break eye contact, almost daring the officer to question his platoon's ability.

As Duc began to outline the sappers' mission, he sensed Thanh's resentment. He stopped and asked the battle-tested veteran for his own solution. Thanh nodded in acknowledgement of Duc's unspoken challenge. Without hesitation, he described how his platoon would carry out its mission. He used the mock-up, much as Duc had done, to illustrate his plan. "Comrades, I propose sending my brave fighters against the cowardly imperialists just after dusk, which will give them more than enough time to infiltrate the position. I do not expect any difficulty. My *Dac Cong* are thoroughly trained, and the American defenses are weak. An assault arrow, made up of three four-man cells, will precede each company," he said, surprising the officers with his articulate presentation. "The penetration cells will mark paths through obstacles for your infantry and disarm any booby traps and mines they encounter." Thanh smiled inwardly, pleased with the impression he was creating. *Do these foolish officers think they're the only ones who can talk intelligently?* he mused, then continued. "After my *Dac Cong* pierce the imperialist lines, shock cells will pass through and destroy the targets with demolitions. Rocket-propelled grenades from the fire cell will support them. My sappers will open the gate for you," he added in a rather condescending tone, and then he compounded the mistake by smugly adding, "You should not have any trouble overcoming the remaining opposition." Turning to Duc, he came to attention and asked impertinently, "*Trung Ta*, do you have any questions?"

Duc stared intently at Thanh, his eyes smoldering with anger. "*Trung Si*, don't be so smug. The Americans are worthy opponents. You, of all people, should know that," he said mockingly, alluding to Thanh's drubbing in the bunker complex. The color drained from the sapper leader's face as he registered the insult, but he remained stiffly at attention, comprehending that there was nothing he could do—at the moment.

You've gone too far, elder brother, Thanh thought. *The confusion of a night attack might provide an opportunity to get even. A bullet out of the darkness could make things right.*

Closely observing the exchange, Minh noted the glint in Thanh's eyes. He wondered if he had found an ally.

33

Reconnaissance Team Knife Edge, 1500, 13 September—Gunfire erupted from the undergrowth, sending the recon Marines scrambling for cover. "Shoot back, shoot back!" Wilson shouted over the roar of the low-flying helicopter and the rattle of small arms fire. As he hit the ground, the team instantly responded, pouring out a heavy volume of automatic weapons fire in an attempt to keep the enemy from rushing the small perimeter. The Marines reacted instinctively, falling back on the hours of grueling immediate-action drills that had taught them how to counter ambushes. Their rifles and machine guns added to the cacophony of deafening sound in the close confines of the jungle streambed. It was impossible to hear their leaders.

The NVA had made a major tactical blunder by directing most of their fire at the helicopter. This gave the Marines on the ground time to organize.

Gunny French crawled from man to man, directing their fire, pointing out targets, and reassuring them with his calm presence. Meantime, Wilson attempted to establish contact with the gunships that circled protectively overhead. Grabbing the handset from his radio operator, he called urgently, "Gunslinger, this is Knife Edge. Seaworthy's hit and we're taking fire. We need help. Over."

"Roger, Knife Edge. We copy. Where are you?"

"We're right under Seaworthy. Blast anything 50 meters outboard of him," Wilson transmitted, and then shouted at his Marines, "Take cover!"

"Edge, this is Gunslinger. Keep your head down. Here we come."

Violent explosions rocked the jungle as the gunships cut loose with salvoes of 2.75-inch rockets. Shock waves rolled over the prone Marines, bouncing them up and down in the detritus of the forest floor while shrapnel ripped through the foliage over their heads, showering them with vegetation.

"Jesus Christ! That was close," Wilson exclaimed as he coughed on the cordite that permeated the air and left an acrid taste in his mouth. "Damn rockets rang my chimes," he mumbled, shaking his head to clear the dramatic effects of the powerful detonations. Using his rifle for support, he rose shakily to his knees and called out anxiously, "Anybody hurt?" He expected the worse, but the team signaled that everyone was fine, just shaken up.

It was then that Wilson noticed how quiet it had become. It was as if someone had turned a loud radio off. There were no Vietnamese voices, no chattering AK-47s—just the faint sound of Seaworthy limping away. *The rockets must have gotten them*, he thought, and shouted, "Gunny, saddle up. Now's the time to get the hell out of here, before the gooks recover."

"We're running, Gunslinger," the radio operator panted into his handset as the recon team trotted along the rough trail that paralleled the stream.

The two gunships rolled in to blast the area with rockets and machine gun fire, hoping to cool the ardor of any pursuit and give the team a good head start. Moments later, the lead pilot transmitted, "Knife Edge, this is Gunslinger. You've got bad guys about 30 minutes behind you, moving fast. We tried to slow them down, but they pushed right through. Tough little bastards. You must have pissed them off."

"Gunslinger, would it help to apologize?" the operator cockily replied.

The gunship pilot chuckled and keyed the intercom, "The kid's got more balls than brains; I'd be scared shitless if I were in his shoes." His co-pilot nodded enthusiastically, then pointed to the fuel gauge.

"Knife Edge, this is Gunslinger. We have to depart the area. Bingo fuel and bullets. Sorry, but you're on your own. Good luck."

"Roger, Gunslinger. Thanks for your help. We're going to miss you," the operator broadcast, sounding a lot more confident than he felt.

***

"Shot," Wilson repeated, standing in the middle of the team's defensive circle, listening intently for the sound of the artillery round.

They had been on the run for more than an hour and had been forced to stop for a break. Sensing that the hunters were closing in, Wilson had turned to the heavily breathing man beside him. "Gunny, we've got to slow them down. We can't keep this pace up much longer."

"You're right there, Lieutenant. I'm the meanest muther in the valley and I'm a tad played out."

Wilson smiled despite himself. The gunny was never out of character. "Let's see if a few dozen rounds of artillery will take some of the starch out of them."

The two men carefully studied Wilson's tactical map before agreeing on a rough approximation of their position. After calling in the urgent fire mission, Wilson listened for the fire warning: "Shot."

He involuntarily hunched his shoulders at the tell-tale *pop* and ripping sound of an incoming round, hoping the coordinates were right. This was not the time to have a friendly round land in their laps.

"*Wham!*" The sound of the explosion reverberated through the dense jungle growth, making it difficult to pinpoint its location.

"What d'ya think, Gunny?" he asked. He needed a second opinion before he would fire another round.

"Shit, Lieutenant, what've you got to lose—except maybe your ass. Drop 400 and no deflection. We're on the gun-target line," he replied. Then he shrugged his shoulders and grinned.

Wilson looked intently at French for a moment, then made his decision and nodded. The operator called it in.

Muted explosions sounded behind them as they hurried along the trail. The gunny's correction had been right on, although a little too close for comfort. Shrapnel had damn near killed one of them when he lifted his head to see what was going on. A large shard glanced off Campbell's helmet, knocking him on his ass and denting the hell out of the steel pot. He became an instant celebrity—and the brunt of a great deal of good-natured ribbing, which Wilson took as a good sign; morale was good, despite their fatigue.

The gunny had taken the lead again, setting a fast pace, which had everyone breathing hard within minutes. *The old fart's like a Timex—takes a lickin', but keeps on tickin',* Wilson thought to himself as he forced himself to keep up. He looked at the others and saw the same determination on their faces. *No quitters on this team. It'd be a cold day in hell before they let that old man best them.*

At the faint sound of voices, French stopped in mid-stride and froze, unconsciously taking a firing stance—rifle extended, butt pressed tightly under his arm, muzzle aligned with his body, finger taking up the trigger slack.

The column stopped, each man holding his position, screening a designated sector of the jungle. They all tensed, feeding on a subliminal message of danger.

The gunny slowly sank to the ground and wormed forward toward a bend in the trail, sweat pouring off his body from the exertion and the adrenalin-stimulated tension. Suddenly, the realization that he was totally exposed—all alone—hit him, the overwhelming fear threatening to paralyze him. *What the hell's the matter with me?* he thought as he struggled to overcome the frightening sensation. *This has never happened to me before.*

He stopped altogether, fighting to gain control of his emotions, just as he felt someone grab his ankle. Panic seized him as he savagely twisted around, gun at the ready—and looked directly into Lieutenant Wilson's startled eyes.

"Jesus Christ, you scared the shit out of me," he whispered emotionally. "I almost blew you away!"

Wilson swallowed hard as he realized how close he had been to dying, staring into the business end of the M-16. "Sorry Gunny," he croaked softly. "I didn't like the idea of you out here by yourself. Next time, I'll honk," he added, attempting to make light of the deadly serious encounter.

"Do that, Lieutenant," French replied abruptly, still too keyed up to laugh it off.

The two leaders carefully moved off the exposed trail into the foliage, working their way up the slope toward the Vietnamese voices, which now included the unmistakable sound of digging. Their progress was measured in inches, as they silently crawled the last few meters to the top of the hill, acutely aware that the smallest amount of noise meant discovery and certain death.

A light breeze wafted over the two infiltrators, bringing the tell-tale stink of fish and wood smoke, which seemed overpowering even in the dense vegetation. The proximity of danger sharpened their senses, and even the slightest odor and the tiniest sound were magnified tenfold.

They reached the edge of the brush line and moved into the cover of a large ground fern, which rendered them virtually invisible in the shadow of its fronds.

Holding his breath, Wilson gingerly parted the foliage and saw five heavily camouflaged Vietnamese digging a pit less than 30 feet away. A second group was at work several meters to their right, and a third team was busily setting up a mortar in a brush-concealed pit to the left.

Wilson allowed the fronds to straighten. In that few seconds of observation, he had seen enough to know that he was looking at an NVA 82mm mortar platoon.

At that moment, French squeezed his arm in warning. Several men were on the move through brush, right toward them.

There was nothing they could do except lie there and pray.

A large creepy-crawly dropped off a leaf and landed on the back of French's neck, sending a spasm of loathing to his brain. *I hate fucking bugs*, he cursed silently, fighting the urge to reach up and slap the shit out of the damn thing. He hated that he was lying face-down, defenseless, as Vietnamese closed on his hiding place. *Shit. I won't even see the fucker who kills me*, he thought.

At French's side, Wilson looked at the gunny and marveled at how calm he seemed, even as a damn huge bug crawled over his neck.

That's all I need, Wilson mused. *I hate bugs.* He was certain that he wouldn't have been able to keep from slapping the shit out of it. His heart beat wildly against the ground, so hard he wondered whether the NVA could feel the tremors.

Five heavily laden North Vietnamese infantrymen passed within three feet of their hiding place without even glancing in their direction, too busy shooting the shit to notice the concealed Americans.

As soon as the NVA had passed, Wilson reached over and flicked the loathsome creature off the gunny's neck, smiling maniacally. The two exchanged meaningful glances and slowly backed out of the position, concentrating on keeping as quiet as possible.

As he prepared to defend himself, he caught a glimpse of an NVA soldier carrying a bayoneted AK-47 just as the guy dashed past, so intent on some errand further down the hill that he didn't notice them.

Spurred on by this second close call, they quickly retraced their route, assembled the team, and moved into the thick undergrowth.

"Gunny, what do you make of this?" Wilson asked, to see if the older veteran's input matched his own assumption.

"Lieutenant, I don't think that mortar platoon is just on a training exercise. They're setting up to hit someone, and my guess is it's Lima Company."

Wilson nodded. He spread out his tactical map and pointed to the NVA's location. "The range of an 82mm is something like three thousand meters. Lima's hill is two thousand meters from the mortars, and there aren't any other targets in this damn jungle."

"The question is, Lieutenant, what are we going to do about it?"

"I'll tell you what we're going to do, Gunny; we're getting the hell out of here—but quick, before the rest of the gooks show up."

34

Lima Company, Hill 540, 1500, 13 September—Anderson spotted Coffman as the major sauntered toward him. He knew by the way he walked that something was up. They had been together so long that body language was an important part of their vocabulary.

"Andy," Coffman cheerfully asked as he approached, "what do you want first—the good news or the bad news?"

"Major, why do I think I'm going to get screwed regardless of which one I choose?"

Acting as if he were offended, Coffman said with a lilt, "Captain, I resent your inference that a field grade officer would do such a vulgar thing to you. I'm quite disappointed. In my day, junior officers were more respectful of their seniors."

"'In my day,' ha," Anderson retorted. "With all due respect, sir, you were a company grade officer last week. As I recall, you were just promoted, but, what the hell, give me the good news first."

Coffman suddenly turned serious. "Andy, I'm spending the night."

"That's great, sir. You're welcome anytime," Anderson replied with genuine enthusiasm. "I can use the help, especially if the gooks hit us."

"I wasn't finished," Coffman added. "I'm not going to be alone. The colonel is also staying."

Anderson started to smile, thinking it must be a joke. But the look on the major's face convinced him it was true. "Christ sir, I thought you said the colonel wouldn't stay in the field."

"I did," Coffman replied, "but it's promotion time, and he figures a little action will help his cause."

"'A little action,'" Anderson sputtered. "Does he have any idea what we may be in for if the gooks get real serious?"

Coffman looked Anderson in the eye and replied levelly, "Andy, the colonel doesn't have a clue. He's never seen action. He thinks it'll be a little small arms fire, maybe a mortar round or two, and then he'll write himself up for a decoration. I'm telling you; this guy has his head up his ass."

Anderson thought for a moment before responding in a disgusted tone, "Now I know why he didn't want us to evacuate this hill. He wants a fight so he can look like a hero."

"Captain," an approaching voice cut in, "your men still look like hobos. Why haven't they cleaned up?" Aldine demanded, stepping angrily to Coffman's side.

Anderson was at a loss. He had the entire company busting its ass to complete preparations for the expected enemy assault. There simply was no time for the battalion commander's foolishness. *I'd rather have dirty troops than dead ones*, he wanted to say, but he knew that would just further infuriate the colonel. Instead, he answered, "I'm sorry sir. I'll get right on it as soon as we're dug in,"

"See to it, Captain. I won't have slovenly troops in my battalion," Aldine pompously replied and stalked off to the foxhole his radio operators had dug for him.

Anderson stood still for a moment to watch the senior officer walk away. He wondered how the man had gotten so far in the Corps. The system had failed to weed him out, and now the men he was responsible for were saddled with an incompetent commander. *Christ we're lucky to have Ron Coffman with us*, he thought. *We'd be up shit creek without a paddle.*

***

"Major," Sergeant Major Richards asked as the officer patted another shovelful of dirt onto the berm of his foxhole. "Where will you be if the shit hits the fan?"

The radio operators had volunteered to dig Coffman's hole for him, but he had refused their offer. He was a field Marine through and through, and he would damn sure dig his own hole.

Coffman stood up to button his blouse despite the sweltering afternoon heat. The colonel had just chewed him out for taking it off even though shoveling was hard work in the root-filled soil. "Sergeant Major, I'll take one of the radio operators and join Captain Anderson. He may need help."

"Okay, sir. I'll take the other operator and stay with the colonel. He may need help too."

The two men looked at each other, completely understanding the hidden meaning in the comment. At that moment they were interrupted by Aldine's strident call: "Sergeant Major, would you come over here?"

186

"Be right there, sir," Richards answered, as Coffman leaned over and extended a hand to help him. The older man took it and stepped out of the waist-deep hole, maintaining the clasp as he stood up, face to face with the officer. "Be careful, Major," he said with feeling. "You're a fine man, and I'd hate to lose you." Then he solemnly shook Coffman's hand, picked up his shotgun, and walked off toward the colonel's foxhole, leaving the surprised officer feeling like he'd just been awarded a medal.

Aldine sat with his back against a tree stump as he wrote on a message pad. "What kept you?" he brusquely demanded, not bothering to look up.

"Sorry, sir," the battalion's most senior enlisted man replied with a trace of anger in his voice. "The major and I were finishing a discussion."

Aldine looked up when he heard the irritation and sarcastically countered, "Sergeant Major, do I have to remind you who the senior officer is in this battalion?"

The older man stiffened and stared down at him, eyes now blazing with anger. *This is too much*, he thought. *I'm no goddam boot, and I don't intend to be treated like one.*

"Colonel," he said in a composed, blunt voice. "I think we need to get something straight between us. I asked to serve in this battalion because I wanted to finish my career as an infantryman, and I thought my experience could be of some help to the younger Marines."

Aldine started to interrupt, but the sergeant major held up his hand. "Allow me to finish, sir. When I rotate back to the States, I'll retire on 30. This is my last assignment, so nothing you can do can hurt me. On the other hand, if you continue to shit on me and the Marines of this company, I'll go to the regimental commander and drop a dime on your head. Your call."

Aldine stared up at the man, seething with anger. "Who the hell do you think you're talking to?" he raged as he scrambled to his feet.

Unruffled, Richards responded calmly, "Sir, with all due respect to your rank, we both know who I'm talking to. You couldn't lead a Girl Scout troop to the head, and you know it."

Aldine's furious retort died stillborn. The sergeant major's derision hit home, piercing the man's fragile self-confidence like an arrow through a balloon. He shrank before the unwavering gaze of the senior enlisted man, seeming to fold into himself as he struggled for some semblance of dignity.

The sergeant major's facial expression betrayed nothing, but inwardly he sifted through a variety of emotions, ranging from pity to revulsion before finally settling on disgust. After all, this officer had accepted the responsibility for the lives of hundreds of Marines even though he knew he wasn't up to the task. And for that, Richards had no compassion. Finally, making up his mind, he addressed his commander, showing all the deference due an officer,

"Colonel, I suggest you talk with the regimental commander when we get back about a command more in line with your talents."

Aldine stared at the ground, unwilling to look his subordinate in the eye. He simply nodded before turning around and walking dejectedly toward his foxhole.

Sergeant Major Richards watched him go, thinking that in all his years of service, he had never experienced anything even remotely close to this. He suffered a momentary twinge of doubt, but at that moment he looked up the slope and caught sight of the company commander striding purposely toward a group of his men—and he knew he had made the right decision. Combat was no place for a weakling; men's lives depended on strong leaders. Men like Aldine needed to be mercilessly weeded out.

***

Anderson looked over the assembly of officers and noncoms, wishing he could give them a good reason why they were sitting on this godforsaken knob, but nothing came to mind. The damn place was just like every other no-name hill and hardscrabble patch of ground they had humped over for the past four months. It wasn't worth the sweat off a good Marine's brow, but here they were, on this rock pile, and nobody was going to kick them off. With that thought firing him up, he got back to the business at hand—a last brief before dark.

"Okay, you all know about the gooks Edwards greased this morning and the luminous markers we found in front of the 3rd Platoon. It's pretty obvious they're checking us out. I think it's a definite indication they're going to hit us."

The mortar section leader interrupted. "Skipper, do you think the gooks'll attack tonight?"

Anderson eyeballed the man and scoffed, "Does a bear shit in the woods?" The quip brought out a few belly laughs at the expense of the young NCO, but they cut through the tension.

Anderson continued in a serious tone. "If it's anything like that time in the DMZ, they'll hit us after midnight, when they think we're crapped out. That's why I want 50-percent alert—one man in every foxhole bright-eyed and bushy-tailed."

He looked at the inexperienced Napoline and Littleton before saying, "Platoon commanders, I want the lines checked every hour. Set up a rotation. I don't want some damn gook running around inside the perimeter because somebody doped off."

Turning back to the group he asked, "Any questions?"

Gunny Smith spoke up first. "Skipper, how many listening posts do you want?"

"I want one per platoon," he replied. "First and second platoons cover the trail, Third Platoon include the gully where we found the comm wire—"

The cry of "Chopper inbound!" interrupted his brief again, just before the faint sound of rotor blades caught his attention.

"One last thing: I don't want anyone shooting, especially the machine guns, unless they're actually attacking. Use grenades. You all know how they like to pinpoint our positions so they can knock them out before the assault." He paused, finishing with, "okay, that's it for now. I'll check the lines after the chopper leaves."

The CH-46 hovered over the wreckage-strewn LZ as the crew chief maneuvered the external sling load of supplies and ammunition toward a small cleared space along its edge. It was a tricky maneuver, because the rotor wash stirred up clouds of dust and debris, limiting visibility and creating an updraft. After several anxious moments, when it seemed as if the rotors would clip the trees, the crew chief finally winched the load down until it hit the ground. A Marine immediately jumped up on the pile and disconnected the cable hook, freeing the cargo net.

The helicopter rose to orbit the LZ as a working party hurriedly carted the supplies away and the stretcher bearers prepared the wounded for evacuation. That done, a radio operator signaled the helicopter to return.

Anderson nervously watched as the first of them was winched aboard the helicopter. Next up was Frazier, who lay unconscious at his feet. Anderson prayed that the young man would make it alive to the field hospital. The doc had done a great job of keeping him alive, but it was still touch and go. Frazier required extensive specialized medical treatment—immediately. They strapped him into the Stokes litter, and Anderson patted the battered officer on the shoulder as he rose upward. "Hang in there, Dick. You're going to make it," he shouted over the engine noise, trying to convince himself that Frazier still had a chance.

Faster than Anderson thought possible, the rest of the wounded were hoisted up until only Block and Harry remained. "This is going to be damn tricky," Anderson remarked to one of the stretcher bearers as he watched the dog stand guard over his handler. "Both of them can't be lifted at once. We've got to separate them."

One of the young Marines studied the animal, analyzing what it would take to subdue the huge brute. "Poncho," he confidently announced, and explained his plan.

Four volunteers moved close to the growling animal, each holding an edge of a poncho. On the count of three they sprang forward and threw it over the dog, struggling to wrestle him to the ground without getting bitten. The big dog reacted violently, lunging forward in attack despite the poncho over his body. The Marines kept their grip and, under their combined weight, forced Harry to the ground. They quickly wrapped the ground cloth around his head and used belts to tie his legs together, completely immobilizing the animal. Then, they secured the enraged beast in the litter and signaled the crew chief to hoist away. One of the volunteers shouted out, "Don't mean nothing, Harry," then shook his head and declared, "I'd hate to be the sucker that unwraps that puppy." Harry's furious growls echoed over the sound of the engines as he was winched up. Block followed moments later, and then the helicopter departed with its load of wounded.

Anderson heard his name called and turned to see his radio operator running toward him lugging the PRC-25. "Skipper, it's Knife Edge Actual," he said as handed over the handset. "He wants to talk to you right away."

"Knife Edge, this is Lima-Six. Over," Anderson responded, wondering why the reconnaissance officer was calling him.

Wilson's ragged voice instantly filled the airwaves. "Lima-Six, there's beaucoup NVA on our ass and they've got us on the run. We're headed for your position. Please don't shoot us as we come in. Over."

"Roger, Knife Edge," Anderson quickly responded, knowing this wasn't the time to find out what the hell was going on. "Which way you coming in and what's your ETA?"

"Lima, we're about 20 minutes away, on a trail heading north toward you. Over."

"Okay, Knife Edge. Hold up when you get to the bottom of the hill and sing out so we know you're there."

"Roger, Lima. On the way. Out."

"Somebody screwed up," Anderson mumbled as he headed toward the 2nd Platoon's lines. "I didn't even know the team was close to us."

35

Reconnaissance Team Knife Edge, 1900 13 September—"This is not good, Lieutenant," French panted as he jogged alongside Wilson. "I'm done in and I know the rest of the men are about finished."

The past three hours had been a nightmare. The North Vietnamese pursuit had forced the team to keep going without rest, and now Wilson's Marines were at the end of their endurance.

"Gunny, there's nothing we can do except keep going," Wilson answered between gasps. "We're almost to the hill."

Both men were burdened with extra gear from the men who couldn't carry it any longer because they were being half-carried, half-dragged by their teammates. It was just a matter of time before the NVA ran them to ground. Both men knew that, once that happened, it was all over; the enemy soldiers would surround them, cut off their withdrawal, and overwhelm them. They *had* to keep going.

"Lieutenant, give me your grenades and extra ammo," French suddenly demanded in a voice that suggested the request wasn't up for discussion. Misunderstanding the man, Wilson replied, "Gunny, I'm okay. I can pack my own load."

"I know that, Lieutenant. It's me that can't go on," he revealed in a matter-of-fact tone. "I'm losing too much blood."

Wilson stopped in mid-stride. "Gunny! Are you hit?"

"Through-and-through. Right side below my rib cage," French replied unemotionally, as if this were a clinical discussion. "Didn't hit any major organs, but I can't stop the bleeding."

"Shit. Why didn't you say something?" Wilson asked. "The doc could have helped."

"No time. The gooks would have gotten us. Now give me the ammunition; I'll need it to hold them off until you get away."

"No way," Wilson replied vehemently. "We aren't kamikazes."

French looked him in the eye. "Face up to it, Lieutenant. I can't keep going at this pace. The gooks'll kill the whole team. Someone's got to slow them down, and I'm it. I'll hold them off for a while, then escape and evade to Lima's position."

Wilson struggled with his emotions. Leaving Gunny French would be the most difficult decision he had ever taken in his life. He felt like a coward, because he was running out on one of the best men he had ever known, leaving him to die all alone. Despite what French said, both men knew there was little chance for survival. The best French could hope for was to kill a few of the pursuers and slow the others down before they killed him. The two argued back and forth until Wilson realized the gunny was going to stay, with or without his approval.

They left French behind a large tree root, where he had a clear view of their back trail. The team had taken two Claymores and placed them in a position to sweep the footpath. They also passed the gunny their extra magazines and grenades. The NVA would pay hell to take the position.

Before leaving, Wilson tried to express his feelings, but French would have none of it. "I don't like wakes, Lieutenant," he whispered. "They make me sad. Now get the hell out of here before I change my mind."

At that, the two men solemnly shook hands. Wilson touched Gunny French on the shoulder and said, "See you on the hill, Gunny."

Keeping up the charade, French replied, "Right, sir. I'll be right along, just as soon as I dust off a few gooks."

Wilson stood upright at attention and brought his right hand to the brim of his jungle hat in a crisp salute. Then he turned and jogged up the trail.

Wilson had barely caught up with the team when he was startled by the sound of muffled explosions, which could only mean one thing: Gunny French had set off the Claymores. The implication staggered him, not because the ambush was unexpected, but for what it represented—French was fighting their Alamo. As the reverberations died away and Wilson could hear the clatter of automatic weapons, he experienced an overwhelming urge to go back. Unconsciously, he looked back over his shoulder and shuddered, weighed down with the burden of the gunny's lone fight. He knew the drama would follow a deadly choreographed maneuver of ambush and counter-ambush, with only one possible outcome.

More explosions, smaller than the first ones, interrupted Wilson's thoughts. Grenades. But whose? Then he realized it didn't make any difference. The real significance lay in the fact that hand grenades were close-in weapons. The NVA were creeping in for the kill. More explosions followed, a final burst of automatic fire, and then silence.

Tears ran unabashedly down Wilson's cheeks. It was all over. French's sacrifice had only bought them a hard-earned 30 minutes.

The gunny's death cast a fatalistic pall over the young officer that threatened to undermine his effectiveness. Physically and mentally exhausted by the strain of the last few days, he was functioning on automatic pilot, and he was close to the edge. His face reflected the pressure, but it was his eyes that told the real story. Rimmed by dark circles, giving his face a haunted, skull-like appearance, they were sunk deeply into his head, seemingly fixed on some far-off vision only he could see. Combat veterans called it "the thousand-yard stare."

The column halted, and he walked into the Marine in front of him. "Shit," he swore under his breath, experiencing a fleeting moment of anger. "Why'd you stop?" he whispered.

"Lieutenant," the man replied in a low voice, "we made it. We're at the bottom of Lima's hill."

36

Lima Company, Hill 540, 2100, 13 September—Anderson lay concealed in the grass, studying the ghostly figure approaching the line of foxholes in the moonlight. It was deathly quiet as the scout warily made his way carefully along the edge of the dirt trail. Whether he was Vietnamese or American was impossible to tell in the darkened shadows, but 2nd Platoon wasn't taking chances. A dozen rifles covered the intruder as a whispered challenge ordered him to a stop.

He slowly raised his weapon above his head, muzzle pointing straight up, a non-threatening angle.

"Knife Edge," he called softly, his voice full of apprehension.

A command voice called out softly of the darkness, "Come on in Knife Edge. How many are you?"

"Twelve," the scout replied as he started forward. The rest of the team appeared out of the darkness, trailing in his footsteps.

Anderson tensed. This was the risky part of the link-up. The North Vietnamese had been known to tag along behind a patrol as it entered the lines, then shoot the hell out of the unsuspecting defenders. A savvy outfit counted patrol members in and shot extras without warning. Lima's experienced troopers kept their fingers on their triggers while they counted.

The whacked-out team staggered into the perimeter, too numb with exhaustion to feel relief after their narrow escape. They stood motionless, hunched over from the weight of their packs, afraid to sit down because they might not be able to get up. They waited for their lieutenant to tell them what to do.

Wilson was as tired as the rest but had to report to the company commander before anyone could relax. As the team leader crested the hill, Anderson stepped out of the dark and grabbed his hand, welcoming him back to the dubious safety of the company's position. "Congratulations Herb," he said enthusiastically. "You did a great job bringing Frazier out. I never thought we'd see him again."

Wilson hesitated for a moment before answering in a halting voice, "Thanks, Captain. My men did well, and we got lucky, but my gunny didn't make it."

"I'm sorry," Anderson replied, reaching out to grasp him on the shoulder, offering solace while the younger man struggled to gain control of his emotions. Wilson's fragile resilience broke down. "It was my fault, Captain," he declared. "I left him behind."

"How the hell did that happen?" Aldine's voice barked out of the darkness, startling both men, who had not heard him approach. "Lieutenant, you were sent out there to bring back two dead men, not leave another one."

Even in the darkness, Anderson could see Wilson recoil, as if he had been struck across the face. Anderson tried to interject a mollifying comment, but he was cut off. "Captain, don't interrupt me when I'm talking," Aldine exclaimed in a loud voice. Turning back to Wilson, he asked scornfully, "Lieutenant, I'm waiting to hear how a Marine Officer left one of his men behind. You do remember, don't you, that Marines bring everyone back!"

Outraged by the accusation, Anderson could no longer contain himself, "Colonel, I don't think that's fair. Lieutenant Wilson and his team performed heroically. They rescued Dick Frazier and—"

"That's enough, Captain," Aldine shouted, shutting him off. "If you say one more word, I'll relieve you." He turned to the lieutenant. "Wilson, I want to hear your excuse."

Before the man could answer, Sergeant Major Richards appeared and softly called out to Aldine, telling him the regimental commander wanted to speak with him right away.

"We'll continue this conversation later," Aldine spat as he stalked off.

Anderson struggled with his emotions. One part of him wanted to go after the worthless son of a bitch and have it out, but another, more rational, section of his brain cautioned patience. *Don't mean nuthin'*, he thought, using Major Coffman's euphemism. "Aldine will get his," he mumbled. In the meantime, he had a company to run, and right now he had a mentally wounded lieutenant to get back in the fight.

"Okay, Herb, how about telling me what happened out there?" He spoke as gently and calmly he could, sensitive of the young officer's badly bruised feelings.

The big man slumped, head down, staring at the ground as he related the story, blaming himself over and over for the gunny's loss. He was barely coherent, the words tumbling out. It was obvious he was mentally and physically exhausted. All of a sudden, he stopped talking, as if gathering his thoughts. Then he looked up, directly at Anderson. "The gunny was wounded and couldn't keep up," he uttered desolately. "He knew the gooks would get us if we carried him, so he stayed behind to hold them off. I tried to argue him out of it, but he wouldn't budge. He told me to get the hell out of there. Captain, I didn't know what to do. The gooks were closing in. I had to make a decision." He stopped talking and waited for Anderson to say something, hoping for the veteran's understanding and approval of his actions.

Anderson hesitated before replying, struggling to find the right words to reassure the uncertain young officer. Several trite phrases came to mind, but he rejected them. This wasn't the time or place for hackneyed platitudes. Wilson deserved an honest answer, straight from the shoulder, no bullshit.

"Herb, we all have to live with the decisions we make. Often men die as a result," he began. "You made the best one you could under the circumstances, and you can second-guess yourself from now till hell freezes over, or you can live with it. Your call. I'll tell you one thing though. If you go around like some limp dick, you're not worth a shit to yourself or your men, and my advice is to get out of this Marine business. It's not going to get any easier. You're a grunt, and until you rotate, you're going to have to make the tough call—just like Gunny French. Now get your men together and dig in. We're going to have a rough night, and I need you to command the reaction force."

Wilson stood stock still for a moment before he replied, "I don't like men dying because of my decisions."

"You don't have to like it, but you do have to do it," Anderson snapped back. "It's called small-unit leadership, and that's what we get paid for."

"Yes, sir," Wilson answered following a moment's hesitation, and then he walked off into the darkness.

With that, Gunny Smith stepped out of the darkness where he had been listening to the conversation between the two officers. "Jesus, Skipper, empathy ain't your strong suit, is it?"

"Well, what did you expect me to say, Gunny?" Anderson snapped. "This is the big leagues. It's no place for amateurs, and you know it. The NVA will chew you up and spit you out if you aren't tough enough to take it. Wilson's a tough guy; he just doesn't know it yet. He did a hell of a job getting his men back, and I don't intend to mollycoddle him because he had a few knocks. Now, let's go and check your lines. I want to see where you put that listening post."

Smith smiled in the darkness and shook his head. He knew who the tough guy was in this company.

37

1st Battalion, North Vietnamese Army, Assembly Area, 2200, 13 September—Duc waited calmly in his command post, a small brush-free patch of ground near the center of the battalion assembly area. His officers were due to report.

The plan was in motion. There was little for him to do except get in the way, and he was determined not to do that. He learned a long time ago that a commander should allow subordinates to do their job without over-supervising them. Besides, after so many battles, he could tell if things were going well—and tonight, everything seemed to be dropping into place. The movement to the assembly area had gone well, although a little more slowly than planned because of the dense jungle. Fortunately, he had allowed extra time for this possibility. The last platoons were arriving with enough time to get ready for the assault

A sergeant of the headquarters platoon reported that Duc's blackout shelter was ready. It was more a poncho-covered frame than a shelter, but at least he could use a filtered flashlight without it being seen. The small hut, just big enough for four men, contained the mock-up of the hill and two telephone handsets, one connecting him to Regiment and the other to the mortar position. It could be quickly dismantled if they had to leave in a hurry. Several men squatted nearby, ready to carry messages and protect their commander, should the need arise. Duc hesitated to go inside the stuffy enclosure. He preferred to remain outside until his all men reached the assembly area.

Muted sounds of movement caught Duc's attention as the lead elements of the Glorious Victory Company moved into position around him. Lieutenant Doi's reconnaissance platoon guides had led them along routes marked by luminescent wooden arrows to pre-selected assembly areas close to their assault positions. They moved with an easy familiarity, comfortable with the darkness, unlike the cowardly foreigners, who were afraid at night and never left their fortified positions.

Duc was pleased with the battalion's excellent noise discipline. The Americans would never hear them, even though hundreds of men were moving through the undergrowth.

A sorely hurting Senior Sergeant Thanh led his platoon into the assembly area, where they quickly stripped off their khaki uniforms, leaving on only loin cloths or black shorts. By shedding their uniforms, they ensured the cloth wouldn't catch on obstructions or make a distinctive noise as they crawled through the grass. They smeared mud over their bodies, making certain that all exposed skin had a thorough coating. Even to an especially alert defender, the camouflage made them virtually invisible against the jungle undergrowth. The men were armed with an assortment of weapons and explosives, but most carried assault rifles, Chicom grenades, and satchel charges. Three men carried RPG-7s to support the assault if it was discovered. Without command, the well-drilled platoon broke into three-man cells and prepared to move out. There was no need for further orders; they had spent several hours studying the mock-up of the American position and rehearsing the infiltration. Every man knew his assignment down to the last detail. All they needed was Senior Sergeant Thanh's signal to go.

The sapper leader stood alone, clutching a tree to keep from falling as an intense spasm of pain gripped him. He clenched his teeth to keep from crying out, thankful the darkness hid the tears that coursed down his cheeks. His leg wounds were causing him fits, something he tried to hide so the cadre wouldn't send him back to the hospital. With a great effort, he forced himself to ignore the pain and concentrate on the *Lo dits* who had caused him such misery—the Americans. He wanted them to die, to be trampled into the ground, buried in nameless graves so their spirits would never know peace. His anger was so great that he momentarily forgot the pain, glorying in the vision of their destruction.

A hand clasped Thanh's arm, startling him. "*Trung Si*, it's time," Duc whispered in his ear. "*Merde*," Thanh swore to himself in French, angry that he hadn't heard the commander approach.

"Yes, *Trung Ta*. I'll send them forward." As he painfully made his way over to his men, another vision came to mind—his hands around the throat of that foul dog turd. *Trung Ta*, he thought murderously, *I hope you're ready to join your ancestors, because you'll see them soon*. Without realizing it, Thanh slipped his hand into his pocket and rubbed the dead pilot's identity discs for luck.

One of Thanh's NCOs stepped forward from the group as he approached them. "*Tien len*—forward," Thanh whispered encouragingly. "For victory and the Fatherland."

Thanh checked the time with his new watch as his men left the assembly area. The watch was so much better than his old, cheap Russian import. It even had a luminous dial. He smiled, remembering the satisfaction he felt as he had slipped it from the dead pilot's wrist. *It was cheap*, he thought, *just the cost of* Bac Ho's *bullet. The My have too much.* He recalled the rich trove of loot they had taken off the flyer. *It makes them soft, and that's why we'll beat them.*

He slipped the pilot's .38-caliber pistol from his pocket and checked the action, trying to get a feel for the unfamiliar weapon. His hand easily fit around the grip. The pistol felt light in his grasp as he brought it up and sighted along the barrel, imagining Duc as the target.

A figure appeared out of the darkness and he stiffened, recognizing Major Minh's profile. "*Trung Si*," the political officer whispered, "is that an American weapon?"

"Yes, *Thieu Ta*. It used to belong to an American pilot, but he has no use for it anymore," Thanh answered as he stuffed the weapon into his pocket.

"You should be very careful with a foreign weapon, *Trung Si*. It could go off accidentally and hurt someone," Minh cunningly replied, eager to see if the sinister brute picked up on the implication.

Thanh hesitated before he answered, carefully considering his response. He was on dangerous ground; the political officer could shoot him out of hand for making a disloyal statement, but he knew there was no love lost between Minh and Duc. "*Thieu Ta*, I know of one instance where a senior officer was killed in a tragic accident."

"How did it happen?" Minh innocently asked, certain that the sergeant had understood his meaning.

"Someone mishandled a captured weapon during a night attack and shot the officer at close range," Thanh replied, keeping up the charade.

"What happened to the offender?" Minh probed.

"Nothing," Thanh answered back. "It was judged to be an unfortunate accident."

"Yes, I can understand," Minh agreed. "Regrettably, those things happen in combat."

Duc finally entered the shelter and reported that all the units of the battalion were in position and prepared to attack on schedule—in little more than 45 minutes. The regimental commander acknowledged the information and reported that a rocket company would attack the combat base at the same time with 107mm projectiles—to obliterate the American artillery. Duc was pleased with the news, but he was too much of a realist to believe the rockets could do that much damage. He knew they were an area weapon and most probably wouldn't even hit their target. But any help was better than nothing at all if the sappers were prematurely discovered.

The three infiltrators slipped noiselessly into the undergrowth and began working their way toward the American hilltop position 500 meters away. There wasn't much time; Duc's *Bo doi* were scheduled to attack at 0200, which gave the sappers only five hours to penetrate the defenses. Thanh was concerned. He had once led an attack that took six hours to cover just 200 meters, but that had been against a tangled maze of barbed wire and mines. Here, there were only listening posts. But timing was everything. Once the battalion gathered in the assembly area, it would be terribly exposed to imperialist artillery and bombers. It fell upon the sappers to blast a hole in the enemy's defenses at the right time so the infantry could push through and overrun the imperialists before they could react.

Combatant Toan froze, detecting the unmistakable smell of unwashed bodies in front of him. *Must be the American advanced position*, he thought. Toan knew the foreigners used small groups of men in front of their lines as scouts, but they were often careless. They made too much noise and smelled like buffalo shit. Once he had actually seen one smoking, the red dot of his cigarette acting as an aiming point. Toan looked up the slope and made out the turtle-like shape of an American helmet against the skyline. *How stupid*, he thought, *The* Do cho *doesn't even know how to properly conceal himself.*

He signaled his two comrades to remain behind, as he inched forward to locate the booby traps they often placed in front of their position. Sweat broke out on his face as his hand touched the thin metal posts of the Claymore mine. It was all he could do to keep from jerking away from the deadly device. Even though he had done this several times, it was still a shock to face one with the knowledge that it might explode at any moment. He reached out to disarm the device. All he had to do was unscrew the blasting cap, but at the last minute he decided to turn the Claymore around. The thought of the Americans setting it off and committing suicide made him smile as he carefully eased it out of the ground.

Combatant Toan held the Claymore in his hands, inches from his face, when it detonated, vaporizing his upper torso in a spray of flesh and blood. His two comrades were luckier. Even though both were killed, their bodies were at least recognizable. The M18A1 Claymore fragmentation mine contained 1.5 pounds of composition C-4 military explosive, which burned at 24,000 feet per second and produced one hell of an explosion. The blast hurtled 700 steel pellets in a 60-degree arc 2 meters high, which usually killed everything in its path up to 50 meters out and wounded up to 100 meters.

The explosion brought a hail of grenades from the American position, which caused several casualties among the unprotected sappers. One screamed in agony before a comrade smothered his cries and, in the process, put him out of his misery. Their discovery and the sudden American onslaught momentarily stopped the sappers, but they quickly reorganized and attacked.

There was no other choice. They drove relentlessly forward toward the perimeter foxholes, ignoring casualties, understanding that they had to blast through before they were annihilated.

Duc grabbed the field phone to the mortar platoon and ordered them to blanket the hilltop with high explosive. The crews turned to with a will. As the first round cleared the tube, another took its place, until four shells were in the air before the first even hit the ground. Red flashes marked every impact, as round after round exploded inside the American lines. Jagged shards of red-hot metal tore through the air in a cone-shaped arc of destruction.

Support troops fired rocket-propelled grenades. The back blasts winked like huge fireflies, while their rocket boosters trailed red flame as they flashed toward the ill-fated bunkers. Their detonations added to the weight of metal falling on the hilltop.

Carefully sited machine guns sprayed the perimeter with a heavy volume of automatic fire. Green tracers streaked out of the night, converging on pre-selected targets with overwhelmingly accurate fire.

American weapons answered, but they were quickly smothered, their crews killed or wounded. One foxhole after another succumbed, leaving a large undefended gap in the perimeter defenses.

Bo doi infantrymen swarmed forward as the machine gun crews shifted their fire to cover the flanks of their penetration. The noise was staggering, an overwhelming cacophony of sound that numbed the senses. Above the din, Duc yelled, ordering his soldiers forward into the mêlée. "*Chung ta ra di!*" he bellowed. "*Tien len, Tien len!*"

38

Lima Company, Hill 540, 2330, 13 September—Anderson was leaning back against his pack, dozing, when he sensed someone approaching. "What do you need?" he called out softly, instantly awake, a habit he had developed since taking command.

His radio operator answered, "Skipper, Lima Three's listening post hears something."

The captain stifled a grunt as he scrambled to his feet. The damn wounds were causing him fits. They kept breaking open, spotting the bandages with a mixture of blood and pus, and they stung like hell when he moved. He felt a little woozy and knew he was running a fever because of the infection. *Maybe the doc has got some aspirin*, he thought as he took the handset.

"Gunny, what have you got?" he asked without preamble.

Smith quickly reported that the listening post heard movement near the fake position they had set up earlier that evening.

Anderson pictured the location. It was just a few meters from the North Vietnamese markers and about 50 meters below the 3rd Platoon's foxhole line. During his tour of the lines, just before dark, the gunny had introduced him to the fire team that would man the listening post. He clearly remembered the lance corporal in charge, a big, rawboned southern boy who seemed as steady as a rock and not at all fazed by the threat of facing North Vietnamese sappers.

"Skipper, I lost contact with the LP right after they reported hearing movement," the gunny reported.

***

Lance Corporal Billy Straight's senses were on full alert. The NVA were out there; he could hear them. And that knowledge sent an involuntary shiver down his spine. As they crawled closer, he concentrated on the barely audible rustle in the grass, trying to estimate the probability of his team's getting out of there without getting its ass shot off.

The three of them were holed up in a clump of grass 50 meters in front of their lines with orders to report anything unusual. Straight figured the assholes crawling through the grass qualified, so he passed the word to the gunny and immediately turned the radio off, fearful that the bad guys could hear its low-volume hiss. *Time to beat feet before the pricks box us in*, he thought as he reached out to signal his men—just as the moon came out from beneath the cloud cover.

The moon's light highlighted a man's shape in front of the dummy position they had constructed to conceal their own location.

"Got ya, you stupid son of a bitch," Straight mumbled to himself, thinking the guy was bush league for being caught out in the open like that. "Should a watched the cloud cover."

Then, to Straight's amazement, the darkened figure began to mess with the Claymore, and that action triggered a violent response.

Straight mashed the plunger, sending a small charge of electric current through the wire into the blasting cap. "Run for it!" he screamed over the noise of the blast. The three leaped to their feet and charged up the hill, shouting over and over, "Don't shoot! Don't shoot! It's the listening post."

Corporal Rodriquez's 60mm mortar section sprang into action as the Claymore blast reverberated across the perimeter. Most of the mortar crewmen had been catnapping in the mortar pits—circular holes, ten feet in diameter and three feet deep—when the night exploded. There was a flurry of activity—"assholes and elbows," in Corps lingo—as they threw off poncho liners, clapped helmets in place, and leaped into position, ready to drop three-pound high-explosive rounds into the tubes. The cardboard ammunition canisters were open, base plates seated, and aiming stakes deployed, night-firing devices showing a red dot against the blackness. All they needed was a fire mission.

"Corporal Rodriguez, give us some illumination," Anderson shouted, and was rewarded a moment later by the solid thump of a mortar round leaving the tube. Anticipating the order, the mortar section leader had been holding a round suspended in the tube, ready to drop.

The first round—illumination—burst high above the hilltop, bathing it and the surrounding jungle in an eerie glow. The flare slowly descended, oscillating from side to side beneath the small parachute, casting shadows that made it difficult for the anxious defenders to discern targets. The murky half-light played havoc with everyone's imagination. Shrubs grew into skulking figures and shadows hid threatening shapes, as the Marines on line stared wide-eyed down the slope, waiting for a solid target.

206

As the illumination round sputtered and threatened to burn out, a gunner launched another one, the burning propellant briefly highlighting the man as the shell burst out of the tube. That flash of light unintentionally pinpointed the mortar position, making it a priority target for annihilation by unseen assailants. The two other 60mm crews anxiously stood by with high-explosive shells, knowing it was just a matter of time until they got the order to fire.

"Come on, come on!" Straight shouted impatiently, verbally lashing out at the two laggards behind him. "Move it out. Twenty meters, and we're home free," he yelled encouragingly, even though he couldn't shake the feeling that he was going to take a round in the back. *Shit, we're never going to make it*, he thought as he glanced back and saw his mates falling farther behind, victims of the steep slope and heavy equipment. "Son of a bitch," he swore aloud and slowed up to grab the last straggler by his belt suspenders. The man was breathing like a steam engine and about out of gas. "The fucking gooks are going to open up any minute," he snarled. "Don't give up on me." He renewed his grip and pulled the man along, forcing himself to keep running despite the pain in his lungs.

"Cover them," Smith yelled to the Marines in the nearest foxholes. Four grenades sailed down the slope, landing well behind the three riflemen, far down the hill, before they exploded in a succession of bright flashes and violent, earth-shattering detonations. As the explosions died away, horrifying screams erupted from the blasted area, revealing the presence of the concealed sappers.

"Come on, Straight! Get your ass in here," Smith bellowed as an AK-47 opened fire, its muzzle flashes standing out clearly in the darkness, pinpointing the NVA rifleman's location. Return fire erupted from the perimeter, blanketing the spot with a hail of 5.56mm ammunition. Smith's machine guns joined in despite his admonition to fire only on his orders.

"Son of a bitch," the gunny swore. "Now they've given their position away."

There was a burst of fire and a fleeing Marine crumpled to the ground, screaming in pain. Straight tried to jump over the prostrate figure but caught his foot and fell heavily, dragging his human burden down with him. For a moment they all lay still, stunned and exhausted. Then, Straight gathered himself together. "Stay down," he whispered and crawled over to examine the wounded man.

"It hurts bad," the boy cried as Straight felt for the leg wound in the darkness.

"I know, but you've gotta be quiet, or the gooks'll find us," he murmured as he slit the uniform fabric with his K-Bar knife and slapped a battle dressing on the oozing wound. He heard someone coming through the dry grass and made a desperate grab for his rifle. As he brought it up to shoot, he saw the gunny standing there, calmly looking down, as if he didn't have a care in the world. The older man chided Straight in his gruff voice, "Could you hustle it up? We don't have all day."

Straight heaved a sigh of relief. "Damn, Gunny, you scared the shit out of me," he croaked, thanking his lucky stars the old veteran had come out for them.

"I'm not leaving anybody behind. Now gimme a hand," Smith directed, bending over so Straight could help put the casualty onto his shoulders. "You cover us on the way back to the perimeter," he instructed and, with that, stepped off without a backward glance.

The first salvo of 82mm mortars exploded without warning, catching several men in the open. Seconds later a second volley came in, followed by a third and a fourth—twelve violent detonations in the space of a minute. No sooner had the sounds died away than the cries of wounded men echoed across the perimeter. At the first shout of "Corpsman!" the company aid men were up, ministering to the casualties despite the threat of another salvo. They struggled feverishly to treat the injured, but they faced a daunting task because of the extent of their injuries.

Doc Zimmer found a man lying in the grass, bleeding profusely from a head wound. He raised the man's head up to apply a battle dressing and watched as a large gob of brain tissue slide out of the broken skull. There was nothing he could do; the Marine was beyond saving, and there were others who stood a better chance. Swearing softly, he quickly tied the dressing and moved to another man, practicing his own rough brand of battlefield triage. It wasn't until much later that he found out how devastating the barrage had been. Five Marines had been killed outright and ten had been wounded, three seriously.

Major Coffman heard Lieutenant Colonel Aldine's shrill voice calling out his name. Trying hard to ignore the flying steel, he ran over to the battalion commander's foxhole. *Christ, I hope this is important,* he thought as another explosion rocked the ground. *Maybe the colonel's finally got his act together.*

He found Aldine in his hole, with only the top of his helmet showing. "Yes, sir," he reported.

"Major, it's my pistol," Aldine whined, catching Coffman completely off balance.

"Your *pistol* sir? What about your pistol?"

Aldine pointed to a shrub a few feet away and said, "Major, my pistol is hanging from that bush. Would you get if for me?"

Coffman was dumbfounded. He simply could not believe what he had just heard. Aldine pointed again and repeated the request.

Major Ron Coffman had *never* refused to obey an order in his life, and he wasn't about to start now, so he stalked over and retrieved the holstered .45. But he grew angrier by the second. *The cowardly son of a bitch is afraid to leave his own hole while good Marines are being killed and wounded.*

"Here's your fucking pistol," he raged, throwing it forcefully and striking Aldine on the forehead. The blow opened a three-inch gash that spurted blood.

Coffman stalked back to his foxhole and called to L Cpl McMillan, his radio operator. "Come on, Mac. We're going over to help Anderson." He reached over to help the radioman as he scrambled to gather his equipment.

"Christ, Major, I can't find my damn notebook," the NCO nervously replied. "I think I kicked it into our hole."

Coffman knew the book, containing critical radio frequencies and call signs, would be needed in an emergency. "I'll look while you get your gear on," he said and shined his red-lens flashlight into the foxhole. "I see it," he said and jumped down into the waist-deep pit. As he bent over to retrieve the small notepad, mortar rounds impacted, hurtling deadly fragments throughout the interior of the perimeter. McMillan grunted in pain and collapsed on top of Coffman, pinning him in the bottom of the foxhole. Unable to move under the weight of the unconscious man and his heavy radio, he pushed mightily, trying to get to his feet, but without success. He swore in frustration and tried again as he felt McMillan's dead weight being lifted.

The rescuer turned out to be Sergeant Major Richards, who helped Coffman to his feet. "You okay, Major?" he asked with concern in his voice.

"I wouldn't be if I hadn't retrieved McMillan's notebook," Coffman answered and then quickly added, "How is he?"

"He'd be a lot worse if the radio hadn't been strapped to his back," the sergeant major replied. "It stopped most of the shrapnel, but it's KIA."

The mortar section was blanketed by high explosives. Two of the pits suffered direct hits that wiped out both crews, including Corporal Rodriguez. Both mortars were unsalvageable. Thus, two-thirds of the company commander's "artillery" was out of action in the first minutes of the fight, attesting to the accuracy of the enemy's gunners. The four unwounded survivors regrouped under the command of Private First Class Jimmy Davis, the senior man left standing. Although he was an ammo humper with only one month in-country, Davis stepped into the leadership vacuum and took charge. The makeshift crew was pretty shaken up, but it managed to keep the illumination going while scouring the area for salvageable equipment and ammunition. After surveying the damage to the shallow emplacements, the four unanimously agreed to renovate their pit, so, while two manned the gun, the others energetically dug for America.

An explosion knocked Gunny Smith on his ass, momentarily putting him down for the count. Vaguely aware of several more closely spaced detonations, he wasn't lucid enough to recognize how close they had been. As he returned to full consciousness, he picked himself up and saw the foxhole beside him was nothing but a smoking crater. A mortar round had detonated in the bottom, mangling its two occupants, who seconds before had been vibrant young men. Most of the blast had been contained by the foxhole, which saved him from serious injury. Shaking his head, he staggered over to his foxhole to look for his radio operator. As he did, several more mortar rounds exploded inside the perimeter. He dove into the hole and landed on the headless remains of his hapless radioman. Struggling to push the dead body away, he shuddered with revulsion as his hands came in contact with the gory mess. "Sorry, Frank," he said to the corpse as he manhandled it roughly out of the hole to get at the radio underneath. He found the handset, sticky with blood, and brought it up to his face, praying the damn thing worked. "Skipper," he transmitted in a voice charged with emotion, "the fucking gooks are murdering us!"

A jolt of adrenalin hit Anderson's bloodstream like a bombshell. *Son of a bitch! If the gunny's shook up, this is some serious shit!* An overwhelming feeling of helplessness engulfed him as he realized the situation was spinning out of control. All he was hearing about were dead and dying Marines, the climbing toll of a devastating mortar barrage, and the threat of an NVA assault.

"Captain, what do you want me to do?" Smith's insistent voice shouted, snapping him out of the self-defeating nightmare.

Jesus Christ, I'm a fucking hypocrite, he thought as he stared into the face of Herb Wilson, the victim of his "limp dick" speech. Despite his guilt, Anderson grinned. Nothing like a good ass-chewing, to get a man going—even if it's self-inflicted.

Wilson couldn't believe his eyes. Anderson was incredible. The guy was *smiling*. He was really enjoying all this bullshit. "Hold on Gunny, I'm sending reinforcements."

"Herb, take your men and reinforce 3rd Platoon's lines. The gooks have knocked the hell out of them," Anderson ordered, no longer smiling.

The reaction force held the key. If they could beat back the NVA, the company might stand a chance.

"Roger, Skipper. I'll round up the troops. But we've got to knock out those mortars. They'll murder us," Wilson shouted over the crack of several explosions. "I think I've got their coordinates. If I do, can you get artillery on them?"

Anderson replied, "Give them to me. I'm already trying to get artillery to help us, but the base is under rocket attack and they're busy with counter-battery fire. All we've got left is the one mortar."

39

Sapper Platoon, North Vietnamese Army, 0200, 14 September—*"Trung Ta, Trung Ta,"* the runner panted, "our victorious *Dac Cong* are inside the *My nguy* lines."

Duc acknowledged his report and picked up the field phone to the mortar position. "Major Co, stop firing," he shouted over the sound of the fighting. "Our sappers were detected but are inside at heavy cost. I have ordered the 3rd Company forward to exploit their success. Be prepared to support us if you see a green star cluster."

Co read between the lines: the plan was in jeopardy and Duc was telling him to be prepared to cover a withdrawal.

Co replied formally, his way of letting Duc know that he understood the significance of his comment. "I understand, *Trung Ta*. We will not fail you. *Di may* man."

After carefully replacing the phone in its cradle, Duc shined his red-filtered light on the mock-up of the hill and thought about the American commander. "What will he do?" he pondered aloud, putting himself in the defender's shoes. "The unfortunate man has his hands full with the mortar fire and the threat of an infantry assault."

Thanh's aggravating voice came from darkness, startling Duc. *"Tu Lenh* forget he has to deal with my *Dac Cong."*

Furious at the overtone of superiority in Thanh's voice, Duc interjected but nevertheless managed to remain civil. *"Trung Si*, how effective do you think they will be without your presence?"

The contemptuous remark cut Thanh to the quick, challenging the abilities of his men and, by inference, his own competence. The reference to his absence on the battlefield was particularly galling; Duc wasn't referring to his wounds but how he got them—after being bested by the Americans. Thanh struggled to keep his composure. He wanted to crush the insufferable little insect here and now, but that satisfaction would have to wait, for the time being. "*Trung Ta*, my sappers will not fail you. They will force the *My nguy* to fight in two directions at once."

Duc had to agree. "I would not want to be in the American commander's place when they destroy his machine gun and mortar positions."

As he walked away, Thanh responded chillingly, "His distress won't last long. One of my best teams is going to kill him."

Sapper Doi and his cell moved swiftly across the perimeter despite the flickering light of the flare. This was no time for stealth. The *Bo doi* infantry were right behind him, so he had to move fast to destroy the American command post. Doi likened his mission to cutting the head off a snake, leaving it writhing helplessly and easy to kill. They headed toward the middle of the hill, where the stupid Americans always located their command posts, thinking they could protect their commander by doing so.

Hearing strange voices, Doi stopped to get his bearings. *How loud the Linh My are*, he thought as he listened to them jabber in their strange language. "They have a radio. It must be the commander," he whispered to his compatriots, smiling to himself. This was almost too easy. The three men melted into the trampled grass and crept to within a few feet of the American position. Doi pulled the fuse of the ten-pound satchel charge, rose to his knees, and flung it into the hole. There was a shout as one of the occupants tried to scramble out—only to be tossed into the air like a rag doll as the charge detonated.

Doi's team slithered away to seek out another target.

Binh Nhat Tang crouched in the grass a few meters from a mortar position, preparing to throw a Chicom grenade into the pit. He was the only survivor of his cell; one had been killed outside the perimeter and the other died as he tried to toss a satchel charge into a foxhole. The alert occupant had shot the comrade before he could pull the fuse, so now it was up to Tang alone to destroy the enemy weapon. Slightly wounded in the left hand during the attack, he had trouble removing the wooden cap that protected the fuse, but he finally succeeded. He pulled the friction cord and threw the stick grenade into the emplacement, where it landed with a loud metallic clang. Just before the missile exploded with a muffled thump, Tang heard a shout, as if something had smothered it. Realizing something had gone wrong, Tang attempted to throw a second grenade, but he fumbled it because of his injured hand. As he reached into his pack to pull out another, a terrific blow to the chest knocked him down. He lay semi-conscious in the grass, wondering why he couldn't move.

Two other teams worked their way along the line of foxholes—from the inside, behind the unsuspecting defenders. The advance of one of the teams was executed perfectly; two men provided cover with their rifles, while the third man threw either a grenade or satchel charge. Two positions fell quickly, their occupants killed before they realized the sappers were there. Unfortunately, as the sapper team advanced on the third position, an alert defender spotted it and opened fire, hitting a demolition charge that one of them carried. It blew up with a terrific explosion, instantly killing him and a comrade, and seriously wounding the third.

The second team was pinned down in the grass by several defenders who opened up a withering volley of automatic weapons fire. One man raised up to shoot, but he was struck in the head and died before he could press the trigger. Another loosed half a magazine and was rewarded by a scream. But before he could fire the remaining rounds, one of the light American bullets ricocheted off the ground and struck him in the face. Its tumbling action carried his entire jaw away, clogging his throat with blood and tissue, leaving him struggling to breathe through the ghastly wound. The third sapper in the team hunkered down in the grass and waited until the firing stopped before he crawled away, out of the killing zone.

Doi heard a foreigner shout above the battlefield noise and veered toward the sound, closely followed by his two compatriots. He strained to see where the voice was coming from, but he finally spotted the tell-tale dirt spoil of a recently dug hole. The flares gave him just enough light to make out the shape of an American helmet as it bobbed up and down. "Just like an animal peering out of its burrow," he mumbled. "Another easy victim." He crept forward, focused on the kill, ignorant of a low, grass-covered mound a few feet away on his left. Lulled by a false sense of superiority, the three sappers advanced together in blatant disregard of Sergeant Thanh's training. As they passed the mound, a ghostly figure rose up and fired three times—so rapidly that the blasts merged into one continuous explosion. Doi was the first one hit; eight double 00 buckshot pellets tore through his side, rupturing arteries and causing massive internal bleeding. The pellet strike lifted him off his feet and threw him to the ground, where he soundlessly bled to death within minutes. The second shotgun blast decapitated the nearest sapper, and the third round hit the remaining man in the stomach, causing excruciating pain. He cried out to his comrades, but they were in no position to help.

Major Minh cowered unseen in a hastily dug hole after he slipped away from Duc and the foolhardy attack up the hill. Wounded *Bo doi* streamed past him on their way to the temporary aid station, uttering the occasional moan or soft cry for help. Their plight had a terrible effect on the political officer's shattered nerves. He wanted to escape this terrible place of death and destruction, but the fear of being caught by the ruthless *San Bat Cuop*—bandit hunters—stopped him. They would show him no mercy and, after finishing with him, they would go after his family. There was no place to hide; he was stuck in this hell hole until the *Linh My* were destroyed. But that thought gave him a glimmer of hope. *If the old fool takes the hill, I'll take credit and parley it into a position with the* Tong Cuc Hau Can *out of harm's way. If he fails, I'll disavow his plan, but the cadre will still hold it against me.* Minh was in a box with only one way out. The Americans had to die, and Duc was the key. The major's blood ran cold at the thought that Thanh was on the loose, swearing to kill Duc in the confusion of the battle.

***

Thanh hobbled back through the underbrush toward Duc's command post as quickly as his wounded legs could carry him, determined to crush the insect in the confusion of the attack. No one would notice one more shot in this hellish din. *What the hell,* he thought, *maybe I'll get lucky and the Americans will kill the son of a bitch.* But then he realized it would deprive him of the pleasure of peering into the man's eyes as he died. Thanh slowed and crept toward the position, using every bit of cover he could find to approach it unseen.

When he heard Duc speaking with one of his runners, he stopped. He didn't want to have a potential witness. *Don't hurry,* he cautioned himself, *there's plenty of time. Wait until he's alone.*

The messenger finally moved off, leaving Duc momentarily unguarded. Thanh stood up and quietly stepped out of the shrubbery with the American pistol raised. Duc's back was turned and he seemed not to have heard Thanh's approach.

"Turn around, commander," Thanh ordered harshly, his finger tightening on the trigger. Duc slowly turned, seemingly not surprised by the sergeant's sudden appearance. "What do you want, *Trung Si*?" he asked in a calm tone despite the pistol pointed at his head.

"I have come to rid the fatherland of a traitor," Thanh replied as he stared into Duc's eyes, waiting to see his fear at the realization he was about to die.

The officer's eyes took on a murderous glint. "You miserable dog. Don't you think I've dealt with fools like you before?" Duc spat in contempt. He nodded his head slightly, and a single shot rang out. Thanh's head erupted in a spray of blood and bone fragment. He collapsed, dead, before he could pull the trigger.

Ha si Thai, Duc's trusted bodyguard, stepped out of the undergrowth, where he had been patiently waiting for the *Lo dit* to try something. He wrenched the American pistol from the cadaver's outstretched hand and offered it to Duc, who shook his head. "Thank you, old friend, but keep it as a reminder that not all our enemies are foreigners."

40

Lima Company, Hill 540, 0200, 14 September—"Skipper, I've lost half my platoon," Gunny Smith whispered urgently into the handset. "We need help quick, or it's Little Big Horn time!"

Before Smith could say more, an impossibly loud blast erupted from one of his front-line foxholes. "Son of a bitch! A direct hit," he exclaimed, taken aback by the violence of the detonation. But, in the flash of the explosion, he identified the unmistakable profile of an NVA soldier and instantly realized it wasn't a mortar round but an NVA sapper team. Clods of dirt and debris rained down, forcing Smith to duck. He lost sight of the sapper, but he quickly scooped up the radio, shrugged into the harness, and climbed out of his fighting hole, intent upon alerting his men to this new threat.

As far as Gunny Smith could determine, the 3rd Platoon survivors were probably hunkered down in their holes, ducking the mortars. They wouldn't have expected to be grenaded, especially from behind. "I've got to warn them," he muttered as he charged across open ground toward the nearest hole. For the second time that night he was knocked on his ass by an explosion, which destroyed his destination. "Fucking assholes!" he screamed, bouncing to his feet, beside himself with rage. Recklessly he charged ahead, opening fire from the hip when he saw three shadowy forms crouching in the grass. The gunny instinctively aimed for the nearest one and loosed three quick rounds, hitting the man square in the body. The first shot struck a rib and tumbled, ripping through the sapper's chest cavity. The second punched into the satchel charge he was carrying over his shoulder and detonated its contents, instantly vaporizing the soldier. The blast also took out the rest of the team, killing one and mortally wounding the other. Smith's third shot was wasted: there was nothing left to hit.

***

"Christ, Major," Anderson exclaimed, "unless we get artillery support, we're screwed."

Coffman nodded, having had several close calls as he made his way across the perimeter to the command post. He had arrived in time to hear Anderson's conversation with the gunny and knew they had to have help quickly. "Okay, Andy. Let me see what I can do," he volunteered. "Where can my radio operator and I set up shop?"

"Use that foxhole over there," Anderson replied, pointing to a half-destroyed foxhole about ten meters away. "It belonged to my mortar section leader, and he won't need it anymore."

Coffman scrambled off, trailed by his radio operator. Within two minutes, they were requesting an emergency artillery fire mission. Coffman's first call for fire was denied without explanation, which raised his blood pressure and his temper. "Put your Six on, right now," he demanded from the hapless operator at KCSB, adding, "I'm Northtide Three," which identified him as the 3rd Battalion operations officer. Moments later, a new voice came up on the net and, without preamble, again denied the request, citing a higher priority mission. Coffman came unglued. "That's bullshit," he shouted into the handset. "We've got gooks inside the perimeter, and we're expecting a full-out attack any moment. Now give us the goddam support."

He barely got the comment out before his radio operator shouted a warning and tried to scramble out of the foxhole, only to slip on the parapet and fall backward, pinning Coffman against the wall with his body. There was a brilliant flash and a thunderous explosion as a satchel charge detonated in the bottom of the hole, throwing the radioman into the air but not before his body absorbed most of the blast.

***

"This one's dead, Captain," Doc Zimmer whispered, as he turned to help haul the mangled corpse out of the smoldering foxhole. Next, Zimmer carefully eased into the hole to check the second body for vital signs while Anderson stood guard. The crumpled form was scrunched up against the side, forcing Zimmer to straddle it as he extricated an arm to check for a pulse. "Skipper. It's the Major, and he's alive," he reported. "But we need to get him out of here, so I can take a good look."

After struggling for several minutes, the two finally managed to lift the unconscious officer out of the hole. Coffman's breathing was shallow, and he was bleeding from several minor wounds, but it was the threat of internal injuries that worried them the most. "I don't know, Skipper," Zimmer speculated. "His helmet and flak jacket may have protected him, but I can't be sure. The only thing I can do now is treat him for shock and try to get him evacuated as soon as possible."

Anderson took another look at his friend before replying, "Doc, I don't think we'll be evacuating anyone for a long while. Do what you can for him and the other wounded."

***

Aldine's persistent voice annoyed the hell out of Sergeant Major Richards, but he wasn't about to expose his position by responding. The old veteran knew "the little gook bastards" were inside the perimeter just as soon as he heard the explosion of their satchel charges. Besides, he had told the colonel, in no uncertain terms, to keep his mouth shut, stay alert, and shoot anybody that wasn't a Marine. *That's pretty simple*, he thought at the time, underestimating the battalion commander's not entirely irrational fear of being alone in the dark. Soon, though, Aldine's insistent whisper of "Sergeant Major" made him want to duct-tape the officer's mouth shut. Richards couldn't help concluding, *The gutless son of a bitch will give away our position.*

Another illumination round burst overhead. In its light, Richards made out the profiles of three NVA as they headed for the colonel's position. "It's show time," he muttered softly and carefully inched the Remington 870 Express into his shoulder, so as not to attract their attention, and sighted in. The pump-action 12-gauge shotgun was loaded with five double 00 buckshot shells, each containing eight pellets that were meant to kick some serious ass at close range. *Calm down*, he cautioned himself as his wildly pounding heart threatened to disrupt his aim.

The sergeant major—a veteran of Guadalcanal, Iwo Jima, Inchon, the Chosin Reservoir, and an earlier Vietnam tour—waited until "the little shits" were in front of his position, not more than ten feet away. "Take your time. Hold 'em and squeez'em," he chanted to himself without realizing he was muttering out loud.

Now! He fired, racked in another round, and fired again, racked, fired, racked, fired, racked, all in a swift, self-assured flow of hostility, and so rapidly that the individual blasts merged into one long roar. Flame belched from the muzzle, momentarily ruining his night vision, but when it returned all three Vietnamese were on the ground.

***

"Hustle up! Hustle up," Wilson shouted repeatedly as he led his nine-man reaction force toward the 3rd Platoon's shattered line. He pushed the ragged formation hard, trying to make it to the perimeter foxholes before the main NVA attack. They had to get into cover quickly, before they were spotted. The illumination didn't help; its crazy patchwork of light completely exposed Wilson's team to the enemy gunners who were creating so much havoc on the 3rd Platoon.

As the reinforcements shook themselves out, another illumination round burst over the hill, replacing one that had burned out. The bright light exposed three half-clothed figures in its glare, startling the hell out of the Marines. Recovering quickly from the unexpected encounter, one shouted, "Gooks! Gooks," and raised his rifle as he skidded to a halt.

The Vietnamese dropped into the waist-high grass just as Wilson's men opened up a withering fire, pounding the ground around them with the deadly small-caliber 5.56mm bullets. One enemy soldier was killed instantly and a second was severely wounded, but not before he got off half a magazine and hit a Marine in the legs. The third NVA miraculously escaped injury and slithered away.

Wilson dropped two men off to treat the wounded man and pushed the others forward, overrunning the bodies on their way to cover in the battered foxholes. In the confusion, they didn't notice that one of the enemy soldiers was missing.

"Christ, am I glad to see you, Lieutenant," Gunny Smith gratefully acknowledged as the two huddled in the bottom of a foxhole.

Green tracers flashed overhead; several ricocheted erratically and left trails of light as the incendiary tips burned out. An occasional RPG round detonated and shook the ground and sent shrapnel whining above their heads.

"Damn! This isn't good," Wilson pronounced resignedly, raising his head slightly above the foxhole's parapet to peer out. "I only got eight men, lost one coming over." A bullet impacted the ground beside his head, splattering his helmet with dirt. "Those bastards are going to be the death of me yet," he exclaimed indignantly, pulling himself entirely below ground level.

Smith chuckled, "Hell, Lieutenant, you want to live forever and end up looking like me?" He doffed his helmet, exposing his bald head, and then flicked his dentures out with his tongue. The outrageous act was so incongruous that Wilson simply stared for a long moment, and finally broke out laughing, giddy with stress and fatigue. "I love this shit," he managed to utter before he lapsed once again into uncontrolled laughter. Unable to keep a straight face, the gunny joined in, chortling in his distinctive throaty, low-pitched voice.

A sudden burst of sustained rifle fire, which erupted from the perimeter foxholes, stopped the hilarity short. As the pair cautiously raised their heads above the parapet, they saw a group of dim figures emerge from the tree line. "Here they come," Wilson muttered to himself as he brought his rifle up. Gunny Smith grabbed the radio.

"Skipper, we got a whole shit pot full of gooks coming in on us," Smith shouted excitedly into the handset, as dozens of NVA regulars advanced up the hillside. "It looks like somebody kicked over a damn anthill." As he watched, a swarm of Vietnamese materialized out of the wood line, at least a company—more NVA than he had ever seen at one time—and they were *all* headed right for him. "Jesus Christ," he exclaimed and then transmitted, "We're going to need help."

Beside Smith, Wilson leaned against the side of the foxhole, his rifle propped on the parapet, calmly firing disciplined three-round bursts into the enemy formation. Burning hot spent cartridges bounced off the gunny's helmet, except one errant piece of brass that went down his shirt, burning his neck.

Smith swore mightily as the pain hit and jerked upright, fumbling to open his flak jacket. "Are you hit, Gunny?" Wilson inquired with shouted apprehension, thinking the older man's gyrations signified a wound.

"Damn, Lieutenant, between you and the gooks, I'm surely headed for sickbay," he responded peevishly as he retrieved the cartridge and burned his fingers in the process. A sudden thought went through his mind: *I can't believe I'm worried about a little burn when the damn gooners are going to tear me a new asshole.*

***

"Fire mission," Anderson requested, starting the urgent call for fire that meant the difference between life and death for Lima Company.

"Come on, come on," he chided impatiently, waiting for the nameless voice on the radio to confirm the fire mission. Instead, the operator broadcast, "Wait. Out."

"Motherfucker," Anderson blurted, infuriated by the delay. "The fucking gooks'll be carving their initials on my chest with a bayonet if they don't hustle."

Following a long pause, the operator resumed the conversation: "Lima Six, your fire mission has been disapproved. It's too close to friendlies." Anderson almost broke the handset in frustration. "We are being overrun. I say again, we are being *overrun!* Fire the goddam mission."

Moments later a vaguely familiar voice came up on the air. "Lima Six, you seem to be in a habit of getting your ass in a sling."

"Who the hell …" Anderson started to ask, and then he remembered the asshole from the previous night who had wanted him to accept responsibility for the fire mission. "Roger, arty. Trouble seems to be following me," he growled, anticipating the same runaround.

"Don't worry. We're going to bail you out. Stand by for your mission."

So, maybe he isn't such an asshole.

"Pour it on, arty, or it may be my last request," he implored.

Realizing he couldn't do everything himself, Anderson made a critical decision. He switched to Napoline's frequency and barked into the handset, "Tom, turn your platoon over to your platoon sergeant and get your ass over here. I need you to work the fire-support radios."

In a matter of moments, the breathless forward observer was huddled beneath a poncho with the company commander, shining a red-filtered flashlight on a tactical map. Anderson pointed out where he wanted the targets fired, including the hill on which Wilson said he had seen the NVA 82mm mortars. Napoline wrote the coordinates in large, bold, grease-penciled numbers on the edge of the map and memorized the location so he wouldn't have to refer to it again.

"Two things Tom," Anderson recited, looking directly into Napoline's eyes. "I want constant illumination over the hill *and* all the fire support you can get me. Without it, we're all dead meat."

Napoline burrowed deeper into the hole as he shouted the description of a new target into the handset—"Enemy mortars. Reverse slope"—and completed the call for fire. He received a "Stand by," as the information was frenziedly translated into firing data for the cannoneers.

Within a minute two 105mm howitzers from Charlie Battery, 13th Marines, were trained on the coordinates and ready to fire. "Shot," the operator announced as two thirty-pound 105mm howitzer shells left the muzzles, followed by eight more as fast as the sweating gunners could load and pull the lanyards. Napoline acknowledged the completion of the mission and hoped that the 300 pounds of high explosives he had fired would do the job. He imagined the variable timed fuses exploding over the hill, sending a rain of shrapnel down on the surprised NVA mortar men. He didn't have time to dwell on it, though; other targets demanded his attention. "Fire mission," he began again as he concentrated on the next target.

No one knew how it started, but the four surviving mortar men were bellowing "The Marines' Hymn" at the top of their voices. In an act of defiance born out of desperation, they repeated the three stanzas over and over. The act was spontaneous, inexplicable, and, at any other time, would have been ridiculed. But Death had visited these young men, killing and wounding three out of four in the section. They had lost good friends, buddies with whom they had shared other moments of danger, but nothing as horrific as this.

The sudden, devastating NVA mortar attack had destroyed their sense of invincibility and forced them to face their own mortality. The Hymn, learned and taken to heart early on at boot camp, was the glue that held them together in the face of death.

They all expected to die, but they were individually and collectively determined to go down doing their jobs, honoring their traditions. None of them was above the age of 20.

***

With the loss of their NCOs, Private First Class Mike Davis had stepped into the leadership vacuum, as was the Marine Corps' prime directive. He simply took charge, organizing the battered survivors into a functioning team that served the gun in a disciplined frenzy.

Switching from illume to high explosives, they dropped round after round into the forest right in front of the 3rd Platoon, falling into a mindless rhythm that kept them from dwelling on the dangers. The young men were exhausted, bathed in sweat, running on raw emotion, but they remained gamely in the fight.

"Grenade!" Davis shouted frantically as the deadly missile stuck the mortar baseplate and bounced onto the dirt in the bottom of the pit. Startled, the others broke rhythm and froze, paralyzed by the sudden, unexpected warning. Davis screamed, "Get out of my way!" and roughly shoved the gunner to the side. Then he flung himself on the Chicom, just as it exploded, absorbing the entire blast with his body.

The heroic feat galvanized the remaining gunners into action. One snatched up his rifle and shot their attacker, catching him in the act of hurling another grenade. The other two huddled over their unconscious comrade. They quickly rolled Davis over. Even in the dim light, they could see that he was terribly wounded. His right hand was completely gone, and the left was missing several fingers and was horribly gouged. The front of Davis's shredded jungle utilities, beneath his open flak jacket, was covered with dark splotches. The shadowy illumination masked the blood's color, but not the torn flesh. The youngsters were stunned. Nothing in their training had prepared them to handle anything like this. Both yelled, "Corpsman!" at the same time, then tore into their first aid pouches for battle dressings.

Davis cried out as intense pain brought him back to consciousness. "Mike, you're going to be all right," he heard someone say, but he saw the horrified look in the man's eyes and knew it was a lie.

Another spasm of pain took his breath away. "Oh, God," he murmured weakly as the tremor passed. "It hurts."

The voice came back more urgently. "Hold on, Mike. Hang with us." Rough hands poked and prodded, causing him more pain. He sensed urgency in their actions, and that scared him.

"Am I going to die?" he asked feebly, struggling with the thought.

"You're okay, Mike. Just wounded," the same voice shakily answered—with absolutely no conviction.

His chest hurt. Someone was pushing it up and down. "I don't want to die," he mumbled softly to himself as he struggled for breath. But his body was shutting down.

With a final gasp, he went limp. The corpsman slowly stood up, wiping his bloody hands on a used battle dressing. "He's gone," he murmured to no one in particular. "I couldn't stop the bleeding. He was all torn up inside. There was nothing I could do," he added apologetically, seeking their understanding.

"It's okay, Doc," one answered lamely and patted the corpsman on the shoulder. "You did your best."

Then why do I feel like shit? the doc thought. *Why do I feel so terribly guilty for losing their buddy?*

A short time later, Anderson stood on the parapet of the mortar pit, looking down at the three dejected Marines who were gathered around Davis's body, which was wrapped in a poncho on the grass. "Get back on the goddam gun," he bellowed. "The gooks are still out there. Now get off your dead asses and make 'em pay." His hard-nosed order was like a slap in the face, shaking them out of their stupor.

They leaped to their feet and took position. The new self-appointed gunner shifted the bipods of the small mortar, aligning it with the azimuth of the pre-registered target in front of the 3rd Platoon. His number-two passed him a shell and the third crewman broke out additional rounds. Seconds later, the first HE round left the tube, on its way "downrange."

41

1st Battalion, North Vietnamese Army, 0330, 14 September—Disorganized groups of *Bo doi* emerged from the jungle and charged madly up the hill, goaded on by their officers, who knew the best chance for survival lay in getting inside the American position before they could react. The premature discovery of the sappers had thrown off the timing of the plan, catching the 1st Company out of position and forcing its commander to launch the attack before his men were fully deployed.

Lieutenant Colonel Duc's careful planning evaporated like the early morning dew as harried leaders pressed their men forward, ignoring tactical integrity in the mad rush to take the hill. Confusion mounted as intermingled units tried to sort themselves out in the jungle darkness, slowing the momentum of the attack. Platoon leaders rushed about in an attempt to restore order, but they succeeded only in confusing the situation even further with their conflicting commands. "*Tien len, Tien len,*" several shouted, even as elements of the 2nd Company advanced too quickly and ran into the laggards of its sister company, causing both groups to bunch up in a densely packed throng.

Sensing a glorious victory, the first wave rushed up the slope. "*Caca Dau, Caca Dau*—kill, kill," they screamed, steeling themselves against the defenders' weapons. Here and there one of their number fell victim to American small arms fire, but not enough to stall the advance. "*Tien len, Tien len.*" Then, without warning, mortar rounds detonated in the middle of the lead wave, cutting down several *Bo doi* and forcing the rest to take cover. The sharp crump of the explosions cut through the battlefield din and stalled the advance.

Alone among his men, *Trung Uy* Chiem remained erect, clearly visible in the light of the parachute flare. He stumbled a few steps, and then slowly turned toward his cowering men, his features etched with pain. As the troops watched, mesmerized by the sight of the severely wounded officer, who stood alone in the maelstrom, Chiem pointed toward the hilltop and shouted "*Tien len*" before he crumpled to the ground. The company sergeant broke cover and ran to help, but it was too late; his officer was dead.

In a fit of rage, he tore open Chiem's pack and took out the company's banner, a square silk flag sporting a yellow star on a red background. The pennant had great importance. It had been presented to the company by hamlet elders before its departure down the Ho Chi Minh Trail and served as an emotional tie to their families. The sergeant tied it to his rifle and, in a suicidal act of bravery, stood up and waved it back and forth, catching the attention of every man in the company before he advanced up the hill. "*Tien len.*" As one, 1st Company leaped to its feet and swept forward behind the banner, through the deadly mortar and small arms fire, ignoring casualties in the mad rush to get at the Americans.

The banner man staggered, hit by a burst of fire, but he refused to go down until relieved of his precious burden. The new bearer was also hit, but another *Bo doi* grabbed the flag and ran it forward, followed by a group of emotionally charged soldiers. Reaching the line of foxholes, he stabbed downward, impaling a defender before he collapsed into the hole himself, the victim of a gunshot that robbed him of his victory. Others quickly followed him into the breach, intent upon exploiting the penetration.

The remnants of one platoon forged straight ahead. They aimed to destroy any American command and control personnel who had survived the sapper attack.

Meantime, survivors of the 1st Company's other two platoons tried to widen the gap. One platoon attacked left and the other veered to the right, following a carefully rehearsed plan to roll up the imperialist flanks. *Binh Nhat* Mo, the toughest fighter in the left platoon, led the attack. He was in the forefront, firing his AK-47 and hurling fragmentation grenades, when he spotted a defender trying to clear a jammed rifle. "*Caca Dau!*" he screamed and ran forward to bayonet the defenseless man. As he lunged, the *Linh My* leaped aside, grabbed the muzzle of the weapon, and pulled Mo forward, throwing him off balance. Before Mo could recover, the enemy soldier wrenched his weapon away and turned it against him. Then, the slayer ducked out of sight and took Mo's comrades under fire, killing one and forcing the rest to take cover. Unnerved by the spectacle of Mo's grisly death, the platoon hung back, reluctant to renew the attack. Fear became their enemy. They took refuge in the captured foxholes, content to snipe at anything that moved. The momentum of their attack was lost.

The eight survivors of the center platoon gathered around their leader, *Thieu Uy* Tran Van Doan, and waited for his orders. A crushing weariness sapped their strength as they came down from the adrenalin burst that had fueled them to this point. The mad dash up the hill had taken an appalling toll on their physical and mental strength—two of them suffered from mild shock, and one was so traumatized he could barely function. Doan also struggled, unable to comprehend how he could still be alive after so many close calls. At the start of the attack, a lifetime ago, the platoon had mustered 19 *Bo doi*; now the bodies of two-thirds of them dotted the hillside. The horrific experience threatened to overwhelm him, until an insistent voice penetrated his dazed brain. "*Thieu Uy*, please give us your orders?"

The words of the veteran sergeant snapped him out of his lethargy. Doan replied, "*Trung Si*, take three men and destroy the imperialist mortar. I'll take the others and attack their machine guns—*Di may man.*"

Trotting rapidly over the shell-pitted ground, Doan led his men in search of the imperialist's machine guns. In his haste, he tripped over a dead body and fell heavily to the ground. Just then, a helmeted figure rose from concealment and opened fire. The fall saved Doan's life, but the men who followed him weren't as lucky. Two were killed instantly, and the third was knocked to the ground with wounds to the chest and neck. Jumping to his feet, Doan rushed the assailant, screaming obscenities at the top of his voice. He lunged with his bayoneted rifle and felt a jarring blow in his arms as he drove it into the enemy's body. His forward momentum carried him into the hole, where he fell heavily against the side, too stunned to move. Before he could recover, his intended victim straddled his chest, grabbed him brutally by the neck, and squeezed. Doan clutched at the powerful hands and tried to tear them loose, bucking and twisting violently in an attempt to throw the man off. His frantic efforts didn't work. The pressure increased, crushing his throat. In desperation, he reached up and tried to poke out the attacker's eyes, but he succeeded only in raking the man's face. Doan punched and flailed, his legs drumming the ground, without effect. His oxygen-starved body grew weaker and finally went limp. He blacked out.

The badly injured survivor of the center platoon crawled to the lip of the foxhole and cautiously eyeballed the interior. His officer lay crumpled in the bottom of the hole in the tell-tale slack-jointed position of the dead. A foreign soldier was propped up against him, showing little sign of life except for the slight rise and fall of his chest. His hands were tightly clasped over his side. It was obvious he was gravely wounded and helpless, yet he stared straight at the Vietnamese soldier, eyes unblinking, revealing no trace of fear. Unnerved, the weakened *Chien Si* struggled to drag his rifle into position, finally resting it on the ground to sight in, the muzzle only three feet from his enemy's face. For a long moment he stared knowingly into the other man's eyes, and then his finger tightened on the trigger. His prey whispered hoarsely in his strange language, just as the rifle fired, abruptly cutting off the sounds. The effort of firing the rifle seemed to take all the strength out of him and he slumped over the parapet.

The team on the right wiped out the first American bunker and advanced on the next, braving increasingly heavy small arms fire that reduced them to four unwounded survivors. As they prepared to rush the position, three defenders came at them, shooting wildly from the hip. A bullet struck *Chien Si* Hoang in the chest and exited his lower back, inflicting a sucking chest wound that left Hoang struggling for breath. Blood and brain matter exploded from *Binh Nhat* Ti's head when a small-caliber round pierced his right temple and killed him instantly. *Trung Si* Liem squeezed the trigger of his AK-47, sending half a dozen 7.62mm rounds toward the *Linh My*. A single bullet hit one of the defenders, who crumpled to the ground. Before Liem could fire again, an American struck him in the head with the butt of his rifle, knocking him to the ground unconscious. *Binh Nhat* Loc managed to disarm his opponent in a vicious hand-to-hand struggle, but he tripped over Ti's body and fell. He felt the defender's arm around his throat and a terrible pressure that forced his head back until everything went black.

It was now up to the 2nd Company to take advantage of the 1st Company's sacrifice.

Duc was furious. *Trung Uy* Khuong was nowhere to be found, and his company was still tangled up on the edge of the jungle, unable to advance. "*Do moi ro,*" Duc swore to himself. He waded into the mass of disorganized infantrymen, shouting directions and shoving troops toward the hill.

Helped by several *Quan Linh*—veterans—Duc quickly restored order. With a triumphal shout, he sent the 2nd Company forward. "*Muon doc lap phai do mau*—For freedom you have to spend your blood. *Tien len.*"

Just as the lead platoon moved into the open, thunderous explosions rocked the jungle behind them. Duc collapsed as shrapnel felled several men round him, their screams of pain lost in the rattle of small arms fire and the sharp crack of grenades. Hardened veterans threw themselves to the ground in panic and fear. This deadly, totally unexpected threat had effectively taken them out of the fight.

It was a decisive moment. In desperation, the *Bo doi* looked for someone to lead them, but no one stepped forward. The battalion had lost its spirit.

Another salvo detonated in the treetops, filling the air with deadly shards of steel and wood splinters. No one moved, except to burrow deeper into the soft, yielding soil.

Duc leaned back against a tree to try to clear the fog from his brain. Then, out of nowhere, someone was shaking him. As Duc struggled to regain full consciousness, his clerk kept trying to bring him around. "*Trung Ta,*" the man shouted anxiously. "Wake up, wake up! The imperialist artillery is destroying the battalion."

Finally registering what he was hearing, Duc struggled to his feet. "There is no time to lose. Help me get the men up." As the pair worked its way through the undergrowth, Duc called out to the dispirited men, encouraging them by setting the example. He recognized several of the older veterans in the faint light of the illumination and called out to them by name. "Come on my, friend. *Bac* Ho expects us to do our duty. Show the young comrades how to fight. *Tien len.*" shamed, the veterans rose and followed their venerated elder brother.

And then a third salvo exploded overhead. This time, instead of going to ground, the company pressed forward, caught up in the spirit of the moment.

Duc led the fresh troops up the slope toward the fire-swept hilltop, maneuvering around the lifeless bodies of their comrades from the 1st Company.

Behind them the jungle continued to explode. Duc knew there was no turning back. The attack had to succeed. "*Tien len.*" Bullets flayed them, dropping some noiselessly while others fell with screams and cries. But the survivors continued to advance, bent forward as if breasting a heavy wind.

Duc motioned the dwindling company onward. His lungs were on fire, but he forced himself to keep going. "*Don't stop,*" he scolded himself. "*Muon doc lap phai do mau. Tien len.*"

Just ahead was an enemy foxhole, a corpse sprawled on the parapet, impaled by a comrade's rifle. Duc grasped the AK-47 and, with an effort, pulled it out, amazed to see the 1st Company's honor banner tied to the barrel. Raising the weapon high over his head, he waved it from side to side so the pennant streamed in the wind. His *Bo doi* swept past him, screaming manically. "*Caca Dau! Caca Dau!*"

42

Lima Company, 0400, 14 September—"Get some," Smith screamed between shots, as mortar rounds exploded in the midst of the enemy formation. "Pour it on!" he bellowed. "Kill the bastards."

The line of attackers disappeared. They all went to ground—except for one figure, who remained standing even as 60mm shells detonated around him.

"That asshole is leading a charmed life," Smith mumbled, as he sighted in, trying to ignore the snap of bullets whizzing past his head. He recited the old rifleman's mantra, "Hold 'em and squeeze 'em," as he acquired the target, aiming for the NVA soldier's chest—center of mass, to the professional shooter—and squeezed the trigger.

"Fucking A," he muttered with satisfaction as the enemy soldier sank to the ground.

"That's one *good* son of a bitch." Wilson's shout caught Smith's attention. "Come on, Gunny. We better check the lines before the gooks recover." The two scrambled out of the foxhole and each took a section of the lines. They intended to meet in the middle and compare notes. Neither man saw the enemy soldier rush over to the gunny's kill.

Wilson slid into the nearest foxhole, landing on top of one of its occupants. "Sorry," he whispered apologetically as he untangled himself, "I didn't see you in this crazy light."

The man didn't respond, and neither did his partner, who was leaning forward against the parapet, on top of his weapon. "Hey, Marine, you sleeping?" Wilson asked flippantly, taking him by the shoulder. Suddenly aware that something was terribly wrong, Wilson pulled him back. "Oh shit," he exclaimed as his eyes settled on the bullet hole in the man's forehead and noticed the pool of half-congealed blood where his head touched the earth. As he peered into the man's lifeless eyes, he tried to recall the boy's name but failed, unable to recognize the distorted face. He allowed the corpse to fall backward into the hole while he examined the other occupant: no pulse, head shot, died instantly, never knew what hit him. A chill went through Wilson's body. *How many more are going to die in this shit hole?*

Someone shouted, "Here they come!"

Looking up, Wilson saw a line of attackers as it charged up the hill, directly at him.

The M-16 bolt went home with a metallic clunk, signaling an empty magazine. With practiced efficiency, Wilson pressed the release, ejected it, and slapped in another 20 rounds. He pulled the charging handle to the rear and let it slam forward. The bolt stripped a fresh cartridge from the magazine and seated it in the chamber. Leaning slightly forward to steady his aim, he pulled the trigger, hardly aware of the weapon's recoil as it fired on full automatic. Shiny brass cartridges spewed out, cascading down on the two dead Marines in the bottom of the hole.

In mid-burst the weapon stopped firing. The extractor had torn the lip off the base of a cartridge, leaving it jammed in the chamber, blocking the next round. Wilson swore in helpless frustration. He needed a cleaning rod to clear the damn thing, but he didn't have one. He heard a wild shout and saw an enemy soldier charging toward him, bayoneted rifle extended to run him through. There was no time to think. As the Viet lunged, Wilson instinctively stepped aside, grabbed the weapon with his left hand, wrapped his right arm around the assailant's neck, and started to choke the shit out of him. He put all his considerable adrenalin-stimulated upper-body strength into the hold and felt the man's neck snap. He released the body and, in a fit of combat-induced rage, took the AK-47 and bayoneted the corpse again and again. Finally coming to his senses, Wilson jumped into a foxhole and used the new weapon to take the NVA under fire.

"Skipper, they've broken through," Smith shouted into the radio handset against the roar of small arms fire and explosions. "We can't stop 'em. Most of my men are down. We need help."

The gunny stopped short at the sight of a pith-helmeted figure above him. Dropping the handset, he fell back against the side of the foxhole and fired half a dozen rounds into the surprised gooner's chest. The body collapsed and fell on Smith's head and shoulders, shoving him to the bottom of the hole, just as another Viet appeared and fired twice as he ran past. The bullets hit the corpse but didn't penetrate. Throwing off the dead body, the gunny rose to his feet and shot the passing NVA in the back. "Asshole," he shouted and quickly swiveled around, checking to make sure there weren't more of the sneaky bastards out there, determined to keep him from retirement. Satisfied that he was safe for the moment, the gunny bent over and picked up his handset in time to hear Anderson anxiously calling him: "Hang on, Gunny, I'm coming over with Littleton and half his platoon. Out."

230

"Come on, John, hustle your men up!" Anderson shouted. "We don't have much time. The gooks are overrunning 2nd Platoon."

Littleton was trying to get his men sorted out in compliance with the most succinct order he'd ever received: "Get your ass over here to my CP with half your platoon. Now!"

Knowing that the skipper didn't suffer laggards well, he responded with a "Yes, sir," as any good lieutenant should, grabbed the men, and beat feet. In one of his smarter moves, he invited Petrovitch and assistant gunner Edwards to join his little band of fighters. The big machine gunner understood the significance of the summons, so he quickly festooned himself and Edwards with belts of 7.62mm ammunition and made sure his assault pouch was fully loaded before joining the exodus. After a short attention-getting brief by the skipper—"The fuckin' gooks have broken through the Second Platoon, and we're going to kick their ass and throw 'em the fuck out"—they double-timed across the perimeter, trying to ignore the snap of incoming small arms fire.

Just before cresting the ridge behind the breach, Anderson stopped and spread the troops out into a line. He faced the small group and ordered, "Fix bayonets!"

Anderson withdrew his own eight-inch knife from its scabbard and attached it to the bayonet lug in a dramatic gesture of bravado. For the men—of whom not one had ever used a bayonet for its intended purpose—the very act of attaching it, of hearing the metal-on-metal snicks of other bayonets being affixed to rifles, jump-started their adrenalin pumps. It meant they were going to "close with the enemy," the formal mission of the infantry. As one smartass later reported, "It was like a cold shot of piss to the heart!"

"Follow me!" Anderson screamed at the top of his lungs as he charged over the concealing crest of the ridge. In an instant, two dozen amped Marines were close on his heels.

My God, Littleton mused as he conjured up visions of Doughboys going "over the top." *This is right out of World War One.* He looked right and left, along the line of men, and felt an enormous sense of pride as they pressed forward into the inferno. There were no laggards, no shirkers. Not a single man faltered. "OOH RAH!" he bellowed over and over, in the emotional release of his young life. His men picked up the yell, turning it into a war cry that carried them toward the mass of Vietnamese infantry scrambling up the slope toward them.

A Marine pitched forward without a sound, tumbling over several times before he came to rest against the mangled remains of a Vietnamese sapper. The line swept past. All hands simply ignored the dead man in their rush to reach cover in the 2nd Platoon's battered fighting positions before the NVA occupied them.

231

With an agonized cry, another Marine dropped to the ground, clutching his leg. A buddy grabbed him by the flak jacket and dragged him to safety.

Littleton suddenly came face to face with a Vietnamese and reflexively butt-stroked him in the head without even slowing down.

Anderson saw Gunny Smith waving his arms and veered toward him, jumping into the hole feet first, followed by his radio operator—just as a line of machine gun bullets stitched the ground beside them. "Christ, I'm too old for this shit," the captain wheezed, feeling light-headed from the exertion and effects of the infected wounds.

Littleton thundered past and slid into an adjacent foxhole, landing on top of a body, which he unceremoniously pitched over the parapet.

Slowed by their load of ammunition, Petrovitch and Edwards fell behind as the rest of the men reached the holes and took cover. Exposed and alone on the fire-swept slope, the pair clambered on as bullets snapped past, tearing up the ground around them, but neither was touched. In a final burst of speed, the two men vaulted into a silenced machine gun position and set to with a will. Edwards threw the destroyed M-60 out of the hole, while Petrovitch lifted one of its dead crewmen onto the front parapet to act as a sandbag, offending Edwards's moral sensibilities.

"Corporal, do you have to do that?" Edwards asked, the revulsion evident in his voice. Petrovitch ignored him for a moment—as he heaved another body onto the bulwark.

"They're already dead. Nothing can hurt them anymore," the big man replied matter-of-factly, as he rhythmically set up the gun and folded himself behind it to shoot. He flashed his assistant a sinister smile. "I'll use anything to keep this gun in action, including your fat butt. Now keep feeding ammunition. We got gooks to kill."

Petrovitch squeezed the trigger of the M-60, expertly firing in steady ten-round bursts, sweeping the ground from left to right and back again. The 7.62mm steel-jacketed bullets flung Vietnamese into the air in every direction. As the weapon's deadly automatic fire scythed through the attackers' ranks, its stream of red tracers pinpointed the position and brought a torrent of small arms fire down on the two gunners.

Edwards flinched as bullets thudded into the improvised "sandbags," the sickening realization dawning that, without their grisly protection, he would be dead. He wanted nothing better than to curl up in the bottom of the hole and hide. Instead, he concentrated on feeding ammunition belts into the gun, making certain that each link was free of dirt and kinks; this was no time for a jam. He watched Petrovitch work the gun like he didn't have a care in the world, marveling at the man's composure—even with the bullets impacting all around him.

Suddenly, the big man jerked back into the hole. "Down," he shouted, dragging Edwards with him as a terrific explosion erupted in front of their position. The blast bounced them up and down, covering them with dirt and debris.

"RPG," Petrovitch said matter-of-factly as he returned to his position behind the gun. "Bastards are serious about taking us out."

Half-stunned by the blast, Edwards peered over the parapet and was shocked to see another enemy soldier raise a launcher to his shoulder and sight in. "Oh shit," he muttered, expecting to see the warhead up close and personal. Instead, the Viet flew backwards, driven by the impact of half a dozen 7.62mm bullets. The assistant gunner heard Petrovitch shout triumphantly, "Get some."

"Jam," Petrovitch shouted, throwing open the feed cover when the weapon stopped firing. In the dim light of a flare, he could make out that it was a cartridge stuck in the chamber. He knew it was ruptured. "Cleaning rod," he demanded brusquely as he first attempted to pry it out with his K-Bar. Edwards scrambled to find the steel rod in the jumble of expended cartridges and ammunition boxes in the bottom of the hole. "Hustle up, goddamn it!" Petrovitch barked impatiently. "The gooks are almost on top of us."

Spurred on by fear and pride, Edwards finally discovered the device pressed into the dirt beneath his own feet. "I got it," he cried—and froze, shocked by the sight of an NVA soldier lunging at Petrovitch with a bayoneted rifle. It happened so quickly that Edwards could only watch with horror as the triangular-shaped weapon stabbed downward.

But it never connected. Petrovitch blew the son of a bitch away with two .45 bullets that destroyed the Viet's face. The body collapsed as if it had been pole-axed.

"Clear the jam," the NCO ordered, like nothing had happened. "I'll keep the bastards off you." Edwards tried to concentrate, even though he expected to die at any moment. Then he heard the .45 bark in his ear. His heart sank. He couldn't pry the damn thing out. The gun was hard down, and the NVA were too close.

"Here, take this," Petrovitch shouted, tossing Edwards the dead NVA's assault rifle. "Use it in good health."

"Funny, Corporal. Very funny," Edwards muttered as he caught the unfamiliar weapon and pulled the bolt to the rear to make sure there was a round in the chamber. Petrovitch then handed him four fully loaded banana-shaped magazines that he stripped from the body—120 rounds.

"Make sure every shot counts. That's all we got, except for our .45s—and that's our last defense."

Targets, Edwards thought as he opened fire on the dozens of figures running up the hill. *They're just targets.* The AK-47 kicked him hard in the shoulder, which surprised him in view of the light recoil of an M-16 and made it difficult to hold the muzzle down.

My God, there's so many, he thought, his heart beating wildly. Panicking, he pushed the selector switch to automatic fire and emptied the magazine in one long burst. He fumbled with the release for a moment but finally ejected the empty and inserted another. Three magazines left. Then two. And one. After firing the last round, Edwards dropped the useless rifle and drew his service automatic as the Vietnamese reached the perimeter foxholes.

One screaming attacker ran right at Edwards, shooting his rifle in bursts of fire. Caught off guard, Edwards found himself staring directly into the muzzle. It was the last thing he saw. A powerful blow struck him in the head and he collapsed without a sound.

"No!" Petrovitch bellowed as Edwards crumpled under the impact. Beside himself with rage, he shot the attacker dead with his pistol and climbed out of the foxhole to get at the other. One ran straight at him, intent on skewering him with his bayonet, but he never got the chance. Petrovitch killed him instantly with one shot. He snapped off two shots at another enemy soldier, also dropping him, his blood lust spurring him on like a man possessed. Swearing and shouting insults, he motioned for the Vietnamese to come to him. He wanted to kill. He emptied his pistol as several enemy soldiers ran by.

A shot hit Petrovitch in the hip, knocking him down, providing two of the enemy with an opportunity to move in for the kill. But they weren't quick enough. Grabbing an entrenching tool, Petrovitch struggled to his feet and smashed it into the nearest NVA soldier, nearly severing the man's head. Desperate, the other NVA managed to stab the big man in the side. As if the bayonet were no more than a needle, Petrovitch grabbed him by the throat and crushed it. The man slumped to the ground, dead.

The enraged gunner struggled upright as three more of the attackers surrounded him, closing in for the kill, intent on finishing him off with their bayonets. Unarmed, Petrovitch glared at them, defiance in his eyes, daring them to come closer. It was a standoff until one yelled a command and they all charged.

"Gunny, something's happened to the machine gun!" Anderson yelled. He spotted Petrovitch as he emerged from the position firing his pistol. "Cover me. I'm going to help."

The company commander scrambled out of the foxhole, followed by his radio operator, just as three Vietnamese converged on the big gunner. Anderson dropped to one knee, quickly aimed his M-16, and fired three times at the closest attacker. His first shot took the Vietnamese high in the chest, and the next two bullets hit him in the stomach, folding him up on the ground, mortally wounded. Smith dropped the second. The third man made the mistake of trying to take Petrovitch by himself, but he didn't make the cut. He ended up staked to the ground with his own bayonet.

"You okay, Petrovitch?" Anderson yelled as the three Marines dropped back into the hole. "We gotta have your gun or we're dead meat."

Petrovitch looked up from examining his dead assistant. "Don't worry, Captain. I'll be there when you need me," he said in a cold, flat voice as tears ran unashamedly down his cheeks. He rammed the cleaning rod down the barrel with all his strength, freeing the jammed cartridge. Then he jacked the first round of a 200-round belt into the gun and sighted in.

"I'm ready, Skipper," Petrovitch said in the same cold, flat voice. "Let's get some!"

Jesus Christ, this guy's the meanest muther in the valley, Anderson thought as he shoved his radio operator into the assistant gunner's position. "You ever been a machine gunner before?" he asked the surprised man.

"No sir," the kid nervously replied.

"Well, there's no time like the present to learn," Anderson quipped, handing him the end of the machine gun belt.

***

Aldine was scared shitless, feeling naked and exposed, his imagination in full cry. Every sound was magnified; every shrub hid a Vietnamese infantryman who at any moment would jump out and bayonet him. Unable to get control of himself, he shook with fear and started to hyperventilate. The poor light of the illumination flares cast eerie shadows on the sergeant major's triple kill, making the twisted corpses appear to be crawling toward him. The battalion commander scrambled to find his pistol. Never in his wildest imagination had he ever thought he would have to defend himself, but now he fumbled with the weapon, which lay holstered somewhere at the bottom of the foxhole, sealed in a plastic case to keep it free from grime. He struggled with the zipper, which he managed to pull off its track, jamming the fastener. Using all his strength, he finally managed to force the teeth open enough to pull out the .45. As if to get even with the damn thing, he threw the case as hard as he could. He tried to pull the slide to the rear, but his hands were so slippery with sweat that he couldn't get a good grip. Sobbing with frustration and panic, he rubbed his hands on his uniform blouse, then tried the slide again. He succeeded in getting it back, then let it go forward. This stripped a bullet from the magazine and pushed it into the chamber, arming the pistol. Aldine fell back against the rear of his hole, exhausted with the effort but no longer defenseless.

The sergeant major saw them coming—four NVA advancing purposely across the open ground, fully alert and professionally dispersed. *Got to make every shot count*, he cautioned himself. *Only five rounds in this baby*. Raising the shotgun into a firing position, he waited until the advancing soldiers were in range and pulled the trigger just as the lead man tripped. *Missed, goddammit!* He shot at him again, then swung to the next man and fired. Then the next. He blasted the last man with his fifth round—first to last shot within ten seconds.

***

Sergeant Major Richards dropped the empty shotgun and grabbed for the .45 on his hip as a Vietnamese rose screaming from the ground, charging at full speed. "Shit," he muttered resignedly, knowing it was too late. In the next instant the man drove a spike bayonet through the flak jacket, piercing Richards's rib cage just below the heart. The assailant fell heavily against the side of the parapet and dropped limply into the bottom of the hole. The sergeant major flew backward, stunned but feeling no pain. He reflexively grabbed the assault rifle protruding from his side. With a great heave, he pulled it out.

Blinding pain lanced through his body. He cried out, "Colonel! Help me. I'm wounded." And, with that, he fell upon the Vietnamese, grabbing for his neck. The man fought desperately, but the sergeant major had the advantage in weight and leverage, even though he was getting weaker from loss of blood.

"Help me, Colonel," he called feebly. With the last of his strength he succeeded in crushing the NVA's windpipe and fell off the corpse, completely spent, unable to move, except to clutch at the hole in his chest. "Help me," he muttered.

"My God it hurts," Sergeant Major Richards groaned as a wave of pain swept over him. His insides were on fire. Even taking a breath was agony. "Help," he croaked in a weak voice.

Aldine ignored the cry for help, too wrapped up in his own fear to do anything but cower in his foxhole. At one point, he covered his ears to keep out the terrible fighting sounds coming from the sergeant major's foxhole. And now, how was he supposed to respond to the desperate call? *You want too much!* he wanted to shout. *Leave me alone. I can't help you.* Shamed by his own weakness, Aldine clutched the pistol and struggled to act, but he couldn't force himself to move. Tears streamed down his cheeks and his body shook with silent grief.

"Damn the man," Richards swore between rolling waves of sheer pain. "He's going to let me die." Thoughts whirled through his head as he pictured his wife of 28 years. *She'll take it hard. We have so many things planned ….* Another wave of pain hit him and he momentarily blacked out. When he recovered and opened his eyes, he looked directly into the face of his killer. "All right, you son of a bitch. Get it over with," he muttered defiantly, having come to terms with his own mortality.

43

1st Battalion, North Vietnamese Army, 0430, 14 September—Duc followed his men as they penetrated deeper into the enemy position. Fire poured in on them from all sides, and he realized the Americans had him in a trap unless he could break through their lines.

"*Tien len,*" the battalion commander shouted, but the few *Bo doi* who responded were immediately shot down. They were pinned down, unable to advance.

It was time to withdraw and save what was left of his beloved battalion, even though the cadre would censure him for failure. He would deal with them if he survived.

Turning to his runner, Duc ordered him to fire the signal to withdraw. Corporal Thai raised the flare gun and fired a green star cluster into the early morning sky. The act brought down a hail of gunfire that killed him instantly. As Thai collapsed, an American .38-caliber pistol dropped from his belt into the grass.

Duc's men attempted to withdraw but the heavy curtain of fire made it worth a man's life to move. They needed support. "Where are the mortars?"

***

Major Co listened to the sounds of the battle and anxiously watched the sky for the signal to withdraw, sensing the fight was reaching a climax. He worried that it was not going well for Duc's *Bo doi*, so he alerted the mortar crews to break out more ammunition. The men turned to with a will, opening up container after container of the deadly 82mm shells and stacking them within easy reach of the mortars. The crews worked quietly in the open gun pits, secure in the belief that the darkness hid their work.

Co heard distant explosions and shuddered, imagining the merciless American artillery pounding his exposed comrades. Suddenly, he heard two distinct, far-off *pops*—the sound of incoming artillery—and knew they were headed for his position. "Take cover," he shouted frantically, throwing himself behind a log as a terrific blast erupted over his head. Something slammed into his back and he lost consciousness.

Four more salvos screamed in to detonate over the exposed gun pits, battering the crews and setting off the ready ammunition. The secondary explosions killed those who weren't slaughtered by the artillery.

Duc managed to gather a dozen men together in a small depression that afforded them some protection from the hail of small arms fire that cracked overhead. They were a mixture of youngsters in their first action and old veterans, most of whom he knew by name. As he studied them in the early dawn light, Duc saw the terrible strain of the last few hours etched on their faces. He met the eyes of a veteran sergeant, a comrade of many years, who nodded his head in recognition. "This is our last battle, old friend. *Di may man*," Duc mouthed and reached out to touch him on the shoulder, feeling an intense sense of comradeship.

With dawn fast approaching, American reinforcements were bound to be on the way. Duc knew his battalion was lost. There was only one option left. He wouldn't surrender.

"*Muon doc lap phai do mau!*" he yelled. "Get ready." He signed for the men to prepare to throw their remaining Chi-Com grenades.

"Now," he shouted, and watched the deadly missiles spin through the air toward the American lines. The men gathered themselves for the attack. The sound of the first explosion reached them. "*Tien len*," Duc roared and leaped to his feet, firing the banner-draped AK-47 on full automatic, leading his men in assault.

***

Lieutenant Doi gathered the remnants of his platoon in a depression that provided them shelter from the incessant American artillery. The attack was going badly and he did not want his men with the assaulting infantry. This was not their battle; his men were specialists, not cannon fodder. He would save them. *What a waste*, he brooded. *Why does the cadre throw our men away?* It sickened him, and he felt powerless to do anything about it. *They're nothing but merciless slugs.*

An enraged voice interrupted his thoughts. "*Trung Uy*, why do you sit here doing nothing?" His heart sank. It was the political officer.

"Major Minh, I am waiting for orders from the commander," he lied, hoping it would satisfy the *Lo dit*, and maybe he would go away.

"I speak for him," Minh rejoined. "Take your men and attack the Americans—immediately," Minh shouted and gestured toward the hill. Doi was thunderstruck; his worst fears had been realized. His men would be sacrificed for no good reason.

"But, *Thieu Ta*, my men are not trained for this," he pleaded.

Minh's hand went to the holster at his side and drew out his pistol. "For freedom, you have to spend your blood. Now go," he ordered, leaving no doubt in Doi's mind that Minh would shoot him if he didn't respond.

Doi led his platoon out of the fire-swept jungle, losing three men in the process. On the grass-trampled slope, a torrent of small arms fire cracked through the air around them. Suddenly, the man on Doi's right cried out and tumbled, motionless, onto the torn-up sod. Another fell without a sound. Doi swore in helpless frustration as they surged upward into the mêlée.

A stream of bullets erupted from a half-concealed position. "Down," he shouted, but only the three men nearest him heard his warning. The others were mercilessly cut down.

When the machine gun abruptly stopped firing, Doi and his comrades jumped to their feet, intent upon destroying it. Their blood lust was up as they pressed forward.

A huge, ghostly figure rose out of the ground. "No," Doi screamed and stopped cold, paralyzed with fear because of the apparition, his worst nightmare. He left his men to charge forward without him.

Hours later, Doi was startled by the loud clatter of a helicopter. He looked up in time to see the huge machine fly directly over his place of refuge. He lay motionless in the bottom of a crater with the remains of two comrades who were already starting to decompose in the mid-morning heat, adding their stink to the fetid air. Gray cordite-impregnated soil swathed him completely; he blended in with the crater's wall, unseen by the tired-eyed defenders. Physically and emotionally played out, Doi struggled to maintain a grip on his sanity as images of the horrific fighting crowded his thoughts. When he pictured the political officer Minh brandishing his pistol, hate welled up within him. *Minh killed my men*, he thought. At that moment he knew what he must do.

Doi slowly rose to his feet, hands above his head, and shouted "*Chieu Hoi*—I surrender."

44

Lima Company, 0445, 14 September—Anderson was beyond tired, running on pure adrenalin, as his body reacted to the combat-induced stress. He was still on his feet, able to function, but he was having trouble remembering specific details of the long night. His wounds—severely infected and draining continuously— were giving him fits, causing him a great deal of pain, which he tried to ignore. Although he knew there would be a price to pay for ignoring them, right now there was no other choice.

Lima was holding on by an eyelash. The Vietnamese had penetrated deep into the perimeter and were trying to flood the breach with reinforcements, even though they were taking heavy casualties from Napoline's artillery fire. His counterattack had stopped them, but pressure had gradually forced them back across the perimeter. He worried that the next onslaught might break the line.

His thoughts were interrupted by the frantic yell of his radio operator: "Skipper, take cover! Lieutenant Napoline says we got an airstrike coming in on the gook assembly area."

Suddenly, the night was lit by dozens of massive explosions, followed by a series of shock waves that rolled over the perimeter, bouncing everyone off the ground. The effect was absolutely numbing; it literally took their breath away.

"What the hell was that?" Anderson exclaimed as he strove to recover from the shock.

"The lieutenant says he just hit the gooks with a mini Arc Light strike"—a mass bombing run by friendly fighter-bombers and attack aircraft.

Enemy fire dropped off. During the lull that followed, Anderson gathered his command group to plan out a last desperate effort to save the company. The Marines had to hold on until dawn, a scant hour away. Reinforcements and air support were scheduled to arrive at first light.

"You two look like shit," Anderson quipped genially as Smith and Littleton slid into his "command foxhole." His attempt at humor barely raised a grin between the two desperately exhausted veterans, who were about played out. They stared at him, hollow-eyed, bearded, and dirt encrusted.

At length, Gunny Smith spoke up. "Well, Skipper, you ain't no beauty contest winner yourself."

The three got down to business. "Seal 'em off," Anderson grunted, pointing to a rough sketch he had cut into the bottom of the foxhole with his K-Bar. "John, swing your left flank around here and, Gunny, do the same on the right. I'll stay in the middle with Petrovitch. We'll have the fuckers trapped between us. Questions?" Both men simply nodded. "No? Then go do it," he ordered with finality.

As the two Marines scrambled out of the hole, Anderson called after them. "Kick some ass!"

"Grenade! Hit the deck," someone hollered as a shower of Chicoms erupted from the Vietnamese positions. Anderson instinctively hunched down against the side of the foxhole and waited for the explosions. The detonations were still reverberating across the perimeter when heavy firing broke out. Several dark figures rose from the ground and ran toward the Marine foxholes, their assault rifles spitting fire. Within seconds most were knocked down—except for two, who made it to the line of Marine foxholes before a thoroughly frightened 18-year-old private emptied his magazine into them at point-blank range. One of the bodies tumbled into the youngster's hole and nearly impaled him on a bayonet. When the young Marine recovered, he saw a flag attached to the rifle and took it as a souvenir. He heaved the corpse out of the hole and, as it rolled against the other body, a hand flopped out to rest on its shoulder.

For the first time in hours, there was no gunfire. The silence was unnerving, almost frightening. Everyone was on edge—still in their fighting holes, fingers on the trigger, surprised to be alive.

As the sky brightened, the stillness was broken by the sound of a single-engine Cessna. Anderson's radio came alive. "Lima Six, this is Southern Hotel, your eye in the sky, checking into the net."

"The last time you said that we stepped into deep shit," Anderson replied grumpily. "Go away. With friends like you …."

Harper smiled. He had good guys to help. Bomber Reed was a little dinged up, but he was fundamentally okay. Life was good.

Anderson settled down. Help had arrived. His mood lightened up and he called for another command group meeting.

The hill exploded with activity; there was no slack for the grunts. Weary Marines, nearly dead on their feet from the after-effects of the adrenalin that had for hours flooded their systems, combed the hill for enemy holdouts. Casualties were prepared for evacuation, and working parties formed up.

There was no time to dwell on lost friends or the horrors of the night. That would come later.

"Here he is, Captain." Anderson followed the Marine's pointing finger and saw the badly disfigured corpse, a shotgun lying beside it in the bottom of the hole. "The sergeant major put up a hell of a fight, sir. There's dead gooks all over the place."

Anderson then looked over to where they had found the colonel's remains and shook his head. The battalion commander had taken his own life. "What a dichotomy," he said, half aloud. "One man's nerve and the other's desperation."

"Look at this," a Marine called out after rolling over the Vietnamese body with his foot. He picked up a pistol and held it out for his buddy to see. "What is it?" he asked, trying to find identification markings. "Son of a bitch, look what's stamped on the barrel—Smith and Wesson. It's an American .38. I wonder where he got it?" he remarked as he showed it off to the rest of his fire team.

Medevac helicopters shuttled in, taking out the dead and wounded.

***

Doc Zimmer was so mad, his handlebar mustache quivered. "Skipper, I'm telling you for the last time, get on the helicopter."

"Calm down, Doc. I'm going just as soon as I take care of a few things."

The corpsman just stared at him and shook his head. "Sir, with all due respect, you piss me off," and stomped off. But he returned a few minutes later with reinforcements.

Gunny Smith eyeballed the scruffy figure in front of him. "Andy, you look like shit. Get on the fucking helicopter."

Anderson stared back through pain-filled eyes and nodded. "All right, you old fart. Looks like you got yourself a rifle company."

45

1st Battalion Remnants, North Vietnamese Army, Hill 450, Dawn, 15 September—North Vietnamese wounded streamed through the trees in the gathering daylight, heading for the dubious succor of the battalion aid station, which was already overwhelmed with casualties. Their path from Hill 540 was strewn with dead and dying men, gruesome signposts of a monumental defeat. Here and there, an unwounded survivor helped a comrade forward, but, for the most part, the wounded were on their own, a glaring indicator that the 1st Battalion was in desperate straits. Veterans could not recall a time when there weren't enough men left to sweep the battlefield.

Several of the walking wounded were dispatched to alert headquarters and send back carrying parties, but that would take hours. The Americans were sure to arrive much sooner.

The walking wounded were ordered to head further into the jungle. One of them, an officer, approached an overworked medic and demanded a wound tag, pointing to a dirty bandage wrapped haphazardly around his head. Taken back by the officer's abrupt manner, the medic hesitated, then stepped forward to exam the wound.

"Just give me the tag," the officer demanded, and reached out to take it from the medic's hand.

"Sir, I can't issue one until I verify the wound."

"Are you refusing my order?" the man challenged, his hand conspicuously resting on the butt of his pistol.

The frightened aid man handed over the tag without another word.

Minh congratulated himself. The wound tag provided a legitimate excuse for going to the rear. He could claim a head wound and now had sufficient proof. No one would question him too closely. Who could blame him for losing the battle when he was wounded before it began? Maybe he'd get that assignment in the rear after all.

Shouts caught his attention. He looked up to see several wounded soldiers pointing upward through a break in the canopy as one of the small American spotter planes passed overhead.

"Get down, you fools!" he shouted. But the soldiers just stood where they were. Suddenly, there was a loud *whoosh* and an explosion that splattered the clearing with white phosphorous.

Minh's heart raced. He turned to run, only to be enveloped by a huge splash of molten fire that engulfed and consumed everything and everyone it touched.

46

White House, Washington, D.C., 2200, 25 May 1968—The South Lawn of the White House echoed with the sounds of military commands as the ceremonial company of the Marine Barracks took its position on the immaculately cut grass. Off to one side, a section of the President's Own struck up a selection of John Philip Sousa's martial music, lending an aura of patriotism to the occasion while serving as entertainment for those guests who had arrived early. The precision marching and military bearing of the young Marines was in sharp contrast to the crowd of spectators, who casually ambled toward the comfortable VIP seating that faced the line of colorfully uniformed men. Sprinkled here and there among the visitors were junior officers in dress uniform who served as escorts for a select group of dignitaries, identified by special passes embossed with the Presidential Seal. Several of these numbered passes had been given to Marines sporting bandages and casts—wounded veterans brought in for the ceremony. Several male guests, whose posture and bearing marked them as former military, subjected the injured Marines to a great deal of attention—one Marine to another, a band of brothers.

An old-timer struck up a lively conversation with a pajama-clad patient sitting in a wheelchair. "Well, son, you look like you came out second best in an ass-kicking contest," he said as a warm smile brightened his face.

"Yes, sir, you could say that," the younger man hesitantly replied, over-whelmed by the sight of the medal suspended from a light blue band around the stranger's neck, a singular decoration that identified him as a recipient of the Medal of Honor. The older man continued the conversation, seemingly oblivious to the attention. He stuck out his hand and introduced himself.

"What brings you here?" he asked, genuine interest evident in his voice.

"I'm Dick Frazier, sir. I'm here to see my company commander get decorated by the President."

At that moment, the band struck up "Hail to the Chief," interrupting all conversation. The guests rose to their feet and assumed a respectful silence, while the military members came to rigid attention and rendered a hand salute. On command, the line of troops executed a rifle salute, their chrome-plated bayonets glinting in the late morning sunlight.

The President strode purposefully to the podium and waited until the band had completed honors before he turned to recognize the couple that was ushered to his side. He warmly shook the man's hand and then, in an act of compassion, put his arm around the woman's shoulders, squeezing gently to let her know he understood her sorrow. After a long moment, he stepped back slightly and faced the couple as a narrator read the citation.

The stilted formality of the citation's language was in sharp contrast to the bewildered, grief-stricken couple standing forlornly, alone despite the crowd, trying to adjust to the loss of a son.

"The President of the United States takes pride in presenting the Medal of Honor posthumously to Private First Class Michael L. Davis, USMC, for service as set forth in the following citation:

"For conspicuous gallantry and intrepidity at the risk of his life above and beyond the call of duty while serving with Company L, Third Battalion, Twenty-Sixth Marines, Third Marine Division (Reinforced), in action against a numerically superior North Vietnamese Army force near Khe Sanh, Republic of Vietnam, on 13 September 1967. When the leaders of his mortar section were put out of action, Private First Class Davis immediately assumed command of the surviving crewmen and kept the weapon in action. During this engagement an enemy hand grenade landed in the position. In a valiant act of self-sacrifice, Private First Class Davis cried a warning and unhesitatingly threw himself on the deadly missile, absorbing with his own body the full and terrific force of the explosion. His exceptional valor, his courageous loyalty and unwavering devotion to duty in the face of grave peril reflect the highest credit upon Private First Class Davis and the Marine Corps, and uphold the highest traditions of the United States Naval Service. He gallantly gave his life for his county."

As the narrator concluded the reading, the woman struggled mightily to control her emotions. Tears ran unashamedly down her husband's cheeks. A military aide stepped forward, holding an open box, which the President took and presented to them with his own hands, offering words of condolence in his homey south Texas twang. In keeping with the solemnity of the simple ceremony, he did not take the opportunity to deliver his usual stump speech about saving South Vietnam. Rather, he spoke as a father with children of his own. Those in the front row swore that the hard-scrabble Texan had tears in his eyes, but who could be sure, for he was known to have a certain political acumen. Two military aides stepped forward and gently escorted the couple to seats in the front row of the reviewing area.

A Marine captain in Blue white dress—blue blouse and white trousers—aiguillettes dangling from his right shoulder, stepped forward, leading a similarly attired captain, minus the aide de camp insignia. In accordance with the ceremony's instructions but in violation of Marine Corps protocol, they approached the Commander-in-Chief uncovered. Instead of saluting—Marines don't salute outdoors without a cover—the two officers halted and came to rigid attention, facing the President, who looked intently into the eyes of the award recipient. In the same even tone as he had used moments earlier, the narrator read the citation.

"The President of the United States takes pleasure in presenting the Medal of Honor to Captain Andrew J. Anderson, USMC, for service as set forth in the following citation:

"For conspicuous gallantry and intrepidity at the risk of his life above and beyond the call of duty as Commanding Officer of Company L, Third Battalion, Twenty-Sixth Marines, Third Marine Division (Reinforced), in action against a numerically superior North Vietnamese Army force near Khe Sanh, Republic of Vietnam, on 12–13 September 1967. Captain Anderson's company came under intense fire from a large well-concealed enemy force. Severely wounded, along with the other members of his command group, he continued to direct the activities of his company. Discovering one of his officers was missing, Captain Anderson advanced into the enemy position, killing several before being forced to withdraw. Upon reaching the relative safety of a hilltop, he refused evacuation, established a defensive position and supervised the evacuation of casualties. Assaulted the next evening by a large enemy force, Captain Anderson led his men in repulsing the attack, killing and wounding an estimated 300 North Vietnamese. His indomitable courage and unyielding fighting spirit in the face of almost insurmountable odds reflect great credit upon himself and the Marine Corps and uphold the highest traditions of the United States Naval Service."

The President then stepped forward, took the medal in hand, and draped it over the officer's head—the reason for being uncovered—so the five-pointed star hung just below the gilded top button of his dark blue blouse. The officer instinctively lowered his head to make it easier for the President, but the gesture wasn't necessary—Lyndon Johnson was a tall man. Stepping back, the President grabbed the surprised officer's hand in his own and firmly pumped it up and down. No limp-dick squeeze for this man. "Loosen up, Captain, I'm not going to shoot you," he chuckled, greatly amused by his own joke and the obvious discomfort of the Marine. "I thought nothing bothered you Leathernecks. At least that's what I heard when I was in the Navy in the big war."

Jesus, Anderson deliberated. *Do I yank the Commander-in-Chief's chain? What the hell. No guts no glory*, he decided. "Sir," he began aloud, "with all due respect, 'navy' is a four-letter word."

The big man guffawed loudly. "I can't wait until I tell that one to the Secretary of the Navy."

Oh shit, I'm screwed, Anderson muttered to himself. *I'll be guarding penguins in Antarctica for my next assignment.*

The first notes of the "Marines' Hymn" interrupted his thoughts and he came to attention. To his great pleasure, he saw the President's posture straighten, a mark of respect to the Corps' sacred anthem. Emotion welled up within him as he thought of the men left behind in that god-awful jungle. His eyes filled with tears. *I'd do anything to bring them back,* he agonized. For the first time he felt the medal around his neck and recognized the heavy responsibilities that came with it. *This is for their sacrifice, and I'll never forget it,* he swore.

At the last note of the music, the President departed within a phalanx of Secret Service agents, leaving Anderson among the crowd of well-wishers. As quickly as he could, he made his way to Davis's parents, dreading the encounter. *Will they blame me for his death?*

"Mr. and Mrs. Davis," he began, and then his voice faltered and all he could get out was, "I'm so sorry."

The woman looked at him for an instant, then stepped forward and hugged him closely, crying into his chest while her husband patted him awkwardly on the shoulder. Anderson held the distraught woman, trying to gain control of his own emotions. Finally, she pulled away, smiling in embarrassment but still deeply affected by the emotional trauma. "Thank you for your concern," she said weakly, "Mike was so proud to be a Marine and wanted to go to Vietnam. In his last letter, he mentioned the company and how good it was—'second to none,' is how he put it." Her husband joined in to share memories of their son with one of the last men to see him alive. Anderson let them talk before he judiciously described several incidents, deliberately avoiding mention of the last battle. Finally talked out, they all agreed to stay in touch, and the couple walked away, still in the capable hands of their escorts.

A familiar voice called out, "Skipper, can you lend me an ear?"

Anderson spun around to see a bandage-swathed officer for the first time since his evacuation. "Dick, am I glad to see you!" he shouted happily and rushed over to the wheelchair-bound lieutenant. After enthusiastically shaking hands—Marine officers don't hug—Anderson stepped back, looked Frazier over, and said, "Dick, you look like shit!"

The wounded officer broke out in a smile. "Damn, Skipper, you haven't changed one bit!"

Awards

Captain Andrew J. Anderson USMC

The President of the United States in the name of The Congress takes pleasure in presenting the Medal of Honor to Captain Andrew J. Anderson for service as set forth in the following citation:

For conspicuous gallantry and intrepidity at the risk of his life above and beyond the call of duty as Commanding Officer of Company L, Third Battalion, Twenty-Sixth Marines, Third Marine Division (Reinforced), in action against a numerically superior North Vietnamese Army force near Khe Sanh, Republic of Vietnam, 12–13 September 1967. Captain Anderson's company came under intense fire from a well-concealed enemy force. Severely wounded, along with other members of his command group, he continued to direct the activities of his company. Discovering one of his officers was missing, Captain Anderson advanced into the enemy position, killing several before being forced to withdraw. Upon reaching the relative safety of a hilltop, he refused evacuation, established a defensive position and supervised the evacuation of casualties. Assaulted the next evening by a large enemy force, Captain Anderson led his men in repulsing the attack, killing and wounding an estimated 300 North Vietnamese. His indomitable courage and unyielding fighting spirit in the face of almost insurmountable odds reflect great credit upon himself and the Marine Corps, and uphold the highest traditions of the United States Naval Service.

Private First Class Michael L. Davis USMC

The President of the United States in the name of The Congress takes pride in presenting the Medal of Honor posthumously to Private First Class Michael L. Davis for service as set forth in the following citation:

For conspicuous gallantry and intrepidity at the risk of his life above and beyond the call of duty while serving with Company L, Third Battalion, Twenty-Sixth Marines, Third Marine Division (Reinforced), in action against a numerically superior North Vietnamese Army force near Khe Sanh, Republic of Vietnam, on 13 September 1967. When the leaders of his mortar section were put out of action, Private First Class Davis immediately assumed command of the surviving crewmen and kept the weapon in action. During this engagement an enemy hand grenade landed in the position. In a valiant act of self-sacrifice, Private First Class Davis cried out a warning and unhesitatingly threw himself on the deadly missile, absorbing with his own body the full and terrific force of the explosion. His exceptional valor, his courageous loyalty and unwavering devotion to duty in the face of grave peril reflect the highest credit upon Private First Class Davis and the Marine Corps, and uphold the highest traditions of the United States Naval Service. He gallantly gave his life for his country.

First Lieutenant Richard D. Frazier USMC

The Secretary of the Navy takes pleasure in presenting the Navy Cross to First Lieutenant Richard D. Frazier for service as set forth in the following citation:

For extraordinary heroism while serving as a Platoon Commander with Company L, Third Battalion, Twenty-Sixth Marines, Third Marine Division (Reinforced), in action against a numerically superior North Vietnamese force near Khe Sanh, Republic of Vietnam on 12 September 1967. Wounded when his company came under intense fire from a large well-concealed enemy force, First Lieutenant Frazier continued to direct the activities of his platoon. When several North Vietnamese infantrymen pinned down his platoon, he single-handedly assaulted the position, killing the occupants, which allowed his men to withdraw without additional loss. In the hand-to-hand fighting, First Lieutenant Frazier was knocked unconscious and captured but was subsequently rescued and returned to friendly hands. By his courageous fighting spirit, bold initiative and unswerving devotion to duty at great personal risk, he upheld the highest traditions of the Marine Corps and the United States Naval Service.

Gunnery Sergeant Norman A. French USMC

The Secretary of the Navy takes pride in presenting the Navy Cross posthumously to Gunnery Sergeant Norman A. French for service as set forth in the following citation:

For extraordinary heroism while serving as an Assistant Patrol Leader with Company B, Third Reconnaissance Battalion, Third Marine Division (Reinforced), in action against a numerically superior North Vietnamese Army force near Khe Sanh, Republic of Vietnam on the evening of 12 September 1967. Gunnery Sergeant French volunteered for a highly dangerous patrol to recover the remains of two Marines killed in action deep in hostile territory. While infiltrating the area, his patrol discovered and killed eight enemy soldiers, recovering a Marine Officer who had been taken prisoner. Gunnery Sergeant French was severely wounded during the subsequent retrograde and voluntarily stayed behind to cover the withdrawal of the hard-pressed patrol. He was last seen engaging the enemy with small arms and hand grenades. By his courageous fighting spirit, bold initiative and unswerving devotion to duty at great personal risk, he upheld the highest traditions of the Marine Corps and the United States Naval Service. He gallantly gave his life for his country.

First Lieutenant Herbert J. Wilson USMC

The Secretary of the Navy takes pleasure in presenting the Silver Star to First Lieutenant Herbert J. Wilson for service as set forth in the following citation:

For conspicuous gallantry and intrepidity in action while serving as a Patrol Leader with Company B, Third Reconnaissance Battalion, Third Marine Division (Reinforced), in action against a numerically superior North Vietnamese Army force near Khe Sanh, Republic of Vietnam from 12 to 13 September 1967. First Lieutenant Wilson volunteered to lead a highly dangerous patrol to recover the remains of two Marines killed in action deep in hostile territory. While infiltrating the area, his patrol discovered and killed eight enemy soldiers and recovered a Marine Officer who had been taken prisoner. In the act of evacuating the former POW, Lieutenant Wilson's patrol was attacked by a large enemy unit and forced to move across country. After successfully eluding the pursuers, the patrol reached the safety of a friendly hilltop position in time to participate in its defense. Lieutenant Wilson personally led a counterattack, which eliminated the immediate threat and provided time for the defenders to rally and defeat a large enemy force. His aggressiveness and heroic devotion to duty reflect great credit upon himself and are in keeping with the highest traditions of the Marine Corps and the United States Naval Service.

First Lieutenant John M. Littleton USMC

The Secretary of the Navy takes pleasure in presenting the Navy Cross to First Lieutenant John M. Littleton for service as set forth in the following citation:

For extraordinary heroism while serving as a Platoon Commander with Company L, Third Battalion, Twenty-Sixth Marines, Third Marine Division (Reinforced), in action against a numerically superior North Vietnamese Force near Khe Sanh, Republic of Vietnam on 12 September 1967. First Lieutenant (then 2nd Lieutenant) Littleton's platoon came under intense small arms fire from a North Vietnamese bunker complex. After evaluating the tactical situation, he led two squads in an envelopment that took the enemy by surprise, enabling Littleton's men to penetrate the position. During the final assault, a machine gun pinned them down, threatening to stop the envelopment. First Lieutenant Littleton neutralized the enemy position and calmly led an assault against the remaining hostile emplacements. By his courageous fighting spirit, bold initiative and unswerving devotion to duty at great personal risk, he upheld the highest traditions of the Marine Corps and the United States Naval Service.

Sergeant Eric S. Petrovitch USMC

The Secretary of the Navy takes pleasure in presenting the Navy Cross to Corporal Eric S. Petrovitch for service as set forth in the following citation:

For extraordinary heroism while serving as a Machine Gun Squad Leader with Company L, Third Battalion, Twenty-Sixth Marines, Third Marine Division (Reinforced), in action against a numerically superior North Vietnamese Army force near Khe Sanh, Republic of Vietnam on 13 September 1967. While in a night defensive position, Sergeant (then Corporal) Petrovitch's company came under attack by an estimated 300 to 400 enemy soldiers, who penetrated the perimeter foxholes. As part of a counterattack force, he placed heavy accurate fire on the attackers, pinning them down until his weapon jammed. Attacked by several enemy soldiers, Sergeant Petrovitch killed three with his pistol and two more in hand to hand combat even though severely wounded. He continued to man the machine gun, despite his wounds, beating back a vicious enemy attack that threatened to overrun the Marine position. He refused medical treatment until the position was no longer threatened. By his courageous fighting spirit, bold initiative and unswerving devotion to duty at great personal risk, he upheld the highest traditions of the Marine Corps and the United States Naval Service.

First Lieutenant Daniel F. Reed USMC

The President of the United States takes pleasure in presenting the Distinguished Flying Cross to First Lieutenant Daniel F. Reed for service as set forth in the following citation:

For extraordinary heroism in aerial flight while serving as a pilot with Marine Observation Squadron-2, 1st Marine Aircraft Wing (Reinforced) near Khe Sanh, Republic of Vietnam on 12 September 1967. Lieutenant Reed was called upon to support a Marine company engaged in battle with an overwhelming force of North Vietnamese, which threatened to overrun it. He called in tactical air support and marked targets for the strike planes. After observing an enemy 12.7mm anti-aircraft gun, Lieutenant Reed unhesitatingly flew into its cone of fire and, despite battle damage, continued to press in on the target, successfully marking it for destruction. He continued to direct ravaging bombing runs on the enemy positions, which allowed the Marines to successfully break contact with the numerically superior enemy force. Lieutenant Reed's remarkable airmanship and bravery was in keeping with the highest traditions of the military service and reflect great credit upon himself, the Marine Corps and the United States Naval Service.

Captain James P. Harper USMC

The Secretary of the Navy takes pleasure in presenting the Silver Star (Gold Star in lieu of Third Award) to Captain James P. Harper for service as set forth in the following citation:

For conspicuous gallantry and intrepidity in action while serving as an Aerial Observer attached to Marine Observation Squadron-2, 1st Marine Air Wing (Reinforced) near Khe Sanh, Republic of Vietnam on 12 September 1967. Captain Harper was called upon to support an embattled Marine company in danger of being overrun by a superior force of North Vietnamese. After assessing the situation, he coordinated strike aircraft and skillfully directed them in attacking the heavily camouflaged enemy positions, resulting in the destruction of several bunkers and fortifications. He identified an enemy 12.7mm anti-aircraft gun and, even though his own aircraft received battle damage, marked the position for strike aircraft. After a friendly aircraft was shot down, he directed a complicated rescue attempt, while supporting the successful withdrawal of the Marine Company. Captain Harper's dedication and bravery at great personal risk are in keeping with the highest traditions of the Marine Corps and the United States Naval Service.

Gunnery Sergeant Michael E. Smith USMC

The Secretary of the Navy takes pleasure in presenting the Silver Star (Gold Star in Lieu of Second Award) to Gunnery Sergeant Michael E. Smith for service as set forth in the following citation:

For conspicuous gallantry and intrepidity in action while serving as a Platoon Commander, Company L, Third Battalion, Twenty-Sixth Marines, Third Marine Division (Reinforced), against a numerically superior North Vietnamese Army force near Khe Sanh, Republic of Vietnam on 13 September 1967. While in a night defensive position, Gunnery Sergeant Smith's company came under attack by an estimated 300 to 400 enemy soldiers who penetrated the line of foxholes. Quickly assessing the situation, Gunnery Sergeant Smith moved to the heaviest point of contact and immediately took the enemy soldiers under fire, killing and wounding an unknown number. He remained in the exposed position until reinforced and then continued to direct fire upon the attackers. His heroic and aggressive devotion to duty reflects great credit upon himself and are in keeping with the highest traditions of the Marine Corps and the United States Naval Service.

Hospital Corpsman First Class Larry D. Zimmer USN

The Secretary of the Navy takes pleasure in presenting the Bronze Star to Hospital Corpsman First Class Larry D. Zimmer for service as set forth in the following citation:

For heroic achievement in connection with operations against the enemy in the Republic of Vietnam while serving as senior Corpsman, Company L, Third Battalion, Twenty-Sixth Marines, Third Marine Division (Reinforced) during the period 12 to 13 September 1967. When a numerically superior enemy force caused numerous friendly casualties, HM1 Zimmer repeatedly and unhesitatingly moved about through a murderous barrage of small arms and mortar fire to render assistance to his wounded comrades. Undaunted by the enemy fire, he skillfully administered first aid, improvising treatment when his medical supplies were exhausted. Zimmer's efforts on behalf of his wounded comrades were directly responsible for saving many lives. His courage and selfless devotion to duty were in keeping with the highest traditions of the Marine Corps and the United States Naval Service.

The following Radio Hanoi broadcast in English was intercepted on 20 September:

The People's Army of Vietnam announced the following awards for outstanding participation in armed combat in the south:

The Liberation War Exploit Order, 1st Class was awarded to the 1st Battalion, 803rd Regiment, 324th Division for outstanding participation in armed combat in the south.

LtCol Pham Le Duc, Battalion Commander, 1st Battalion, 803rd Regiment, 324th Division was awarded the Hero of the People's Armed Forces for exceptionally outstanding achievements in combat.

Major Vu Van Minh, Political Officer, 1st Battalion, 803rd Regiment, 324th Division, was awarded the Order of the Soldier of Liberation Order, 3rd Class for participation in the liberation of the South.

Lieutenant Tran Van Doi, Reconnaissance Platoon Commander was awarded the Military Exploit Order, 1st Class for outstanding performance in combat.

Senior Sergeant Nguyen Ba Thanh, Sapper Platoon Commander was awarded the Glorious Fighter Medal for outstanding performance in combat.

Glossary and Guide to Abbreviations

American terms

A-4 Douglas Skyhawk single-seat jet attack bomber.

AN/PRC-25 U.S.-built short-range, portable, frequency-modulated radio set used to provide two-way communication in the 30 megacycle to 75.95 megacycle band.

AO Aerial Observer, an individual whose primary mission is to observe or to take photographs from an aircraft in order to adjust artillery fire or obtain military information.

Bn Battalion.

CH-46 Boeing Vertol Sea Knight, a twin-engine, tandem-rotor transport helicopter designed to carry a four-man crew and up to seventeen combat-loaded troops. Cruising speed of 11 knots and two .50-caliber machine guns mounted in the waist of the aircraft.

Chicom Chinese Communist (used for NVA hand grenade).

Claymore U.S. directional anti-personnel mine.

CO Commanding Officer.

Co Company.

COC Combat Operations Center.

CP Command Post.

DMZ Demilitarized Zone.

F-4B McDonnell-Douglas Phantom II, a twin-engine, two-seat, long-range, all-weather jet interceptor and attack bomber.

FAC Forward air controller. An individual who controls attacking strike aircraft engaged in close air support of friendly troops or against other targets.

Grenade Launcher U.S.-built single-shot, break-open, breech-loaded weapon.

Ho Chi Minh Trail North Vietnamese infiltration route, known as the Truong Son Strategic Supply Route in the North.

Howitzer, 105mm U.S.-built towed, general-purpose light artillery piece. The M2A1 variant is mounted on a carriage equipped with split box trails and pneumatic tires. It weighs 4,980 pounds, is 19.75 feet in length, and has a maximum range of 11,155 meters with a maximum rate of fire of four rounds per minute.

KIA Killed in action.

Klick Kilometer

KSCB Khe Sanh Combat Base.

LAAW U.S.-built Light Anti-tank Assault Weapon, a 66mm anti-tank rocket system in which a projectile is prepackaged in a disposal launcher.

M-26 U.S.-manufactured hand-thrown bomb, which weighs approximately one pound and contains an explosive charge in a body that shatters into small fragments; it has an effective killing range of 40 meters.

M-60 U.S.-built belt-fed, gas-operated, air-cooled 7.62mm machine gun; weighs approximately 23 pounds without mount or ammunition; has a sustained rate of fire of 100 rounds per minute and an effective range of 1,100 meters.

M-79 "Blooper" Shoulder weapon which fires 40mm projectiles and weighs approximately 6.5 pounds when loaded; it has an effective range of 375 meters.

Napalm/Nape An incendiary, usually air delivered as an anti-personnel weapon.

Ops O Operations Officer.

RPG Rocket Propelled Grenade.

SNCO

Snake-eye U.S.-built bomb designed so that after release fins pop open to act as air brakes, which allow the bomb to fall behind the aircraft, decreasing the risk of blast damage.

Sparrow Hawk Quick reaction force.

WIA Wounded in action.

Vietnamese terms

AK-47 Soviet-designed Kalashnikov gas-operated 7.62mm automatic rifle, with an effective range of 400 meters; the standard rifle of the North Vietnamese Army.

Ao dai Traditional costume of Vietnamese women consisting of wide trousers and full-length tunic with a split up the sides.

Bac Ho "Uncle Ho" or Ho Chi Minh.

Bo Doi North Vietnamese infantry; soldiers.

Caca Dau Kill.

Chinh-Uy Political officer

Chung ta ra di Move out.

Dac Cong Sappers.

Di may man Luck or good fortune.

Do cho de or **Lo dit** Jerk or asshole.

Do mau Yes! Spend blood!

Do moi ro, Do khan Son of a bitch.

Kiem Thao VC/NVA self-criticism session, which concentrated on resolving organizational problems and leadership difficulties.

Lao Dong Communist Party.

Linh My American puppet.

Moi Savage; refers to Montagnard tribesman.

Muon doc lap phai do mau "For freedom, you have to spend your blood."

My American.

My nguy American puppet.

Nam Vung Thoi-Co "Seize the opportunity."

NVA North Vietnamese Army.

San Bat Cuop Bandit hunters.

Thu Ky Clerk.

Tien len Forward.

Tong Cuc Hau Can Rear Services Directorate.

Tu Linh Commander.

Vietnamese ranks

Binh Nhi Private.

Binh nhat Private First Class.

Chien Si Soldier.

Ha si Corporal.

Quan Linh Combatant.

Thieu Ta Major.

Thieu Uy Second Lieutenant.

Thuong si Senior Sergeant.

Trung si Sergeant.

Trung Ta Lieutenant Colonel.

Trung Uy Senior Lieutenant.

Tu Lenh Commander